JESUS TREE

Jesus Tree

Stephen Doster

OPEN ROAD
INTEGRATED MEDIA
NEW YORK

This edition published in 2022 by Open Road Integrated Media, Inc.
180 Maiden Lane
New York, NY 10038
www.openroadmedia.com

PREFACE

This was a difficult book to write. First, it was inspired by the real-life murder of a pastor that occurred during the Great Depression. Because the murder is still a painful subject and a point of contention for those who remember it (even more than eighty years later), the story was reset in the fictional middle-Georgia town of Lamar. *Jesus Tree* doesn't attempt to point a finger at the guilty party of the real murder. It looks at it not from the angle of who would benefit by the death of the pastor, but who would benefit by sending the accused murderer to prison or the death chair.

The second reason this book was a difficult project is that researching and writing about convict labor in the prison camps of the Jim Crow South is not a pleasant task. Abuse by lawmen is rife even today in the age of instant, widespread communication, so it's not hard to imagine the brutality wardens and guards got away with in the remote county prison camps of the 1930s. A number of books served as research material for aspects of convict labor, including *I Am a Fugitive from a Georgia Chain Gang* (Robert E. Burns, Grosset & Dunlap Publishers, New York, 1932), *Twice the Work of Free Labor: The Political Economy of Convict Labor in the New South* (Alex Lichtenstein, Verso, New York, 1996), and *Hard Times on a Southern Chain Gang* (John L. Spivak, Brewer,

Warren & Putnam, New York, 1932), originally published as the novel *Georgia Nigger*.

Which brings up the third reason writing this story wasn't easy to write. I was raised not to use the "N" word. Period. Writing about a black man in a Depression-Era prison camp pretty much guarantees that word will surface at some point. I wrote a draft without using the "N" word, but it didn't ring true, and I debated scrapping the book altogether. I later realized that while the word is offensive, not using it would diminish the achievements of those who endured and overcame the prejudices of that era. Creating "win" stories, when it was "lose-lose" for the blacks and for the society that kept them down, doesn't honor the people who lived through those times. Presenting this tale in the language of the day brings the harsh reality of the moment into focus.

The Wild Man from Sugar Creek: The Political Career of Eugene Talmadge (William Anderson, Louisiana State University Press, Baton Rouge, 1975) provided revealing insights into the life of Eugene Talmadge and Georgia politics of the era. Some trivia: because of a skin condition, Talmadge was referred to as "The nigger who came to town," by his detractors, further proof that the "N" word was as prevalent in the war of words in the 1930s as it is today. Talmadge was an avowed segregationist, yet, as a farmer he worked side-by-side with black fieldhands and broke bread with them at the same dinner table; evidence of the conflicting and dysfunctional forces at work on both blacks and whites.

Two books provided keen insights into the lives of Pullman porters: *Rising from the Rails: Pullman Porters and the Making of the Black Middle Class* (Larry Tye, Henry Holt and Company, New York, 2004), and *Pullman Porters and the Rise of Protest Politics in Black America, 1925-1945* (Beth Tompkins Bates, The University of North Carolina Press, Chapel Hill, 2001).

Lightwood, by Brainard Cheney (Houghton Mifflin Co., Boston,

1939) and *Running the River: Poleboats, Steamboats & Timber Rafts on the Altamaha, Ocmulgee, Oconee & Ohoopee* (Carlton A. Morrison, Delma E. Presley, Saltwater Press, St. Simons Island, 2003), were invaluable resources for depicting the life and times of those living in Georgia's piney woods and making a living on the Altamaha River, post-Civil War through the mid-20th century.

A number of books shed light on the lives and customs of African Americans living in Gullah and Geechee cultures. Among them are: *Drums and Shadows: Survival Studies Among the Georgia Coastal Negroes* (slave narratives compiled by the Savannah Unit of the Georgia Writers' Project, Work Projects Administration, with an introduction by Charles Joyner and photographs by Muriel and Malcolm Bell, Jr., Brown Thrasher Books, The University of Georgia Press, Athens, 1940); *Sapelo's People: A Long Walk into Freedom* (William S. McFeely, W. W. Norton & Company, New York, 1994); *Blue Roots: African-American Folk Magic of the Gullah People* (Roger Pinckney, Llewellyn Publications, St. Paul, 1998); *African Muslims in Antebellum America: Transatlantic Stories and Spiritual Struggles* (Allan D. Austin, Routledge, New York, 1997); *God, Dr. Buzzard, and the Bolito Man: A Saltwater Geechee Talks About Life on Sapelo Island, Georgia* (Cornelia Walker Bailey with Christena Bledsoe, Anchor Books, New York, 2001); and *A Gullah Psalm: The Musical Life & Work of Luke Peeples* (Estella Saussy Nussbaum and Jeanne Saussy Wright, LP Collections, Savannah, 2014).

While *Jesus Tree* focuses on events in Georgia during the Depression, it could have been located in any other state using convict labor at the time. Reading this story, you might develop an appreciation for the blood, sweat, and tears that went into the construction of the back highways crisscrossing Southern states. On a deeper level, the highway, central to this tale, is an extended metaphor for the African Americans of the era who laid down the roadbed and paved the way for those following in their footsteps.

I am indebted to the following people for turning ideas on scraps of paper into a book: Anne Doster, foremost, for her patience and support, and for her edits and comments; Devon Boan provided much needed encouragement as well as insights into African-American culture that were particularly helpful; Tom Dennard took the time to edit parts of the manuscript and gave guidance on the workings of Georgia's judicial system during the 1930s. Bob Stanford's offhand remark that Pullman porters carried contraband up and down the coast by rail, provided a key element that helped move the plot along at a crucial stage. Any of their input I got wrong can be attributed to "artistic license." My agent, Jeanie Loiacono, never lost faith in this story or its message, and I thank her for her perseverance. Aurelia Sands at Deer Hawk Publications had the courage to take on *Jesus Tree* when other publishers shied away from the subject matter. Chelsa Jillard's critical eye put the finishing touches on the manuscript. Many thanks Jeanie, Aurelia, and Chelsa.

Lastly, I'd like to dedicate this book to the men in chains who built the roads we travel on.

JESUS TREE

CHAPTER 1

On the morning of June first, 1972, Ben Jordan boarded a Greyhound bus at the Reidsville stop. Luke, the driver, one of the first blacks hired by the bus line, knew at a glance that the new shoes and oversized suit Ben wore meant he had just been released from Georgia's state penal institution. Luke had picked up enough newly-released prisoners to know which ones served long stretches. It was in their eyes—a mixture of fear and exultation—and in their step—hesitant, unsure, like an aged mariner returned from a long voyage--to find the home of his youth was now a foreign land.

Ben, in his early sixties, gingerly climbed the bus steps as if testing his sea legs on dry land. Luke checked his ticket and told him to take a seat. Ben slowly turned and looked toward the back of the bus, letting his eyes adjust from the bright light of the early morning sun. He could have waited for the bus in the comfort of a small waiting room with other passengers, but declined for fear that one of them might ask where he came from or where he was going.

"Right there's fine," Luke said, pointing to the unoccupied front seat by the bus door.

Ben stared at the spot and froze in his tracks. The front of a bus was reserved for whites. At least, it had been the last time he'd ridden one.

"You sure about that?" he said, almost in a whisper.

"Go on," Luke replied. "Ain't nobody gonna to say nothing. This my bus! I'm the captain."

Ben cautiously lowered himself into the seat, and set the small satchel that contained all of his worldly possessions on the floor at his feet. As the bus pulled away from the station, he gripped the metal rail in front of him like a man who just realized he was on the cone of a rocket ship about to blast off to new worlds.

The forty-mile trip to Lamar, his destination, would take almost an hour with stops in every town, hamlet, and crossroad along the route. Ben looked through the wide windshield of the bus with fascination and horror as the terrain before him flew by like reels on a cinema screen, hurtling him simultaneously forward into the future and far back into the past. Images, half-recognized and rooted in his younger days, were quickly overlaid by newer, strange sights produced by the forty years of progress since he had last traveled the highway. He stared wide-eyed, afraid to blink, scared he might miss something, until it became too much for his mind to process.

He had entered prison during the Jim Crow era—a shackle bound by links in a chain that stretched from the Ku Klux Klan, to Reconstruction, to Freedom, clean back to the first ships carrying slaves to the New World. Ben despised that chain, but understood it. He recognized it in a word, a stare, a shifting of bodies, or dead silence, and he knew how to react. But things had changed while he was inside. The chain was now broken. He had emerged an alien after a forty-year trek. The land he now looked upon was a landscape inhabited by people changed by three wars, equal rights movements, the space race, sex, drugs, and rock and roll. It was a world where blacks drove buses that whites rode on, where black men like him sat up front, where bikini-clad white women spread lotion over their bodies on billboard signs.

"Lawd haff mercy," Ben muttered under his breath as four decades played out on the big glass in front of him. "Lawd in heaven haff mercy," he repeated in the Geechee language he'd grown up speaking on a barrier island.

Up ahead, a stretch of CSX railroad paralleled the highway before curling into a pine forest. It was the first thing he saw left unchanged since his incarceration. He closed his eyes and savored the image in his mind.

But shutting his eyes on a moving vehicle only made him dizzy, a life-long malady that had prevented him from joining his father on the shrimp boats that plied the coastal waters. If it wasn't for that, he often told himself, everything would have been all right. He wouldn't have found work on the land that brought him under the influence of the Cutler family.

In New Branch, Luke stopped long enough for passengers to buy food at a store that also served as the local bus station. While the others disembarked, Ben remained seated, afraid to leave the bus; afraid it would leave without him in a world he little recognized. He looked forlornly at the store window where one poster depicted happy travelers on a bus bound for Florida. Beside it was another display that had been torn so that the man's head appeared to be decapitated.

"Hey, Mister," Luke said, returning with a soda, "you got time to go and get something."

Ben nodded. "I'm okay," he said, gently rocking in his seat.

"Here," Luke began, reaching for his money clip.

"I gots money," Ben said, patting the wallet in his coat. "I just sit here."

Luke looked him over for several moments. "Going home?"

Visions of Hog Hammock, the settlement on Sapelo Island where he had been raised, flashed through Ben's mind. Home was the tin-roofed house with a fireplace that had given heat in the winter, the small patch of ground on which his family had grown vegetables, the shed that housed one milk cow, the two room schoolhouse where he spent his first seven years of learning, and the First African Baptist Church where he heard about good and evil in all-day Sunday gatherings. Five decades after leaving the island, he still thought of it as his home, but he knew he couldn't go there; not yet. He had business in the town where the trouble first began.

"Going to Lamar," Ben replied. "Gots to see a man."

"See a man?" Luke repeated.

Ben rocked several more times and smiled. "Gots to see a man about a soul."

Luke set his soda bottle in a plastic drink holder and let out a long sigh. "That's some serious business."

"It very serious bid'ness," Ben said, the smile disappearing from his face.

Luke made no reply and turned in his seat. He glanced in the mirror at the elder black man rocking to and fro, staring out the window at the storefront.

"There's a bathroom around the side," he said, guessing what was on Ben's mind.

Ben looked at him, then returned his attention to the store.

"Honest," said Luke. "You can use the bathroom. It's okay."

Ben looked at Luke again. He had learned the hard way to hold it in until he found a bathroom for blacks or a tree secluded from view.

"You sho?"

Luke nodded.

"You ain't gonna drive off an' leave me?"

Luke nodded again. "This bus ain't going nowhere without you, Pops."

Ben stepped down from the bus, satchel in hand, and returned a few minutes later.

"Tanks fo waitin' on me," he told Luke.

The driver grinned broadly. "Ain't going nowhere without you, Pops."

A few minutes later, the bus was on the road again.

Ben leaned forward in his seat when it came upon a stretch of road that turned sharply to the west. A mile further on, the highway veered sharply again, this time in a southeasterly direction. Luke shook his head and looked in the overhead mirror at Ben.

"I don't know who laid out this road, but this is the only stretch of highway on the route that has a dogleg in it like that."

Ben said nothing. He, more than anyone, knew the reason for the severe bend in the highway and the titanic struggle of wills between the two men who had put it there. One of those men, the man Ben had waited forty years to see, lived in Lamar.

Luke pumped the Greyhound's brakes when it approached the Altamaha River Bridge, and slowed to a crawl. Midway across the river, the bus came to a full stop. Ben's gaze instinctively followed the river's slow eastward flow as the driver opened the bus door and descended the stairs to investigate the reason for their delay.

Images of river scenes flashed through Ben's mind for the first time in decades. He had traveled the Altamaha's length many years before in a hollowed-out cypress tree trunk. He knew the river's bends and its timeless rhythm. It carried with it the sins of man, the rain-washed blood of those murdered in Georgia's hills and mountains and the misdeeds of countless sinners baptized on its shores. Somewhere over the horizon, the Altamaha emptied into the Atlantic near Sapelo Island where he was born.

"Shoulda never left de island," Ben muttered to himself as he had done a thousand times since the killing took place. The *other side*, the mainland, was full of evil. His mother and the island's elders had warned him and Eli, his cousin.

During his tenure at Reidsville State Penitentiary, Ben had come to view the prison's walls as a shield that protected him from the outside world—a place he comprehended less and less as the years rolled by—rather than a barrier designed to protect society from him. Images from the outside filtered in through radio and television like indistinct shadows cast by sunlight into the cave in which he dwelled. The language, the attitude, and the disrespect the younger inmates brought into the prison, dismayed and disoriented him. The thought of leaving the cell that had become his home for decades, caused him anxiety. Just as everything evil had been on the mainland, the other side when he lived on Sapelo, evil now lurked on the outside, beyond the prison walls.

Freedom, this freedom from imprisonment, would have to be relearned. Ben was unfettered, free to go where he pleased, when he pleased. He wanted to go to only one place, but Sapelo was cut off from him until his mission was completed. One thought—only one thought—sustained him: He had a purpose, a mission that could only be completed on the outside.

"Folks," Luke announced, jarring Ben out of his reverie, "We got a pulpwood truck overturned on the other end of the bridge. They got most of the logs out of the way, but it's gonna be a while before they get the rig upright and open up a lane, so make yourselves comfortable. I'll let y'all know just as soon as we're about to get back underway."

Luke stepped off the bus again and walked past the long line of trucks and cars backed up on the southbound lane.

Ben returned his attention to the river, and watched it gently flow underneath. A lot of water had flowed under that bridge, down the Altamaha, and out to sea since Ben's life changed forever.

"A lot of water," Ben muttered as his thoughts drifted downstream to Sapelo along with the slow moving current, *but not enough to wash away the sin of Pastor Dodge's murder.*

CHAPTER 2

A shooting star from the west blazed across the night sky high over Sapelo Island the evening of January 1, 1910. Old Hattie, the midwife who'd ushered much of Sapelo's population into the world long before Emancipation, glimpsed a reflection of the star's fiery trail in an alligator slough on the way to Hog Hammock, a black settlement on the south end of the island. Her husband, Willis, brought the creaking ox-drawn cart to a halt. The two gazed upward through the overhanging oak branches as the white-hot sphere streaked over the island and out to sea.

"West-to-east," he muttered.

"Ooh, Jesus," Hattie replied, shaking her head, "a wanderin' star."

Three years earlier, she witnessed another shooting star on the night she delivered Ben's first cousin, Eli Wilson. It had crossed Sapelo, moving in the opposite direction.

"Eli born under a lucky star," she said.

"Dat right," Willis agreed.

"He be lucky as long as he stay on de island."

"I know dat's right."

When the ox cart pulled up to Jesse Jordan's clapboard house in Hog Hammock, they heard his wife, Josephine, cry out, deep in the throes of childbirth. Inside the house, Hattie found three of

Josephine's sisters surrounding the bed, holding her arms and legs, and urging her to push the child out. Their voices betrayed their growing panic. The birth wasn't going well. Geneva, Josephine's eight-year-old, stood in a corner of the room with her two younger sisters, Delphine and Rona, observing their mother's and aunts' struggles to bring another Jordan into the world.

"She been in pain fo hours," Jesse told Hattie.

Hattie said nothing as she observed the chaos before her and placed a bag with her birthing instruments on the bed cover.

"Men folk leave de room," she calmly commanded. "You girls step away frum de bed," she instructed the aunts. Everyone in the room had been birthed by the ancient midwife, and so immediately complied. "Don't push, Chile," she told Josephine. "I tell you when to push. You jus' lie still." The sounds of Jesse's and Willis's heavy boots on the wood floor echoed down the hallway. A calm permeated the room. Hattie reached between Josephine's legs and inserted her withered hand into the birth canal.

"Dis chile stuck," she said matter-of-factly. "You girls turn yo sister over."

The aunts hesitated. One of them started to question Hattie's instruction.

"Turn yo sister on all fours!" Hattie said, this time, in a tone that left no doubt as to her intention.

"It ain't proper," one aunt whispered.

"I ain't deaf," Hattie said. "Ain't nuthin' proper 'bout makin' babies. Ain't nuthin' proper 'bout birthin' dem either! You wants a new chile, or you wants yo dignity?"

Geneva watched wide-eyed as her aunts helped her mother turn over onto her hands and knees. Hattie placed a towel beneath Josephine's legs and looked at her watch. The aunts looked at one another doubtfully.

"Okay," Hattie said after two minutes passed, "should be sumtin' happenin'."

"It cumin'!" Josephine called out. "It cumin' out now!"

"Dat right," Hattie said, reaching beneath the mother and feeling the infant's head emerging. "Let de chile come on out. You ain't gots to do nuthin' now. God got him. God an' gravity. Cum on out, li'l one. Cum on to Hattie."

Josephine let out one last cry of anguish and relief as the newborn slid effortlessly from one world to the next.

"Lawd God in Heaven haff mercy!" Hattie said as the baby's head emerged wrapped in two thin layers of the caul. "Dis baby will haff special power. He will see spirits. He may be a preacher or sumtin'."

She worked quickly to tie off the umbilical cord. Hattie had delivered babies in the dark, on boats, even once in the crotch of an oak tree during a hurricane. Her hands knew what to do, moving nimbly and with steady assurance.

"God live in de east, de devil in the west," she said. "Bury de afterbirth on de east side of de house," she instructed Geneva and her aunts. "Burn dat white cloth and put it on the naval 'til dat naval rotten."

The afterbirth—the caul and the umbilical cord—was the first part of an islander that went into the earth. The remains of his connection to his mother's womb went into Sapelo's ground, forever binding him to his ancestors, to the living, to their beliefs and customs, and to the island itself. The rest, the flesh and bones, would come later at death, in an elaborate ritual designed to give rest to the spirit.

"Dayclean!"

It was the first word Josephine's son heard the following morning as she stood over the loose soil that contained his afterbirth and held him tightly in her arms. Dayclean marked a new morning, when life began again, when all of the previous day's trials and absurdities died with nightfall, leaving behind a pristine world— like the first day of creation.

Geneva, Rona, and Delphine sat on the front porch steps watching their mother round the corner of the house pointing to objects and telling Ben the names of everything in creation.

"Ever'ting haff spirit," she said, in the Geechee dialect, a West African-English language spoken on Georgia's isolated barrier islands. "A tree haff spirit. De bird haff spirit. Ever'ting belong to God, an' God give ever'ting he made spirit."

Two hounds emerged from beneath the Jordan's porch and barked loudly, announcing a visitor's arrival. Soon, a small figure emerged from a path that disappeared into a thicket behind the Jordan home.

Tiny Ruth, the island's prophetess, born with power of seeing the future, joined mother and son on a sandy patch of ground that served as the front yard. Josephine had been expecting her. Others would later come to see the child whose entry into the world had been foreshadowed by the shooting star.

Ruth's frail, trembling fingers, which once soothed the brows of her master's infants, caressed Ben's cheeks. She peered through eyes that had foreseen the end of slavery, looking deep into the windows of the child's soul, and began to prophesy.

"Dis chile haff de power to see spirit," she said without hesitation, confirming Old Hattie's observation.

Josephine solemnly bowed her head in agreement. None of the long-time islanders questioned Tiny Ruth's word. "Blue mens will free de slave," she foretold many years before the first shot was fired at Fort Sumter. Some islanders laughed at her then. Years later, Union soldiers dressed in blue uniforms fulfilled her prophecy, and few doubted her after that.

Josephine believed the double-caul that had enclosed her son's head conveyed upon him special gifts unknown to others. Ruth's prediction seemed perfectly reasonable to her. The seer leaned closer and inspected Ben's face and hands.

"I see a tree sproutin' frum de earth," she said. "It a pine tree wiff two heads. Dis baby's soul tied to some'un else. De tree will reach up to de sky. De two cum into dis world together, an' will leave together."

She lightly ran her fingers over his skull then let her hand hover over his head.

"Dis baby a li'l Moses. His spirit will wander fo fo'ty years. He will see de promise land but will not enter it—if he ever leave Sapelo."

Josephine again nodded. Others had left the island for the mainland, the west where the Devil resided, attracted by jobs that paid well, by the all-night juke joints and gambling houses, and by world-wise women who inhabited larger towns up and down the coast. A few had done well for themselves and sent money to family on the island. Others returned to Sapelo, broke and broken. Younger men disregarded their examples, thinking themselves invincible, only to follow in their footsteps.

"If he leave Sapelo," Ruth repeated, looking Josephine in the eye, "he will know no peace."

The next afternoon, Reverend Stiles, the visiting minister to Sapelo's African Baptist Church, stopped by the Jordan home. Stiles, educated at the Atlanta Baptist Seminary, had worked hard to learn the Geechee language and customs. His personal mission was to replace the islanders' superstitious beliefs with sound religious doctrines, and that started with building relationships with the people in their homes.

"I heard about the birth at the landing, Brother Jesse," Stiles said, sitting on a handmade chair covered with sun-dried cowhide. Jesse and Josephine sat across from him while the newborn slept peacefully in her lap. "I look forward to presenting him to the congregation this Sunday. Have you named the boy?"

Jesse, who was born into slavery, had thought long and hard about the surname he took after freedom. He settled on the name Jordan, the river Moses's people crossed to reach the Promised Land. Jesse also devoted a lot of thought in determining the name of his first male offspring.

"He name Ben," Jesse replied, "Ben Jordan."

The pastor nodded knowingly.

To white folks, Ben was just another name. To the progeny of Bu-Allah, a Mohammedan from whom Jesse claimed descent, Ben meant "son of." It was a name found throughout both Jesse's and Josephine's families—a name that spoke both of fear and reverence of Bu-Allah, who prayed five times a day, whose Koran had been passed down from generation to generation, even though his descendants could no longer read its Arabic script. Jesse sat with his feet firmly on the ground. It would have been more comfortable to cross one leg over the other, but to show another person the soles of one's feet was disrespectful, a custom brought from Africa with Bu-Allah and still practiced by his descendants.

After a few more minutes of cordial conversation, the reverend came to the point of his visit.

"Has Doctor Crow come by yet?" he asked, attempting to be casual about the inquiry.

"No, Suh," Jesse replied, shaking his head. "Ain't no Doc Crow cum roun' here yet."

"Good," Stiles said, shifting his gaze between the mother and father. "He has no power over this child. Once we pray over him, he's a child of God."

"I unnerstan," Jesse said. "He in de Lawd's grasp."

"Amen, Brother Jesse. Amen."

The afternoon of the third day, dark clouds hung low and thick over the island, emptying a steady drizzle of rain that soaked the ground and swelled the banks of black water sloughs across Sapelo.

Despite the preacher's warnings, the Jordans knew Dr. Crow would come after three days, and they knew there was nothing they could do to stop him. By late afternoon, the thickening cloud cover cast an early dusk over the settlement. Jesse was the first to hear the donkey's hooves splash through puddles on the road that led to their cabin. In between the constant drips from the tin roof, he heard the splashes grow louder as rider and donkey left the main shell road and approached the Jordans' doorstep.

"He comin'," Jesse said, opening the front door a few inches to peek outside.

Josephine took a deep breath and said a prayer. Sooner or later, the island's root doctor visited every newborn child. Dr. Crow's knowledge of herbs and roots, capable of afflicting unsuspecting victims, had been handed down to him from the first African shaman brought to Sapelo in chains. For a price, he could conjure a hex or lift one, be it for good luck, wealth, love, or revenge. Two weeks earlier, he had chewed a root at the back of a courthouse in Darien. The next day, his client was acquitted of murder charges. No one on Sapelo, including his client, showed surprise over the verdict.

Though his fame continued to grow and he had yet to reach the height of his powers, the root doctor searched for a successor. The knowledge of island flora and their mystical attributes, the language of the unknown tongue, and the collective wisdom of generations stretching back in the mists of time—all had to be preserved.

He, too, had seen the shooting star, and waited for the prophetess and the preacher to have their turns before seeking out the baby Jordan.

Jesse opened door at the sound of two heavy boots ascending the front porch steps of the cabin.

"De boy in back," he said, swinging the door wide. Geneva and her sisters huddled in a corner of the front room as Dr. Crow entered. She stared up at the tall, thin man wearing dark glasses and a tattered raincoat. To Geneva, the root doctor resembled the scarecrow in their vegetable patch. Without uttering a sound, he hung his hat and overcoat on a peg, and proceeded toward the back of the house, leaving a trail of water in his wake.

Jesse followed Dr. Crow to the back room where Josephine stood next to a small mattress made of old rags sewn together, and stuffed with moss. Ben lay on top of the mattress with his face toward the window as if trying to see something beyond.

Dr. Crow nodded to her and bent down on one knee. Water dripped from his pants and boots, soaking through cracks in the rough-hewn floorboards and onto the sandy soil beneath the house.

Jesse leaned heavily on the doorframe, his eyes darting from Ben to Josephine.

"He born wiff de double-caul," the root doctor said.

"Yes," Josephine answered, watching Dr. Crow's every move. Ben continued to eye the window, as if unaware of the stranger's presence.

Dr. Crow removed his glasses, revealing one bloodshot eye and an opaque eye that appeared to be covered with a thin membrane. His appearance was such that otherwise fearless men, white and black alike, turned aside in his presence once the glasses were removed. His powers over death were already legendary, having survived numerous attempts on his life by the victims of his hexes. One prominent tale held that two relatives of a man who suddenly went lame after double-crossing Dr. Crow rowed over from the mainland and sought out his cabin deep in the woods of Sapelo. They filled the tiny structure with lead shot, only to see him walk out moments later, his clothes riddled with bullet holes, but his body unscathed. In another story, Darien's sheriff deputized two black men to bring Dr. Crow in for questioning about a woman who'd died of poison. Their boat never made it across the sound. Two bodies, discovered by fishermen a week later in a tidal creek, bore a single crow's feather embedded in their hair. These and similar anecdotes persisted long after the fact, the supernatural nature of their details growing in prominence with each passing year.

The medicine man leaned down to inspect Ben's face. As he leaned closer, Ben turned to him and stared. The shaman breathed sharply three times in rapid succession, like a feral animal sniffing the scent of prey. He reached out with his right hand.

"Don't you touch dat chile!" Josephine snapped.

"Hush," Dr. Crow snarled, irritated at the interruption. To his mind, the continuation of the shaman line was far more important than a mother's concern for one offspring. He turned his head and glared at her in a manner she found profoundly unsettling. As he continued to stare, she had the distinct feeling he was looking beyond her, through the window boards at her back. She also noticed that Ben, again, appeared to be looking at something beyond where she stood.

After several moments, he returned his attention to the child. He held his bony hand above the baby's head and spoke the unknown tongue, at first in low, measured tones, but increasingly louder and faster until Geneva heard them from the front room where she and her sisters remained huddled together.

Jesse exchanged glances with Josephine as the incantations grew louder. Ben shifted his attention between Dr. Crow and his mother, but otherwise gave no indication of fear or discontent. As abruptly as he had begun, Dr. Crow ended his chant without taking his eyes off the child. A full minute passed by before he slowly rose up and left the room without saying a word.

"Well," Jesse said, standing with Dr. Crow stood on the front steps, "Is he de one?"

The root doctor stared at the ground and slowly shook his head. "No," he emphatically replied without looking up. He was, in fact, relieved that the child born under the wandering star would not be his successor. That person would have to be rooted to the island, someone who could carry on his knowledge of magic spells. "He not de one. He can't know the power of de root. But he gots other giffs almos' as powerful."

Jesse turned back toward the door to make sure he wouldn't be overheard by his wife.

"Can you mek up a root fo protection?" he whispered. "I gots three girls. He my only boy. I-I-I don't want nuthin' to harm him. I can pay you next month."

The root doctor put on his hat and stepped out into the drizzle. He paused, turned, and looked at Jesse for the first time. In the dim light, Jesse could see the permanent stain of various plant juices on either side of Dr. Crow's mouth.

"You don't need no root," he replied, his expression unchanged. "Bu-Allah standin' outside de back window watchin' over yo chile."

CHAPTER 3

Six decades after his death, Bu-Allah's influence still loomed large over Sapelo. His presence lingered in the forest shadows cast during the full light of day and enveloped the island by night, protecting its inhabitants from outsiders who would turn the land into a playground for the rich or beachfront development for emerging middle-class whites. In death, the old-timers claimed, Bu-Allah had become more powerful than in life.

He had been taken captive by a warring tribe in North Africa while on a trek to Mecca, and sold to slavers. Thomas Spalding first saw Bu-Allah when his family fled to Nassau during America's War of Independence. Like other Tories, the Spaldings chose to sit out the conflict rather than take up arms against their fellow colonists or be accused by British authorities of treason. Even as a young man, he immediately recognized the slave's confident air. In his eyes, he saw a reflection of himself—intelligent, determined, imposing in manner, and impressive in speech. Years later, as the master of Sapelo, Thomas purchased Bu-Allah on another trip to the Bahamas, and brought him back to manage his estate.

Within a few years of landing on Georgia soil, Bu-Allah was running operations on the mainland plantation, and in the master's absence, on Sapelo. Tall, with high cheekbones, olive skin, and penetrating eyes, he ran the island with an efficiency marveled at by Spalding's fellow planters. On his head, he wore a fez. As a devout Muslim, he observed the Koran's five pillars of faith. Five times a day, he knelt on his prayer mat facing Mecca, and worshipped Allah.

Ben grew up listening to stories of Bu-Allah's feats; his ability to speak and write in numerous languages, his command of slaves, and the respect whites gave him.

During the War of 1812, when other islands fell to the Crown's forces, Spalding gave Bu-Allah the authority to arm and train his slaves to defend Sapelo from invasion. The British never attacked out of respect for Bu-Allah, the legend held, whose word men obeyed without question. Each year on Ben's birthday, Josephine pulled out a small box containing a few of Bu Allah's possessions and allowed him to touch them. His aunts possessed other artifacts, including their ancestor's Koran.

Bu-Allah's spirit had been known to Ben from his first day of life. As he grew, Ben caught glimpses of it on moonlit nights. The former slave who ruled Sapelo was more than a collection of stories to the impressionable child; he was a founding father to be revered and emulated.

From an early age, Ben found himself equally drawn to his cousin, Eli, like an orbiting moon to its planet. Eli's long limbs, straight hair, lighter skin color, and aquiline nose spoke of a direct lineage to Bu-Allah. His fluid movements and the easy, confident air with which he carried himself, attracted the eye of black and white alike.

Ben's features resembled more closely those of the Ebo warriors from whom his mother descended. The Ebo, some of whom drowned themselves when the ship reached Georgia rather than submit to slavery, were purchased by Spalding when no other planter would have them. The few Ebo tribesmen who survived, fled first to the island's woods, eventually assimilating into the slave population. Their language died with the passing of the last surviving warrior, but the stoic and intractable Ebo ethos passed from one generation to the next.

"He sho 'nuff Ebo," his aunts remarked about Ben when at age five, he willingly accepted punishment in exchange for chores he refused to perform. His father, Jesse, likewise impressed upon his only son, the extraordinary heritage of courage and strength from which Ben could draw to sustain him through any trials life might have in store for him.

"You part Bu-Allah, part Ebo," Jesse repeated throughout Ben's youth. "Ain't nobody ever seen nuthin' like it. Never! Bofe Bu-Allah and de Ebo survive dat trip cross de water frum Africa. Only de strongest peoples live tru dat time. Bu-Allah de sma'test man dey wuz on de coast. Sma'ter den mos' dem planters. Ol' man Spaldin' knowed dat. It tek a sma't man to put a sma'ter man in charge. You gots de strength of de Ebo an' de mind of Bu-Allah. Don't never forget."

Ben attended a two-room schoolhouse run by the Penningtons, husband and wife teachers from the mainland. In addition to his studies, he listened to and learned the lessons of students in grades ahead of him in an effort to keep up with Eli. The two cousins were seldom seen without each other's company. By second grade, his classmates referred to Ben as Eli's echo, an appellation he bore proudly.

The instructors poured their knowledge of the outside world into the students' eager minds. It was, in part, their descriptions of life in Savannah and Charleston, that first sparked Eli's interest, and through him, Ben's curiosity of what lay over the horizon beyond the hunting, fishing, and agrarian lifestyle of their parents and grandparents, beyond the reach and influence of Bu-Allah.

Sundays were all-day events at Sapelo's First African Baptist Church beginning with Sunday school, followed by a service, a covered dish lunch, then more singing and preaching of the Word. A few years after Ben's birth, the First African Baptist Church on Sapelo secured the services of Pastor Renfro Simon. Everyone entered through the same door, but men sat on the left side of sanctuary and women on the right. Young adults and children occupied the middle pews. This separation of genders, his mother assured him, was due to Bu-Allah's Muslim influence. Upon entering the church, the older men and women bowed reverently to a small recess where a statue of Jesus, stolen at the conclusion of the Civil War by a Union soldier, once stood. Here, Ben heard the first negative whisperings about Bu-Allah from older children in his Sunday school class who questioned whether a non-Christian would be allowed to enter heaven.

The summer after Ben's twelfth birthday, he knelt to pray at the anxious bench during church service, signaling that he was ready to seek the Lord and become a full member of the church. A tall, lanky church elder named Rupert Bright was assigned to prepare Ben for baptism and official acceptance into the congregation. Ben liked Rupert because he never raised his voice or glared at children like some elders who kept younger ones in their place with intimidating stares and scolding. He also admired Rupert's position as a deacon whose duties included the serving of communion. One Sunday, Ben saw Rupert stop in front of a man and turn an empty wine glass upside down in a deliberate manner before serving the next person.

"Why he did dat?" Ben asked Jesse after the service.

His father laughed. "Dat man make whiskey deep in de woods an' sell it. De pastor tell him he got to stop, but he ain't stop. He outta God will. He outta de church will. So Brother Bright don't serve him no wine."

"I don't wanna be outta God will. I want Missa Bright to be my mentor."

Ben's father smiled broadly. Rupert Bright had also prepared Jesse for baptism when he was twelve. "You go to he house tomorrow at sunup an' start de learnin'," he instructed Ben.

Shortly after daybreak the following morning, Ben left for Rupert's log cabin to start the three-month process of instruction. By that hour, Jesse had already arrived at the Sapelo dock to board the *Eliza Grey*, the shrimp boat he worked on. Josephine had already left to work at the home of Howard Coffin, the Hudson Motor Company executive who owned most of the island. Ben's mother believed that Coffin's intention to develop other barrier islands into resorts—but not Sapelo—was directly due to Bu-Allah's influence.

"Missa Coffin tink he own de islan'," she often said. "He may run it by day . . ."

But by night the spirits still ruled, and Bu-Allah, who once directed the lives of slaves on the island, ruled above all. Josephine worked under Coffin's roof with the other islanders' approval. They knew she would keep an eye on his activities.

"You know why yo papa sent you here at sunup?" Rupert asked Ben who sat at a small kitchen table in the middle of the room.

"No, Suh."

"What dat say?" Rupert asked, pointing a long, bony forefinger at a verse in the open Bible on the table.

Ben leaned forward and read aloud. "Lazy hands make a man poor."

"Mark it!"

Ben wrote the verse on a piece of paper. He would be expected to memorize each verse they discussed.

"God don't cotton to no lazybones," Rupert said, circling Ben. "Dat why yo daddy make you cum here early. A man who don't get up befo de sun rise up over de trees gonna be a no 'count. You get up one hour befo de next man, an' you get three-hundred-sixty-five hours mo' time den him each year. Dat fifteen full days—mo' dan two weeks—you get over de man who still in bed. God don't tell no one how much time he got to live, so you gots to do yo best wiff de time you got. Gettin' up a hour earlier put you in God's favor. Okay. Dat's dat," Rupert said, putting a stamp of finality on the subject.

"Now," he continued, "any questions?"

On the table before Ben sat a pair of salt-and-pepper shakers and a small ceramic jar with the word "Sugar!" painted in magenta across it. As the deacon spoke, Ben's gaze darted between the Bible text and the sugar jar. Rupert stole quick glances at Ben and noticed his wavering attention.

"Whut heaven like?" Ben asked.

"No man alive knows," Rupert replied. "Mark down Firs' Corinthian two, nine. 'No eye haff seen, no ear haff heard, no mind haff conceive whut God haff prepared fo de ones who love him.' So say de Lawd. Now, you seen dem automobiles Missa Coffin' folk drive around?"

"Yessuh."

"You heard a radio befo?"

"Yessuh."

"No man alive could conceive dem tings a hundred years ago. Tings dat will be made by man a hundred years frum now, cain't nobody imagine today. So, ain't no way we gonna conceive whut heaven like. Dat's dat. Any questions?"

"No, Suh."

"Next lesson. Now, read Matthew, chapter fo."

Ben turned the pages and began to read aloud Satan's tempting of Jesus with all the kingdoms of the world. When he finished, Rupert launched into a lecture on the consequences of giving in to temptation, all the while keeping an eye on Ben whose attention returned ever more frequently to the jar on the table.

"You got a sweet tooth?" Rupert asked at length. Ben nodded eagerly.

"You want sum of whut's in dat jar?" Rupert leaned across the table and lifted the lid to reveal a mound of white crystals inside.

"Yessuh," Ben replied, his mind filled with thoughts of eating refined sugar straight from the jar.

Rupert scooped out a large spoonful.

"Hold out yo hand," he instructed.

Ben did as he was told and watched with keen anticipation as the deacon poured the spoon's contents into his hand. Ben smiled and popped the pile of granules into his mouth. But the smile turned to a look of disgust a moment later. He sputtered and rushed to the sink to spit. Rupert's cackling laugh rang in his ears.

"Dey is a glass of water on de counter already poured. Hep yoself," the deacon instructed, still laughing aloud.

A minute later, Ben returned to the table humiliated and angered at his mentor's deceit.

"Okay," Rupert said, his jovial mood gone, replaced by a solemn face and sober tones. "Whut you learnt?"

"Dat wuz sneaky," Ben replied with resentment in his voice.

"Just like de Devil!" the deacon replied. "He real sneaky. Like a snake. Satan tempt Jesus Christ wiff kingdoms an' mansions. But it wuz all a lie. See? De sugar jar wuz filled wiff salt! Sum tings dat look real good ain't whut dey seem. It called temptation. Temptation cum in all shapes and sizes. It cum at a man all de days of he life. You gots to recognize it, Ben Jordan! Dat why I let you eat salt. 'Cause God love all He creatures—man an' beast—an' I love you. Better you eat a li'l salt an' learn de lesson now den get took in an' lose yo soul later."

Rupert placed a small piece of hard candy in Ben's hand.

"Okay, dat's dat. Any questions?"

Ben stared at the jar before him with enlightened eyes and felt his anger subside. He let the candy roll across his tongue. He had, in fact, many questions that he wanted to ask in Sunday school but was too shy to bring up for fear of being rebuked or laughed down. There, in his mentor's kitchen, he felt he could ask anything without fear of rejection.

"God love all creatures? Mama say ever'ting got a spirit. Trees, animals. Ever'ting. Is dat true?"

"Psalm one-fifty, verse six. Read it."

Ben leafed through the pages and found the text. "Let ever'ting dat haff breath praise de Lawd."

"Mark it! Ecclesiastes three, verse twenny-one. Read it."

"Who knows if de spirit of man rise up or de spirit of de animal go down into de earth?"

"Mark it! Ever'ting on Earth belong to de Lawd. Ever'ting haff spirit. De bones go into de ground, de soul go to heaven, but de spirit stay here on Earth. Okay, dat's dat. Any questions?"

"Yessuh. Sum de older chillren say Bu-Allah cain't go to heaven 'cause he not Christian," Ben blurted. The subject had been preying on his mind for months.

Rupert let out a long sigh. "Okay ... whut you just ax me regardin' a man's soul ... dat a very serious question. Bu-Allah pray to de God of Abraham five time a day. Christians pray to de God of Abraham. De Jew pray to de God of Abraham. Whether Bu-Allah in heaven or not—dat between God and Bu-Allah. Now, dat's dat. Any mo' questions?"

"No, Suh."

"Okay. Next lesson. Firs' Samuel, twenny-fo, verse one through ten. Read it!"

The deacon patiently circled the room as Ben struggled to

find the passage. At length, he read how David spared King Saul's life.

"Why he spare de king?" Rupert wanted to know. "'Cause he anointed by God," Ben replied. "Co-reck! King Saul anointed. David anointed. A preacher anointed. Don't never forget it. You gots to listen to whut de preacher say! A preacher be a holy man, anointed by God frum de time of Abraham. King David coulda slew Saul, but he never done it 'cause Saul anointed. A man who do harm to a preacher is a man doing harm to de Lawd Almighty. Any questions?"

"No, Suh."

"Okay. Next lesson."

Ben's studies continued until noon, at which time Rupert sent him home to memorize what they had discussed. That evening, Ben rushed for the front door when he heard Jesse's heavy footsteps on the porch. He jumped into his father's arms while his sisters pulled at his pant legs, all eager to tell him about their day.

Jesse grinned and slipped Ben a piece of caramel candy wrapped in wax paper while the others weren't looking. When Ben looked at him quizzically, his father's face broke into a broad grin.

"Son, did Deacon Bright teach you 'bout temptation today?"

"Yessuh."

"He put dat ol' sugar jar on de table?"

"Yessuh!"

"Uh-huh," Jesse said knowingly. "He done de same ting to me when I wuz a boy. Took two days to get dat nasty salt taste outta my mouth. Now, you go ahead an' eat dat candy, but don't let no one see you."

The three months of preparation passed quickly for Ben. On the final day, Rupert told him to return to his cabin an hour before dawn. He awoke early, having slept little all night, and left his mother, father, and his three sisters still in their beds as he crept outside and ran to the deacon's home. Spirits, earthbound until Resurrection Day, were visible to Ben beginning at dusk when the worlds of light and dark overlap one another. Some spirits he pitied; others he learned to avoid. This morning, he ignored all of them, secure in the knowledge of the protection promised by scripture and comforted in the belief that Bu-Allah's paternal spirit held sway over all other spirits on the island.

"Now," Rupert told Ben as they walked through his cabin from the front door to the kitchen, "come wiff me."

Ben followed Rupert into the back yard and heard the door shut behind them.

"Okay, tek dat trail into de woods," Rupert instructed.

Ben hesitated, straining his eyes in the dark to find an entrance to the trail.

"Whut de matter?" the deacon asked.

"I ain't never been out here, Suh. I don't know de way."

As Ben spoke, a flame grew bright above him. A moment later, he realized the deacon had lit a kerosene lamp.

"Quick. Tell me whut de Psalms say 'bout de lamp?"

"'Yo word is a lamp to my feet an' a light fo my path,'" Ben answered.

"Dat right, Ben. See de light on de ground? De lamp put out dat light only so far. You cain't see way yonder ahead, but you can see far enough. Dat why God give us de scripture. He don't want us seein' 'til kingdom come. But He wanna light de path we on 'nuff to see where we goin'. Now, lead on."

Ben took the lantern from Rupert and found the trail. Soon, he and the deacon were deep in the forest moving further into the island's interior. Half an hour later, at the very point where Ben knew they would be utterly lost without a light to guide them, Rupert took the lantern from Ben and extinguished the flame.

"Okay," he said, "Second Corinthians, chapter five, verse seven. Whut is say?"

Ben turned toward the voice. "We live by faith, not by sight."

"Dat right. Now, final lesson. Keep walkin' on dis trail. Don't stop 'til you get to de end."

Ben turned back in the direction they had been heading and again strained his eyes to see the trail.

"I can't see nuthin'," he said.

No one responded.

Ben reached out and felt nothing but the leaves of underbrush and tree bark. He quickly realized that he was utterly alone deep in the same forest he'd heard about all of his life where jack-o-lanterns—balls of light—lured unsuspecting islanders deep into the woods, never to be seen again. For a moment, he considered walking back in the direction they had come, but he knew he was being tested. If he returned home, the preparation for baptism would begin again next year. He would be rebuked by the church elders and scoffed at by his peers. More importantly, his mother and father would be disappointed.

"We live by faith, not by sight," he said, nervously as he held his hands out, touching branches, feeling his way along the trail that narrowed with each step. At any moment, he expected Dr. Crow or a demon to pop up and devour him. Perhaps, they would appear together and fight over his soul. More than once, he felt the icy touch of a spirit touching his shoulder. When he turned, he only caught a glimpse of the phantom disappearing into the woods. At just the point where he felt sure he might turn and run, he felt a hand push him forward.

He continued the lonely sojourn for another five minutes until, looking up, he saw the first hints of daylight filtering into the night sky. He kept his eyes heavenward, continuing to feel his way forward on the relatively straight pathway. Ben soon encountered foliage so dense he was convinced he could go no further. He stood in the path looking behind him, and again considered retracing his steps when he heard someone say, "Ben Jordan, come out!"

Ben turned and looked at the wall of palmetto bushes enclosed by cedar trees in front of him. He bent down and gingerly pushed palmetto fronds aside, making his way through the undergrowth until he stumbled and fell forward into a small glade. He jumped to his feet and began to brush the sand off his clothes. His jaw fell open a moment later when he became aware of the twelve men who surrounded him. As his eyes adjusted to the dawn light, he realized the men were Pastor Simon, deacons, and elders of his church. Rupert Bright stood with the deacons betraying no emotion on his face. Next to the deacon stood his father, Jesse, tears streaming down his face.

"I knowed he would make it," Rupert said aloud. "He pass all de tests."

"Brother Ben," said Pastor Simon as he stepped forward, "welcome to de body of Christ!"

CHAPTER 4

Eli stood on the beach and watched Ben and the other candidates, dressed in white clothes and wrapped in white sheets, step forward to be baptized. Reverend Simon submerged each person three times, their sins drifting away on the outgoing tide.

"I baptize you in the name of the Son," the preacher said. Ben let his body go slack as he leaned back, letting the pastor and another deacon immerse him. "And the Father." The second immersion lasted a second more than the first. "And the Holy Spirit!" Ben felt his body go under a third and longer time. When he broke the surface, a warm sensation engulfed him. Though only twelve, he knew he had passed through a threshold of sorts, even if he couldn't put it into words.

"You had Deacon Bright," Eli said with a laugh a few days later as the two boys walked through the woods on the way to a fishing hole.

"What so funny 'bout dat, Cuz?" Ben wanted to know.

"He de hardest Bible teacher dey is. You thought he wuz a easy man. He tough on he students! He tek you in de woods at night?"

"Dat wuz de last lesson."

"De straight an' narrow path lesson . . . I tink dey primin' you to be a preacher."

"Why you say dat?"

"I ain't never had to do it. None of de other boys, too. I wuzn't supposed to say nuthin', but dat whut I tink."

As Ben and Eli matured, their lives revolved around a never-ending cycle of schooling and chores dictated by the seasons and punctuated by day-long Sunday meetings. On the days Jesse and Josephine worked, his sisters kept house and fed the chickens and hogs while he chopped wood and tended the family orchard of orange, grapefruit, peach, and pear trees and a quarter acre where he learned to grow and harvest corn before grinding it into hominy grits.

In their spare time, the two cousins hunted game in Sapelo's woods and dropped fishhooks in its many creeks. The two were equals with the rifle, but Ben's innate talent with a pistol, a discarded .45 caliber firearm they cleaned and repaired, far surpassed his cousin's. By their early teens, they had an intimate knowledge of every slough and tree stand on the island. Jesse taught the boys how to swim at an early age, a skill many children on the mainland never learned. On Sapelo, surrounded by water, it was imperative. They earned money diving at the docks to free shrimp nets tangled on propellers and dislodge anchors hung up on submerged objects, competing with one another to see who could remain underwater the longest.

Nights were spent listening to stories about the ones who had come from Africa, about Bu-Allah's exploits, about spirits—good and evil—that walked the island, and about hags who rode their victims all night to the point of exhaustion.

Before daybreak on Ben's seventeenth birthday, he awoke to the sound of scratching on the window of the room where he slept.

"Ben," Eli whispered. "Let's go!"

"Go where, Cuz?" Ben wanted to know.

"You see!"

Eli, having repeatedly been reminded by relatives that he was born under a lucky star, gradually assumed the attributes of a modern day Achilles, impervious to danger or misfortune. Ben, under the shadow of Eli's aegis, likewise believed no harm could befall either of them. Together that morning, they set off for St. Catherines Island, north of Sapelo, where Eli intended to court a girl of fifteen whom he had met in Darien. Her father had warned Eli to stay clear of St. Catherines, the result of quarrels between islanders going back longer than anyone could remember. But Eli's desires far outweighed the risks, and with Ben as his lookout, he feared no one.

By sunrise, the two were paddling along the tidal river on the island's west bank in a makeshift pirogue they had fashioned the year before by hollowing out a tree trunk. The water was still as they crossed the sound separating Sapelo and St. Catherines. A little over an hour later they reached their destination, a row of tabby structures that had once been slave cabins. In the distance, they heard gunfire.

"Sum'un out huntin' mighty early," Eli said.

Ben stood guard on the shell road leading to the cabins while Eli strutted to the rear of the third one. Ten minutes had passed when Ben heard the sound of heavy footsteps on the road. A moment later, he saw a large man brandishing a shotgun round the bend trotting quickly and breathing hard. He found his cousin behind the cabin talking through an open window to a beautiful girl who seemed to be barely in her teens.

"Cuz! We gots to go!" he said, breathlessly. "A man cumin!"

"It Poppa," the girl gasped, her expression turning from bashful playfulness to alarm.

Eli stood erect and puffed out his chest. "I ain't scared of no man," he said, calmly looking in the direction of the road.

"He got a gun!" Ben said.

"He'll shoot you down!" the girl cried, "De bofe of you!"

By then Ben and Eli could hear the footsteps and heavy breathing of the girl's father leaving the road and heading their way.

"Take de trail," the girl said, pointing to a small nearby opening in the woods. "It tek you back to de road."

Eli smiled, took her hand, and kissed it. "I be back!"

By the time the man reached his cabin, the back window boards were closed, and the intruders were gone. However, two sets of fresh footprints led to the woods.

"I deal wiff you later," he panted, looking at the window.

The cousins scrambled through the woods and quickly found the road. They had been chased before by wild boars and even once by an alligator guarding its nest, but those escapades had been fun, even exciting. This chase was different. The thing after them carried a weapon.

"He haff a shotgun or a rifle?" Eli panted as they approached the beach where they had landed.

"Couldn't tell!" Ben panted back. "Whut it matter?"

"Rifle gots a long range!" Eli answered. "He gots to get close wiff a shotgun!"

Ben jumped into the canoe as Eli pushed off. He immediately saw two shotgun holes that the man fired into the bottom of the craft.

"Huntin' gator nuthin! He shot our boat, an' we leakin'!" Ben shouted.

"Plug it wiff yo foot!" Eli shouted back as the two feverishly paddled.

"Dey is two holes!"

"Plug 'em wiff bofe feet!"

His words were cut short by the sound of the father hurling curses at them from the shore. "Get down!" Eli advised.

A shotgun blast echoed over the water as pellets streaked by, several lodging in the canoe's side.

"Don't stop!" Eli said, laughing. "Keep a paddlin'!"

Another blast resounded from the shore. More pellets streaked by.

"De water comin' in!" Ben shouted.

"Bail it out! I'll paddle!"

Ben scooped the water over the canoe's sides while Eli stroked harder, slowly moving them out of range while the man on the beach reloaded and fired two more ineffectual rounds.

Halfway across the sound, the wind picked up, making the water choppy. Ben attempted to plug the shotgun holes with his and Eli's shirts, but they were forced to abandon their canoe a half-mile from Sapelo's northern shore.

The incoming tide pushed Ben and Eli into an inland river infested with alligators. Both had experienced their fair share of run-ins with gators and gave the matter little thought as they crossed an expanse of marshland and swam across to Sapelo. But when it came to crossing through the island's swamps, they moved quickly.

"De swamp de Devil's doorway to de world," the old-timers believed. "It where he cum up at night. De snake and de gator guard he doorway to de Unnerworld!"

Ben cleaned up at Eli's home using the outside well to wash the muck and cuts acquired during their adventure. He remained at Eli's house until dark. On the way home, Ben thought he saw movement on the road ahead of him. Overhead, dark clouds briefly opened, and a shaft of moonlight filled the forest around him. After several moments, his eyes detected a tall figure in the road staring at him. The man stood erect, like a tree. In the bright moonbeam, Ben could see the man's facial features, the deep-set eyes, high cheeks, and thin, curved nose, like an eagle's beak. On his head, he wore an odd shaped hat. It was his first clear view of the apparition Ben had heard about since he was a toddler.

Just as quickly as they had opened, the clouds closed again, obliterating the specter. Moments later, a steady rain began to fall.

"Boy, where you been?" Jesse demanded.

Ben said nothing. The expression on his face spoke for him.

"He seen sumpin'," Josephine said. "Whatchoo see, Son?"

Ben briefly described the figure in the road. Josephine and Jesse looked at each other.

"Bu-Allah," they said in unison.

The next morning, Josephine took Ben to visit her uncle, Aaron Miles, a man over one hundred years old who lived in the same tabby cabin he had grown up in as a slave. With his permission, Josephine went up a small fight of steps to the cabin's attic and soon returned with a sack. Inside was a box that held another box. Inside the second box was an object wrapped in newspaper dated 1850.

"Is this whut you saw last night?" she asked Ben as she held aloft a fez.

Ben nodded. "Dat it."

Her Uncle Miles smiled broadly, revealing two bright rows of teeth, a source of pride on his part at such an advanced age.

"Dis here hat belong to Bu-Allah," he said, holding it at an angle. "Still see de sweat stain on the brim."

Josephine handed the fez to Ben who held it reverently, as if handling eggshells. He turned it over and saw two faint undulating rows of discolored banding, stained by the sweat of Bu-Allah's brow.

"Go ahead," the old man said. "Tetch it."

Ben reached out a forefinger and ran it along the inside brim.

"You tetchin' Bu-Allah," he informed Ben. "Sum day Bu-Allah gonna reach out an' tetch you."

CHAPTER 5

In the summer of 1928, Ben and Eli joined a work gang on Howard Coffin's property, clearing trees to accommodate a private airstrip for planes to land on.

"You see a snake, shoot it," the white foreman instructed his all black crew, most of whom came from the mainland. "Any of you boys know how to handle a gun?"

"He do," said Eli, pointing at Ben.

"Oh yeah?" said the foreman, placing a tin can on a nearby fence post. "Lemme see you hit that," he said, handing Ben a loaded revolver.

"Where, Suh?" Ben asked.

"The can, Boy! That's where!"

Eli laughed and interpreted for Ben. "He want to know where on the can you want him to hit it."

"Just shoot the damn . . ."

Ben dropped the can from its perch before the foreman finished the sentence.

At first, the mainland blacks looked on with fascination as Ben and Eli asked permission of each tree before cutting it down, but their wonder at the islanders' ways quickly turned into derision as they questioned the cousins on their customs. Before long, secretly, and without telling one another, Ben and Eli began to question their beliefs as well. A few days into the job, both had proven themselves the mainlanders' equals with a crosscut saw and an axe, and their hard work earned the respect of the older men. Ben's expertise with a pistol came in handy as workers dislodged water moccasins and rattlesnakes from their sanctuaries.

Ultimately, the lure of the mainland proved to be too powerful for Eli as the visiting workers spoke of all-night speakeasies in the black districts of nearby towns, of city women, and of the easy money to be had.

"Den why you here on Sapelo?" Ben asked one logger, a brawny man from Waycross named Noble Wise.

"This only temporary," he said, laughing, flashing two gold teeth in a show of wealth. "I'm making money here, but my women are over there." He nodded in the direction of the mainland. "Everything you want is over there. I gots a line on some work after this job is did. You boys wanna leave this island, just come on to Waycross and let ol' Noble know."

Men from tiny backwoods settlements and barrier islands were attracted to Savannah, Macon, and smaller towns like Brunswick and Waycross with their lighted streets and noisy juke joints. Little by little, the mainlanders laughed away Ben and Eli's beliefs, explaining that Jack-o-lanterns were merely swamp gas, a naturally occurring phenomenon. Hags weren't real witches but high blood pressure that could be corrected with diet or medicines.

Toward the end of summer, after the landing strip had been completed, Eli found Ben fishing in a tidal creek with a hand line.

"Let's go," he said as Ben tossed a baited hook into the muddy brine and watched the string slowly sink.

Ben knew what he meant. Eli's time had come. He was ready to enter the other world where airplanes, automobiles, radios, and telephones were changing society. None of that had come into the daily lives of the people on their barrier island. Eli had come to view Sapelo as an insular backwater, chained to its past. The root doctor, the prophetess, their parents, the church elders—all of their ways of thinking and everything they proclaimed was from before slavery. For Eli, the other side of the water represented true freedom.

Ben reeled in the empty fishing line by hand and coiled it up neatly. Eli was ready to leave Sapelo. Ready to strike out on his own. Ready to see what lay ahead beyond Darien, the nearest town. Ben, having reached the ripe old age of eighteen, was also ready.

The boat to the Meridian docks on the mainland left Sapelo three times a day, in the morning, at noon, and before dark. Eli's plan was to catch the first boat the following day and stay overnight at an older brother's house in the Crescent settlement before pushing on to Waycross.

That afternoon, Ben told his parents about their decision to leave Sapelo.

"You cain't leave dis island," Josephine said emphatically as Ben stuffed his belongings in an old Army issue duffle bag. "Eli born under a lucky star. He be lucky long as he live on Sapelo!" she reminded him. "Don't forget whut Tiny Ruth say. She say, 'Dis baby a li'l Moses. He will wander de desert fo fo'ty year. He will see de promise land but will not enter it—if he ever leave Sapelo.' She wuz talkin' 'bout you, Ben Jordan."

Ben spent a restless night. The little sleep he could muster was filled with a dream of grotesque animals that chased him across alien landscapes overflowing with bizarre images and odd-shaped buildings. An unseen but keenly felt presence spurred the animals after him. Ahead of him, a light on the horizon shone brightly, and he headed for it. As he neared the beacon, his resolve turned into doubt. He wondered if, instead of guiding him, the light lured him to an early demise. He wasn't sure if the animals gaining on his heels weren't trying to rescue him or if the presence driving them hadn't sent the creatures to save him. The dream played over and over in his mind like a movie reel with no end.

In the early morning hours, a storm swept crossed the island and moved out to sea. The cool breeze brought with it offered relief, but Ben dared not look out his window. He instinctively knew that the presence in his dream was Bu-Allah, and that the landscape was the mainland. The light and the animals he could not assign to a known entity.

He awoke tired before dawn and crept outside so he wouldn't wake his parents. But Jesse sat on the front step waiting for him.

"Don't look a white man in the eye 'less you know him real well," Jesse advised as they walked to Eli's home. "If a white man tell you to do sumtin', you do it! Don't ax questions. An' don't never be alone wiff a white woman—ever. You say 'yes Suh' an' 'no Suh,' 'yes Ma'am' an' 'no Ma'am.' Dat all you gots to say."

"Yes, Suh," Ben replied.

"Tings in de towns ain't like tings on Sapelo. Even sum de colored folk learnt so much dey don't know nuthin' no mo. Dem peoples don't know nuthin' 'bout de root. Dey don't know nuthin' 'bout de old ways."

"Yes, Papa."

"Watch out who you be wiff. You get in de wrong crowd, dat who you become. You get in wiff bad folk, you gonna be a bad man. You get in wiff good folk, you gonna be a good man. You is who you tied to."

"Yes, Papa."

"An' one last ting," his father said, placing his hands on Ben's shoulders and looking him in the eye. "Dey can tek ever'ting you got. Dey can break yo body. But de spirit, de soul," he said, tapping Ben on the chest, "cain't no man touch dat!"

Jesse left Ben and Eli at the dock and walked away without looking back.

"Engine problems," the dock master informed them an hour after the boat failed to arrive on time. "She'll be here directly."

But the boat didn't show all that morning, nor the better part of the afternoon.

Ben followed the sun's arc across the sky and grew restless as it approached the far horizon.

"Daddy say sunrise fo de breathin' man, sunset fo de spirit man," Eli told him. "Breathin man wake up when de sun rise. De spirits cum alive when de sun go down."

Ben didn't reply. He'd been thinking the same thing, concerned that Bu-Allah might show himself and stop Ben from leaving. The sound of the diesel engine approaching the dock filled him with renewed anticipation of the adventure that lay before them, and he put Bu-Allah out of his mind.

The trip from Sapelo to Meridian was a thirty-minute ride on an aging vessel that had plied the waters of Doboy Sound for years. Halfway to the mainland, the red ball of sun dipped behind the western horizon. Two bottlenose dolphins broke surface alongside the boat, their presence a sign of good luck.

The cousins occupied bench seats on the rear deck with their worldly belongings stowed beneath them. Ben kept his eyes fixed on sun's rays in the western sky. Somewhere over there whole towns would be lighting up and coming alive with spirits of a different kind. He'd never seen a street all lit up. He'd never seen men lit up, stumbling from one bar to the next, falling down drunk on the sidewalk. He hadn't seen women dancing to the live music that could be heard a block down the street every time someone stepped out of a nightclub. He'd heard the stories. Now, he was going to see for himself.

As he watched the sky and dreamed of things to come, a strong offshore breeze sprang up, bringing with it small waves that slowed the boat's progress. Ben felt a hand on his shoulder, pulling him backwards.

"Cuz, stop messin' wiff me," he told Eli.

His cousin, sitting a few feet away, turned and looked at him. "I ain't messin'."

Ben looked around. They were alone on that part of the boat. He had felt the hand once before, walking alone in the dark on the path behind Rupert Bright's cabin.

"Oh," he said, "must be de wind."

But he knew who it was.

So did Eli.

Bu-Allah's spirit had awakened to find one of his progeny missing.

CHAPTER 6

They spent that night at the home of Eli's older brother in Crescent, a small settlement just north of Darien. The brother knew a local pulpwood truck driver who was making a run to middle Georgia and would pass through Waycross, a rail hub where north, south, east, and west lines intersected. Ben and Eli left Crescent the next morning a little after sunup. The driver and Eli seemed not to be bothered by the aging truck's leaky exhaust, which seeped into the cab for most of the trip, but by the time the truck rolled to a stop in Waycross, Ben's head was swimming.

Compared to Macon and Savannah, Waycross was a small town. To two barrier island residents, it seemed a city of large buildings, bustling streets, and almost continuous train activity. Ben and Eli found the address Noble Wise had given them several blocks from the railroad yard. Eli knocked on the door and stepped back as an elderly woman opened it wide enough to see their faces.

"Yes? Speak up!" she demanded.

"Ma'am, Noble say for us to cum see him . . ." Eli replied, serving as the spokesman.

"He took the train to Macon," the old woman snapped.

Ben and Eli looked at each other, taken aback. On the island, if a stranger showed up at your doorstep, he would be given shelter.

"He told us dey wuz work . . ."

"He ain't told me nothing 'bout no work. If they is work, how come he ain't got it? How come he got to go to Macon for to work?"

Ben squatted and breathed in deeply, sure that he would vomit from inhaling truck exhaust for sixty miles.

"He told us on Sapelo . . ."

"I don't know nothing 'bout that," she said dismissively. "You best go on back to Sapelo."

"We cum here fo work . . ."

"You just boys. Grown men lining up for work these days. Go on back home."

Ben fell onto his knees and puked on the gravel. The woman stared at him with contempt.

"Already been drinking," she said, shaking her head. "This early in the day, and you been drinking. Go on from here before I call the police."

Ben threw up once more as the door slammed. Eli stared at the closed door in disbelief, then turned to help Ben to his feet.

"I all right," Ben assured him. "Dat felt real good getting dem fumes out."

"Boys," a voice called from across the street. They turned and saw a well-dressed black man in his sixties. "Go down to the train shed," he said, pointing in the direction they had come. "A man in a truck will come along in a bit. He might have some work for you."

The two followed the road back into town. Near the depot, they found a maintenance shed where train engines were repaired. Behind that, they saw a gathering of black and white men, some of whom were climbing onto the back of a flatbed truck, which pulled away just as Ben and Eli arrived.

About ten men remained as a train pulled into Waycross. The men turned and looked wistfully at black porters who helped men and women on and off the railcars. Ben and Eli stared too.

"Sho wish I was working on that train," one of the men said.

Train porters had the dream jobs. They wore clean uniforms and traveled the country. The men standing around the shed would be happy for a day's employment in the hot sun for a dollar or less. By evening, the lucky ones earned some money to pay rent or buy food, but their bodies and spirits took a beating in the scalding Georgia sun. And the porters would be in a distant city—Miami or Philadelphia, Tampa, or New York—enjoying the nightlife.

"Uh-huh," another man in line said. "Man, they got it made. Riding up and down the line, getting monstrous big tips."

"Selling hooch!" another remarked with a cackle.

Porters occasionally buying Georgia moonshine and selling it for inflated prices to clubs in Miami and New York, was a widely repeated legend among people who inhabited towns along train routes. Whether it could be proven was another story. The men watched to see if any untoward transactions occurred, but the train was soon on its way without the anticipated exchange of ceramic jars for cash.

Ben and Eli occupied the last two places in the line and leaned against the shed, each hugging his luggage. Just as the man they met on the street had predicted, another truck soon pulled up to the shed.

"I need four men to pick onions," the driver called out.

"No, no," Eli whispered. "I ain't left Sapelo to work in no field."

Five men scrambled aboard the truck. It sped off, leaving a trail of dust in its wake.

"Waycross a big town," Eli said, eyeing the buildings. "Dey gots to be work in dere somewhere."

"Yeah, if you white," an older man wearing overalls replied. The remaining men in line, all black, laughed at the remark.

"Where you two from?" he asked, looking Eli and Ben up and down as if they were immigrants from a foreign land.

"We frum Sapelo," Eli said.

"Good Lawd hep us!" the man cried, shaking his head.

"You nigguhs might as well go back to Sapelo," another chimed in. "Ain't no work around here 'cept what comes by on a truck."

Ben spoke up for Eli. "He was born under a lucky star. He can get a job on that train if he want to."

The older man laughed hard. "Man, you . . . you two both crazy. That the best job they is in the whole world, and you think you gonna jump on that train and snatch one?"

The sound of hammers pounding on iron echoed within the shed.

"He can walk in there and get work in two minutes," Ben said. "A man born under a lucky star can do anything."

"Well, go do it," the man replied. "Ain't nobody stopping Mr. Lucky Man."

Eli grinned, nudged Ben with his elbow, and winked. He was, in fact, feeling lucky, a sensation he got sometimes when he knew something good was about to happen. He entered the shed through a back door.

"Who you boys staying with?" the man asked Ben after Eli disappeared inside.

Ben scratched his head and thought for a moment. "We wuz stayin' wiff Noble."

"Noble Wise? He gone. Gone to Macon."

Ben nodded. "We know."

"His aunt don't let no strangers 'round her house."

"We know," Ben repeated.

"They lock you up if you ain't got nowhere to stay," the man said, his voice suddenly serious. "Some of them police 'round here will beat you if you ain't got a place. They don't look kindly on drifters."

"Uh-huh," the others affirmed. "That's right. That's right."

"See that church?" the man said, pointing to an antebellum

structure nearby. "That preacher name is Coghill. He live in back of it. He'll put you two up for a night or two. But you best be having a job and a place to stay before Friday."

At that moment, Eli emerged from the shed smiling broadly. The foreman inside the shed had lost a crewmember the day before and needed a strong back to replace him. The men outside were too old or too simple to handle the work in his estimation. In Eli, he saw an alert, willing mind and an able body.

"I gots de job!" he announced.

"I'll be a son of a gun," the older man said. "Sho nuff?"

Eli grinned and nodded. "Start right now."

"See!" said Ben. "I told you he was born under a lucky star."

"He sho nuff is born under a lucky star," the older man said, rubbing Eli's head. "Give me some of that luck, Boy!"

The other men circled around and rubbed his head in hopes that his good fortune would rub off on them. When they were done, Ben handed Eli his belongings, and told him about the church nearby.

"Leave de bags wiff me," Eli told him. "I'll go see de man 'bout a place fo us to live. You stay here an' get some work, an' I see you back at dis shed affer dark."

The cousins shook hands, and Eli disappeared once again inside the rail shed. A few minutes later, Ben saw a shiny Packard approach. Following it was a logging truck. Both vehicles pulled up to the shed and came to a stop. A white man in his early sixties got out of the car and approached them. The black driver of the truck stayed in the cab and observed.

"Any of you boys know how to handle an ox team?" the white man asked.

"That's me, Boss," one of the men answered.

The white man eyed him up and down with suspicion. "Don't lie to me," he said in a harsh tone that caused some of the men to step back. "I need a man to clear timber. You're the sorriest excuse for laborers I've ever seen. Anyone ever done logging?"

Ben stepped forward. "I reckon I have, Suh," he said.

"Where?" the man wanted to know.

"Over to Sapelo."

"Sapelo? Sapelo Island? Who for?"

"Mr. Howard Coffin," Ben answered.

The man spit on the ground. "That gottdamn Yankee?"

Ben didn't reply. The man eyed him up and down for several moments.

"What kind of work was it?"

"Clearin' land, Suh."

"Clearing land? What kind of trees?"

"Oak an' pine, Suh. Sum cedar."

The man turned and appraised Ben as he would a horse.

"I ain't looking for a damn day-laborer. I'm hiring.

This is full-time work in Lamar. If you ain't worth a gottdamn, you can walk your ass back to Waycross yourself!"

"Yes, Suh."

"Can you handle a gun?"

"Yes, Suh."

"Ever shot a rattler?"

"I know all 'bout shootin' snakes, Suh. Dey is plenty rattlers on Sapelo."

"The work is five days and a half day on Saturday, sunup to sundown. I pay seven dollars every Friday. I take two dollars for room and board if you need it. Still want the job?"

The man in overalls nudged Ben in the back.

"That good money, Boy. Better snatch it up," he murmured.

"Yessuh, I still want de job," Ben replied.

The white man tilted his head toward the logging truck.

"Get in, and follow me," he instructed.

He turned to the driver. "Luther, take him to the lumber yard office."

"Yessuh, Mister Cutler," the driver replied.

The man in overalls whistled aloud after the car had pulled away. "Man, both you boys was born under that lucky star."

Ben asked the truck driver to wait. He ran inside the shed and found Eli holding a large wrench while another man beat on the huge bolt attached to it.

"Cuz, I gots a job!"

Eli smiled. "It our lucky day!"

"Hold it steady, Boy!" the black mechanic scolded. "I'm going to Lamar," Ben said, grabbing his bag. "Where Lamar?"

"Don't know!"

"It's on the other side of Baxley to the river. Now hold the damn thing tight!" the workman said.

"Sorry, Boss," Eli said, grinning broadly.

"I cum see you on Sunday," Ben told his cousin. "Okay," Eli replied returning his attention to the task at hand.

For the first several miles, Luther remained silent, concentrating on negotiating hairpin turns and rutted roads. Ben assessed the diminutive driver who appeared to be in his mid-thirties. He sat on a block of wood in order to see over the steering wheel. Compensating for his lack of height to view the road clearly through the windshield meant that his feet struggled to completely depress the floorboard pedals. Ben looked on nervously each time he pushed in the clutch to switch gears, but it was soon apparent that Luther had developed a reliable system to compensate for his small stature.

"Who dat man is?" Ben asked as they got back on the main highway from Waycross to Baxley.

"Dat man?" said the driver. "What 'dat man' mean?"

"Who dat man who hire me?"

"Boy, where you from?"

"Sapelo."

"Sappa-which?"

"It an island on de sea."

Luther shook his head. "I ain't never seen the sea. You talk strange."

"It de way we talk," Ben replied.

Luther threw his head back and laughed aloud. The new hire, in Luther's eyes, was the closest thing to a foreigner he'd ever met.

"The man is Mister Obediah Cutler. He run a big lumber mill operation at Lamar."

"He made you drive dis truck to pick up one man?"

Luther laughed again. "I done hauled a load of cut lumber to Homerville this morning."

"Whut he like, Missa Cutluh?"

Luther wiped his brow as the truck chugged along the road.

"Mister Cutler is a hard man," he replied. "He come up hard, and he 'spect you to work hard. If you lied to him about you logging trees, he's gonna kick you out of his operation real fast. Logging a serious business. They is a hundred ways to die cutting timber. You can die chopping it down. You can die taking it out of the woods. You can get snake bit. You can die at the saw. A log will fall on you."

Ben nodded in agreement. He'd seen men injured on the Sapelo logging crew. Most of the time, it was when a man was hungry or tired. Sometimes, it was because someone got too complacent and didn't pay attention.

"You never know when a tree gonna fall or which way it gonna fall," Ben said.

"You right about that," said Luther. "A tree might be heavy on one side or up top. You think it going to fall left, but it fall to the right."

"I seen a tree fall and knock down a dead tree," Ben replied, warming to the topic. "De dead tree hit a man standin' fifty feet frum de firs tree."

"I seen a tree kick back and hit a man standing behind the stump," Luther said, shaking his head at the memory.

"Spring back?"

"Yes! Spring back like a sling shot!"

Ben smiled broadly, recognizing a kinship with Luther that extended beyond geographic boundaries. They were fellow woodsmen with shared experiences. Luther felt it too, and opened up to Ben with advice he may not have otherwise revealed.

"Mr. Cutler hard, but he fair. You work hard, he pay you. You slack off, he kick you out. They is plenty nigguhs looking for work around these parts. You come in the yard drunk, he kick you out. You fight, he kick you out. You steal, he kick you out. See what I'm saying? He got a little shed at the lumberyard. It got six beds and a shower for hands who ain't got a place to stay. They is a house across from the yard where you get yo meals. Miss Martha's. She cook real good. Them two dollars he takes out covers her cooking. Tell her Luther Morris sent you over. She'll treat you real good."

CHAPTER 7

The Cutler Land & Lumber property consisted of a one-story-office building, a large sawmill operation, the lumberyard, and on the far end, the tiny bunkhouse where Ben would sleep. Obediah's personal office space was the center of activity for Lamar's power brokers. There, he and his cronies swapped tall-tales during all-night poker games, and made business deals. It was said among locals that more civic projects and business transactions were launched in Obediah Cutler's quarters than in all the banks and law offices of the county. The workers were paid each Friday from the payroll manager's room, a small room on the back steps of Obediah's offices.

Luther stopped at the payroll office long enough for Ben to sign a few forms, then he drove Ben five miles away to a logging operation comprised of an all black crew. Willie Stokes, the foreman, grew up in a black community settled by former slaves a few miles outside of the Lamar city limits. His loggers consisted of blacks who came from the surrounding counties. They located and cut pines and cypress trees in low-lying river bottom areas and then hauled them out. It was hard labor in mosquito and snake-infested areas the white workers didn't want to go.

"You can die of snakebite, heat stroke, or by having a forty-foot log roll over you," Willie told Ben, echoing Luther's litany of death-by-logging. "You can drown, or you can get lost in the forest." His resonant voice reverberated through the woods as he spoke, listing ways of dying like a badge of honor for those who had survived the work. "I ain't got but a few men on this crew who is lasted three years. Some run off in the middle of the day and don't never come back. Some leave the woods on a stretcher. Some leave in a box," he said with pride. The law of the forest separated the weak from the strong.

Ben simply nodded. He and Luther had already covered the topic. Willie threw down the law plainly: Ben would have to prove himself. But the people he wanted to prove himself to weren't Willie and Obediah Cutler. He wanted to impress his mother, father, and Bu-Allah.

The first day, he mostly observed the workers trimming downed trees and preparing them to be hauled to a clearing where they would be loaded onto the truck Luther drove. After sundown, Willie dropped him off at the lumberyard.

The bunkhouse became Ben's first home in Lamar. Three pine bunk beds lined the walls. A ceiling fan provided the only relief from heat during the summer months. Outside, a metal trash barrel filled with wood scraps from the sawmill, offered heat in the winter. Bathing took place outdoors beneath a showerhead hooked up to a hose. A nearby ceramic basin served as a washtub for dirty clothes. Ben cleaned up as best he could and walked across the dirt road to the home of Martha Holland, a rotund woman who cleaned houses by day, served lumberyard workers breakfast and dinner, and made lunches they took to work in tin containers. The mention of Luther Morris's name earned Ben a fresh serving of skillet cornbread.

"You need to put some meat on those bones!" she told him.

"Yessum."

"You come over hear first thing tomorrow morning. I'll have you some fresh biscuits, ham, eggs, and grits. You gonna need somethin' to stick to your ribs during the day."

"Yessum."

The evening of his first night in Lamar, Ben felt Bu-Allah's spirit. He knew it would come. It would find him. He had been waiting for it. The spirit had moved over the face of the waters as he left Sapelo by boat. Now, it had moved across the Doboy Sound and up the Altamaha River to Lamar. Lying in his bunk, he could see a full moon through a window. In it, he saw Bu-Allah's face, the same face he'd seen in the moonlight on his seventeenth birthday. Bu-Allah's blood coursed through his veins. He felt his pulse rising and knew it coincided with the incoming tide at Sapelo.

Ben slept peacefully through the night and awakened to the sounds of other men stirring from their beds. The breakfast Martha promised reminded him of his mother's cooking, and he felt good about his prospects. Though Lamar wasn't as big as Waycross, he liked the people, and thought his chances of prospering were equal to those of his cousin, Eli.

Willie Stokes knew he had reached his career plateau and gave his crewmen the opportunity to advance as far as the times allowed. Luther had joined the crew as a teen, carrying water and tagging trees selected for harvesting. He gradually worked his way up to hauling logs to the Cutler lumberyard, and finally, to area pulp mills that refined the wood into cardboard and paper products. Willie assigned Ben the task of trimming limbs and branches from downed trees, and setting chains on the logs to be pulled from swamps by a team of oxen.

The first week on the job, Ben ran into the same problem with his fellow workers he had experienced on Sapelo. They thought nothing of felling a tree and dislodging its inhabitants, but he'd been raised to believe everything had a spirit. He asked permission of each tree before bringing it down and asked leave of any creatures whose homes were demolished in the process.

Muncie, an older logger whose opinions held sway on his fellow workers, took each instance of Ben's unconventional behavior as an opportunity to have fun at his expense.

"Please fo-give me," Muncie cackled as he sank a cross-saw into the side of tree trunk. "Sorry mama squirrel!" he teased when the tree crashed to the ground.

Some of the other men began to imitate Muncie.

"De Lawd cain't be mocked," Ben said under his breath.

From his work on Sapelo, he also recalled the secret to bringing their ridicule to a screeching halt. The opportunity came late in the afternoon on the second day when Muncie stepped back to observe the best direction to fell a sixty-foot pine. The moment he did, the telltale sound of a diamondback rattler filled the air. The snake, curled up atop a fallen log, fixed its mesmerizing stare on Muncie. From the snake's elevated position, Muncie's leather boots offered no protection.

Cutler Land & Lumber Company issued a pistol to each logging crew. The gun for Willie's crew usually stayed with him.

"Hold still," Willie called out as he rushed forward.

"He fixin' to strike," said Muncie. A quiver in his voice betrayed his otherwise calm exterior.

"Don't move," Willie said as came to a standstill, cocked the gun, and aimed.

He blinked twice as his aging eyes tried to focus on the target. Ben stood next to Willie and saw an unsteadiness of hand. Muncie, frozen in place, saw the gun wavering too.

Without a word, Ben snatched the pistol from Willie's hand and fired from the hip. The gun's explosion was followed by the sound of the snake's lifeless body sliding to the ground.

"Jesus!" Muncie cried as he lunged forward. A cold shiver ran through his body as he turned and looked back at the dead serpent. Bailey, another crewman, picked up the snake, placed it lengthwise on the log, and measured it with his hands.

"Six foot, three inch!" he called out.

"Here," Willie said, handing Ben the holster and gun, "you our snake killer from now on."

No one said a word about Willie or Ben or the snake. But from that moment on, Muncie and the others treated Ben as one of their own.

After a month of working in mud and sweating throughout the heat of the day, Ben could stand his overalls upright by his bunk. One Saturday afternoon, he washed his work clothes in the outdoor basin. After a hard day of work on Sapelo, he could always cool off in a shaded creek or in the ocean breezes that swept through Hog Hammock. In Lamar, seventy miles inland, respite from the heat and humidity was hard to come by. Whites could make use of fresh water swimming holes. Blacks were bound to dried up creeks or the front porches of the unpainted clapboard shacks on the east side of the train tracks. He spread the overalls on top of the shed roof to dry, and went inside the bunkhouse where he put on a white shirt and a pair of cotton pants, the only other clothes he owned.

Luther had invited Ben to his home in Scott Hill, the black section, for the afternoon, but Ben was eager to see Eli, and hitched a ride on the back of a truck. He arrived in Waycross around three in the afternoon and visited the church near the train shed. There, he found Reverend Coghill, who informed him that his cousin had found a place to stay with a family on the other side of town. When he located the house, a man in a white T-shirt answered the door.

"Eli? You mean Lucky Man? He gone for the day," the man informed him.

"Where to?" Ben asked.

"Don't know. He and this other boy were going to the country." The man looked quickly back inside, then turned to Ben and lowered his voice. "I think he got a girl over to Millwood. Somewhere in there."

Ben thought about the young woman on St. Catherines Island. Eli told her he would return.

"A girl?" he asked.

"That boy's a fast mover," the man said. "Ain't seen anything like it. Lucky Man pushing these Waycross women away! Sometimes, he goes to Tifton. I think he seeing a girl over there, too."

"When you tink he cumin' back?"

The man looked at Ben as if he had asked a question whose answer seemed obvious.

"Well, Son, I wouldn't be waiting 'round here for him to get back anytime soon," the man advised. "You hear what I'm saying?"

"Can you tell him he cousin, Ben, cum to visit?"

"Yeah. I'll tell him. It'll be early Monday morning before he gets back, but I'll tell him."

Ben returned to Lamar near dark. As he lay in bed inside the hot shed that evening, Scott Hill, the east side of the tracks where most of Lamar's blacks lived, began to look inviting. Luther had been asking him to visit his church, First African Baptist of Lamar, and Ben decided to attend it the next morning, despite his dialect and the ridicule others heaped on him for it. Martha lent him an oversized coat, which had belonged to her late husband. On the way to church the next morning, he became aware of the mothball-cedar smell emanating from his coat.

He met Luther, who introduced his mother, father, and sister, Saundra, a pretty young woman about Ben's age. Though he felt an immediate attraction, he positioned himself as far away from her on the pew as possible, embarrassed by the odor coming from his coat. Lamar's First African Baptist was twice the size of the one on Sapelo. Instead of men and women sitting on opposite sides of the church, families sat together.

The service began with rousing hymns, during the middle of which, Ben sensed someone looking at him. He stole a glance in Saundra's direction. Her body swayed to the music, her rich alto lifted in song. To his amazement, she turned her head and smiled.

Ben looked away. No one of the opposite sex had shown interest in him before. He had been in Eli's presence since he could remember, and all eyes naturally turned to his cousin. At first, he attributed it to curiosity. He was, after all, an outsider raised by the ocean, which most blacks and many whites in Lamar had never seen.

As the congregation took up a new hymn, Ben found himself unconsciously glancing in her direction, as if drawn by an unseen force—perhaps the same force that connected him to Bu Allah and the spirits of his ancestors. He hadn't been raised to believe in predestination, but in his chest, he felt something stir, like the vibration of a string responding in harmony to the plucking of another. In those brief glances, he drank in her warm, honey-colored skin, her delicate frame, and her luminous eyes that seemed to emit light.

"Someone said there is a depression going on in this country," declared Reverend Douglas, a stocky little fellow with a sparse beard. "But I ain't depressed!"

"No, Suh!" boomed Deacon Thomas from the front row. The deacon was big man with a large, rectangular head. His resonant voice echoed the pastor's thoughts and urged him on as he had done for many years.

"I ain't discouraged!" the minister continued. "Ain't noways!"

"I'm not down!"

"No, Suh!"

"Do you know why?"

"Why you ain't down?"

"Because God's in control!"

"Yessuh!"

"God led the Israelites out of bondage!"

"Tell it!"

"And He led the black man out of bondage!"

"Yessuh!"

"God don't turn his back on His people unless they turn their back on Him!"

"That's right! That's right!"

"God may punish a nation for how they treat the poor, but He'll look out for those poor people even as He plagues the rich!"

"Speak, Sir! Speak!"

"He might not send locusts to ruin a man's crops, but He can sure enough send a curse to ruin a bank!"

"Yessuh!"

"I'm still here! You're still here! We're all still here!"

"Still here, Reverend!"

"We ain't going nowhere! The God of Abraham is still looking out for you and me!"

Ben stole another look at Saundra. Their eyes met for the briefest moment.

"God is in control!" cried the reverend.

"Speak, Suh!"

"Keep your eyes on the Lord, not on your situation!"

"Amen!"

"Don't worry about what that rich man across town has got or what your neighbor has got or what you ain't got!"

"No, Suh!"

"You got what God gives you. If He wants you to have more, He'll give you more. If He wants your neighbor to have more, He'll give him more."

"Oh, yeah."

"The earth and everything in it belongs to God. Anything you got, you just holding it for Him for a little while."

"Just a while."

"When your time is up, you give it all back."

"Give it back. That's right."

"Some folks have been living mighty high on the hog."

"Mighty high."

"They live in big houses and drive fancy cars," the reverend said.

"That's right," echoed Deacon Thomas.

"They live on nice streets paved with new asphalt."

"I know that's right."

"They think they will have their reward in heaven."

"Come on, come on."

"But scripture says the oppressors have already received their rewards here on Earth!"

"Amen!"

"Jesus said the first shall be last and the last shall be first!"

"Listen to Him!"

"You may live in shack compared to some of these fine houses around here!"

"Come on, come on!"

"But God will not be mocked!"

"No, Suh!"

"God is in control!"

"That's right!"

"After the judgment, you shall live in mansions of ivory and walk streets of gold!"

"Hallelujah!"

* * *

Ben turned his head ever so slightly once again as the congregation broke into hymn. Saundra turned at the same time. This time, they held their gazes. Her deep brown eyes reflected more than the smile on her lips. Ben felt Bu Allah's presence, an unseen clasp on his shoulder.

"Look deep, my son," the spirit said. In Saundra's eyes, Ben saw something familiar. He saw Sapelo.

Across the railroad tracks and half a mile away, the pastor delivered a very different sermon at Lamar's all white Methodist church.

DeLong Stanton Dodge had come to the clergy by way of World War I trench warfare. The German mustard gas bombs that brought agonizing deaths to much of his infantry unit, had brought him to God faster than decades of soul searching in peacetime. The detonation of another bomb in a later battle obliterated the hearing in his right ear and plagued him with recurring headaches the rest of his life.

He came from the infamous "carpetbagger" Dodge family known for having evicted squatters from their middle Georgia homesteads in the middle 1800s. DeLong, well aware of his family's nefarious dealings in Georgia, welcomed the opportunity to serve the Methodist church in Lamar. Through him, he felt the Dodge family's name might be redeemed in the same way the Apostle Paul's metamorphosis had restored his character in the eyes of those he once persecuted. Lamar, Georgia, he reasoned, would be his Ephesus.

"Who has woe?" he asked the Methodist congregation that morning. There was no call and response like at First African Baptist. His flock came to receive, not to participate.

"Who has sorrow? Who has strife? Who has complaints?" he asked a small, but devout, congregation. "Who has needless bruises? Who has bloodshot eyes?" he continued. "Proverbs tells us it is 'those who linger over wine, who go to sample bowls of mixed wine. Do not gaze at wine when it is red, when it sparkles in the cup, when it goes down smoothly! In the end, it bites like a snake and poisons like a viper!'"

He pounded his fist hard on the podium. Prohibition had been a failure in his eyes. The anti-liquor laws were useless in the larger cities and even moreso in rural areas. In fact, the problem had grown worse.

"Your eyes will see strange sights and your mind imagine confusing things. You will be like one sleeping on the high seas, lying on top of the rigging. They hit me, you will say, but I'm not hurt! They beat me, but I don't feel it! When will I wake up so I can find another drink?"

Dodge saw his mission in a clear light. Other nations had been brought to ruin by the excesses of their inhabitants. He had fought in a bloody war to keep his country strong and would be damned if he stood idly by while its will and might were incrementally diminished by the great evil called alcohol.

"I've seen grown, able-bodied men standing in line for a bowl of soup and a piece of bread. I've seen the breadbasket of this great nation turn into dust and fly away. I've seen a once vital and powerful people brought to their knees. Why, you may ask? Because we have turned our back on God Almighty! That's why. We have allowed men to turn a nation of doers into a nation of drunkards. They may not feel the blows, but the innocent women and children who depend on them for food and shelter, certainly do. God has punished this nation just as he punished the Jews. He has given us over to our own lusts, like a parent who lets his child do as he pleases. The end result can only be disastrous. We need to get back into God's good graces! We need to turn our face toward Him, not away from Him. We have anti-liquor laws, but the alcohol keeps flowing. The poison that infects one man eventually infects all men. Yesterday, seven men were at work. Today, six men are taking up the slack of the one too inebriated to carry his load. Tomorrow, five men will take up the slack for two who no longer can. They call this a depression. It isn't a depression, my friends. It is God's judgment, plain and simple. Only He can bring a nation such as ours to its knees."

Pastor Dodge stood head and shoulders above most men in town. His presence could be intimidating, and he made the most of that asset when the occasion required. In private company, he came across as soft-spoken and good-natured, almost docile, but behind the pulpit, he called down fire and brimstone with the best evangelists.

"And what are our leaders doing about it?" he asked, his face red, his large fist pounding the lectern. "They pass a few puny laws. But those laws need to be enforced! And who here in Lamar, Georgia, is enforcing those laws? Name for me the pillars of this community who are working to ensure liquor, which flows like a river here, becomes at best a trickle? The bankers? The lawyers?"

He paused for effect.

"The first families?"

Everyone knew he meant the Cutlers.

Obediah had inherited more than one prejudice from his father, Eleazer Cutler. After the Civil War, the Dodges of New York forcibly evicted the Cutlers and other squatters from land they had occupied for decades. Eleazer's preacher did nothing to prevent their removal. In fact, there was nothing he could do. The Dodge patriarch found a sympathetic federal judge who sided with their claim to the land. From that point on, Eleazer regarded all clergymen as mere tools of the wealthy. That bias was instilled in

Obediah as a boy and dictated his thoughts and actions as an adult. He likewise instilled in his only son, Clayborne, a similar disdain for men of the cloth.

"You can't name one, and neither can I!" Pastor Dodge declared, slamming his hand one last time on the podium.

"A depression? No, my friends. Justice! The punishment clearly stated in the Bible. 'A whip for the horse, a halter for the donkey, and a rod for the backs of fools!' Well, *we* are the fools! We let the crime against God continue unabated, so let the punishment fit the crime. Who is punished? Not just the imbiber, but the onlooker and the one who looks the other away . . . you and me."

"Let us pray . . ."

CHAPTER 8

Ben dined at the Morris' table that afternoon, sitting directly across from Saundra. News of Klan activity one county over circulated among Lamar's black communities like wildfire spreading across a prairie. A negro family's home had been burned to the ground overnight; their charred bodies discovered that morning. Two bullet-riddled corpses lay on the front porch, brother and sister shot down in cold blood as they fled the burning building. A wooden cross smoldered on the front yard.

"You watch youself when you out there drivin' them logs," Luther's father admonished.

"Yessuh."

"The KKK raising up its head more and more," the elder Morris said.

"Uh-huh," said his wife. "When a white man get in trouble—he grab the first negro he come across and hang him from a tree."

Ben wasn't following the conversation closely. He had something else on his mind. Saundra sat directly across the table. By then, Luther was aware of their unspoken exchanges and looked on as a spectator while Ben and his sister fell deeply and silently in love with one another.

* * *

Ben's first year of logging for Cutler Land & Lumber was filled with a continuous trajectory of advancement, at least in his eyes. He had left Sapelo with two dollars and the shirt on his back. By mid-summer, he had established himself as a hard worker who could be trusted to complete jobs without supervision. He quickly adapted to the physical demands of the work, and his fellow crewmen appreciated his quickness and accuracy with the pistol.

Ben didn't miss a Sunday at First African Baptist or a Sunday meal at Luther's home. Within a few months, it was apparent to everyone in the community that Saundra and Ben were in love. Though the two wanted to marry right away, they decided an extended courtship would be more proper in the eyes of the church and the community. By the fall of 1930, they set a wedding date for early March of the following year. He saved enough to send a few dollars to his family on Sapelo each month and put away a small sum to purchase a home in the black community of Scott Hill. Things seemed to be falling his way in rapid succession, and he began to wonder if he, too, had been born under a lucky star. He wrote to Eli, asking him to be his best man. A week passed before Ben received a letter from his cousin stating that Eli would arrive in Lamar the day of the wedding.

Though only thirty miles from Waycross, Lamar might as well have been in another state. The two cousins found themselves tied to the boundaries of their work and love interests, neither of which intersected. Eli, too, had his share of good fortune. He had been promoted from shed laborer to mechanic's apprentice. The accompanying pay raise allowed him to spend more on clothes and women, though he found it increasingly difficult to send spare money to his family on the island or find time to write letters.

* * *

Two days before the wedding, news of a rape spread throughout Lamar. An unidentified black man had been accused of attacking a poor white in Two Mile, a settlement named after a creek that fed into the Altamaha River two miles north of Lamar. For blacks and whites alike, the rape charge was code for incest. Blacks across the county stayed indoors after dark and kept loaded shotguns by their front doors. Ben immediately sent word to Waycross for Eli to stay away from Lamar, and he and Saundra postponed the wedding date.

Belinda Cale began to show signs of a pregnancy three weeks shy of her fourteenth birthday. Wealthier white families sent daughters in her condition to distant relatives who oversaw the birth and gave up the unwanted child for adoption. Donan Cale, her father, eked out a living as a farmer and could hardly afford to clothe his seven children, much less send one away to give birth. He couldn't publicly admit that one of his brothers had committed the deed, so he spread the word that his daughter had been assaulted by a young black who attacked her as she was returning from school one afternoon.

Obediah just as quickly spread the word that his black workers were off limits to vengeance-minded whites, many of whom were always eager to vent frustration over their station in life on the only segment of society worse off than themselves.

"Any son-of-a bitch lays a hand on a Cutler Land & Lumber man will answer to me," he said, making sure the message was spread among the poor white communities. He temporarily assigned Willie's all-black crew to the lumberyard until the furor rising among Cale's extended family and friends cooled down.

The trouble ended as quickly as it had begun. Word went out that the Cales found the culprit and dealt with him in the customary manner, though no black family in the county reported a missing relative.

Ben and Saundra exchanged vows before Reverend Douglas and the congregation on the 15th of March, 1931. Eli didn't show, a fact Ben attributed to his cousin's work schedule and active social life.

"He a hard man to get hold of," he told Luther, who stood in for Eli as best man.

Shortly after the wedding, the new couple moved into a three-bedroom shotgun shack three blocks from First African Baptist. The small bed they shared bounced noisily across the wood floorboards each time they made love, prompting Buck Shavers, their elderly neighbor, to kid Ben on his way to work.

"Hey, Boy. You get a new sofa?"

"Nah, Suh, Missa Shavers."

"Well, I sho 'nuff heard furniture moving 'round last night?"

After a few days of listening to Mr. Shavers's remarks and accompanying laughter, Ben bolted the bed legs to the floor.

Obediah's son, Clayborne Cutler, also experienced an upward trajectory that year. The self-assurance that came with being the sole male scion of Lamar's wealthiest resident and largest employer, permeated his persona. At six-one with wavy, golden hair, his steely blue eyes beckoned women and won the confidence of men. After graduating from college, he landed a job in Atlanta with the highway department where he first caught wind of grandiose building plans for small towns across the state—plans designed to pull municipalities out of the depression by their bootstraps. In the early days of railroads, townships that found ways to get rails laid through their borders prospered. Many of the ones that didn't, dried up and ceased to exist. Lamar had managed to get a branch rail line laid to it in the late 1800s, mostly due to the efforts of Eleazer and Obediah, who needed a way to transport timber to market.

Clayborne saw the new highway's promise as well, possibly more so than many others who thought passenger rail would never fade as a mode of travel. He had traveled the northern states where automobile factories churned out vehicles in ever-increasing numbers, and where highway expansion projects were on the rise. More than that, Florida had become a vacation destination for winter-weary northerners. He looked on a map of Georgia and saw the potential to bring a constant flow of commerce through Lamar. He knew that soon powerbrokers up and down Georgia's spine would line up to ensure the new road came through their municipalities.

"The poor dirt farmer," his father once advised him, "don't know beans about economics. But he knows when he's losing a dollar and when he's gaining a dollar. So does every two-bit mayor and county clerk in every one-horse town. You got to find a good fishing hole before the next fella and put your pole in it first. That's how you get ahead."

As he lay in his Atlanta bedroom one night, another vision came to Clayborne. His father had acquired large tracts of land for timber harvesting. He also saw land acquisition as his road to riches, only on a much smaller but more focused scale. The land he coveted would be in the small towns along the new highway. There, he would set up a series of hotels, restaurants, and service stations to house, feed, and fuel the steady stream of travelers passing through middle Georgia. The only thing he lacked was capital. Banks weren't lending, and investors who shared his vision, were scarce.

"Son, I know all about the timber business," Obediah informed Clayborne when he broached the subject by phone the following day. "That's all we Cutlers know. If you want to think big, think about ways this new highway can get our logs to market faster. They're building paper mills from Savannah down to Camden County. Tell me how I can get logs over there faster and cheaper!"

"Daddy, you're not seeing the big picture," Clayborne protested. "These automobiles are going to put passenger railroad companies out of business. People will need a place to eat and sleep, just like they do on Pullmans. I want to be the Pullman car of the road."

"I don't know anything about the rail business," Obediah replied. "I don't know anything about the highway business. You don't even know if that highway will get funded, or if it will come through Lamar. All we Cutlers know is how to grow trees and cut timber. We're smack in the middle of the best timber forest in the world, and you're talking about housing and feeding people in driving machines. I can sit out there on the highway we got now and not see an automobile pass by for an hour."

"That old east-west highway going through town? It's only good for getting out of Lamar. Daddy, this new highway will be a big, fat pipe linking Florida to all those Yankees up north. They may not be worth a damn, but their money sure is, and I intend to take it from them."

"Well, I wish you'd come get rid of one Yankee, this DeLong Dodge bastard. He keeps poor mouthing me for not drying up the flow of liquor around here, as if I give two damns whether or not the government outlaws alcohol, or people make it themselves. First, his family forces us off our land, now this."

"He's that new Methodist preacher, right?"

"Yeah. A preacher and a gottdamn Dodge!"

"Daddy, I can't do anything about that right now. What I need is some money to buy some downtown property."

"All right," Obediah said, weighing the matter in his head, "tell you what I'll do. I'll back you in Lamar. If you can turn a profit on something here, we'll see about investing somewhere else."

That summer, Clayborne married Claudette Boyer, a former beauty queen from Milledgeville who worked in the governor's office. The wedding proved to be the biggest event in Milledgeville since the depression had started. On the way home from the post-nuptial parties, Obediah complained of tiredness and asked his wife to drive the rest of the way. By the time they reached Lamar, his speech was slurred. The doctor put him on medication and bed rest.

With his father's health in decline, the reins of managing the Cutler Land & Lumber Company passed on to Clayborne, and he realized his time in Atlanta was coming to an end. Through Claudette's and Obediah's connections to Governor Eugene Talmadge, he wrangled a position as a county fertilizer inspector, a job that would begin the following year.

CHAPTER 9

The year 1931 began well for Ben and Saundra. She fell in love with Sapelo's enchanting allure on a visit to his parents' home. Ben's oldest sister, Geneva, returned to the island from New York to celebrate the new addition to the family. Her Geechee accent, notably altered to conform to mainland speak, quickly came back to her under the Jordan roof. Her tales of life in the fast-growing Harlem section of Manhattan inspired Rona and Delphine to follow her to the city as soon as they graduated from the eleventh grade.

Eli's parents had no news of their son and fretted that he had succumbed to mainland vices like many before him.

"Like a moth to de flame," Deacon Jones told Ben after church that Sunday. He had shepherded Eli through the baptismal process and took the news of Eli's estrangement hard. "He wuz a goot boy. A real goot boy," said the deacon, his face pained as though wounded inside, "But de world got to him. De world full of shiny, bright, sweet smellin' tings." He shook his head slowly. "I don't unnerstan' it. It not like Eli to cut away frum de fambly like dat."

It was on Sapelo that Saundra first became aware of a nagging cough, which she attributed to the marsh air that enveloped the island, but she had more important things on her mind. In April, she broke the news that she was expecting. The following months rapidly rolled by for Ben, who couldn't wait to get home to his new bride and their home in Lamar. One evening, Ben and Saundra sat beneath a large fig tree behind their house as the first stars became visible in the clear sky. He rubbed Saundra's belly, speculated about their child's gender, and discussed possible names. He thought of Eli and envisioned his cousin carousing in Waycross and surrounding towns—dalliances, his folks called them. In that moment, he felt God's hand on him and smiled, realizing that he wouldn't trade his lot with Eli's. At the age of twenty, he had established himself in the world. He had a steady job at a time when work was scarce. He had married and moved from a bunkhouse into a home. And Saundra carried their first child.

"De hand of de Lawd above on us," he told her as they watched the starry night unfold.

It seemed to Ben that God, indeed, favored him over Eli until he came home one evening to find Saundra on the bedroom floor weeping. He knew the family doctor had come to the house that day to check on the pregnant mother.

"It God will," he said, attempting to console her. "Dey will be another baby."

Saundra shook her head.

"It's not the baby," she said through the tears. "Whut den de matter?"

She replied with an answer that instilled dread into the hearts of all family members who heard it.

"TB," Saundra said, collapsing into Ben's arms.

Clayborne returned to Lamar the spring of 1931, and assumed his father's role as an official member of the local courthouse gang, a loose confederation of power-wielders comprised of the mayor, the newspaper editor, the chief of police, and various attorneys.

Their job was to deliver the votes that kept politicians in office, especially Eugene Talmadge, the governor whose word or pen stroke could fund construction projects or bring new commerce to their towns. The Unit System gave rural counties as much weight in deciding elections as Atlanta and the larger cities. It also made courthouse gang members exceptionally influential in state politics. The Cutlers knew the power they possessed and wielded it according to their needs.

Clayborne's position as fertilizer inspector required little more than taking bribes from companies who produced bags filled with fertilizer and dirt and listening to farmers moan about it.

"I got dirt!" one farmer bitterly complained. "I ain't paying those sons-of-bitches for more of it!"

"There's no way around getting a little earth in those fertilizer bags," Clayborne assured him. "It's all measured to regulation. You're getting the fertilizer you pay for plus a little soil is all. Ain't nothing wrong with that."

"Like hell! I'm paying by the pound!"

"Okay. I'll look into it," Cutler told the man, having no intention of following up on his promise.

Clayborne used the extra income earned as inspector to snatch up properties around town. The store he most coveted stood at what would be the corner of the existing road through town and the new highway. Prominently positioned on the south side of Lamar's main street stood Hoffer's Soda Shop, a former liquor store owned by longtime resident, Salty Hoffer. His liquor store closed a year into Prohibition, but everyone knew Salty sold bootleg alcohol to patrons through a window in back of the building. He often made midnight trips to the coast, where he acquired cases of alcohol smuggled in by train, by boat, and by airplanes from the Bahamas. Often as not, he had to lug cases of whiskey or moonshine from drop-off points to his car, which, at times, could be a quarter mile trek over broken ground. By the summer of 1931, he needed someone to assist in his late night forays.

Cutler made several offers for the property, but Salty wasn't selling. After a third offer failed, Clayborne threatened to expose Hoffer's illegal sales of whisky and moonshine. Like Pastor Dodge, Hoffer had survived the horrors of World War I and didn't scare easily. He walked with a pronounced limp, the result of a wound received during that war. Salty never cared much for Obediah, and resented the younger Cutler returning to Lamar and throwing his weight around. Moreover, Salty had a nose for business opportunities. Clayborne's desire to acquire downtown properties made him suspect that much bigger game was afoot. Before long, his suspicions were confirmed when surveyors came through town taking cursory elevation readings and pounding stakes into the sun-baked soil.

Lamar's First African Baptist Church members donated what they could to send Saundra to a first-class tuberculosis clinic in Atlanta, but the money fell far short of what would be required. The doctor sent her to a state-run Negro Tuberculosis Clinic located an hour from Lamar. It offered little hope. Ben feared that, without expert care, she wouldn't survive long enough to give birth to their child. When he learned Salty Hoffer needed someone to assist on his whisky runs, he jumped at the chance to make a few extra dollars.

"I make a run every ten days," Salty informed him. "That's three trips each month. The pay is five dollars a trip. I pay out soon as the last case is unloaded back here in Lamar."

Five dollars represented almost a week's wages for Ben.

"I'll do it, Missa Hoffer," he said.

"If you get caught, I ain't paying no bail money," Hoffer told him.

"I unnerstan," Ben replied.

"I ain't never seen you before, so don't tell on me. Get it?"

"I get it, Boss."

"And if they catch me, I won't tell on you. Deal?"

"Deal, Boss," Ben replied.

Their first liquor run took them to a wooded area near Savannah. They left Lamar Saturday evening and arrived at the rendezvous point a little before one o'clock in the morning. Ben followed Salty through the woods to a bluff overlooking a tidal river. Hoffer nestled on the roots of an oak tree and lit a pipe while Ben paced the bluff, anxious about what would soon transpire. Two hours passed before a small boat rounded a bend in the river.

"Dat de one, Boss?" Ben asked.

Salty made no reply. A moment later, two short bursts of light projected across the water. Salty produced a flashlight from his coat and turned it on and off twice in rapid succession. A single flash came from the boat in reply. Salty responded with a single flash.

"That's the one," he said.

A few minutes later, Ben saw a man at the oars, quietly propelling the boat toward the bluff. Another man sat at the back, his legs propped on something covered by a dark dropcloth. The boat soon came to a halt beneath the oak.

"Nice night for it," said the man sitting next to an outboard motor used only in an emergency. Even in the moonlight, Ben could tell the man's face bore the permanent ruddy hue of a fisherman, possibly a shrimp boat captain, exposed to sun and wind for days and weeks at a time. "Who's this?" he said, angling his head toward Ben.

"Ain't nobody here but me," Salty replied, leisurely drawing on his pipe. The embers cast an eerie glow on his thick mustache that ran down both sides of his mouth to his chin.

"You got the money?"

Hoffer patted his coat.

"Well," the man said, removing the dropcloth to reveal four cases of whiskey, "tell mister nobody to come and get the goods."

Ben slid down the sandy embankment and unloaded the cases. Bottles lightly rattled in the straw packing as he lifted them from the boat and trudged up the steep bluff to place each case at Salty's feet. When the last case came off the boat, the man looked up at Salty.

"Okay?"

"Count them," Salty instructed Ben.

"Don't you know nigguhs can't count?" the man replied.

"Already done it, Boss. Dey is twenny-fo.'"

Salty pulled a small cloth pouch from his vest pocket and tossed it to Ben, who handed it to the man in the boat. The man opened it and counted. As he did, Ben noticed his companion at the oars held a gun in his lap.

"A pleasure doing business with ya," the man said, content with the amount in the pouch.

He nodded at the other man who shoved off with an oar. Salty kept an eye on the boat until it had moved a considerable distance upstream. Ben trudged up the steep grade of the bluff one last time and gingerly set the last case down.

"Dat man had a gun," he said.

Hoffer patted his pocket. "So do I, Ben. You never know who you're dealing with." He smiled wearily. "Now comes the fun part. Getting this hooch back to Lamar without some damn cop stopping us."

They arrived back in Lamar before daybreak, in time for Ben to wash up and get ready for church. The Right Reverend Douglas delivered a searing sermon on the importance of remaining in God's will and the consequences of living outside of it.

"There is a way that seems right to a man," the reverend said, "but in the end, it leads to death."

Ben felt the five dollars in his pocket grow warmer as the service progressed, and pondered whether or not it would be right to tithe from the night's earnings. He kept the money in his pocket and put money from his logging income on the offering plate.

Saundra gave birth to a little girl, Naomi, late in the year. The doctors gave mother and child little hope of surviving the birth. Luther drove Ben fifty miles to the Negro Tuberculosis Clinic to pick up his daughter. He wasn't allowed to see Saundra, who lay in bed too weak to sit up. She, like the other patients, had been quarantined from the outside world for the duration of the illness.

Two days later, Geneva showed up unannounced on Ben's doorstep. Delphine and Ronda had moved to Harlem and occupied the apartment Geneva left behind.

"I here to raise de chile 'til Saundra return," she said, reverting to the Geechee in her brother's presence.

Ben stood in the doorway holding his crying daughter. Without saying a word, he moved aside to let his sister in.

"Where you bury Naomi's afterbirth?" Geneva demanded to know.

"Dey wouldn't give us no afferbirth. I axed, but dey say dey done thrown it away."

Geneva shook her head in disgust.

"Dem medicine mens don't know nuthin'. Haff you showed Naomi outside?"

"I shown her dayclean dis morning. I told her dey is spirits in all tings."

Geneva nodded approvingly.

"How long can you stay fo?" Ben asked.

"I here 'til Naomi grown," she replied. "Saundra ain't cumin' back, Ben. Dey say no one cum back frum dat clinic."

"I savin' money," he told her, gently transferring his daughter into Geneva's arms. "I savin' to get Saundra to a better place."

"You best hurry up," Geneva replied. "Birthin' make a sick woman weak."

"I workin' on it, Neva. I workin' on it." Late one afternoon that week, Ben and Willie Stokes walked the woods near the Altamaha River marking trees for the next day's harvest. In the near distance, they heard a red cardinal's shrill, insistent chirp. To Ben it sounded like someone repeatedly calling out, "It's here! It's here!"

The two men followed the bird's urgent cries. In a glade near the river, they came across a pine tree bearing a strange sight. At first, Ben thought the bleached bones on the ground were those of an animal. He looked at Willie, who stared at something overhead, his mouth wide open. Ben followed Willie's gaze and saw the cardinal he heard earlier perched atop a limb. Beneath it hung a mummified skeleton dressed in tattered clothing. A rusting wire was wrapped around the man's neck. His head, still perched on top of his exposed spine, twisted at a surreal angle. Both his lower legs and an arm had long since been pulled down by buzzards and carnivorous animals.

Ben immediately recognized Eli's face, staring toward heaven as though beckoning a higher power to rescue him. In that moment, he realized his cousin never received the message warning him to stay away from Lamar.

CHAPTER 10

"God in heaven have mercy on this man's soul," Willie said.

"Dat my cousin, Eli."

Ben spoke softly, unable to avert his eyes.

"He de one cumin' to de weddin'. He born under de lucky star."

Willie shook his head and wiped the sweat from his neck with a white rag.

"Them Cales did this. That's why they got so quiet a while back. I shoulda known they strung up somebody. But that don't matter now. We gonna give this boy a decent burial."

A small plot of ground called the Strangers Cemetery had been set aside next to the black graveyard on the east side of Lamar. Over the years, pine coffins of blacks with no family ties to the area, gradually filled the graveyard. Most of them were workers who died in logging or sawmill accidents. Others were strangers passing through town killed in knife fights or who, like Eli, were simply in the wrong place at the wrong time.

Ben looked down at the bones on the ground, then at the scarecrow of the man hanging above. Eli's afterbirth lay buried somewhere on Sapelo soil, rooting him to the island like an oak. His spirit, Ben believed, had already returned to his birthplace. His body must also be returned to Hog Hammock where the bones of his ancestors lay—where their spirits wandered by night. His bones would join their bones; his spirit would walk with theirs. Ben knew if Eli's remains weren't returned to Sapelo, his spirit would search the island, then, not finding it, wander the Earth until the Resurrection. Either way, Eli's spirit would be in limbo, a fate reserved for the wicked—those who shunned the church elders and turned their backs on the gospel.

"No, Suh," he said, "Eli bound to de island soil. I tek him home."

A river breeze broke the still, humid air, and a shiver ran through Ben. In it, he felt Bu Allah's presence. He began shaking with rage.

Willie saw Ben's hand reach for the pistol and discerned his thoughts.

"Dem white trash folk done this," Ben said.

Willie reached out and stayed Ben's hand.

"Them Cales gonna shoot you and burn your house," he said. "Don't tell no one nuthin . . . not no white man . . . you hear?

"The law oughta know . . ."

"Po-leece ain't gonna do nothing! Ain't gonna be no justice. Best leave it alone."

In slavery, it was said, Bu Allah sought justice regardless of a man's color. Once, Thomas Spalding went to Europe, a poor white from Darien beat one of his slaves. Bu Allah went into town and demanded redress from the justice-of-the-peace. The guilty man was not only jailed and fined, but endured a tongue-lashing by Bu Allah. After his release, he left Darien and never returned.

The Spaldings and Bu Allahs of the world ceased to exist in post-Reconstruction, Jim Crowe Georgia, but a new master had emerged in the form of local community bosses, and every town had one. In Lamar, the new master was Clayborne Cutler.

"I'll let Mistah Cutler know," Willie assured Ben. "He's the only one can do something 'bout it."

Ben said nothing. He had already begun thinking about how to get Eli back to the island. He could have the body shipped by train to Sterling and from there, by boat to Sapelo. But he wanted time with Eli. A thirty-foot cypress with a wide trunk stood near the river's edge not far from where the body hung. The cypress would have to be cut down and hollowed out. He eyed the river current, and gauged how long the journey to the coast would take. As the crow flies, it was a shade over eighty miles, but the river twisted like a giant serpent, making the distance almost two hundred miles. It would take him two or three days, depending on the weather.

He uncoiled a length of rusted wire left behind on the ground, and wrapped it around the base of the tree. Twisting the wire ends around each gloved hand, Ben leaned back and scaled the fifteen feet of trunk to the first limb. He climbed out on it and untied the wire holding Eli's corpse as Willie reached up and carefully helped lower it to the ground.

News spread fast among the black community. By nightfall, a moonlight vigil had begun in the clearing where Eli's body lay wrapped in a tarp and atop a pile of pine straw. Several fires were built to provide light and create smoke that kept the mosquitoes at bay. A number of pines tagged for harvest were felled and served as benches, but the lynching tree remained standing. Food baskets arrived not long after sundown, and continued coming until after midnight.

Willie directed his logging crew to saw down the cypress tree, and supervised as they worked until the early morning hours hollowing the trunk with axes and hatchets. Ben remained seated on a log next to Eli's body, declining food or drink. His eyes remained transfixed on his cousin, oblivious to the activity around him.

A little past one in the morning as the moon crested the tops of the forest, Reverend Douglas arrived and began impromptu sermon.

"The Bible tells us 'If a man have committed a sin worthy of death and thou hang him on a tree, his body shall not remain all night upon the tree, but thou shall bury him that day.'"

Deacon Thomas assumed his rightful place in the gathering, exhorting his minister, punctuating each statement with an affirming response.

"Amen," he said, his deep, resonant voice echoing through the woods, drowning out the sounds of nearby hatchets.

"'For he who is hung on a tree is accursed,'" Reverend Douglas continued. "But I say this man is not accursed!"

"Come on, Suh."

"For this man never committed a sin worthy of death."

"Tell it."

"This man was innocent of the crime he died for."

"That's right. That's right."

"I say cursed is the man who sheds innocent blood!"

"Speak, Suh!"

"He shall seek succor, but shall find none."

"Nobody!" boomed the deacon.

"He shall close his eyes, but he will not sleep."

"No sleep!"

"He shall put food in his mouth, but he will not taste."

"That's right."

"He shall seek refuge, but he shall not rest."

"No rest!"

"Cursed is the man who kills his neighbor."

"Holy Jesus!"

"He shall be allotted months of futility and nights of misery," said the reverend. "Yessuh. Yessuh."

"When he lies down, he will think, 'How long before I get up?'"

"Go ahead."

"He will toss till dawn. My days will be swifter than a weaver's shuttle."

"Amen."

"They come to an end without hope, for his life will be but a breath."

"A breath, Lord!"

"His eyes will never see happiness again."

"No, Suh!"

"The Lord God will frighten him with dreams and terrify him with visions so that he shall prefer strangling and death rather than remain in his body."

"Lord, help him!" said Deacon Thomas.

"His days will have no meaning."

"No meaning, Lord!"

"He will say 'Why do you not pardon my offenses and forgive my sins, for I will soon lie down in the dust?'"

"Yessuh!"

"Brothers and sisters, Ben's cousin, Eli, was hung from this tree just as Jesus was hung from a tree at Calvary."

"Holy Jesus!"

"Some of you may be wanting to take justice in your own hands."

"Uh-huh."

"You may be thinking that you want to repay violence for violence."

"No, Suh!"

"But God is looking."

"Yessuh!"

"He sees your comings and goings. He sees the works of good men. And he sho'nuff sees the works of evil men. The Lord, our God will not be mocked!"

"Can't mock Him!"

"For the Lord has a day of vengeance."

"Yessuh!"

"No one knows about that day or hour, not even the angels in heaven."

"No one!"

"Things that cause people to sin are bound to come, but woe to that person through whom they come. It would be better for him to be thrown into the sea with a millstone tied around his neck!"

"Amen!"

Ben sat on a log beneath the pine, his head down, eyes staring intently ahead. As newly arriving members of the black community appeared, they filed by, paying their respects to the body and giving Ben words of sympathy and encouragement.

He had been half listening to the preacher, half listening to Willie's crew on the riverbank. The tonal quality of the hatchet strikes rose and fell along with the preacher's voice. Soon, the blows became higher pitched as his fellow workers dug through the log's core. In his mind, he envisioned his trip down river and what he would say to Eli. He would remind his cousin of their adventures on the waters around Sapelo, their forays into the deep woods there, and their defiance of elders' admonitions to stay out of the swamps. They felt safe intruding on the Devil's turf. Bu-Allah was there to protect them. He asked Bu-Allah's spirit for protection on the journey ahead, but felt nothing in response. Bu-Allah tried to keep him and his cousin from leaving the island. Why should his spirit reach out now?

Tiny Ruth had warned him not to leave Sapelo. "I see a tree sproutin' frum de earth," she had warned his parents, who passed on the admonition to him. "It a pine tree wiff two heads. Dis baby's soul tied to some'un else. De tree will reach up to de sky. De two heads cum into dis world together an' will leave together.

He spirit will wander fo fo'ty years. He will see de promise land but will not enter it—if he ever leave Sapelo."

He and Eli had set their faces like flint on another world where people didn't believe those sorts of things. The cousins hoped that if they didn't believe them, the prophecies wouldn't come true. But as he sat in the eerie glow of moonbeam and firelight, he realized that Tiny Ruth's divinations were unfolding before his eyes.

Ben remained deep in thought until a commotion interrupted his reverie. He became dimly aware of people fussing over the appearance of a new arrival. He looked up and saw his sister carrying a small bundle toward him.

Without saying a word, she gently placed Naomi, soundly asleep, in her father's arms, and sat next to him. Geneva stared at Eli's enshrouded body as shadows stirred by the campfires danced over it.

"Docta Crow know whut to do 'bout dis," she whispered at length.

"Don't talk 'bout dat," Ben said. "Dese folk don't know nuthin' 'bout Docta Crow. Dey too Christian to know bout de root."

Geneva shook her head even more, swiveling it from side to side as anger swelled inside her.

"Someone on de island gonna haff sumtin' to say bout dis. Dat's all I'm sayin."

Ben kissed Naomi on the head and held her to his chest, rocking back and forth to the rhythm of the hatchet blows. Their reports had grown tinnier as the wood chipped away to within a few inches of the bottom. It wouldn't be long before he was on the water with his cousin.

Naomi stirred at his kiss and fell in and out of sleep, alternately looking wide-eyed at the spectacle of light and moving bodies in the clearing, and lovingly up at Ben, knowing that she was secure.

Geneva got up, walked to the tree from which Eli's body had

been hung, and peeled off a patch of bark. She walked back to where Ben sat and quietly placed it in one of his overall pockets.

"Dis de tree whut hung Eli. He spirit tied to dis tree now. Dis piece go in de grave wiff he body. It not de tree fault. De tree go into the ground wiff him."

Ben said nothing.

The hatchet blows had ceased. He heard Willie instructing two men with adzes to scrape the interior to a smooth finish. Before long, word came that the dugout canoe was almost ready.

The pastor spoke a final prayer over Eli while two men sewed the tarp flaps together using a heavy, waxed thread. All eyes turned to Ben as he kissed his sleeping daughter on the head and carefully handed her back to Geneva. He said nothing as he rose and slowly walked toward the water's edge preceded by two men carrying Eli's enshrouded body. A hundred people followed closely behind in a silent procession. The cypress dugout shone like a ghostly spectre in the moonlight. Shavings and hunks of cypress littered the riverbank. Willie's logging crew stood to one side, their bodies glistening with sweat; watching Eli's body being placed near the bow. A handmade basket, sturdy enough to sit on, had been filled with biscuits, fruits, cured ham, and water. It was placed a few feet from the rear of the vessel. Two paddles and a long pole fashioned from the cypress tree lay inside.

The reverend said a few words in prayer to cover Ben's trip. When he finished, Willie put his arm around Ben's shoulder.

"Take this," he said, placing a small sack in Ben's hands. Ben could feel a revolver inside. A box of .45 caliber bullets rattled as he placed the bundle inside the canoe.

"They is as many ways to die on the river as they is sawing logs," Willie said. "Most river folk are real good people. But the river attract scalawags too, like bees to honey."

Willie edged closer and whispered in Ben's ear. "They will just as soon steal from you or cut you as look at you. Don't be afraid to shoot a scoundrel. I don't care if he black or white."

Another man, much older than Willie, stepped forward.

"This is Mister Dix," Willie said. "He used to pole log rafts all the way down to Darien. Listen to him, now."

Mister Dix cleared his throat and put his hand on Ben's.

"When you ride the river, it like going back in time. They is all kinds of folks on the river."

"Listen to the man," Willie said.

"Stick to the injun side of the river," Dix advised, using a term held over from the days when Creek and other Indian nations occupied lands south and west of the Altamaha. The north bank, where settlers had established themselves, was the *white* side. "The white side always trouble," he continued. "Always follow the strong current. The weak current will take you to dead parts of the river. A weak current is a death current."

Ben half-listened as the old river runner imparted the wisdom of his experiences, about freshets, about wild animals, and about river rogues, but one admonition registered in Ben's memory.

"The river like a snake," Dix told him. "It shaped like a snake. It twist and turn like a snake, and it stick you like a snake. When you ride the river, you ridin' a rattler. You ridin' on his back. See what I'm sayin'? You gots to watch out the whole time, or he'll rise up and bite you." He jabbed two fingers into Ben's hand to drive home the point. "When he bite, they ain't nothin' for it. Ain't nothing'. Lots of bones on the bottom of this river. Many a man taken downstream and never come back. Lots of folk got bit. Lots of folk."

Dix bent down and let his hands dip into the copper-tinted water. He then lifted them over Ben's head and let the water slowly drip through his fingers, over Ben's head and shoulders.

"You now baptized by river water," Dix told him. "The river gonna protect you!"

Ben nodded in acknowledgement, but made no reply. He wanted to thank the people for coming out in the night to stand vigil over a stranger's body. He wanted to thank Reverend Douglas for his words. He wanted to hold Naomi again. He tried to speak, but the words wouldn't come.

Instead, he simply stepped into the canoe and kneeled near the center. Willie shoved the craft out into the water, and Ben paddled to the middle of the river where the current flowed strongest. Without looking back, he stroked the water with his paddle, eager to close the distance between Eli and Sapelo.

CHAPTER 11

After an hour of steady paddling, Ben stood to test the craft's balance. He picked up the long pole and pushed off the river bottom to propel the boat downstream. To his surprise, the canoe handled almost as well as the pirogues he once used around the tidal creeks of Sapelo. From the standing position, he could observe potential dangers further downstream.

Two hours later, a strong wind blew up river from the east. In it, he felt Eli's spirit. After a while, the breeze increased, and he sensed another spirit: Bu Allah's.

He turned his attention to the shoreline and began to see shadowy figures on the banks of the river. He had been born with the power to see spirits. Now, for the first time since coming to the mainland, he again saw the remaining earthly presences of men and women long since dead. How long, he wondered, had their spirits roamed the river paths on either shore?

"You goin' home, Eli," he said aloud. "Yo body soon be wiff yo fambly. Yo spirit soon be settle wiff de old ones."

He glanced at the shoreline on either side of the river. More ghostly images silently gathered on its banks. Some beckoned him to steer closer.

"Not like dese po peoples. Dey ain't gots no home like us."

Ben spoke to his cousin about things past until the first light of day appeared in the sky ahead. Behind him, to the west, he heard the distinct sound of thunder. He vaguely recalled Mr. Dix saying that rains upriver could cause downriver flooding a day later, or was it two days later? He couldn't recall.

One by one, the stars overhead disappeared, and the spirits vanished from the shoreline. By noon, Ben became aware of his hunger. He opened the basket and tore a biscuit in half, placed a slice of ham inside, and began chewing. He followed the sandwich with water, then ate another biscuit.

Decades earlier, the river had been a major thoroughfare, alive with steamboats and log raft flotillas. But railroads and later highways reduced river traffic to the occasional angling or hunting party, mostly northerners on holiday. On this first day of the journey, Ben saw only the occasional poor black or white standing near the river's edge with a cane pole.

By three o'clock, after more than twelve hours of steady paddling, the heat of the day forced him ashore. He pulled the canoe onto the south bank of the river and fell into a deep sleep in which he dreamed he and Eli were running through Sapelo's woods laughing—a wild mother boar close on their heels. After what seemed like an endless chase, they left the forest and tumbled down the steep slope of a beach dune still laughing hysterically.

"Momma boar mad!" Eli said between gasps.

"Momma boar fast!" Ben answered. His remark seemed to be the funniest thing in the world to both of them, and they cackled even harder with delight.

A faint buzzing sound began to emanate from the other side of the dune. As the sound grew louder, the two cousins stealthily crawled up the sandy slope to peer over it. Eli was the first to reach the top. Ben saw him peep over the dune's edge, and watched as his cousin's smile slowly turned to dismay.

"Oh, Ben," Eli said, turning his head toward him. "Whut is it, Cuz?" Ben asked.

"Oh, Ben," Eli repeated, his voice filled with anguish and remorse.

In the dream the buzzing noise steadily increased.

Ben crawled up the slope and looked over the top. He felt heat pulsing from Eli's body and noticed bands of white sand that clung to the sweat on his cousin's arms. As he pushed aside a small stand of sea oats and lifted his head above the dune's crest, the buzzing intensified to a deafening level.

Ben awoke from the dream to the sound of mosquitoes swarming around him. When he saw the crumpled sheeting at the canoe near his feet, the reality of Eli's death struck him like a shotgun blast in the chest. The day before, he had been in shock over the grisly discovery. This was a different kind of shock, one tempered by sleep and reflection. Some dreams Ben could recall in the past were strange or terrifying, and waking to the reality of the day had been a relief. This time, the dream had been his refuge. Reality was the horror.

"Oh, Cuz," he said, reaching out to his cousin. Tears formed in his eyes and rolled down his cheeks. "Eli, forgive me."

It wasn't Ben's idea to leave the island, but now, in hindsight, he felt he could have done more to discourage their leaving. He recalled the invisible hand trying to pull him back to Sapelo on the boat he and Eli took to the mainland. Both cousins ignored the warning.

"We shoulda listened to de old folks, Eli. Dey wuz right. De old folks know. Old Hattie. Tiny Ruth. Mama. Docta Crow. Dey told us no to leave de islan'. We shoulda listen."

Overhead, a crow cawed three times. On the island, a crow's call signaled impending danger. Ben reached into the sack Willie gave him, and pulled out the gun. He listened intently, but heard nothing out of the ordinary. He had been asleep for hours and nightfall was settling in. Ben knew why the crow had cawed even though he couldn't see it.

"Bad spirit roaming de woods," he informed Eli.

Ben launched the canoe into the river. "Dey wakin' up and lookin' fo a soul to tek a holt. Well, dey ain't gettin' none of us."

A few yards from shore, he turned and saw several spectral images taking shape, standing on the bank where he had just been. He paddled hard and scanned the treetops, looking for the crow, but saw nothing.

"He know," Ben said to his cousin. "Docta Crow know you cumin' home. He lookin' out fo us."

A little after midnight, he felt the river's pace quicken. The storm he heard the day before poured rain into the Oconee and Ocmulgee Rivers that fed the Altamaha. In the waxing moonlight, Ben soon saw that the canoe had risen almost to the height of the shoreline on either side. The current strengthened and didn't let up throughout the night.

The next day, as Ben negotiated a turn in the river, he heard dogs barking on the north bank. He paddled the boat around the bend and proceeded along a stretch where the river widened to over five hundred feet.

"Hoy!" someone called out from the bank to his left.

Ben looked but saw no one.

A minute later, he heard the person call again, this time about hundred yards ahead.

"You in the boat. Over here!"

Ben squinted in the white-hot sunlight that reflected off the water. At the water's edge, he saw a white man gesticulating feverishly with his arms.

"You in the boat. If you're a God-fearing man, pull over and help a fellow Christian!"

Ben placed the revolver in the hip pocket of his overalls. As he paddled closer to the riverbank, he heard the dogs baying in the distance.

"Hurry, Man!" the stranger called out, his teeth clenched in a forced smile. He looked nervously over his shoulder in the direction of the barking.

"Folks affer you," Ben stated matter-of-factly as he neared the shore. He stopped the canoe ten yards from riverbank. The man stood a little over six feet. He had a high forehead, a pronounced but thin nose, and penetrating dark eyes. Red, wavy hair hung down to his shoulders. His clothes were those of a dandy—someone used to fine living. But Ben noticed the pants and patent leather shoes were mud splattered, and sweat covered the man's freckled face.

"Wild dogs, Sir," he said with an accent Ben had never heard before. "These woods are crawling with them. They've been chasing me for the better part of an hour. I thought I had shaken them, but as you can hear, they now bear down upon me. If you will be so kind as to take me to the other side of the river, I will be much obliged."

Ben had never been called "sir" before, not by a white man. No white man had ever asked Ben to do anything either. They commanded.

"You don't even have to take me straight across. You can let me off downriver. It won't be out of your way at all."

Ben sat on the basket and eased the canoe forward, pulling up parallel to the bank. He put his hand on the gun in his pocket as the man got in and sat between Ben and Eli's body. After he settled in, Ben pushed off with his paddle.

"The name's Billy," the stranger said, dipping a handkerchief into the river and wiping his brow. "Billy Waters. God bless you for stopping."

"My name Ben. Ben Jordan."

The baying grew louder. Though Ben directed the boat toward the opposite shore, the current pushed them further downstream. By the time they reached the middle of the river, the man had eyed the contents of the canoe with interest and suspicion.

"Where are you headed?" he casually asked. Ben pointed down-river. "To de sea."

"The Atlantic? Where are you coming from?" Ben jerked his head back. "Upriver."

Billy licked his lips and eyed the basket beneath Ben.

"What's . . . what's in there?" he casually asked.

Ben put the paddle down. He squatted, and with one hand, lifted the basket's lid. With the other, he handed Billy enough food to satisfy a hearty appetite. The man dug into his meal with an eagerness that betrayed his casual air.

"You wouldn't happen to have any extra water, would you?" he asked.

Ben produced a bottle topped with a cork, which Billy quickly gulped down.

The barking grew very distinct, followed by the low rumble of horses' hooves.

"Missa Billy," Ben said, increasing the frequency of paddle strokes, "I believe dey is mo' dan wild dogs affer you!"

Billy smiled and brushed a hand through his sweat soaked hair. "Ben, you've done me a good turn, so I'll be straight with you. A few days ago, I had a little . . . um . . . misunderstanding, shall we say, with certain gentlemen in the town just north of here. No doubt you will see several of them very shortly. It is my firm belief that they didn't track me down to inquire about my health, if you take my meaning."

Ben paddled quickly and forcefully, turning once or twice to glance at the white side of the river. "I tek yo meaning, Missa Billy. It a priv'lege to hep a man in need. I can tek you mo' downriver if you want."

Billy stretched out and yawned. "Thanks, but I'm heading south to the Okefenokee. It is an excellent place to lie low. Dogs can't track you, and gators keep the law away something beautiful," he said as one speaking from experience.

"De Devil himself live in de swamp," Ben said.

Billy laughed aloud. "I can see you're a Christian, Ben. A Christian doesn't fear the Devil. Old Scratch should fear you! As for me, I'm too far-gone. Satan got his clutches into me long ago. If he does inhabit that place, I will be right at home there."

The canoe had closed to within a hundred feet of the south bank when shots rang out across the water. A hail of bullets splattered the woods ahead of Ben and Billy. Ben drowned out the sounds of men shouting loudly with the final thrusts of his paddle. They reached the far shore as another round of bullets zipped through the trees above their heads. Billy jumped from the dugout and pulled it onto the bank.

"Come on," he instructed Ben. "Take cover behind these trees until it stops raining lead."

Ben jumped out of the canoe and crouched with Billy behind a fallen tree that had washed downriver and snagged on the bank. From their vantage point, they could see six men on horseback. One of them, wearing a broad brimmed hat and riding a grey mare, looked through binoculars in their direction. Some of the men seemed to be cursing while four hound dogs nervously sniffed the ground trying to pick up a scent. In drought conditions, the men could have crossed on horseback. A few may have even attempted to swim across during normal river levels, but thanks to the upstream rains, the current flowed too swiftly to attempt such a feat.

It had flashed though Ben's mind that the rain was sent by God to speed his journey to Sapelo. Now, he wondered if the rains had been sent to aid in his new companion's escape.

"They must have split up," Billy said "There were a dozen or more men after me last time I checked."

"Whut dey want you fo, Missa Billy?"

Billy pulled a deck of cards from a vest pocket and smiled impishly.

"Missa Billy, is you a scoundrel?"

Billy laughed so hard the men on the opposite bank heard him and started firing in their direction again. After the gunfire ceased, Ben repeated the question. Willie had told him to be wary of men like Billy, but he couldn't help liking him.

"Ben," said Billy, "I am indeed a scoundrel, among other things which I have been called—a rapscallion, cad, rascal, rake, rogue, and blaggard. I am all of these and more. I am not, however, a liar, a thief, or a murderer. Anything I do, I do in the open and in plain sight. See those men over there on horseback? They represent the pillars of society. South Georgia's finest. And how do they make their living? By cheating their fellow man one contract at a time. They do it the coward's way—with lawyers and bankers. It's all legal and proper. And they have the unmitigated gall to attend church each Sunday and pretend they are God's elect. But God help the man who takes that ill-gotten money back from them using only his wits. Well, Ben, if those gentlemen over there on the opposite bank are the Lord's chosen ones, then give me the Devil, because I, for one, can't tell a hair's bit of difference between people like them and people like me."

Ben studied Billy and looked at the men across the river. They were a cut above the whites who killed Eli, but they were no different when it came to taking the law into their own hands.

"It wuz mens like dat hung my cousin."

Billy looked over Ben's shoulder at the canoe. "That's his body there under the tarp?"

"Yessuh. I'ze tekin' he body home fo to bury."

"I'm sorry to hear that," Billy said after a moment's pause. "I truly am. And I thank you again for saving my neck. Now, I must be getting on. If I recall from my last trip through this part of Georgia, there is a ferry about ten miles downstream. They will be on my trail again before the day is out."

"Hold on, Missa Billy," Ben said.

He crawled to the canoe, emptied the gunnysack, then filled it with food and crawled back to Billy.

"Here. Tek dis. Dem Lamar womens giff me 'nuff food fo three mens."

"Ben," Billy said as he tied the handkerchief around his neck, "I once wanted to be in the ministry. But I was too good at cards and too fond of women. God and the Devil waged an epic battle for my soul, and I don't need to tell you who won. But I do know this much, as sure as God is in Heaven and the Devil is in Hell, you are a good man, and God is watching out for you. And if ever I am in a position to do so, I will repay you for your kindness."

As Ben handed Billy the sack, a final volley of gunfire descended on the woods around them. He turned just in time to see the men on horseback gallop out of sight on a trail that paralleled the river's edge. When he turned back around, he saw Billy ascend a small rise in the woods. He paused at the crest and waved to Ben before disappearing over the other side.

Ben waited half an hour for the horsemen to move further downriver, and considered his options. He couldn't wait where he was for too long. He knew they would cross the river downstream and return to that spot to pick up Billy's trail. The current was too strong for him to paddle upstream. Crossing to the opposite shore proved problematic as Billy had mentioned there were six other men after him, and they might appear any minute. His only option was to continue downstream and hope the riders had already crossed.

Billy's recollection of a downstream ferry proved to be accurate. A few hours later, after what seemed like never-ending bends, the river narrowed, increasing the current's speed. As Ben navigated a sharp turn, the current shot his canoe like a cannonball toward the north bank where three men stood waiting. Behind them, he saw horses tied to saplings and hound dogs sniffing the ground. Straight ahead, he saw a steel cable stretched across the river. On the southern shore, men were repairing a flat-bottom boat that had been damaged by the rising waters.

"Come here!" a stocky man shouted from the northern landing as Ben approached. He, and his three companions, took aim at Ben. "Pull over here, nigguh, or I'll shoot!" he barked, his face red with anger.

The river at that point narrowed so much that he would be easy prey. If they didn't get him, they could easily fill the boat with holes. Ben had no choice but to angle toward the northern landing.

Within moments, they had the canoe on land and dumped all of its contents, including the hamper, Ben, and Eli's body, onto the ground.

"Where'd he go?" the stocky man demanded. He put his leather boot on Ben's neck and shoved the rifle end hard into the back of his head.

"Just shoot him, Sonny," said another, a thin man with a mustache.

"What did you do with Billy Forest?" Sonny shouted.

"I don't know no Billy Forest," Ben answered.

One hound sniffed Ben's feet while the others began to ravage the food that spilled from the basket. The thin man poked the outline of Eli's body with his gun's barrel. At that moment, Ben knew what Eli's last hour of life had been like. No one had come to Eli's rescue. Ben knew he had helped Billy escape a severe beating or worse, and he wasn't about to give him away to the real scoundrels Willie had warned him about.

"We got a body over here," said the thin man. He pulled out a knife and began to cut through the waxed stitching.

"Well, well," said Sonny, applying more pressure with his boot on Ben's neck as he pulled the pistol from Ben's overall pocket. "Looks like we got us a murderer as well as a thief's accomplice."

"I ain't never kilt no man," Ben said.

Sonny glanced up and spied a tree limb a few yards away. "Jimmy, get the rope," he ordered. "We're going to have us a hanging today after all."

Jimmy, who looked to be Sonny's twin, continued to stare at Eli.

"Looks like this one has already been hanged," he said. He opened the covering to reveal Eli's mummified remains.

"Christ, God-a'mighty," Sonny said. "Jimmy, where's that damn rope?"

"You ain't using my horse," Jimmy replied.

"I don't want no nigguh on my hoss either," said the thin man.

"Fine," Sonny answered, letting up pressure on Ben's neck. "We'll drown his sorry ass. Tie that rope to the tree."

"What are you boys doing over there?" boomed a voice from across the river.

"Don't you worry 'bout it! Just fix the damn ferry, and pull us over!" Sonny shouted back.

"Boy, if you believe in God, start praying," the thin man told Ben as he tied the rope around his chest. He tied Ben's hands behind his back.

"Stand up, nigguh," Sonny commanded Ben.

Ben slowly rose to his feet and stared with sad eyes at his cousin's remains. He feared that both his and Eli's spirits would wander the banks of the river until the Resurrection, searching for their bodies like the lost spirits he saw at night.

"I sorry, Eli," he said as the sound of horse hooves approaching caught the men's attention.

"I'm gonna give you one last chance," Sonny said. "Tell me where that son-of-a-bitch Billy Forest is headed."

"I don't know nothin' 'bout no Billy Forest," Ben replied.

"All right," Sonny replied, shoving Ben into the river. "Have it your way."

The fast moving current immediately swallowed Ben. He felt his body simultaneously falling toward the bottom and rapidly moving downstream. Almost instantly, the rope snapped taut, squeezing his chest until he thought his lungs would explode. He struggled for the surface, but the force of water pushed him down and back into the riverbank where sunken tree limbs scratched his face and torso.

Moments later, he became aware of another force at work. As he struggled among the branches, he had the distinct impression that his body was being drawn upstream. He believed that it was his spirit leaving his body and being drawn back to Eli. Soon, he felt his life slipping away and ceased struggling. Just as Ben was about to lose consciousness, his head broke the surface of the water. He gasped for the life-giving air and swallowed a quart of Altamaha River.

"Keep going!" he heard a voice shout above the din of water swirling around his head.

Half a minute later, Ben felt his shoulder hit dry land and was conscious of his body being dragged up onto the shore.

"Whoa! Whoa!" a voice yelled. Twenty feet away, a grey mare came to a stop. The rope tied between Ben and the horse slackened. He rolled onto his knees and regurgitated river water before collapsing onto his own vomit, gasping for oxygen.

"What the hell, Sonny?" said the man wearing the broad brimmed hat. A pair of binoculars hung from his neck. "I leave you alone for half an hour, and you're hanging someone!"

"He's the one helped Billy Forest get away!" Sonny shot back. "I'm telling you, Hugh, they're in cahoots! Besides that, he's carrying this here pistol, and he's got a dead man in the boat. He's a murderer!"

"That's right," Jimmy chimed in.

Hugh dismounted, removed his hat, and wiped his brow with a shirtsleeve.

"The only one guilty here is me for going on this fool's errand with you. You're the one who got hoodwinked by that card shark. If you weren't my brother, I'd have left you back upriver like the others did."

"You saw him paddle Forest cross the river! And he's got a dead man in his boat. Plus, he's carrying a gun. What else do you need?"

"Did you ask him about the body?"

"Hell no. Why should I ask a nigguh . . ."

"Use the sense God gave a goose, Sonny! If he killed a man, would he be carrying him around in a dugout canoe? No! He'd bury him in the first loose patch of ground he comes across."

"He wouldn't answer because he's guilty. We caught him red-handed!"

Hugh looked down at Ben.

"Do you know this man, Billy Forest?" he asked. Ben, still breathing heavily, didn't look up.

"De man I hep name Waters. Missah Billy Waters."

"Waters, Forest, it doesn't matter," Hugh replied.

"These charlatans got a new name for every town. Have you ever seen him before?"

"No, Suh."

"Did he say where he's headed?"

"He ain't said nuthin," Ben lied. It was a lie designed to save another man's life. "He say he been chase by wild dogs, so I hep him."

"What about this body?" Hugh asked. "What are you doing with it?"

Ben lifted his head, and slowly raised himself into a sitting position.

"He my cousin. Dey hang him fo no reason. I tekkin' he body home fo to bury."

"Where's home?"

"Sapelo. To de sea."

"She's coming over!" boomed a voice from the opposite bank. The cable spanning the river pulled taut as the ferry began a steady crawl across the water.

"Where are you coming from?" Hugh wanted to know.

Ben tilted his head upstream.

"Lamar. I works for Missa O. C. Clayborne."

"You hear that?" Hugh said to his brother. "He works for Obediah Clayborne."

"I bet his cousin had it coming to him," Sonny snapped. "They are both guilty as sin as far as I'm concerned. For all you know, they killed a white man, and this one," he said, pointing at Ben, "got away!"

"Just stop!" Hugh said, holding up a hand. "No more. I've about had enough of your nonsense for one day. I've got better things to do than going around killing innocent men."

The others agreed.

"Not you, too, Jimmy," Sonny said.

Jimmy looked at the ground, then at the man on the ferry pulling on the cable. "We'll be lucky to pick up his trail by dark."

Sonny threw his rifle on the ground in disgust. "I don't believe this!"

"We ran his butt out of town," the thin man replied. "That's enough. Ain't no shame in losing him at the river."

"He's right, Sonny," said Hugh. "Let him go."

Ben watched the dogs eat the last of his food as the men loaded Eli's body back into the canoe. He got in and pushed off from the shore just before the ferry arrived. As he rounded another bend half a mile downstream, he looked back to see Sonny and his horse crossing on the ferry.

CHAPTER 12

Ben steered the dugout downriver through the night and all of the next day, pausing occasionally to seek shade under overarching tree limbs along the riverbank. Just before midnight on the following day, he brought a handful of river water to his mouth and detected a hint of salt. The mighty Atlantic, pushing its tides upriver, was not far off. Almost mystically, as if passing through a doorway, the scenery turned from a tree-lined river, to open expanses of marsh grass. Before long, the old rice fields of the Butler Plantation appeared on his right. A little further on, the Darien docks came into view on his left.

He entered the Altahama Sound as a rising full moon laid down a carpet of white light on the water, like a lighthouse beam guiding him home. Two dolphins darted across the water, possibly, he thought, the same ones that accompanied him and Eli when they left the island.

"We see yuh," he called to them. "Go tell dem Eli an' Ben cumin' home."

He paddled for over an hour against a light breeze before reaching a landing on the west side of Sapelo. Ben stepped from the canoe and collapsed on to the ground, clenching and releasing fistfuls of the rich, dark loam in both hands. He lay still, his head pounding from lack of food and sleep and days of exposure to the elements.

Minutes passed before he felt the presence of a solitary figure standing above him on higher ground. He thought it might Bu-Allah or Eli's spirit, or his father, but his eyes quickly adjusted to the moonlight that filtered through the oak branches high overhead. Above him stood Dr. Crow. In the shadows, he looked even more intimidating than Ben recalled, like a walking scarecrow, more spirit than human. How Dr. Crow knew he was coming or when and where he would arrive, Ben didn't even question. The voodoo master always seemed to be there, summoned by unseen powers.

"Show de body," Dr. Crow said, pointing a bony finger toward the dugout.

Ben slowly rose to his feet and spread open the tarp that enshrouded his cousin's body. Dr. Crow walked down the embankment and pulled a small pair of shears from his breast pocket. He leaned forward and snipped a lock of Eli's hair. Without saying a word, he walked back up the incline and blended into the forest shadows.

Ben carried Eli's body to his cousin's home and laid it at the front doorstep. It was the last thing he remembered before losing consciousness.

The next afternoon, Ben awoke from a deep sleep to find that he was lying in his old bed at his parents' house. Homemade poultices covered his face and arms where his skin had begun to peel.

"Eli home," his father, Jesse, told him. "Yuh done good."

Ben raised his head.

"When de burial?"

"'Morrow."

Josephine came into the room carrying a bowl of chicken broth she'd been simmering on the wood stove. "Hep him up, Father," she instructed Jesse. "De boy need nourishin'."

Jesse helped Ben raise his head as Josephine tilted the bowl toward his mouth. He drank it down eagerly and asked for more. Josephine soon returned with another bowl of broth and some homemade bread, which he quickly devoured.

"Mo, please, Mama," he said, wearily.

She returned a few minutes later to find him sound asleep once again. When he awoke, it was dark outside, and the house was still. He got out of bed cautiously, testing his limbs and carefully placing the poultices aside. The moon had come up again. Slowly, he pushed open the shutters and looked outside, fully expecting to see Bu-Allah. Instead, he saw only tree branches swaying in the night breeze.

He knew that Eli's body lay on a cooling board in the front room of his parents' house. Most of the island's residents would have already come and gone, bringing food and offering condolences to the family.

The next morning, Deacon Rupert Bright showed early up at the Jordans' home to check on his former baptismal student.

"You remember yo Bible lessons, Ben?" he asked. "Yessuh, Missa Bright. You taught me real good."

"How 'bout Eli? Did Eli remember he Bible lessons out in de world?" Ben paused.

"I cain't say, Missa Bright. Didn't see much of Cuz affer we got to Waycross."

A pained expression clouded the deacon's face. Ben's hesitation and response told the elder Eli had gone astray according to the church's standards, and it grieved him to hear it.

"De world pull on a man all de time, Ben," he said. "It pull on him real hard where you livin'. Not so much on dis island, but real hard over on de other side. De world pull on a man 'til it pull him down. Unnerstan'?"

"Yessuh."

"It pull a young man down real fast."

"Yessuh."

"Sin crouchin' outside yo door, Ben. He waitin' to jump on yo back."

"Yessuh."

"If sin get on you, you bring it in de house, an' it get on ever'one in de household. Hear whut I'm sayin'?"

"Yessuh."

"You got a mat outside yo front door?"

"Yessuh."

"How cum?"

"Fo to wipe de dust of de world off my feet befo cumin' in de house."

"Dat right. But sin cum inside de home ridin' on yo back. Don't let sin get in yo house, Ben."

"No, Suh."

"When you cumin' home, Ben? When you bringin' dat bride and li'l girl to Sapelo an' settle down?"

"I don't know, Missa Bright. Mebee some day."

"Someday ain't no day. When you cumin' home?"

"I don't know Missa Bright. Saundra real sick right now. She gots de TB."

"Okay. I been prayin' fo her."

"Tank you, Missa Bright."

"Don't forget yo lessons, Ben."

"No, Suh."

"Dese folks here on Sapelo . . . dey is yo folks!"

"Yessuh."

"Dem folks over dere . . . dey don't unnerstan' our ways."

"Dat de trufe, Missa Bright."

"Don't forget whut I say, now, you hear?"

"No, Suh. I won't forget."

"All right. Let's go bury yo cousin."

The funeral procession began shortly after Deacon Bright's visit. An ox-drawn cart bore the pine coffin that held Eli's remains. The Jordans followed on foot, closely behind Eli's family. Ben walked stiffly at first, but the walk and the morning sun quickly restored life to his sore limbs.

"We ax leab fo to enter dis cemet'ry," a church elder called to the spirits there, asking permission to come inside the grave-yard gates.

Two hundred voices filled the air with a hymn, "Low Down the Chariot and Let Me Ride," as each person filed through the cemetery gates. The island's newest pastor, Reverend Isaac Williams, offered a similar homily to the one delivered by his counterpart in Lamar, Reverend Douglas. Ben half-listened as he had done during Eli's impromptu wake in the woods on the river's edge. Before, it was due to shock. This time, he found himself distracted by the nagging feeling that someone was watching.

"'To me belongeth vengeance,' saith the Lord," the reverend reminded the people. "'I will repay.'"

Revenge had been on Ben's mind for much of the journey home. He grappled with the idea, at once attracted and repulsed by the thought of seeking vengeance.

"'In due time their foot shall slide,'" the reverend quoted, "'for their day of calamity is near and their doom rushes upon them. Wait for the Lord, and He will deliver you!'"

"Dat right," Rupert Bright said.

"The body—Eli's body—is a temple," Reverend Williams continued. "Tear it down, and the spirit will rise up again!"

The service concluded with "My Soul, Be at Rest" as a group of men carefully lowered the casket into the ground. Eli's mother approached the graveside. In her hand, she held dirt from where his afterbirth had been buried. She reached out and let it slide gently from her hand onto the pine box. Ben, too, stepped forward and carefully tossed in the piece of pine bark from the tree on which Eli had been hung.

Two men with shovels quickly filled in the grave and formed a small mound on top. A plaster headstone was put in place. On it, Ben saw the image of a shooting star over Eli's name. After they were done, his family members approached the grave and one-by-one left objects on the burial mound. Each article—a shaving jar, an alarm clock, an Errol Flynn figurine—were broken, symbolizing that a life, one of the Creator's vessels, had been broken. Shards of colored glass were sprinkled here and there to discourage haints from walking over Eli's remains. Eli's father was last to approach the grave. He bent over the headstone and hung from it a fractured Christmas ornament in the shape of a star.

As Ben left the cemetery grounds, he heard bushes rustling, and straggled behind while the others made their way back to Hog Hammock. After almost everyone was out of sight, he walked stealthily back toward the graveyard and peered through the wands of a palmetto bushes to see Dr. Crow's donkey tied to a cemetery gatepost. Inside the burial grounds, the old conjurer kneeled beside a preacher's grave, uttering words Ben could not understand. The root doctor reached out with long, sinewy fingers that more closely resembled claws than human digits, and took a pinch of dirt from the grave mound. He repeated the ritual at Eli's grave, placing the dirt from both burial sites inside a small pouch. As he walked back toward the gate, Dr. Crow paused and turned to look in Ben's direction. He sniffed the air and waved a hand three times by his waist before mounting his donkey. A minute later, Ben was alone save the chattering of squirrels and birds.

He decided at that moment to leave the island before dark,

before Bu Allah's or Eli's spirits awakened. More than that, he had an odd feeling about the root doctor. The preacher admonished patience, to let God's vengeance take the place of man's. Ben wavered on this matter, but he knew where Dr. Crow stood. He had not met Ben at the landing just to pay his respects. He knew the root doctor had been collecting ingredients—a lock of hair, dirt from graves—to make a conjure. Ben wanted to be gone before Dr. Crow could get to him.

When he returned home, Josephine and Jesse questioned Ben about his insistence on taking the next boat to the mainland.

"Why you got to go, Ben? You ain't healed up," his mother protested.

"Listen to your mother, Son," Jesse added.

"Docta Crow affer me," was all he replied. His parents knew what he meant and didn't pursue the matter any further.

Ben arrived at the dock just as the ferry pulled into view. On the dock between Ben and the boat, stood Dr. Crow.

"Here," he said, handing Ben a crumpled piece of discolored paper and a stub of pencil, "write de name on dis paper."

Ben looked quizzically at the scrap of paper in the root doctor's hand.

"Preacher say vengeance is fo de Lawd," he said.

"Hmph," Dr. Crow replied with a scowl. His disdain for the island's clergyman, a mainlander temporarily transplanted to Sapelo, was evident. "A t'ousand year be like a day to God! You wants to wait 'til kingdom come, Boy, or you wants justice now?

"Preacher say . . ."

"God give de preacher a book," Dr. Crow interrupted. "God give me the root! He give me de learnin' and de power to use He plants. Write down de name ob de man whut kilt Eli!"

Ben took the paper and pencil in his trembling hands.

"Make de name right," Dr. Crow instructed.

Mainlanders dismissed the conjurer's alleged feats as coincidences, but on the island, his prowess with the root remained undisputed. His power lay in placing hexes, removing conjures, or creating roots to bring good fortune, money, love, and he seldom displeased his clients.

In Ben's mind, he had no choice but to follow the commands lest the root doctor place a hex on the Jordan home.

Dr. Crow pulled a small cloth-enshrouded object from the inside pocket of his frayed raincoat. He opened a flap to reveal the cloth had been stuffed with roots of various kinds, brightly colored powders, grave dirt, and Eli's hair, which had been singed with a flame.

"Whut dis root do?" Ben asked.

Dr. Crow looked at him, his one good eye glazed over and red.

"Dis one called de Destroyer. Dis de most powerfulest root dey is. Ain't nuthin else like it. It got pepper in it. Pepper hot! It got rainwater in it. Water bring a flood. I blowed in it, so it got wind, too. Fire, water, and wind. Dey all is in de root. All o' dem. De root will bring de man down by fire, flood, or storm. Cain't no man stop it once it in de ground. You gots to be careful wiff dis conjuh. Don't drop it in de water. Anyone wiff de name on dat piece of paper up and down de river be kilt! An' don't keep it wiff you too long. It will turn on de owner if it ain't buried quick! You hear? It will turn on you. You gots to get rid of it tonight. An' don't bury it at de wrong house. It might kill a innocent man."

Ben hesitated. Though his minister in Lamar and the one on the island admonished patience, Dr. Crow offered Ben a route to justice without direct confrontation. He could plant a bomb on Cale land, one sure to kill the intended victim, without ever being suspected.

"De blood on me!" Dr. Crow said, divining Ben's thoughts.

"Any blood shed be on my head, unnerstan'? It cum to me and pass out to de dark spirits. De dark spirits tek it to Satan where sin cum from. De sin return home to evil, unnerstan'?"

Ben paused a moment longer before scribbling the letters C-A-L-E on the piece of paper. He handed it over.

The witch doctor spat on the paper without looking at the writing, and stuffed it into the cloth. He then produced a needle already threaded, and expertly sewed the root shut. Finally, Dr. Crow turned and chanted words from the unknown tongue over it. After the chanting stopped, he held the root out to the spirits. A full minute passed before he placed it in Ben's hands. At that moment, the otherwise sunny day seemed to grow darker, as if an unseen shadow blanketed the sky.

"Don't let dis root leave yo sight," Dr. Crow admonished. "Bury it on de man's land befo sunrise. Unnerstan'?"

"I unnerstan," Ben replied, delicately placing the root in his pocket. As he turned to leave, Dr. Crow grabbed his arm.

"Tek dis," he said, "placing another object in Ben's hand. "Dis here called a am'let. Put it in yo shoe. It mek you invisible an' keep de dogs frum barkin' when you cum to de house fo to bury dat root."

Ben looked down at a square of red velvet. It had been folded over and sewn together to form a thin patch almost the size of a postage stamp.

"Dis proteck you frum de Devil hisself," he told Ben, knowing he would need something to provide the boldness to plant a hex on the murderer's land.

Ben didn't speak to anyone when he boarded the ferry. As it crossed the sound, he looked for the dolphins, hoping they would escort him to the other side, but none broke surface. Perhaps, he thought, the root kept them away. He could feel it in his pocket, growing warmer as the ingredients inside came to life.

From Meridian, he caught a ride to Brunswick where he boarded a train. By late afternoon, he was back in Lamar. Geneva greeted him at the front door, holding Naomi in her arms.

"How Naomi?" were the first words out of his mouth.

"De chile fine long as someone holdin' her tight. De minute you put her down she cry. It becuz she were snatch frum her momma. Here," she said, passing Naomi to Ben, "we gonna haff a mess o' folks here fo long. Let me clean up dis place."

Ben held Naomi while Geneva prepared the house for a stream of visitors about to arrive. Word that Ben had returned from his trek wouldn't take long to get around Scott Hill.

"Hi, li'l girl," he cooed to his daughter. "Papa home."

Naomi wriggled in his arms and looked up at him, smiling.

"Papa home for good," he told her. "Mama be home soon."

As Geneva had foreseen, a steady stream of people soon showed up carrying food dishes.

Deacon Jones took up a position on the front porch, serving as the official greeter. His rich, resonant voice filled the house as he greeted new arrivals eager to hear of Ben's journey to Sapelo. Some of them spoke about Eli, a man they'd never met alive, in exalted tones, comparing him to Christ. The pine tree he'd been hung from likewise assumed an elevated status. Local blacks called it the Jesus Tree because a man died on it for other men's sins.

Reverend Douglas showed up a few minutes later. Ben greeted him warmly, but hoped he wouldn't bring up the topic of revenge. Dr. Crow's root had made the journey most of the way home in Ben's hip pocket. Halfway to Baxley, riding in the crowded negro section of the train, he felt a burning sensation at his side. He had almost forgotten the root was there. He put his hand on it. It felt hot, like a rag on fire. He pulled it out for just a moment and glanced at it. Some of the contents had leaked and stained the outer surface of the cloth. When he stuck it back into his pocket, his eyes met those of a white haired woman. She looked at him, her eyes filled with alarm at the sight of the conjure, and quickly moved to another part of the railroad car.

Reverend Douglas spoke encouraging words to Ben about his wife's recovery and raising Naomi into a fine Christian woman, but Ben's thoughts remained on the root. He had placed it inside a bucket in the shed behind the house, unsure what to do with it.

That night, while Geneva and Naomi slept, he lay awake in bed. Every time he closed his eyes, he felt as if he was floating downstream in the dugout canoe, another bend in the river approaching. When he opened his eyes, he recalled the lynching he almost received, which brought visions to his mind of Eli's final moments. The more he thanked God for sparing his life, the more he recalled both preachers' sermons on forgiveness. But their words only stirred up thoughts of Dr. Crow holding out the root for him to take.

"It will turn on de owner if it ain't buried quick!" the root doctor had warned.

Ben sat up in the bed. Sweat rolled down the back of his neck.

"De blood on Docta Crow," he said softly.

"De sin return home to evil," he heard Dr. Crow's reply as clearly as if he stood in the room beside Ben's bed.

"Sin return to evil," Ben whispered. "De blood on Docta Crow."

He repeated this mantra as he put on his overalls and boots. He placed the red amulet in his left sock for protection. He knew he wouldn't sleep again until the root had been disposed of. Looking out the back door, Ben noticed the shed seemed to glow in the dark. He realized that holding onto it would put his family in danger.

"De blood on Docta Crow," he said again, crossing the railroad tracks with the root in his hip pocket and a shovel in his hand. He circled the outskirts of Lamar through darkened wood trails. Though the night air felt cool, sweat dripped from his brow. The root was warming. After a few minutes, he thought the root might burn a hole in his overalls. Ben pulled it from his pocket and carried it on the shovel.

He walked the distance to the Two Mile community in twenty minutes. He well knew the surrounding woods. Cutler land bordered it, and he'd logged trees on much of that ground. He knew exactly where Cale property abutted the Cutlers'. A string of dilapidated fence posts, connected by rusted barbed wire, marked the boundary that once kept Cutler cows from straying. Obediah Cutler had run-ins with Cales in the past, and more than once, accused them of cattle rustling. Willie's crew, too, had experienced altercations with the family who, in turn, accused Cutler of logging on their property.

"Dis here Cale land," Ben told himself, coming to a halt. He placed one hand on a fence post and looked down the darkened tunnel of the tree-lined pathway. Somewhere on the other end of the tunnel, stood Donan Cale's home.

Ben ignored the mosquitoes that lighted on him as he stared ahead.

"Dis de Destroyer. De sin return home to evil."

Ben turned, half expecting to see Dr. Crow standing next to him, speaking the words.

He slowly lifted one leg over the wire, then the other.

"De blood on Docta Crow," he muttered.

Ben mumbled the words again as he moved silently down the dark path. He knew that if he was caught on Cale property, he would end up hanging from a tree like Eli. He also knew that he was as good as dead if he didn't get rid of the root.

After a few minutes, he came to a small clearing. For a fleeting moment, he thought of turning back, but he put his head down and kept walking. He had come too far to turn away.

He almost walked up on the house a minute later. The one story, rambling structure had been built eighty years earlier on the Conyers Plantation. Rooms had been added as the Cale family grew. The woods, which came almost to the back door, had once been open fields.

Ben froze in his tracks when he realized he stood exposed in the moonlight. Had someone been sitting on the back porch, they would have easily spotted him. Most likely, a number of dogs were sleeping on or under the front porch, but none of them detected his presence, which he attributed to the amulet.

He slowly bent down and dug a shovelful of dirt, pressing hard on the handle, and compressed the dirt forward. With his left hand, he let the root slip behind the shovel to the bottom of the hole, then he eased the shovel out of the ground. Ben stepped on the dirt with his right foot, and stealthily retraced his steps to the property boundary, all the while listening for the sound of barking hounds.

Ben thought about what he'd done all the way back to Scott Hill. A little past two in the morning, he arrived home exhausted. He took off his boots and overalls and hunched over the kitchen sink, letting a slow drizzle of cold tap water fall from the faucet onto his head. After he had cooled down enough, he stripped his clothes and eased back into bed. No longer did the visions flash before him when he closed his eyes. He fell asleep almost as soon as his head hit the pillow. Just before losing consciousness, he heard another voice in his ear. This time, it was Deacon Bright.

"You remember yo Bible lessons, Ben?"

CHAPTER 13

The fires kindled during the years that federal anti-liquor laws were in effect, still burned brightly in churches across the land. No flame burned brighter or hotter than the one in Pastor DeLong Stanton Dodge's pulpit. His vitriol toward drinkers and purveyors of alcohol increased during the dry, deathly-hot summer, a period hard-scrabble dirt farmers talked about for years. Creeks dried up, big rivers slowed to a trickle, and it seemed nature had forgotten how to make rain.

The night of Ben's return to Lamar, Obediah Clayborne lay on his deathbed, his frail body yielding to the final assault of pancreatic cancer.

"Clay, they're just waiting for you to slip up," he told his son. "Every son-of-a-bitch between Waycross and McRae is going to come after you. Bankers, lawyers, preachers. They're all gonna want something—a business investment, a donation—you name it. Every one of them will tell you they have your best interest in mind. Don't you believe it! They'll tell you about how 'me and your daddy go back a long ways.' Show those bastards the door."

"Yes, Sir."

"Them paper mills starting up around here are gonna want to buy up Cutler land. Lots of people want Cutler property around the town square. Don't you let them have it! Me and your granddaddy fought hard to get it. Them lots is hard to come by."

"I know, Daddy. Hoffer won't give up his corner for anything."

"I never cared much for Hoffer. If you nab that property, I'll rest easy in my grave. And watch out for old Donan Cale out at Two Mile. His daddy and my daddy came out of the same woods, and look where those Cales ended up—dirt poor, thieving no-accounts. He's held a grudge over that. Most of all, and I don't care how you do it, run that son-of-a-bitch, Dodge, out of town. That's the one thing I regret, that he's still breathing Lamar air, and I'm lying here about to die."

Obediah raised his head from the pillow.

"Get him, Clay." He looked his son in the eye. "Any way you can. You hear me?"

Since returning to Lamar, Clayborne realized that, while he would inherit his father's holdings, he would not inherit the respect Obediah had earned in the surrounding community. Clayborne heard the snide remarks about being born with a silver spoon in his mouth, about how he was just a mama's boy who wouldn't be able to fill his daddy's shoes. His grandfather had knifed a man over a card game. His father had also killed a man, an emaciated bandit wearing a tattered Confederate cap, who tried to rob Obediah on his return from a log-rafting trip downriver. Both murders were done in self-defense and stood as a private badge of honor passed down from Cutler father to son. Clayborne had yet to kill his man, but pioneer Georgia, where frontier justice prevailed, was a thing of the past. The state had become civilized, connected by rails and roads. The rule of law—for whites, among whites—prevailed.

Clayborne carefully considered his response. A deathbed promise would have to be kept.

* * *

"I'll get him, Daddy. Don't worry about that." Four hundred people, black and white, showed up for Obediah Clayborne's funeral a week later. A few days after the burial, peals of thunder rumbled in the distance, teasing growers with the promise of rain that never came. Clayborne lay in bed and considered his options.

"Something's got to give," he said to himself absent-mindedly, thinking of the rain. It occurred to him that something had to give in the town's growing debate over the issue of strong drink. It was no secret that part of Pastor Dodge's vitriol was directed at Salty Hoffer. In the same instant, a bolt of lightning ignited the sky in the distance, Clayborne realized the solution was simple. If the good reverend somehow came to an abrupt demise, Hoffer would become a suspect. With a little help, he could be a prime suspect. All Clayborne needed was an accomplice—someone who could do what needed to be done without questioning.

The next morning, as Willie's men harvested trees, Clayborne paid the crew a visit on horseback while surveying the company's timber holdings. Ben was trimming a tree with an older logger named Bailey, when he looked up and spotted Cutler light a cigarette. A sunbeam poured through the trees, bathing Clayborne in a brilliant light that seemed to set his golden hair afire. His tanned face and blue eyes reminded Ben of a Greek god he'd seen in a book the Penningtons once brought to Sapelo's two-room schoolhouse.

"Dat de purtiest man in de whole worl," he said.

Bailey laughed. "Him? That's ol' man Cutler's son, Clayborne. He the one in charge now."

Ben continued to stare at Clayborne until the stillness of the morning was shattered by a piercing cry.

"Snake!" a crewman called out.

Ben turned and saw men scatter left and right, revealing a large diamondback coiled, its tail moving rapidly, creating the distinct sound that made a man's stomach turn and his heart race. Three feet away stood a logger who'd been on Willie's crew for just a few months. He'd bent down to pick up a steel wedge when the rattler revealed itself. The man remained in a half-crouch, frozen in fear at the sight before him.

"Don't move, Nate!" Willie called out. "Ben coming!"

At the sound of the initial cry, Clayborne's head also jerked up. He watched Ben pull the pistol from its holster on his back and fire from the hip. A moment later, the snake's head exploded, and the menacing rattle ceased. In that same instant, Clayborne knew he found the man who would help him keep the deathbed promise to his father.

"Who's that?" he asked Willie, pointing to Ben. "Him? That's Ben Jordan."

"The one whose cousin was lynched?"

"He the one."

"Is he a good worker?"

"He good, Boss. He's the best. He's the best at what he do."

"He handles a gun pretty well."

"Best shot out here, Mista Cutluh. Best man with a gun I seen—white or black. But he different, Boss. He from Sapelo."

"What's that got to do with it?" Clayborne asked.

"Nothing, Mista Cutluh. But them Sapelo peoples is different is all I'm saying. They ain't like most folk."

"He got family here?"

"He got a wife and li'l girl. The wife over to the Negro TB clinic. She not doing too good."

Bailey stretched the snake out on a log and measured it.

"Seven foot, two inch!" he called out.

Clayborne said nothing more about Ben to Willie. On the way home, he worked out the final pieces necessary to fulfill the promise he made to his dying father.

One crisp, October evening, Clayborne stood on the back porch of the Cutler Land & Lumber payroll office, watching crew members file by with their weekly earnings. Willie's crew received their pay last. When Ben walked by with his earnings, Clayborne called him aside.

"Ben Jordan, I need you to shoot a snake for me," he said in a low tone so he wouldn't be overheard. He pulled a pack of Lucky Strike cigarettes from his coat pocket and lit one. "Meet me in that empty lot behind the water tower tomorrow night at eleven o'clock sharp."

"A snake, Missa Cutluh?"

"Yes."

"At night, Boss?"

"Yes."

"I go shoot dat snake now, Missa Cutluh!"

"No. Not now!" Clayborne replied harshly. "Just be there like I told you, and don't tell anyone."

"'Leven o'clock tomorrow night?"

"That's right."

"Okay, Boss."

Clayborne narrowed his eyes.

"Tell no one, you hear? Not your wife, not Willie—no one!"

With most any other white, Ben might have asked questions, but Clayborne Cutler wasn't any other white. He was the president of Cutler Land & Lumber and a pillar of the surrounding community. In the Depression South, when a white man of prominence told a black man to do something, he did it. Ben well understood this unwritten rule.

"Yessuh, Missa Cutluh," he answered, "I won't tell no one."

Clayborne's stern gaze instantly relaxed, transforming into one of benevolence. He eyed the week's pay in Ben's hand.

"This little job could earn you a lot more money than what you're holding there, Ben Jordan." A smile crept over his face. "A whole lot more. Enough to get your wife out of that two-bit TB clinic into a *real* facility."

Clayborne flashed a large wad of cash in front of Ben's eyes, then quickly put the money away. Ben felt his knees go weak.

"You can make it happen, Ben. Be there like I said. But if I find out anyone else knows about it, the deal's off."

"No, Suh! Won't no one know 'bout it, Boss."

To be singled out for such a job by the wealthiest man in town was somewhat of an honor. For the rest of the evening and throughout the next day, the idea of meeting to shoot a snake at night seemed to Ben an odd proposition. The secrecy made it even more perplexing, and the honor more dubious, but he did as Cutler had instructed and told no one.

At eleven o'clock the following evening, Ben arrived at the designated spot, and waited. He pulled a sweater on top of his overalls as the first cold snap of autumn descended on Lamar. After half an hour of waiting, he heard a voice from the woods at the edge of the property.

"Ben. Over here," the voice said. It was Cutler. "I'm coming, Boss," Ben called out.

"Keep your voice down!"

"Sorry, Boss," Ben whispered.

When he reached the treeline, he saw Clayborne in the moonlight that filtered through the branches. Ben immediately saw the .45 caliber pistol in Clayborne's hand. It was brand new, not one that belonged to the company, at least, not one Ben recognized. Clayborne, having carefully planned the evening far in advance, purchased the gun on an overnight trip to Columbus, Georgia.

There, in the dark of the woods' canopy, Clayborne lit a cigarette. Though Cutler normally smoked Lucky Strikes, Ben noticed he held a pack of Camels as the match burned brightly. For the first time, with light projecting from beneath Clayborne's face, Ben saw the antithesis of a Greek god. What he saw reminded him more of the gargoyle sketch his teacher had once shown the class.

"Ready to kill that snake?" Clayborne asked. "I ready, Boss."

"This won't take a second to do, but I need your word that no one will ever know about it."

"Okay, Missa Cutluh."

"Swear on your mother's grave?"

"She ain't ded, Missa Cutluh."

"Swear on your grandmother's grave?"

"I swear I won't tell no one, Boss!"

"Okay. Your word is good enough for me. You have my word, too, Ben."

"You wants me to shoot a snake wiff dat?" Ben asked, eyeing the gun.

"That's right," Clayborne replied, handing it to Ben.

"Know what I got here?" he said as he extracted an envelope from his pocket.

"No, Suh."

Cutler handed Ben the book of matches.

"Strike one," he said.

Ben tore off a match and feeling with the tips of his fingers lit one. In the brief moments that it burned, Clayborne flashed a small stack of twenty-dollar bills before Ben, whose eyes grew wider as the flame burned. Clayborne knew he could order one of his workers to do just about anything without them balking, but the job at hand required some extra insurance. Sweetening the pot with a little money seemed prudent. He smiled upon seeing that the money had produced the desired effect.

"Missa Cutluh," Ben whispered. "Dat got to be all de money in de whole wide worl'!"

"That's five hundred dollars, Ben," Clayborne replied. He stuffed the money back into the envelope and placed it in Ben's chest pocket. "There's five hundred more for you after we're done. You can get a lot of doctoring for your wife with that kind of money."

"And all's I haff to do is kill a snake?"

"That's all. Nothing to it. Won't take you but a second. Follow me."

Ben clutched the gun in one hand and pressed firmly on the envelope in his pocket with the other. His feet seemed to float on a cushion of air as he followed Clayborne down a narrow trail. Saundra's health had steadily declined. He had been praying for a way to get her into a better tuberculosis clinic. Now, it seemed, God had answered his prayer. The day of deliverance from the world's burdens was at hand.

Clayborne also thought his day of deliverance had arrived. The promise to his father would soon be fulfilled. The Cutler family was finally to be avenged of the wrongs imposed on them by the hated Dodges of New York.

Both men privately mused on diverging tracks of thought as they followed the trail that curved south and east toward the preacher's home. The Methodist rectory had been purposely situated a quarter mile from town so that its occupant could meditate in peace and quiet.

Ben remained deep in thought about how best to spend his earnings when he first saw the lights of the house ahead of him. Clayborne came to a standstill behind the rectory, and paused to take a final drag on the Camel before snuffing it out on the heel of his boot and dropping it onto the ground.

"Why we stoppin' here, Missa Cutluh?" Ben asked.

"Sshh! Don't use my name!" Clayborne hissed. He pointed at the light coming through a window.

Ben looked inside and saw a den lined with cedar. Shelves filled with leather-bound books covered one wall. Near the window was a cluttered desk. On it were sheets of paper. Ben could see a large figure pacing the room.

"Look," Clayborne whispered.

As he said this, Pastor Dodge approached the desk and sat down to make some final changes to the next day's sermon.

"There," Clayborne said, "is your snake."

Ben looked at Reverend Dodge, then at Clayborne, unable to comprehend the full import of Cutler's meaning. He looked again at Dodge and saw an aura surrounding him.

He turned back to Cutler.

"Dat ain't no snake, Boss. Dat Passuh Dodge!" Clayborne turned toward Ben.

"I say it's a snake," he said. The words came out slowly, deliberately, bitterly. "Now, shoot it!"

Ben recalled the advice his father had given him. "If a white man tell you do sumtin', you do it. Don't ax questions." Jesse's advice had served Ben well until that moment, but every instinct was repulsed at the thought of carrying out this command.

"But he a preacher man, Missa Cutluh! A preacher anointed by God. He a holy man."

Clayborne looked at Ben with all the affectation of compassion he could muster.

"Look," he said, putting a hand on Ben's shoulder. He had anticipated the possibility that Ben would balk even with a monetary incentive, and still had an ace to play. "I didn't want to tell you this, but this so-called holy man knew all about the rape Cale and his kinfolk accused your cousin of perpetrating. You know and I know that one of those Two Mile poor whites raped her. When that baby comes out, he's not going to look like your cousin or any other black man. He's going to look like a Cale because he is a Cale.

That bastard Dodge knew it, too. And what did he do to stop it? Nothing. My daddy put a man with a shotgun at the lumberyard gate and personally told Cale to leave you black workers alone. Remember? That son-of-a-bitch Dodge . . . Look at him . . ."

Ben glanced over at the window where Dodge had resumed writing.

"He didn't do a thing to stop the lynching. He could have done something and didn't raise a finger. And what's worse, he hasn't said anything since. Sits there writing sermons like it never happened. He sits there now working on tomorrow's sermon. Tells folks to love their neighbor and to do unto one another, but when it comes right down to it, all he does is talk. Is that holy?"

"No, Suh," Ben replied, the thought that Eli's lynching could have been prevented angered him.

"Is that righteous?"

"No, Suh." He felt hatred welling up inside of him like sap rising in a tree.

"Is that his Christian duty?"

"No, Suh!"

"There's plenty of other reasons why he should die, believe me," Cutler concluded. "Lots of other people want him dead. I don't have time to go into that now."

Ben's lower lip trembled with rage. His chest heaved.

Cutler leaned over and whispered his coup de grace in Ben's ear.

"One thousand dollars for one second's work. Isn't your wife's good health worth it? A man has to do what a man has to do for his family."

He turned Ben's shoulders square to the window. "Just pretend you're picking off a rattler."

Ben set his jaw firmly and raised the revolver. The breath came hard and fast through his nostrils like an enraged bull about to charge. The shot was an easy one from under twenty yards. He'd killed many a snake from further distances. His forefinger slowly squeezed on the trigger.

"Snake!" Clayborne said.

Ben pulled the trigger, but nothing happened. He pulled again before realizing that his finger wouldn't bend. A tingling sensation originating in the tips of his fingers quickly ran down the entire length of his arm, causing it to shake.

"Come on," Clayborne said impatiently. "Do it!"

Sweat broke out on Ben's forehead as he struggled to steady the pistol with both hands. He summoned all of his strength to remain composed. After several more moments, he managed to squeeze off a shot. As he did, he felt a hand push his arm aside.

To Ben, the gunshot sounded like a dynamite explosion. It was with some sense of relief that he noticed the bullet had slammed into the window frame instead of reaching its intended victim.

"Christ, God all mighty!" Cutler whispered loudly and angrily. "You shot the house!"

"What fo you push me?" Ben asked.

"I didn't push you, gottdammit!"

Clayborne snatched the gun from Ben's hand. "Stupid, gottdamn nigger! Get outta my sight!" Inside the rectory, Dodge got up from the desk and went to the front door. His hearing had grown worse since coming to Lamar. He thought a car had backfired in the drive leading up to the house.

"Go wait at the water tower, and don't move until I get there!" Clayborne commanded Ben.

Ben tried to run, but his legs suddenly felt like they had turned to rubber. It was only with great determination that he remained upright and moving forward. After a quarter mile, he could go no further and fell to the ground where he curled into a fetal position. He felt like throwing up.

At the rectory, Dodge returned to his desk to make some

finishing touches on the sermon he would deliver the following morning. Clayborne couldn't believe his luck. He had anticipated that Dodge would come to the backyard where he would shoot him down, but not before cursing him to his face. Now, it was as if nothing in his plan had changed. The only difference was that he had a witness. The idea came to him that he might have to kill Ben as well, but he had one more errand for Ben, one that was too risky for Clayborne to make.

As Ben lay paralyzed on the ground, he realized the hand that pushed his arm didn't belong to Clayborne. He knew that Bu-Allah and the collective spirits of his ancestors had reached out across the miles of water separating Lamar and Sapelo. The son of Jesse, the great-grandson of Bu-Allah, couldn't kill a preacher in cold blood.

A searing pain tore through his head when he heard the weapon fire again. He felt as though an iron clamp had tightened around his skull. The shot sounded faint this time, like a child's cork gun, accompanied by an echo. Ben let out a howl that likewise echoed through the woods. His cry was met by the growl of an animal nearby.

Minutes later, he heard footsteps and called out, but it was too late. Clayborne tripped over him and fell down.

"Damn useless coward!" Cutler growled. He arose and dusted off his clothes. Then he reached down and snatched the envelope from Ben's overall pocket. Ben was glad to be rid of it.

"We done a evil ting, boss," Ben lamented. Tears streamed down his cheeks. "We kilt dat preacher. You an' me. I guilty as you, 'cause I didn't stay yo hand."

"Shut up! Now, listen. We didn't kill Dodge, you hear? Hoffer did it."

Ben sat up and stared up at Clayborne.

"Missa Hoffer?"

"That's right. Salty Hoffer. I started to leave, but then I looked back, and there's Salty standing behind the house. I heard the shot, same as you."

Ben continued to stare at Clayborne with a mixture of relief and suspicion.

"Why fo Missa Hoffer wanna kill a preacher man?"

"I told you! Plenty other people want to see that Dodge bastard dead. Hoffer sells liquor. Dodge is always preaching against alcohol. Now, come on. I have another job for you."

When they reached the water tower, Clayborne handed Ben the gun.

"You, Ben Jordan, put a slug in the rectory window frame with this gun. If they match that bullet with this .45, you're good as dead. I want you to throw it in that swamp over on the other side of the colored section. Do you think you can do that without messing things up?"

"Yessuh, Missa Cutluh."

"And remember, you made a promise. I never saw you out here. If you get caught with that gun, you never saw me out here. Okay?"

"Okay, Boss."

"Shake on it."

Clayborne held out his hand. Ben hesitated. He had never even touched a white man before. Slowly, cautiously, he stretched out his arm. An icy chill ran down his spine when his hand clasped Cutler's. In his mind's eye, he saw Rupert Bright's kitchen table. On it sat a sugar jar. Inside the jar he saw Cutler's roll of money.

"I done failed de firs' lesson," he said, not realizing he had spoken aloud.

"Don't worry about it," Clayborne replied. "It worked out okay anyway. You just get rid of that gun like a told you."

CHAPTER 14

"A man tormented by the guilt of murder will be a fugitive till death!" Reverend Douglas shouted from the dais of Lamar's First African Baptist Church the following morning.

"All right," Deacon Thomas replied, his voice rolling like thunder down the aisles and echoing off the back wall.

"Let no one support him!"

"Come on."

Ben slumped in his seat as the reverend's words pierced like fiery daggers, burrowing deep into his flesh. *He know,* Ben thought. *He a holy man like Dodge.*

He might not know who done it, but he know.

The first thing Ben's eyes focused on that Sunday morning had been Dr. Crow's tiny red amulet that sat on a small bedroom table. He'd neglected to take it with him to meet with Clayborne Cutler. In hindsight, he realized it was a grave mistake. The paralysis he felt while running from the Methodist rectory still lingered on his walk to church.

Even though it was a sunny day, a dark pall hung over his world, much like when he stood in Dr. Crow's presence. Somehow, it seemed wrong that the sun still came up and songbirds still sang after the evil that had been committed.

Geneva noticed Ben's aloofness on their walk to church. He seemed distant, as if in another world.

"Whut wrong?" she asked, carrying Naomi in her arms.

"Nuttin," he said.

He hadn't thrown the murder weapon into the swamp like Clayborne instructed. Ben had another idea, one that required digging. He'd run home after the murder and taken a shovel from the shed, then disappeared into the night. Two hours later, he returned. As he crossed the railroad tracks, he thought he saw someone. More to the point, he thought someone, a white man, had seen him, but he couldn't be sure. Now, as he replayed the previous evening's events over in his mind, that seemingly inconsequential encounter loomed large. He was a black man carrying a shovel on the night of a murder.

Naomi squirmed in Geneva's arms and reached out to her father.

"Naomi want you," his sister said.

"Not now," he replied. "Papa tinkin."

Ben refused to make eye contact with his fellow worshipers. As he sat in the pew, fervently praying for forgiveness, those looking thought he was praying for God's healing touch on his wife.

"One touch from you, oh Lord, and even the dead will rise up," Reverend Douglas said.

"All right," Deacon Thomas chimed in.

"A word from your lips, and legions of afflicted will stand up out of their sick beds."

"Amen."

"One thought from you . . ."

"Come on . . ."

"And nations will arise, whole and new!"

"We praise you, Lord!"

Naomi lay in the pew next to Ben. She swiveled her head from side to side, taking in the movements of people around her as they reacted to music and the sermon. Ben's attention drifted in and out of sync with the congregation. He expected at any moment for the church doors to burst open and men to carry him away for his crime. Somewhere along the way, the sermon shifted from the afflicted to murderers and thieves.

"The devil prowls around like a roaring lion looking for someone to devour!" the reverend said.

Ben slowly nodded. He'd heard something growling in the woods as he waited for Cutler to return from the rectory. At the time, he thought it might have been a bobcat. Now, he knew better.

"The wicked man earns deceptive wages!" Pastor Douglas called out. "But they will not go unpunished!"

Ben had to rest his head in his hands. For the first time, the full weight of what had transpired, began to sink in. He'd brought sin into his home. His daughter and sister would suffer for it. He realized that he couldn't return to Sapelo to face his parents, Rupert Bright, or the other church elders.

"Whoever refuses to strike hands in pledge is safe," said the reverend, as if revealing, play-by-play, Ben's evil acts to the entire congregation.

Ben recalled shaking Cutler's hand in the dark, forever binding himself to the deed he could have prevented but did not.

At the end of the service, Ben tried to rise, but his legs failed him. He pulled hard on the pew in front of him and finally stood shaking, his body covered in sweat.

"Go home and get some rest, Brother Jordan," the reverend told him outside the church's front doors. "Go on home, now."

Ben couldn't look Douglas in the eye. He knew that the news of Pastor Dodge's murder would pass like wildfire through Lamar at any minute. He didn't want to be standing on holy ground with a holy man when it reached Scott Hill, but it was too late. He saw it coming. Like a strong wind presaging a storm, he saw people talking loudly near the street. They turned and spoke hurriedly to the people around them. The news was afoot and heading his way.

"Reverend Douglas," one of the flock called out. He approached Ben and the pastor. "Did you hear about them Cales over at Two Mile?"

"No," the reverend replied. "You talking about the people that hung Ben's cousin?"

"Yes, Sir. They dead," the man said. "Every last one of them. All of them dead in a house fire. Oil lamp fell over." He stood back smiling, proud to be the deliverer of the news. The news landed on Ben like blows from a heavyweight fighter.

"God have mercy on their souls," the preacher said.

"Lawd fo'giff me," Ben tried to say, but the words wouldn't come out. He knew an oil lamp didn't start the fire. It was Dr. Crow's root.

"Wife, children, the old man, all of them," the man continued. "His cousin, the lame one, too."

"Lawd, Lawd," Ben cried, falling down on both knees. He pitched forward and fell to the ground, covering his face with his hands. It had not been the news he expected, and it hit him harder than the thought of being an accomplice to murder.

It took two men to help Ben home. They put him on his bed where he lay unable to move for most of the afternoon. He stared at the ceiling while guests entered the house and testified with Geneva about how Reverend Douglas was always right and that, in the end, God's vengeance would take place at the time of his choosing.

God and Docta Crow, Ben thought as he listened to their voices from his bedroom.

He waited silently for the next wave of news to wash over the community.

* * *

When Pastor Dodge failed to show up for the Methodist service, Miles Avery, a church member who served on Lamar's police force, went to the rectory with his son, Miles, Jr., to find him. The front door was unlocked. When he entered the study, Miles saw Dodge slumped over the desk. At first, Avery thought the pastor might be the victim of a stroke or heart attack, but something didn't look right.

"Stay here," he told his son, who watched from the doorway while his father entered the room. He immediately knew from the hole in the window and the wound on the back of the pastor's head, that he'd just walked into a murder scene. The blood had dried and turned black, indicating the crime took place sometime during the night. A fountain pen was in Dodge's right hand. Beneath the body was paper with writing on it.

"Jesus," he said under his breath. He felt the pastor's neck for a pulse.

Avery reached for the telephone, but pulled his hand away, realizing that he was probably the first to enter the room since the crime took place.

"Come on, Miles," he scolded himself, "get it together."

He was tired, having been up most of the night investigating the Cale fire. All the evidence there pointed to an overturned kerosene lamp. That had been an accident. Standing in the rectory study, he knew a murderer was at large in the Lamar area.

"Is he dead, Daddy?" Miles, Jr. asked.

"Run on down to the Mobley's, Son. Tell Miss Mobley to call the police chief and Doc Ellis. You got that?"

"Yes, Sir."

"Go on, now."

Avery knew that finding the killer might be quick, or he may never be found. Lamar's police files contained a number of unsolved murder cases going back forty years. Several of those

STEPHEN DOSTER

cases remained open due to evidence having been destroyed by well-intentioned relatives or incompetent first-responders, but he was going to make sure that only law enforcement and the county coroner would be privy to the evidence he found. He hoped that, sooner or later, someone might blunder and say something that only the real killer could know.

Miles peered through the hole in the window to get an idea of where the gun might have been fired. He saw an open spot in the woods where a path allowed easy access to the rectory's back area. On the ground, covered with pine straw, he spied a small, white object the size of a cigarette butt.

Ben's next door neighbor, Lucille, planted herself in his front room after lunch to help Geneva tend to the steady flow of visitors who came to celebrate God's justice on behalf of Ben and his cousin. Lucille had barely settled in when she heard the sound of feet racing up the front steps, followed by an agitated rat-a-tat knock on the doorframe.

"Come on in," Lucille called out through the open door.

One of the neighbor's sons, a thirteen-year-old named Victor, entered. All conversation halted at the sight of the young man who stood in the doorway partly out of breath.

"He dead!" he exclaimed excitedly. "Mama told me come over and tell y'all."

"Who dead, Chile?" Geneva asked.

"Methodist preacher! Someone shot him dead!" Lucille reacted by jerking upward in her chair and covering her mouth with one hand. From his bed, Ben let out an imperceptible moan.

"That preacher? Dodge?" Geneva asked.

"Uh-huh. He the one. They found him dead! Miss Clarice went up to the house. She his maid, but they wouldn't let her up the drive. The police got it all roped off."

"Okay, Honey. You done told us," Geneva replied. "Is dere anything else, or is dat all you know?"

"That all I know," Victor replied. "All right, now. You tell your mama we appreciate her sendin' you 'round, you hear?"

"She want me to tell the Wilsons and the McDermotts, too!"

"Well, you go on now. And tell your mama tank you."

"Good Lawd," Lucille said, as Victor ran down the walk and through the open gate. "What in God's holy name happening around here? This sure is a day of judgment in Lamar!"

Naomi lay in Geneva's lap, oblivious to the events transpiring around her.

"A preacher!" Lucille said.

"And a holy man!" Geneva added.

Ben was thankful he'd been lying down when the latest news came. The same nausea and headache he had experienced the night before overcame him once again. He lay on his back with a wet cloth on his brow. Victor had brought them the screaming headline, but Ben knew the full story with all its gory details would soon follow in his wake.

A few hours later, after most of the visitors had left, he got up slowly, went to the back yard, and sat under the fig tree. Exposure to the fresh air and shade renewed his strength a little, but he felt his spirit sink down into the depths of the earth. It wasn't too long before he heard someone else enter the house followed by excited voices. Ben knew the latest edition of Pastor Dodge's murder had arrived.

"Lord have mercy on this town!" cried Clarice Clarendon, plopping down on a chair to catch her breath.

"All right now," Lucille said. "Calm down, and tell us what happened out to the rectory."

"Lord have mercy on all of us," Clarice gasped, fanning her face with one hand.

"Settle down now, Honey," Geneva told her. "Ain't no fire. Catch yo breath. You wants some water?"

"No, thank you. I might need something more powerful than water before this day is through!"

Ben listened intently as the voices traveled down the center hallway and outside to where he sat. He couldn't make out all the words, but from the tones, he knew the import of their content.

"They tried to keep me from going in that house," Clarice continued, "but I told that one little policeman, you know the one trying to grow that mustache . . ."

"Bloom?"

"That's him. I told him that little man, 'I know where everything in this house go and if anything is missing, so just step aside.' Then that other policeman, Avery, he says, 'Tell her come on in. I got some questions for Miss Clarice.' So I go in the house and—Lord, God in Heaven—I seen them carrying the pastor's body out on a stretcher. He all covered up except his feet, but I know it him from the outline and from his shoes, which I done polished just two days ago on laundry day.

"'Now, Miss Clarice,' Avery says, 'When was the last time you saw Pastor Dodge?' So, I told him, 'Two days ago.' Then he starts asking me about who else has been by to visit the preacher and did I know anyone he had quarrels with, which is lots of folks in Lamar who like to drink. But all this time, I'm listening to the police chief, Hawkins, talking to Doctor Ellis. You know most men can't be in a conversation and listen to another one at the same time."

"I know that's right," said Lucille. "Mens can barely stay up with what one person telling him."

"But I'm talking with Mister Avery," Clarice went on, "and listening to his questions with one ear and listening to Hawkins and Doctor Ellis with the other. Doc tells him, 'I'd say he's been dead about twelve hours, but I need to do an autopsy to narrow it down.' And I hear the chief say, 'Do you know anyone who smokes Camels?' And the doctor says a number of his patients do, and the chief says, 'I want a list of them.' Then he calls over to where we're standing and he tells Mister Avery, "Go to all the stores in town and find out who smokes Camel cigarettes." Then Avery tells me to go home, and don't say anything about what we discussed or anything I seen 'cause I might be called upon to witness in court."

"Wuz any ting missin' frum de place?" Geneva asked.

"Nothing! Not one little thing. Everything was right where it always is. Police chief finally let me in the study to look around and tell him was anything missing. But ain't nothing missing. I been cleaning that house for years. Something move an inch, and I gonna know about it. Ain't nothing moved. Not one little thing."

"Ooh, Clarice, did you see blood?" Lucille asked.

"I didn't see no blood. And they wouldn't let me go 'round back of the house. Officer Avery took me outside, and that young fella, Bloom, took me back down the drive. There was lots of folks down there watching. Some of them asked me what I saw, but I remembered what Avery told me. And you can't say anything about this to anyone, 'cause I told him I'd keep my mouth shut, but I had to tell someone. What if them killers came after me? I wanted to tell you what I know, so you can tell the police."

"But you don't know anything," Lucille pointed out. "You told them everything you know."

"I know that, and you know that, but them killers don't know!"

"Lawd, Lawd," Gevena said, shaking her head. "Dis sho nuff be a day of judgment on dis town."

CHAPTER 15

The following evening, three white men showed up at Ben's house. Geneva answered the door and recognized one, a resident of the Two Mile community who bore a white vertical scar above his right eye. She only knew him as a no-account named Caleb. The second man, a stranger, was shorter and leaner with closely-cropped red hair. The third, she knew as Seymour, one of the Cales' extended family members. He stood with his back to the other two as though on guard.

"We're here to see Ben Jordan," the stranger said.

Caleb looked over Geneva's shoulder into the dark front room behind her.

"He too ill to come to . . ."

"Go get him," he demanded.

He pulled a pistol from beneath his coat and showed it to her.

"You mens can wait in de front room . . ."

"I ain't goin' in no nigguh's house!" the stranger said.

"Bring him to the door," said Caleb in a calm but menacing tone.

Two minutes passed before Ben slowly shuffled down the hall. He cracked open the door and leaned heavily against the doorframe.

"Tell your wife to take a walk," the stranger said.

"She my sistuh."

"Tell her to disappear."

Ben turned to Geneva and told her to leave. "Dey gots a gun!" she whispered.

"Go on," he quietly replied. "I know whut dey want."

"She gone," Ben told them a few moments later.

"I'm gonna say this once," the stranger began. "Someone shot that nigguh-lovin' preacher, Dodge. The man who shot him was Salty Hoffer."

Ben made no reply.

"You love your little girl and your sister, don't ya, Ben?" the man asked.

"Yessuh, I do."

"Then you remember what I just told you. Salty Hoffer killed that preacher. Anyone says anything different is gonna be damn sorry he ever was born. He might come home from work and find his family dead and his house burnt to the ground. He might even find a burning cross in his front yard. Your sister and your little girl can move up north, but we'll find them. Them big city apartments catch on fire all the time. This house can catch on fire. A house like this can burn to the ground in about thirty minutes."

"It's happened before," said Caleb.

Ben recalled Luther's father talk about KKK activity and the burning of a black family's home.

"We don't want it to happen again, do we?" said the stranger.

"No, Suh," Ben replied.

"We have an understanding, don't we?"

"Yessuh, we do."

Caleb stared Ben in the eye for several seconds. "Take some friendly advice, Ben Jordan. Don't tell no one about this here little discussion. You ain't never talked to us, and we damn sure ain't never talked to you. You got that?"

Ben nodded. He watched the men leave his tiny front yard and climb into the cab of a flatbed truck. When the sound of the truck faded in the distance, he closed the door and turned to see Geneva standing next to the window in her bare feet and holding a loaded shotgun.

"Who dey is?" she asked, lowering the gun. Ben said nothing.

"Dey is KKK, ain't dey?"

He looked away.

"Whut de Klan want wiff you, Ben? Why dey on yo front doorstep an' tellin' you who done dat murder?"

"Neva," he said after several moments had passed, "I ain't never seen no mens on de front step, an' neither is you."

"You said you wuz goin' out fo a walk de other night. De night de preacher kilt. Where wuz you?"

His silence told Geneva more than she wanted to know.

"If you mixed up in dis, Ben, you gots to hide. You gots to go to Sapelo an' hide in the deep wood like dem Ebo done way back. If you mixed up with white men, dey gonna put de law on you!"

But Ben had already made up his mind the day before while sitting under the fig tree. His real crime was one nobody would ever know about and one he could never be convicted for. Visions of the Cale children trapped in the fire burned into his brain, and, like hot embers, the vision erupted anew all day long until he could think of nothing else. In his mind, he deserved punishment. He could live with man's judgment. It was God's wrath he feared.

"I done it," he blurted. "I kilt dem. All of dem."

"Kilt who?"

"Dem Cales. Docta Crow giff me a root."

"Jesus haff mercy."

"He give me a root, an' I planted it out to de Cale place."

142

"Whut kind of root?"

"He gimme de Destroyer. I had to plant it. He say it would up an' bite de owner if he ain't get rid of it. I had it in de shed . . ."

Geneva's eyes widened upon realizing the root had been so close to home.

"You done the right ting getting' rid of it," she said. "Dem Cales is de ones hung Eli. Dat between Docta Crow an' dem. It ain't yo fault!"

"But I de one rooted dem. Docta Crow say de blood on him, but de blood on me, too! De root kilt all dem Cales, not just de mens."

Geneva let Ben's confession sink in.

"Ain't no one can blame it on you," she said at length, shaking her head. "Ain't nobody 'round here believe in de root. Ain't no white man gonna believe Docta Crow root started no fire."

"But you know, an' I know!"

"Whose to say it weren't de oil lamp? It wuz a cold snap Saturday night."

Ben rocked back and forth in his chair, absorbing Geneva's words. She was right. No one would believe his story. A white judge would laugh him out of court, but it didn't ease his mind. The guilt was on his head.

"Dat li'l chile," he said, staring that ground. "Dat li'l chile wuz innocent."

"De father wuz one o' dem Cales. He de one rape dat girl."

"De chile innocent."

Geneva threw up her hands in frustration.

"De chile gonna grow up like all dem other Cales!

Dey nigguh-hatin' white trash, an' good riddance is whut I say."

Ben continued to rock and stare forward.

"Dat ain't all," he said after some time had passed. "Oh, Lawd Jesus," Geneva sighed.

"I kilt him, too," he whispered.

"Whut you mean you kilt him, too? Now who you talkin' 'bout, Ben?"

"De preacher, Neva. I kilt de preacher when you thought I wuz out walkin'. I wuz in de wood behind de Dodge house."

"You kilt Pastor Dodge?"

"I fired one time. But Bu-Allah stay my hand," he said, clasping his right forearm with his left hand, "just like you reaching out and pushing my arm."

"If you ain't kilt him, who den?" He shook his head.

"We mek a pact."

"It a pact wiff de Devil!"

"De Devil wuz in dem woods, Neva! I heard him growlin' like a lion, just like Reverend Douglas preach it. I heard him!"

"You strike hands wiff a white man who gonna kill a preacher?"

"I ain't seen him do it. All I know is I didn't stay anyone hand like Bu-Allah stay mine, an' dat as good as killin' him."

Geneva clenched her fists. "It dat Cutler, ain't it?" Ben said nothing.

"It Cutler. I knew it!" she said, slapping her thigh in anger. "He a white man. De richest white man in town. An' he trick you into goin' out to de preacher house, didn't he?"

Ben made no reply.

"He offer you money?"

"I giff my word."

"Yo word ain't worth spit to a white man! He de one sent dem three KKK to put fear in you. Dey Cutler's insurance. He gonna blame Hoffer, den he gonna point de finger at you. Dey gonna hang you, sho! You gots to run. Go back to Sapelo an' hide in de woods like dem Ebo!"

Ben shook his head defiantly.

"I ain't runnin'. I cain't go to Sapelo. I done evil in de sight of

God. An' you cain't say nuthin' 'bout dis to de law. You heard dem men on the porch. Dem men gonna burn down de place an' get you an' Naomi. De blood on my hand, Neva."

"We gonna get you a lawyer, Ben. Reverend Douglas will know whut to do."

"Ain't no lawyer can help. Tiny Ruth done prophecy. It all cumin' true."

"But dey hang you. De law gonna do you like dey done Eli!"

Ben shook his head slowly. Tears trickled down his cheeks.

"Cain't no one help me. Eli didn't deserve no hangin'. I do."

Ben knew the day-of-judgment for his crime was bound to come, and he didn't have to wait long. That Saturday afternoon, he stood at his kitchen sink staring out the back window, lost in thought. Geneva sat at the tiny kitchen table feeding Naomi, when a sharp rap on the front door broke the silence. Ben flinched.

"Someone at de door," Geneva said.

Ben didn't reply. He turned and took Naomi from her and held his daughter tightly.

There was another rap, this time on the back door.

"Ben Jordan!" a police officer said. He opened the door and entered the kitchen. "I'm arresting you for the murder of Pastor DeLong Stanton Dodge."

The next moments were a jumble of confusion for Ben, as though a grenade had exploded in his tiny kitchen. Someone pulled Naomi from his arms and placed him in handcuffs. Naomi, terrified at the scene unfolding before her, cried hysterically and reached out for her father as he was led outside.

Someone sent in an anonymous tip that led the police to Salty Hoffer. The next day, an elderly white came forward to say he saw Ben walking with a shovel in his hand on the night of the murder. For Police Chief Hawkins, it was all the evidence he needed to link the two. Separate trials were scheduled for May when the next trial court would be in session.

One day into Ben's incarceration, he awoke to the sound of a metal key turning in his jail cell door. The door swung open, and Clayborne Cutler walked in. He was in Atlanta making sure he was out of town when the anonymous tip pointed the finger at Hoffer. When he learned that Ben, too, had been arrested, he rushed back to Lamar.

"You got ten minutes," the jailor said.

"I'll call you when I'm good and ready, you hear?" Cutler replied.

"Okay, Mister Cutler. But the chief said . . ."

"Don't worry about the police chief. Just give us a little privacy."

Clayborne leaned against the door after the jailor left. He made sure they were alone before speaking.

"Jesus, Ben," he whispered, squatting down, "I never knew you made liquor runs with Salty."

"Yessuh. I needed money fo Saundra. She gettin' awful weak, Missa Cutluh."

"Okay, okay. I'll see about moving her to another clinic."

"You shouldn't a cum here, Boss. Dey gonna connect you wiff me."

"You're one of my workers, remember? Daddy always took care of his negroes. I'm just looking out for Cutler Land & Lumber's interests. Now, tell me, did they ask you anything about Salty Hoffer?"

"Dey sho did. I told dem Missa Hoffer a goot man, Missa Cutluh. I ain't never seen him kill no one."

"But I told you I saw him behind the rectory, remember?"

Ben leaned back and rested his head on the cool cement wall.

"I 'member, Boss. You told me you seen Salty shootin de preacher. But Missa Cutluh, why don't you tell them police? I ain't seen nuthin'. You de one who seen him."

"No, no! I've got a reputation to upkeep. I don't want the Cutler family name being dragged into this. Think about Willie and the other negro workers at the lumber company, Ben. If I go down, the company goes down, and everyone working there—Willie, Luther, Muncie—all of them will be out of work."

Ben leaned forward.

"Boss," he said, "three white mens cum to my house. Dey gonna burn it an' kill my sister, Neva, and Naomi if I don't say Missa Hoffer done de killin'. But I ain't never seen him do it."

"Just don't say anything."

"I cain't lie, Boss. Whut if dey ask me whut I seen." Clayborne sighed and stood erect.

"You know who those three men were, don't you?"

"Yes, Suh. Dey is KKK."

"That's exactly right. You better think about your family, Ben. A good lawyer might get you out of this mess. But there aren't any lawyers can keep those men away from your and your family."

"But you could, Boss. You the biggest man in Lamar."

Clayborne shook his head. "I'm the biggest man in town until the sun goes down. These guys work at night. There's nothing I can do about it. But don't worry about that right now. You need an alibi. Now, you've been in those woods behind the rectory before haven't you? It's a short cut from Scott Hill into town, right?"

"Yessuh. I been in dem wood befo'."

"Just tell them you were in those woods when you heard a shot. You don't have to say anything else. You just heard a shot. And that's the truth."

"I done told dem I fire at de window."

"What? Christ, Ben!"

"Dat de *real* trufe, boss."

"The truth? That's what I pay lawyers for!"

"Yessuh. But dey axed me all dem questions." Clayborne ran his hands through his hair and rubbed his forehead, deep in contemplation.

"Well, you sure as hell won't get a fair trial in Lamar, now. I'm gonna get you a decent attorney and see about getting your trial moved to Baxley. If you're lucky, the jury will give you life in prison."

"Boss, I don't tink I gonna see no trial. Dey is folks outside all day sayin' dey gonna pull me outta here an' hang me."

"Don't worry about that. I'll take care of it. Just remember our deal."

"I remember, Boss. But I mo' worried 'bout de Klan. Dey cum to my door an' say dey gonna burn de house an' kill my li'l girl, an' my sister, Neva."

"Okay, okay. I'll take care of that, too. Now, just don't say anything until you got a lawyer by your side. Got that?"

"Yes, Boss."

CHAPTER 16

In the weeks leading up to the trials of Salty Hoffer and Ben Jordan, while the lawyers interviewed people, gathered evidence, and selected the jury, Geneva traveled back to Sapelo with Naomi. She had been advised not to leave the county until Ben's trail was over, but her faith in the law and lawyers of any stripe had long before been trumped by her belief in the power of the root. Dr. Crow's ability to secure an innocent verdict for blacks along the coast was legendary. She'd known men and women who'd been taken to court in Darien. Some of them had white lawyers, but the ones who invariably got off the hook, had another advocate on their sides. Dr. Crow might not be able to personally attend Ben's trial, but he could work up a potion that would work on a prosecuting attorney, a jury, or even the judge.

Geneva made the trip to Sapelo the same day Ben was moved to the Baxley jail. The next morning, she left Naomi at the Jordan Home in Hog Hammock, and made the long walk to the interior of the island where Dr. Crow resided. A drizzle began as she moved cautiously down the long, narrow path leading up to the shanty he called home. Two large oaks towered over the hut, providing protection from wind, rain, and scorching heat. A small pen surrounded by a fence made of palmetto fronds held his donkey. As she walked up to the dwelling, the surrounding area seemed to come alive with birds and rodents that scattered at her approach. Large ferns growing on the roof draped over the eaves, lightly dripping water to the ground. Geneva reached up to knock on the door, but it opened before she could touch it. She stepped inside and saw Dr. Crow across the room sitting in a cowhide chair, facing the door.

"I cain't cum to de trial," he told her before she spoke a word.

The door behind her slammed shut with a loud thud that startled her. An assortment of dried herbs, leaves, and grasses hung from ceiling rafters. To her left was a long counter covered in jars filled with the remains of reptiles, plants, and colored liquids. Above the counter were more glass containers brimming with brightly-colored powders. Her eyes fell on an oblong object that rested on the center of the counter.

"De power get weaker away frum de island," he informed her. "De furder you go, de weaker de power get. Dem city peoples don't believe, so de power is lesser, unnerstan'?"

"I unnerstan," Geneva replied, her eyes darting between the witch doctor and the root sitting on the counter. "Dey wanna hang Ben."

"Dey ain't gonna hang him," Dr. Crow assured her.

"If dey don't hang him, dey gonna giff him life on de prison farm."

He shook his head. "Maybe dey give him life, or maybe dey giff him sumtin' else."

"Like whut?"

Dr. Crow grinned as the rain outside turned into a downpour. He held up four fingers.

"De judge gonna sentence yo brudder to fo'ty year in de prison camp. I cain't be at de trial, but I will send a messenger. Keep yo eyes an' yo ears perk. De messenger will cum."

"Fo'ty year a long time."

"He still a young buck. He be out befo he dead. It de best I can do."

Geneva pulled ten dollars from her shirt pocket. "Tank you," she said.

He shook his head. "Don't want ten dollar." Geneva hesitated. "Whut you want?"

He pointed in the direction of Hog Hammock.

"De girl," he replied.

"No," she said, shaking her head. "She Ben li'l girl."

"She got de power. I can feel it. She in line to learn de unknown tongue and de magic frum old times. Dem times even de people fergit. De white man don't know. De black man fergit. But I know, an' I pass it to de next one. De chosen one. De girl gots de power just like her daddy. But de power ain't no goot 'less you be on de island!"

Geneva pulled ten more dollars from another pocket.

"It all de money I have," she said. "Dis or nuthin'."

In the semi-light of his darkened shack, Geneva sensed Dr. Crow's authority over aspects of nature. She knew that he held her life in his hands. He flashed a brief, fiendish smile, arose from his seat, and walked to the counter, stooping to avoid the plants hanging overhead.

"Cum over yuh," he commanded.

Geneva's eyes fell once again on the root. A small needle with thread stuck out one end of the velvet fabric. He opened a drawer and pulled out a scrap of paper and a broken pencil.

"Write he name on de paper," he instructed.

"Who name?"

Dr. Crow paused and looked into Geneva's eyes. A chill ran through her body.

"De one who point de evil finger at yo brudder." She shook her head in protest. "De root you give Ben kilt dat whole fambly. All dem Cales. Ever one."

"Yeah," he replied, bobbing his head up and down, "dat were de most pow'ful conjuh dey is. Ain't no mo' killin' cum frum dat fambly."

Geneva hadn't lost any sleep over the loss of the Cales. She believed they were of one mind when it came to blacks, but she wasn't prepared to be burdened with the guilt of destroying Cutler's relatives.

"I don't want no part of killin' a whole fambly," she said.

"Dis root don't kill," Dr. Crow answered. "It wear de victim down like water drippin'. Li'l bit here; li'l bit over dere. Dis one work on him fo many year. It break de man health li'l by li'l. Now, do as I say. Write de firs name an' de last name."

Geneva took the pencil and stared at the paper scrap. From the moment the three white men appeared on Ben's doorstep, one name popped into her head. Only one man in Lamar was powerful enough to order Ben to do something that violated the basic tenets of his beliefs. The white system might not get justice for his transgressions, but the old ways, using Dr. Crow's powers, could.

Dr. Crow turned his back as she bent down and reached for the paper. She pulled it closer to her and wrote C-L-A-Y-B-O-R-N-E C-U-T-L-E-R.

"Fold it twiced," he instructed, "an don't let me see de name."

Geneva did as he said. He took the note from her, spit on it, and spoke words over it she couldn't understand. He bound the spell by spitting on it once again, this time, violently. He then slipped the piece of paper inside the root and sewed it shut.

"Dis one I call de Black Widder. It destroy a man a li'l bit at a time like a spider bite. Plant it under de house of de man who name on de paper. De magic spread like a root under dat house. Ain't no 'scape. Ben go to prison dat got a fence. Dat man go to prison in he own body. Dey give yo brudder fo'ty year; de man get de same sentence. Ben get fo'ty year; dis man die in fo'ty year."

Dr. Crow crooned several mournful, almost inaudible incantations over the root while Geneva stared at it, mesmerized as though looking at a live viper made of gold, an object at once dangerous and desirous. As she looked on silently, the full weight of her actions came into her consciousness, and doubt crept into her thoughts. She had no proof that Clayborne Cutler shot Pastor Dodge.

"De blood on me. Hear whut I'm sayin'?" Dr. Crow reassured her. "But you gots to plant it in de dirt. Don't do no good just tossin' it under de house. It cain't tek root an' spread if it ain't in de soil. A old dog cum along an snatch it up. Run off an bury it somewhere else. Den de root no good!"

He placed it in a rough-hewn cedar box whittled into the shape of a tiny coffin.

Geneva grabbed the box and placed the twenty dollars on the counter. The moment she did, the front door opened.

"You tink hard 'bout de li'l girl," he said, referring to Naomi. "I de last one, 'cept Tilly. An' she do de white rootin'. Ain't no one cumin' affer me. De island have no root man when I be gone."

"I tink on it," she replied. She turned and exited the shack and ran home in the rain.

"Mama," she said to Josephine when she reached the Jordan home, "Where Naomi?"

"She in de back asleep, chile. Whut wrong?"

"We gots to catch de boat. Docta Crow want Naomi! We gots to get off de island."

Jesse and Josephine quickly packed Geneva's belongings and hurried her to the dock without asking questions. They knew Ben had been born with supernatural abilities and that his powers could be passed to his progeny. They also knew the witch doctor still sought an apprentice.

Jesse heard the ferryboat motor rumble to life before they could see the dock.

"Run on ahead," he said. "I slowin' you down!" He handed Naomi to Geneva.

"Go on," he told Josephine as he stooped over, panting for breath. "You too."

He rose up and squared his shoulders.

"Jesse, you cain't stop Doc Crow!"

"Go on! Dis de onliest way to de dock."

"Go on, nuthin'!" Josephine said, also gasping for air. "I stayin'!"

"Bye Mama! Bye Papa!" Geneva called out as hurried off with her suitcase in one hand and Naomi wrapped in a sling on her shoulder. She sprinted the final hundred yards, and leapt onto the boat just before it pulled away from the dock.

A little while later they were clear of the island. As the ferry picked up speed in the river, she heard the distinct "CAW!" of a black crow. She turned and saw the old voodoo practitioner standing on the dock. Naomi, snuggled tightly against Geneva, lifted her head at the sound.

"No, Chile!" Geneva said, pushing Naomi's head down. "Don't look 'round. Ain't nuthin' back dere fo you."

Twenty minutes later, the diesel ferry plowed toward the Meridian dock on the mainland. Geneva had just begun to feel at ease when she became aware of a presence overhead. She looked up and saw a black object circling in the air above the boat. She let out a scream when she realized it was a large crow.

"Whut de matter, Miss Geneva?" asked one of the deckhands, an islander named Reed.

Geneva, too startled to move, pointed at the apparition overhead.

"Dat crow botherin' you?"

"Dat ain't no crow," she said. "Dat de root doctor. He affer de girl!"

"Dat so?" Reed replied, malevolently eyeing the bird. "Docta Crow mek up a root against my daddy long years ago. I fixin' to mek up a li'l sumtin' fo him!"

He grabbed a coiled rope, tied a lead weight to it, and swung the line in a tight, concentric circle. He slowly released the rope through his fingers until it extended into a six-foot arc that cut the air with precision, emitting a loud "whoop-whoop" with each rotation. The turns increased in speed as Reed waited for the crow to circle again and pass directly overhead. When it came within range, he released the line with one hand and held onto the end with the other. The piece of lead shot past the crow, missing it by inches.

"CAW!" the bird cried in surprise. It called out twice more before breaking away from the boat and heading back to Sapelo.

"Yeah. Go on back to de islan' old crow!" Reed called after it. "Dat one fo Papa!"

He turned to Geneva and Naomi. "You okay now. Ain't no one gonna bother nobody while I on dis here boat."

CHAPTER 17

Salty Hoffer's trial began in Lamar the second week of May, 1932. He acquired the legal services of Art Ruggles, a Macon attorney who didn't come cheap.

Also in the courtroom sat Dan Pendarvis, an Atlanta lawyer retained by Cutler to serve as Ben's legal counsel. Pendarvis had successfully petitioned to have Ben's trial moved to Appling County. He wanted to observe the first trial in person since Salty's testimony could impact his client.

Ruggles used his opening remarks to position the evidence against Hoffer as weak and circumstantial. He told the jury he would prove beyond a reasonable doubt that while Salty Hoffer might be guilty of violating Prohibition laws, he was doing just that—illegally transporting liquor from Kingsland, on the night in question. Ruggles based the crux of the defense on the fact that Salty had been pulled over by a Waycross patrolman the night of the murder on his way to Kingsland. The officer's testimony placed Hoffer south of Waycross heading southeast toward Kingsland around eleven o'clock in the evening, the approximate hour the coroner established as the time of Dodge's murder. He could not, therefore, be behind the Methodist rectory at the same time. He also pointed out that another set of prints besides Ben's were found.

That person, Ruggles asserted, was the real killer: Someone who had yet to be identified.

Bob Owen, the solicitor general who would prosecute both trials, immediately forged a case for motive. His paunch belly, receding hairline, and slovenly dress belied a quick mind well versed in the law and attuned to the local populace's way of thinking. After presenting testimony by Lieutenant Avery and Police Chief Hawkins, he questioned several of Lamar's longtime residents including one of Dodge's church members. On day two of the trial, he called Salty Hoffer to the stand.

"Mister Hoffer," Owen said in his best backwoods Georgia accent, "these upstanding citizens of Lamar, whose reputations are above reproach, have established the fact that Pastor DeLong Stanton Dodge was violently opposed to any form of alcohol consumption and routinely voiced his opinion from the church pulpit and in public. Now, of all the people in Lamar, you, a former liquor storeowner and a known bootlegger, clearly have the most to lose by the good pastor's continuous assault on the very thing that you depend on for your livelihood. That's one hell of a good reason . . ."

"You'll watch your language in my court," interrupted the presiding judge, Everett Johnson.

"'Scuse me, Your Honor," Owen replied. "That's one *heck* of a good reason to kill a pastor in my book, Mister Hoffer. Wouldn't you agree?"

Salty rubbed his lower jaw pensively.

"But that doesn't make any sense," he replied after a few moments. "Preachers all over the country rail against the evils of alcoholic spirits, and no one is shooting them. I may be guilty of hauling liquor, but I must say, Pastor Dodge wasn't hurting business any. In fact, business has been pretty good. Some of my best clients are here in this courtroom right now."

At this comment, a number of onlookers in the courtroom shifted uncomfortably. One man sitting cross-legged jerked his leg uncontrollably, striking the seat in front of him with a thud.

"Ben Jordan certainly wouldn't have a reason to shoot Dodge based on your reasoning," Hoffer continued. "I'm the one who paid Ben, and none of Dodge's sermons had the least effect on my ability to do so."

A murmur of approval rippled through the white observers in the courtroom and among the blacks who occupied the balcony. For rural blacks and whites alike, murder trials represented the most entertaining spectacle for months or possibly years to come.

"Now," Owen continued undaunted, "you claim you were pulled for speeding in Waycross at the time of the murder."

"I entered the ticket as evidence. It's right there . . ."

"Well, it coulda been you, Mister Hoffer," Owen began, "or maybe it was someone who looked like you. You were pulled over on a dark highway. Now, the patrolman had a real good recollection about your truck. He told us about the dent in the bumper and the cracked windshield and all that. He was real clear about those things. But he wasn't so clear about you. He recollected you looked a lot like the man he pulled over, but *a lot like* ain't the same as *definitely* the man he pulled over."

"If it wasn't me driving my truck, then you produce the fella who was!" Hoffer replied much to the courtroom's amusement.

"Can you prove it *was* you in the truck, Mister Hoffer?"

"Don't have to. You have to prove it wasn't me. Hell, I can't prove my mama birthed me, but I'm pretty damn sure she was there."

"Mister Hoffer," Judge Johnson intoned, "your language . . ."

"I'm sorry, Your Honor," Hoffer replied. "I didn't mean no offense."

Owen smiled broadly. "No offense taken."

"I didn't mean you! I'm talking to the judge!"

A wave of laughter radiated throughout the room.

Owen, trolling the waters with a baited hook and waiting for Salty to take the lure, laughed the loudest, but Hoffer remained on his guard. He had developed a nose for police raids on remote moonshine stills and cow pastures where illegal spirits were brought in by plane.

"Your Honor," Owen said as the laughter died down, "I believe we have a hostile witness."

"Mister Hoffer," Judge Johnson said, "the prosecuting attorney was just doing his job. I advise you not to take things personally."

"He's trying to hang two innocent men, Your Honor! I take it *very* personally."

"Let me put it to you like this," the judge said as he leaned forward, his voice sterner than a moment before. "I run a civilized court. I expect everyone here to use a civil tongue. There are consequences for those who don't. Is that clear enough?"

Hoffer looked at Ruggles who signaled for him to settle down.

"Yes, Your Honor," he replied.

"Good. You may proceed," the judge told Owen. "Thank you, Your Honor. Now, Mister Hoffer, regardless of what you know or think you know, it is just barely possible that someone else was in that truck—a look alike—while you were somewhere else. That is not beyond the realm of possibility, would you not agree?"

"Prosecution is speculating, Your Honor," Ruggles interjected. "If there is a look-alike, let the prosecution produce this person."

"I agree," the judge said. "Either produce this person, or move on."

"I concede that we haven't yet found the individual in question," Owen replied, still working the jury in an attempt to cause doubt on Hoffer's whereabouts before moving on to evidence that placed him at the scene of the crime. "It's a big state. He could have hired someone from Atlanta. I appreciate the court and this jury's indulgence for allowing me to broach the question of Hoffer's activities on the night of the murder. Now, Mister Hoffer, can you tell the court what brand of cigarette you smoke?"

Hoffer nodded. "I can." Owen stood and cocked his head at Salty. "You're not going to help me with my case, are you?" he said, with a chuckle. "Okay. What brand of cigarette do you smoke?"

"Camel."

"Thank you!" Owen replied with a deep sigh. Another wave of laughter went through the court. The judge lightly rapped his gavel.

"Keep it moving," he said.

"It turns out, Mister Hoffer," the prosecutor continued, "that the police in Lamar found a single cigarette butt behind the rectory in the exact spot from which the fatal shot was fired. And you do know what brand of cigarette it was?"

"Let me guess. A Camel?"

"Yes! It was a Camel!"

Owen held aloft a small, transparent bag that contained the cigarette butt in question.

"And you know what else the Lamar police did?

They interviewed every doctor and shop owner in town—on both sides of the tracks—to find out who in Lamar smokes Camels."

"We've already heard the police chief's testimony, Your Honor," Ruggles said.

"Agreed. Get to your point," the judge told Owen.

"I'm already there, Your Honor. I just wanted to re-establish for the jury the fact that there are less than a hundred regular Camel smokers in and around Lamar. Of those, thirty are women."

Owen looked at Hoffer and raised his voice as he made the next thrust.

"Of the remaining Camel smokers, only ten are over six feet tall, the height of the killer as established by police ballistics, and of those ten, only nine have honest to goodness, air-tight alibis!"

"Well, then go arrest that last guy," Hoffer fired back without batting an eyelash. "'Cause I'm one of those nine fellas with the airtight alibi!"

Judge Johnson pounded his gavel as loud laughter erupted throughout the room. Only one person, Pendarvis, looked on in stony silence. He knew what everyone in the courthouse knew, from blacks in the balcony, to Judge Johnson, to the least attentive juror. Hoffer was a white man with a plausible alibi. Ben was a black man with virtually no cover story. He already admitted to the police to having fired a shot at the rectory and had been seen with a shovel in the early hours of the morning. Other than that, Ben wouldn't elaborate on his movements. In his work on similar cases, Pendarvis knew other forces were at work, and suspected that the Klan was behind Ben's reticence.

Owen didn't laugh along with the rest of the crowd this time. He leaned heavily against the jury box rail, staring at Hoffer as if to imply it was the solicitor and the jury against the accused.

"They did a fine job with the ballistics," Owen continued. "I won't go into detail about the police chief's and Officer Avery's testimony. They did a real fine job measuring the distance of the shooter to the house, the angle at which the bullet was fired, and the approximate height of the man who fired the shot. Like I said, there are only ten men who fit the description laid out before us by the police. In fact, they narrowed the height of the killer to six-two."

Owen paused and turned his head toward the jurors, then back to Salty.

"How tall are you, Mister Hoffer?" he asked.

Salty looked away in disgust.

"Six-two," he replied.

"Six feet and two inches!" Owen echoed loudly. "A six-foot-two man who smokes Camel cigarettes. I have no further questions for the witness, Your Honor."

Owen smiled at the jury and sat behind the prosecutor's table, satisfied with the outcome of the questioning. Art Ruggles rose from his chair and smiled at the jury.

"Mister Hoffer," he began. He sighed as if to apologize for an innocent man having to endure the accusations that had been leveled against him. "Have you ever been to the Methodist rectory before the night of the murder?"

"No!"

"And how would you get to the back side of the rectory coming from the direction of the woods?"

"I have no idea. I've never been in those woods."

"And you've lived in Lamar for how long?"

"Twenty years, just about."

"You mean to tell me that in all the time you've lived here, you never once have been in those woods behind the Methodist rectory?"

"Why would I? I got no business there."

"Don't you hunt?"

"Yes, but not that close to town. No one does."

"So, you wouldn't even know how to get to the rectory from the trails that run behind it?"

"No, Sir."

"And if, for some reason, you finished smoking a cigarette while you were out in the woods, what would you do with it?"

"I'd snuff it out with my foot."

"Please describe that for us."

"I throw the butt on the ground and crush it with my heel."

"Why is that?"

"So it won't start a fire."

"And yet," Ruggles said, turning to the jury, "Lieutenant Avery testified that the cigarette butt he found had been snuffed out, probably on a boot heel, *then* tossed onto the ground. In fact, he saw it from the rectory window, sitting on top of the pine straw path, not ground down into the path, which any smoker would naturally do. I find that interesting. It's almost as though someone wanted that cigarette butt to be found."

"He's speculating, Your Honor," Owen said. "Agreed," the judge replied.

"Just pointing out to the jury the curious manner in which the Camel cigarette was left behind. Now, Mister Hoffer," Ruggles continued, turning slowly to the jury to make sure they were all paying attention, "my esteemed colleague failed to bring to the jury's memory another interesting fact both Chief Hawkins and Lieutenant Avery told us about: They also found some fresh footprints in the soft soil of the trails in those woods. In fact, they found some very good, distinct size twelve shoe prints. There's no mistaking that. We've seen the plaster casts, and we've heard the expert testimony about that. Now, would you please, Mister Hoffer, hand me your left shoe."

Salty hesitated, then reached down, pulled off a well-worn shoe, and handed it to Pendarvis.

"Thank you. Now," Ruggles said, lifting one of the plaster casts presented earlier as evidence, "would you tell the jury what size shoe you wear?"

Salty cleared his throat.

"I'm a size eleven."

"Size eleven!" Ruggles repeated, placing Hoffer's left shoe over the plaster cast. The shoe was almost half an inch shorter than the impression, and slightly wider at the toes. Ruggles walked slowly past the jurors, holding the plaster cast and the shoe out at arm's length so each person could get a close look at it. He then held it out for the court to see.

"Room to spare," he said. "Room to spare. And as you can see, the plaster impression isn't as wide as Mister Hoffer's shoe."

He returned the shoe to Hoffer and placed the plaster back on the evidence table before returning to the jury box.

"It's interesting to note that my client's arrest came on the heels of a tip phoned into police—a tip that was the result of a rumor going around Lamar which no one seems to be able to trace to its original source. The evidence presented so far clearly proves Mister Hoffer wasn't present at the scene of the crime. Who are you going to believe? An officer of the law who pulled my client over during the hour of the murder, or a cigarette butt conveniently left behind at the scene? Let me put it to you another way: It's no secret in Lamar that my client has enemies. It's just possible that one or more of those enemies intentionally planted the Camel butt where it could easily be found so as to frame Salty Hoffer! It was a heavy-handed, clumsy, too obvious act designed to cast suspicion on him and *not* on the real culprit. The only problem with that is you know and I know that Salty Hoffer was on the other side of Waycross heading south at the time of the murder, and didn't return to Lamar until well after midnight."

CHAPTER 18

"I hear tell you're pretty good with a pistol," Bob Owen said.

Ben sat on the witness stand of the Baxley courthouse a week after Salty Hoffer's acquittal. Salty would serve some time for bootlegging, but he had been cleared of the murder charges.

Dan Pendarvis succeeded in having the venue of Ben's trial changed, but he knew it would be anticlimactic. His client had already admitted to firing a bullet into the rectory, yet he wouldn't disclose who told him to shoot at the pastor or why he was carrying a shovel the night of the slaying.

Geneva was allowed to visit him a few days before his trial on the condition that she not bring Naomi with her. "Tek her away," Ben had told his sister.

"I cain't tek Naomi to Sapelo. Docta Crow affer her!"

"Send her to New Yoke. Rona an' Delphine tek care of her up dere. When she old 'nuff, tell her dat her daddy dead."

"Dat ain't de trufe."

"It *is* de trufe! Her daddy die on de river tekkin' Eli body downstream," Ben said, his head sinking into his hands. "I ain't de same since Docta Crow give me dat monster root. He say de blood on him, but it ain't. De blood on me!"

He looked up at Geneva. "I done evil, Neva," he said matter-of-factly. "I gots to pay fo it. Naomi don't need to know her daddy hang fo murder."

"Docta Crow say you gonna get fo'ty year."

"Den I still be in prison. Naomi don't need to know. Tell her I her cuzin or sumtin."

"Dat a lie, Ben."

"De trufe worser! I don't never want her see her papa in prison. Never."

"I said, you're pretty good with a gun, aren't you?"

Owen repeated. He was working with a new judge and jury, and came at Ben with both barrels. If he couldn't nail Hoffer, at least, he could take down his accomplice.

William "Stone Eyes" Pembroke, the judge, earned the moniker for his ability to preside over court proceedings like an immovable, unblinking marble bust, interrupting only when necessary to move the trial forward. His talent for displaying impartiality was honed in a hundred poker games during his army stint in the Spanish-American War.

"Yessuh," Ben replied in answer to the prosecutor's question.

"I hear tell you can kill a snake with a single bullet from fifty feet. Is that right?" Owen asked.

"Dat 'bout right, I reckon, Suh."

"That's some pretty good shooting. Would you agree that a man who can shoot a snake head the size of my fist from fifty feet, can put a bullet through a man's head from the same distance?"

"I ain't never shot no preacher," Ben said, slowly shaking his head.

"You didn't? But you admit to firing a slug into a window frame just a few feet from where he was sitting!"

"Yessuh."

"So you admit you were there the night of Dodge's murder, but you didn't fire the fatal bullet?"

"No, Suh."

"You heard the fatal shot, but you didn't see who fired it?"

"Yessuh."

"What were you doing with a shovel the night of the Dodge murder, Ben?"

"I bury sumtin'."

"You were burying something. What were you burying? The murder weapon?"

"I don't 'member."

Owen turned to the jury and smiled.

"He doesn't remember. My, my. Do you forget a lot of things? Or is this just a one time deal where you forgot what you were doing with a shovel in the middle of the night, a night on which a murder took place?"

"I don't 'member nuthin' 'bout dat, Suh."

"You don't. Do you remember being behind the Methodist rectory that evening?"

"Yessuh. I 'member dat."

"Okay. And do you remember what happened while you were behind the rectory?"

"Yessuh. I fire a shot in de window frame."

"And do you remember why you fired a shot in the window frame?"

"Yessuh. A hand push me. It push my arm."

"Whose hand?"

"A spirit hand. A hand frum way back."

"A spirit hand? You mean, not a real hand, but a hand, like a ghost?"

"Yessuh. Dat whut it wuz. A ghost hand."

"And why were you firing at the window in the first place."

"I wuz tryin' to kill Missa Dodge. I mean, Pastor Dodge."

"And why were you trying to kill him?"

"A man told me to."

"A real man, or a ghost man?"

"A real man, Suh. A real man, flesh an' blood like you an' me."

"And is this man in the courtroom today?"

Ben looked up and slowly, deliberately, scanned the room. Clayborne Cutler had been absent at Hoffer's trial as a show of indifference over its outcome, and he remained in Lamar during Ben's trial, finalizing the purchase of Hoffer's corner property from the bank. In the eyes of the community, he'd done enough for his employee by hiring Pendarvis to defend him.

Three faces stood out as Ben looked over the gallery. They belonged to the white men—Seymour, Caleb, and the stranger—who came to his porch the day after Dodge's death. Sticking out prominently from the stranger's mouth was an unlit match.

"Naw, Suh. De man ain't here."

"How about Salty Hoffer, was he there at the time of the murder?"

"I ain't never seen Missa Hoffer at de rect'ry. I heard de gunshot dat kilt de preacher, but I ain't seen who done it."

"Let me get this straight, you fired once into the window frame, but you weren't there when the fatal shot was fired?"

"Dat right, Suh."

"And who was the man who told you to fire the bullet at the reverend in the first place."

"I don't 'member."

"You don't remember? You remember firing a shot at the pastor, and you remember hearing the fatal shot fired, but you don't remember who told you to fire the bullet that you fired, and you don't remember what you were doing with a shovel a few hours later?"

Ben slowly shook his head.

"Naw, Suh."

Owen spent another half an hour futilely repeating the scenario and grilling Ben on the particulars, but failed to get any answers that differed from the initial questioning or the testimony he had given the police.

"How tall are you, Ben?" Dan Pendarvis asked after Owen sat down.

"Five-ten, Suh." Ben replied.

Pendarvis turned toward the jury box.

"Members of the jury, I ask you to recall the evidence presented by Lamar's police and the forensics experts that testified at the beginning of this trial. All of them, to a man, agreed that the person who fired the bullet into the window frame had to be between five-foot-eight and five-foot-eleven inches tall. Certainly less than six feet. They measured my client every way a man can be measured—barefoot, in shoes, in boots—and they all, every one of them, agreed that he could not have fired the bullet that killed the Methodist minister. The real killer is over six feet tall. What we don't know is whether or not the pastor was standing, sitting, crossing the room, or staring out of the window. Those are details the police have not revealed. Why? Because even they know the real killer is still at large, and only he knows those particulars."

"I object, Your Honor," Owen said, rising to his feet. "Counsel for the defense is speculating on law enforcement's intentions."

"Agreed," Judge Pembroke said. "Stick to the facts, please."

"Yes, Your Honor," Pendarvis replied. "The facts are, members of the jury, that all of the experts—to a man—have testified that the killer is over six feet tall. Ben Jordan is not only *not* over six feet tall, he's *not* six feet tall. He is, in fact, two inches shy of six feet and therefore, according to the expert testimony of law enforcement, not the killer. But he freely admits to being at the scene of the crime on the night in question. Ben, please tell the jury what you were doing behind the rectory that evening."

Ben glanced up and saw the three men staring at him. He returned his gaze to the pine flooring.

"I don't 'member."

"Ben, is it that you don't remember, or are you trying to protect someone?"

Pendarvis knew the answer. Only a white man or men could instill enough fear into Ben that he was willing to die rather than name names. He might not be able to save Ben's neck, but he could at least ensure that the jury suspected the same thing.

"The witness will answer counsel's question," the judge said.

Ben shook his head.

"I don't 'member."

"Are you protecting the identity of the real killer?"

Pendarvis asked. "Naw, Suh."

"Has anyone come to you and told you not to reveal the name of the real killer?"

Ben briefly looked up. The stranger pulled the match from his mouth and slowly turned it upright in a deliberate and menacing manner. The law, Ben knew, couldn't guarantee his or his family's safety outside the courthouse or the local jail. If he pointed the finger at Cutler, Naomi and Geneva would be dead by morning. He also felt that whatever punishment the jury meted out for him, was deserved. He was an accomplice to Pastor Dodge's murder, which he could have prevented. Even more damning to him, were the deaths of the Cale family. In Ben's mind, he was on trial for their deaths—for their murders.

Ben slowly shook his head.

"I don't 'member, Suh," he replied.

"Is it possible that your life and the lives of your family members have been threatened unless you keep your mouth shut as to who the real killer is? Is that just barely possible?"

"I don't know nuthin' 'bout dat," Ben answered hesitantly.

"And is it just barely possible that you have been threatened not to discuss the matter of the shovel that you were seen carrying later that night?"

"I don't know nuthin' 'bout dat," Ben repeated.

Pendarvis sighed and stared at his client. From the start, Ben had done nothing to help his own case. There was nothing more he could do for Ben Jordan.

CHAPTER 19

On the final day of the trial, the sun rose over thin cloud cover, casting an eerie glow over middle Georgia, but by mid-morning, a steady wind from the west cleared the sky.

Geneva arrived at the Baxley courthouse amidst a throng of blacks, most of whom had walked into town or caught rides on the rusting trucks of black farmers. In her purse, she carried the coffin-shaped box that contained Dr. Crow's root. The box hadn't left her sight since leaving Sapelo. In her mind, she carried a time bomb. In the wrong hands, it might do just as much damage as the Destroyer had done to the Cales.

She recalled Dr. Crow's promise that he would send a messenger. Throughout the trial, Geneva looked for the conjure man's messenger to arrive, but no one came. She scanned the crowd, searching for anyone resembling a resident of her island.

Half a block from the town square, as her hope began to waver, a dark object soaring high above, caught her eye. She looked up in the harsh glare of sunlight and saw the silhouette of a large crow as it alit on the apex of the courthouse roof. Others around her saw it, too, and pointed.

"That old crow is a sign," the woman next to her said, "An omen."

"They gonna hang him," a man replied.

"Sho 'nuff," someone else replied.

Two masses of people, blacks and whites, approached the town square from different directions, like two rivers briefly flowing side-by-side. The waters parted as whites entered through the front double doors of the building while the blacks entered single file through a narrow side entrance that funneled them to the balcony seating.

Owen wrapped up the prosecution's case with an impassioned plea to the jury to do the right thing and convict the accused for taking the life of an innocent man, a preacher, no less. He pointed out that while the evidence against Salty Hoffer had been circumstantial, Ben Jordan, who once made liquor runs with Hoffer, admitted to putting a bullet in the rectory window frame.

"He admits to being an accessory to murder," Owen concluded. "You must convict!"

Dan Pendarvis spoke in an equally fervent manner and appealed to the jury's civic and moral duty to find the defendant innocent.

"This man's life is in your hands," he told them. "He's a hard worker. Never misses a Sunday church service. His wife lies dying in a TB clinic, and he's raising a newborn. You know as well as I do he didn't fire the fatal bullet. You know as well as I do someone— very likely a white man—put him up to it. Even then, he couldn't complete the evil deed. He's too good. Too decent. Too honorable to kill. The jury in Lamar didn't condemn Salty Hoffer based on a rumor and flimsy evidence anyone could have planted. They know if that's all that is required to convict a man, then none of us are safe. Don't condemn Ben Jordan just because he was following someone's orders, yet still refused to fully carry them out. If there is any doubt in your mind, you must find this man innocent!"

At that moment, Geneva heard the distinct sound of claws scraping on wood high above where she sat.

"CAW! CAW!"

All heads turned to see the shrieking crow as it paced across the wide sill of an open window.

A murmur spread throughout the balcony section. The judge lightly rapped his gavel.

"CAW!" screeched the crow before the judge could instruct the bailiff to escort the jury out of the room. The huge bird cocked its head in the direction of the twelve jurors.

Judge Pembroke didn't look lightly on interruptions during his trials. At this crucial juncture, he found the disturbance intolerable. The case being tried had already received a lot of press in the newspapers. He didn't want to see his reputation and the integrity of the court denigrated by the antics of a crow. He turned to the bailiff and said some words. The bailiff looked up at the window, too high above to reach. He shrugged.

"Well, throw a shoe at it!" Pembroke replied, his voice loud enough for Geneva to hear. "I'm trying to run a trial here!"

The bailiff picked up a wooden doorstop and stared up at the window.

"You better not miss," said the court clerk. "That window cost a pretty penny."

"CAW!" the bird cried out a fourth time, again in the direction of the jury box. It glared at them for several moments before turning its back on the court and flying away just as the bailiff released the doorstop. It missed the opening and shattered the large pane of glass above it, causing an eruption of laughter from the gallery.

Geneva smiled. The crow, Doctor Crow, had called out four times. She looked at Ben and discreetly raised four fingers. The messenger had arrived. The verdict had been revealed.

The jury deliberated for almost an hour before returning to the courtroom.

Judge Pembroke entered the room from the judge's chambers and resumed his place on the bench.

"Has the jury come to agreement on a verdict?" he asked.

The jury foreman, his bronzed face framed by white hair and a snow-white mustache, stood.

"We have, Your Honor," he said, his voice shaking.

The courtroom fell silent for the first time since the opening day of the trial as the foreman fumbled for his glasses.

"How do you find?" the judge asked.

The foreman cleared his throat.

"We find the defendant . . ."

"Hang the nigguh!" a voice called out from the gallery.

The judge rapped his gavel hard.

"Any more outbursts of that nature," he warned, peering down from his seat in the direction of the offending voice, "and I will clear this courtroom."

He scanned the gallery for several more moments before settling back in his chair and motioning the foreman to continue.

"We find the defendant, Benjamin Nathan Jordan . . .

The entire gallery, black and white alike, sat on the edges of their seats, holding their collective breaths.

"Guilty of murder . . ."

The words were followed by howls of enthusiastic approval from the white gallery. More cries for hanging rang out. Word soon reached the overflow crowd on the courthouse grounds, and their cheers filtered into the courtroom. The judge rapped his gavel in an attempt to restore order.

Those sitting in the balcony looked on silently and awaited the sentence. They knew he would be found guilty. What they really came for was to see just how far justice had come to middle Georgia.

The judge knew that clearing the room at this point might initiate a riot. He stared at the gallery, waiting for them to quiet.

Sooner or later, they would realize that the sentence had not yet been pronounced.

Another minute passed before the crowd settled down. He turned to the court bailiff and told him to get the jury and the defendant out of the room as soon as the sentence had been passed.

"The defendant, Benjamin Jordan, will rise," the bailiff announced a few moments later.

Ben and Pendarvis stood up at the same time.

The judge turned to the foreman.

"Has the jury agreed on a sentence?"

The man nodded. "We have, Your Honor."

He handed a note to the bailiff, who walked it over to the judge.

Pembroke unfolded the paper and read aloud. "Benjamin Nathan Jordan," he began, "The jury finds you guilty of serving as an accomplice in the murder of Reverend DeLong Stanton Dodge with a person or persons unknown. The jury sentences you to serve a term in the state penal system not to exceed forty years."

CHAPTER 20

A small phalanx of lawmen ushered the jury out of the courtroom as men and women in the gallery cheered their approval of the verdict. Two more hustled Ben to a holding cell in the courthouse basement as soon as the judge delivered the sentence. Once outside, those who had found the jury's decision unsatisfactory began calling for a hanging.

Before they could transport Ben to the city jail, angry whites, mostly from Two Mile and other settlements near Lamar, blockaded all the entrances. Blacks quickly scattered before the crowd turned on them. Ted Thorpe, Baxley's chief of police, sent calls out to area law enforcement agencies for assistance. His outnumbered lawmen inside knew that once it turned dark, they would be forced to hand Ben over to the hostile crowd.

Shouts for his release to the mob became increasingly loud and insistent. Twice, Thorpe tried to calm the crowd from the front steps. Twice, he retreated inside unable to appeal to their sense of reason.

"They ain't gonna wait 'til nightfall," Ben heard a voice say from down the hall, near the heavily-bolted entrance to the courthouse holding area.

"They'll be drinking before too long, working up courage," another voice said.

Ben recognized the voices as Ferrin Joyce and Roy Smiley, the Baxley policemen who had escorted him from the courtroom to the ten-by-ten cell he now sat in. They had been assigned to prevent his escape. In a few short minutes, their roles had changed to that of protectors.

"The hell if I'm stickin' around when they come through that door," he heard Roy say. "I don't give a damn what the chief says. I told him we shoulda brought more police in from other towns. We're outnumbered ten to one."

A commotion on the courthouse lawn briefly interrupted their talking. They craned their necks to peer outside through a barred window.

"They're gettin' serious," said Ferrin. "I saw a gun."

Ben heard more outside voices calling for the police to send him out. He prayed that Geneva had gotten away without incident.

"They're gonna be in here before the hour's out," said Roy. "How much you want to bet?"

"I'll take that bet. How about a dollar?"

"You're on."

"Shake?"

"Ain't no need to shake. My word's good."

"Okay. But let's get it straight. You're betting in less than an hour, they'll be inside the courthouse . . ."

"Anywhere inside. Doesn't have to be this door."

"Fine. Anywhere . . ."

"You boys okay down there?" Thorpe called from the floor above.

"We're okay," Ferrin hollered back. "They got guns."

"Don't worry about that! Just stay at your post. We got it covered. Waycross is sending some backup."

"Waycross?" Roy muttered. "What about Jesup or Hazlehurst? They're a lot closer."

The rowdiness outside took on a carnival-like quality, as if a

great show was about to begin, one that each man would personally participate in.

"Waycross ain't coming," Ferrin said, his voice lowered. "Mark
my words."

Ben sat in his dark cell rocking in time to the rhythm of the
collective gyration of the crowd outside. As he rocked, he contem-
plated what he had seen that day. The crow cawed four times.
Geneva raised four fingers. A moment later, the jury sentenced
him to forty years. Dr. Crow, he knew, was behind this, but there
was more to it than that. Tiny Ruth, the island prophetess had
foretold these events the evening a wandering star passed over
Sapelo on the night of his birth. Her prophecy had come true
before his eyes. It was as unalterable as an incoming tide. For the
first time, he saw his life not as an incongruous and unconnected
chain of events, but an orderly series of occurrences set into motion
by an unseen hand. Everyone and everything connected to his
life—Tiny Ruth, Dr. Crow, Clayborne Cutler, Eli, Salty Hoffer, the
meteorite that plunged to Earth the night of his birth—all were bit
players in a larger drama. He saw that as clearly as he saw his hand
in front of his face, as clearly as the metal bars that imprisoned
him or the damp stone floor beneath him. Knowing this truth, a
calm came over Ben. He had just been sentenced to hard labor in
a prison camp, a death sentence in its own right, but he remained
at peace. He would not die that day. He could not die. It had been
predestined by his Maker, foretold by a prophetess, and executed
by Dr. Crow and the jury. A rush of euphoria overwhelmed his
senses. He felt a power he couldn't name swirl through and around
his body like a gentle wind. Only the thought of being separated
from Naomi, Geneva, and his family on Sapelo, brought him
back to the harsh reality of the moment. The thought of what he
had done to the Cales and what he hadn't done to save Dodge's
life, further tempered his exultation, but his faith in his destiny

remained unshaken. Feelings of ecstasy and desolation rocked his soul, tossing him up and down like ocean waves to the point where he could barely catch his breath. A battle raged inside him until tears of joy and grief mingled and streamed down his face.

"It okay," he called out to the guards when he could speak again.

He heard shuffling feet, followed by the sound of footsteps approaching his holding cell.

"What you want?" Ferrin asked, cradling a pump-action shotgun in one arm. Though he was a large, barrel-chested man, a trace of fear in his voice betrayed his seeming nonchalance. Perspiration covered his forehead and sweat stains filled the crease of his armpits.

"It okay, Boss. Dey cain't harm us."

Ferrin stared at Ben for a few moments, then walked back to his post.

"Prisoner's losing his mind," Ben heard him tell Roy.

"What'd he say?"

"He says they can't hurt us."

Roy snickered nervously.

"Does he, by God? Well, I feel a hell of a lot better now."

An occasional stone banged loudly on the metal door.

"Can't hurt us, huh?" Roy said loud enough for Ben to hear. "I'm glad we got you here to protect us!"

His laughter was interrupted by the voice calling down a second time.

"What's going on down there?" Thorpe called out. "Nothing, Chief!" Ferrin replied.

"Who's Roy shouting at!"

"The prisoner."

"Keep it down, you hear! I don't want to hear a peep unless you got trouble."

"Yes, Chief."

"He's getting rattled," Roy said a few moments later. "It won't be long. Them boys out there know Waycross is on the way. They ain't gonna wait for reinforcements to get here. I bet they got the roads into town blocked off."

"Hell," said Ferrin, "Waycross ain't even coming." Their conversation continued along the same lines for another half hour as the pace outside the courthouse picked up. Ben peeped through the ventilation to his cell. He could tell from the quickened footsteps on the turf outside, that things would soon to come to a head.

He heard someone descend the stairs from the floor above.

"They cut the phone line," the officer stated matter-of-factly. It was a new voice Ben hadn't heard before.

At that moment, a loud noise shook the back door and reverberated throughout the basement. The battering ram, a railroad crosstie, was no match for the door, but the pounding brought another officer down the stairs.

"Don't worry about that door," he said confidently. "Can't no one bust it down."

"Why don't you put some buckshot into them from the window above?" Roy asked. "It's getting a little intense down here."

"Chief said stay away from the windows. Just keep your guns on the door. Ain't no one outside willing to die for no nigguh."

"Ain't no one inside willing to die either," Roy said after the two others left.

Ben continued to rock in his cell, smiling and humming a song he grew up singing in his church, secure in the knowledge that no harm would befall him. He heard footsteps moving quickly on the floor above and on the lawn outside. Shouts emanated from the throng and from the first floor to the basement. The moment of no return was about to be breached. Yet, he smiled as the world around him spiraled toward anarchy.

"De Lawd in control," he said, drawing on teachings he grew up with. "I cum frum Bu-Allah. Bu-Allah and de Lawd protek me. I in de valley, but I don't fear no evil. Dey can tek my body, but dey cain't touch de soul."

The mayhem surrounding Ben would soon reach an apex, a point after which everyone inside and outside of the courthouse knew unfortunate events would transpire. Too many men on the lawn had made promises to "get the nigguh" to back down now. Someone rigged the crosstie to his truck and drove up to metal door, which began to buckle under the strain as the driver rocked the truck back and forth.

"We got us a situation!" Ferrin called upstairs.

No reply came back. Sounds of glass shattering and men running filtered down the stairs.

"Okay," Ferrin said with a sigh, "get yourself ready."

He cocked his shotgun.

"Let's just give 'em the nigguh!" Roy said.

"Keep your gun on the door, dammit!"

At the precise moment, the lawmen expected the door to cave in, the banging ceased. To their amazement, they soon heard the truck slowly back away.

"Now what?" said Roy, still suspicious and expecting the worst.

The cacophony outside quickly, eerily died down by degrees, like a tornado trailing off into the distance. Soon, there was nothing but silence—even more unnerving than the noise it replaced.

"Christ! I can't take this!" Roy said.

"Shut up!" Ferrin replied. "Listen!"

Upstairs, a new commotion took place. Footsteps were followed by voices were headed toward the staircase. "Who's that with the chief?" Roy asked.

"I don't know. But they're coming this way."

"I bet he's handing the prisoner over to them. How much you wanna bet?"

"Hush up!" Ferrin replied, his gun still aimed at the back door.

Ben, too, heard the voices approaching. Even from a distance, he recognized one of them. The voices grew louder as two sets of footsteps descended the stairs. He heard feet shuffling at the bottom of the stairwell to make room for the new arrivals to pass. A few moments later, Clayborne Cutler, dressed in a white seersucker suit, stood in front of his cell.

"Give me about five minutes, Chief," he told Thorpe, a man who stood a head taller than Clayborne.

"Open the cell," Thorpe ordered Ferrin.

"Can't. Bailiff's got the key."

"I don't need to go in. Just give us a little privacy," Cutler said.

"All right, Boys. Let's give them some room," Thorpe commanded.

Ben gazed at Cutler, who seemed to glow. On the night of the murder, his persona resembled a demon in Ben's eyes. There, in the dark of the basement holding area, Clayborne looked like an angel dressed in white.

"Where you been, Boss? I ain't seen you at de trial."

Clayborne glanced toward the stairwell to make sure he couldn't be heard.

"Been busy, Ben. But I've been following the proceedings. What I want to know is why you didn't say you were in the woods taking a shortcut into town like I told you?"

"Dat a lie, Boss. I put my hand on de Bible and swear to say de trufe. Ever bit of it."

"And look where it got you. These yahoos want to string you up!"

"Dey cain't tetch me, Missa Cutluh. De die been cast long time ago."

"I heard they gave you forty years. I thought they would give you life."

"No, Suh. Dat also preordain. Fo'ty year." Clayborne briefly hung his head.

"You did real good not bringing my name up," he said.

"We made a pack, Boss. I kep' my word. I ain't said nuthin' 'bout you being out dere on dat night."

"I'm sorry about the way things have worked out, Ben, I truly am. If there's anything I can do, just let me know."

"You can, Boss. Saundra need good medicine. My sister, Neva, gonna need work. She been tekkin' in laundry, and now I ain't makin' no mo' money fo de house."

"I'll see your wife gets into a better facility. And don't worry about your sister, I'll get her work. Old Millie is getting to be about worthless around the place anymore. Can your sister keep a house?"

"She keep a clean house, Missa Cutluh. She keep de most cleanest house dey is. You can go by an' see fo yo'self. De flo clean enough to eat on."

"All right. I'll talk to her. Now, remember what I said. The police aren't closing the book on this case, so don't say anything to anyone, you hear? Otherwise, those three men are gonna come back to your house, and there ain't a damn thing I can do about it."

"I hear ya, Missa Cutluh. I hear ya, Boss."

"Okay. Right now, though, we got us a little problem outside. Now, I'm gonna get you out of here. You ready?"

"I ready, Missa Cutluh."

Clayborne looked Ben in the eyes knowing full well their paths were about to diverge in ways he didn't think the man behind the bars fully comprehended. He knew Ben was going to a hellhole for a crime he didn't commit, but it was for a greater cause. *For the people of Lamar*, he told himself, a mantra he repeated in his head all day, every day, since the night he pulled the trigger.

"I'll take care of your family, Ben," he said

"I know, Boss."

CHAPTER 21

A minute later, Ben found himself shackled at the hands and feet, shuffling up the stairs to the first floor. The enormity and finality of his conviction began to sink in as he climbed each step. He slowly shook his head.

"I ain't get to see her," he mumbled. "Ain't never gonna get to say goodbye to my li'l girl."

"Hush up," said Roy, walking behind Ben. His armpits and the back of his shirt were soaked in sweat. Ferrin walked in front, following the police chief and Clayborne.

When Ben reached the top step, he saw what Thorpe and his men were up against: A sea of white faces. Some people clad in T-shirts and jeans, some wearing seersucker suits, surrounded the courthouse like a roiling tidal wave poised over a tiny atoll.

"You sure grow 'em mean in Lamar, Cutler," the police chief said.

"Yeah, well . . ." Clayborne began, surveying the scene outside. Since his father's death, he'd been waiting for an opportunity to solidify the respect he knew he'd need to establish himself as a force in Lamar and the surrounding area. "They're mean sons-of-bitches, but so was my daddy. You just gotta know how to handle them."

A quick glance around by the deputies revealed that reinforcements hadn't arrived.

"I knew Waycross wasn't coming," Roy whispered.

Ferrin cut him a look that said he didn't want to hear anymore about it.

"You sure about this?" Thorpe asked Clayborne as they approached the front doors.

The crowd outside had remained relatively quiet after Cutler entered the building, but it was apparent from the increasing calls, that they were getting restless.

"Yep. But you got to hold up your end of the bargain."

Thorpe gritted his teeth. The police backup he was expecting hadn't arrived. He knew any delay would prove fatal to Ben and perhaps, to some of his men.

"I'll keep my word."

"Good. Now, when we get out there, have your boys ready to get in their cars and get the hell out of here quick-like. We get just one shot at this."

"Okay, Scotty," Thorpe said to an officer nearest the doors. "Open 'em up."

A deathly silence enveloped the mob when Clayborne stepped out onto the front step. Chief Thorpe and two lawmen followed, then Ben, accompanied by Roy and Ferrin.

"They're 'round front!" someone shouted from the side of the courthouse.

Within moments, men who had been watching the back entrances, hurried to find viewing positions. Clayborne held his hands up and waited until the stragglers pushed to the front.

"He ain't your nigguh no more, Cutler," a voice yelled.

"Like hell!" Clayborne shot back, his face transforming in an instant, becoming blood red, his eyes and neck veins bulging. The man who called out stepped back and into the person behind him.

"Let's get one thing straight," he said in a loud, defiant voice, "this man may now be a convict and a ward of the state, but he is and always will be a Cutler hire. My daddy himself hired him, and I'll be damned if anyone is going to lay a hand on him!"

"He killed the preacher!"

Clayborne turned to the man who spoke. He knew him just as he knew most of the faces standing there.

"He never killed that preacher, Joey! You know good and well it was someone else. You, too, Sully. And you, Gordon. All of you know someone put him up to it. I know you boys want to string up the killer same as me, but this boy ain't the one. You got the wrong guy."

A hush fell over the men as Clayborne surveyed the crowd. He pointed at a small group to his right. Ben kept his eyes fixed on the steps. He didn't dare lift them to meet the eyes of a white man as it would be perceived as an affront.

"Purvis, Jimmy, Tinker," Clayborne said, calling each man by name, "and the rest of you, you know better. You gonna shoot these lawmen for one black, and he didn't even pull the trigger that killed that preacher? You gonna risk doing serious time?"

"I ain't. Not for no damn nigguh," Tinker said.

"Now you're talking sense!" Clayborne fired back. He had one man on his side, and he saw other men shift their feet. A few moments earlier, they had stood firm, like an immovable object made of one mind and one body. Now, the immovable object was showing cracks. Obediah knew how to work a crowd, and he had taught his son well.

"You've done enough," Clayborne continued, heaping praise on the men surrounding him. "If I was stuck at the Alamo with ten thousand Mexican sons-of-bitches crossing the plain, I'd want every one of you boys by my side. You made yourselves heard loud and clear, and . . ." He paused and looked at several busted windows, "you done went and did a little damage," he added with a broad grin.

Laughter rippled throughout the crowd. The immovable object was crumbling.

"Keep going," Thorpe whispered.

"Okay," Clayborne continued, holding his hands up. "You had a little fun. But you also broke the law. Now, the police chief here is an understanding man. He's willing to overlook things on account of emotions running high and all that, aren't you, Chief?"

"That's right," Thorpe replied.

"I will personally cover the damages," Clayborne went on. "You boys don't have to worry about jail or paying fines. Isn't that right, Chief?"

Thorpe clenched his fists behind his back and drove the fingernails into his palms.

"That's exactly right," he said, belying his true emotions.

"All right," Clayborne continued, "we got just one more order of business to settle. We got to get this prisoner to that prison camp north of here."

"I thought you were taking him over to the city jail," said the courthouse clerk. "You can't take this man to the prison farm without the proper paperwork."

Thorpe turned and stared him down. "Tyler, you want to come out here and explain it to these boys?"

The clerk swallowed hard. "No. But I've said my piece. This isn't how things are done."

"Objection noted," Thorpe replied. "I'm trying to save this courthouse of yours from being burned to the ground. The paperwork can wait."

"Is there a problem?" Clayborne asked.

"No!" Thorpe answered. "Keep it going."

"Okay," Cutler said, turning to the crowd once again, "we need you boys to make a path to the squad cars."

"Ain't gonna do you no good. We done busted the tires," Purvis cackled.

More laughter.

Clayborne laughed along with them.

Thorpe stepped close to Clayborne. "I'll deputize some men and take their cars," he said.

"Well now, there is something you can do to help make things right," Clayborne called out. "The chief of police is gonna deputize some of you boys to help us escort the prisoner."

"Ain't no one lettin' no nigguh ride in his car," Tinker said.

"You got a truck, Tink," Clayborne fired back. "He can ride in back. Now we need a lead car. Someone in front."

"Hell, I'll take the lead," Jimmy volunteered.

Roy nudged Ferrin. "He's got *them* working for *him* now."

"Shut up before someone hears you!"

"Good!" Clayborne said. "Now, we're gonna need some vehicles for the police."

"They can ride with me," someone else offered. "I'll go just to make sure the sumbitch doesn't escape."

"That's very civic-minded of you," Clayborne replied. "Anyone else?"

"I'm in," several more voices shouted.

"Okay, anyone who wants to help us get the convict to the prison camp come on up here and get yourself deputized."

Thorpe quickly swore in a contingent of men and dispatched his officers to various vehicles. He turned to one of his men and instructed him to stay behind.

"Go over to the hotel, and make sure that Atlanta lawyer gets out of town alive. I don't want the city papers down here."

Clayborne escorted Ben to the truck that would take him to the prison farm fifteen miles on the other side of the Altamaha River. "Some of you boys join me and the police chief in my car," he said. "The rest of you follow Tinker's truck. Anyone tries to stop us, don't be afraid to open fire."

The police chief smiled at Clayborne's quick thinking. In just a few minutes, he'd turned an angry mob bent on hanging Ben, into guardians determined to see him safely to his next point of incarceration.

"For a moment there, I was afraid I was gonna have to open up on you boys," Roy told several men as he approached one of the police cars. Ferrin held his tongue and slid in behind the wheel.

CHAPTER 22

Forty minutes after leaving the Baxley courthouse, Ben was staring at a man lying in a fetal position on the ground before him, his wrists tied to his ankles. Ants crawled over his body. He was young, Ben thought, maybe in his early twenties. His eyes were closed. The man's eyelids twitched, and an occasional spasm shook his body.

The ride to the prison camp had been a slow parade, complete with honking horns and cheers from people passing by.

"Take a good look at him," said Hoke, a big-boned guard with large jowls and short-cropped hair. "That one tried to escape."

A shorter, burly guard named Jeder approached, pushing a wheelbarrow with a pick and shovel in it.

"Sumbitch is good as dead," he said, nudging the dying man with the heel of his boot.

"Go ahead and strip down," Hoke ordered Ben. "Suh?" Ben replied.

"You talkin' back to me?" Hoke said, cocking his shotgun.

"No, Suh. I ain't talkin' back. I didn't unnerstan' whut you say."

"Strip down, damn you! Take them clothes off!" Hoke shouted.

Ben had worn his Sunday suit to the trial. He hesitated a moment, then undid the button holding up his pants and let them drop. He kicked off his shoes and stepped out of his pants.

"Come on! We ain't got all day!"

Ben reluctantly removed his coat and shirt while Jeder squatted and cut the cord that bound the dying man's hands and feet.

"Underpants and socks, too," Hoke instructed. "Then put his clothes on."

"Suh, why I cain't . . ."

Ben staggered but didn't fall as the flat part of the shovel landed square on the back of his head. A second blow by Jeder put him on the ground.

A hundred feet away, a wild cheer erupted. Clayborne and most of the others who had participated in the convoy to the prison camp, watched from the entrance where they had dropped Ben off. The yard boss agreed to take Ben in the warden's absence. His was one of a hundred and forty prison camps in Georgia, and the facility was already overcrowded. That meant more stress for his guards, who reacted with extreme violence at the least sign of resistance, but the Lamar contingent had arrived on a good day. The yard boss felt sure there would soon to be a vacancy.

When Ben regained his senses, he saw the dying convict's eyes briefly open. He stared straight at Ben. His lips trembled as if he was trying to say something, perhaps to warn Ben of what lay ahead. Then, he slowly closed his eyes. In the glare of the Georgia sun, with flies buzzing around the man's head, Ben saw his spirit leave the body.

"God bless de dead man soul," Ben softly said.

"Come on, and get up," Jeder ordered, kicking Ben hard in the leg.

"I gettin' up, Boss," Ben said. His teeth felt as though they would fall out.

"Get them drawers off and put his clothes on!" Hoke ordered loud enough for the men lining the fence to hear. "This ain't no hotel."

Drops of blood from Ben's head splashed on the ground as he crawled to where the dead man lay. He slowly removed the black and white horizontal-striped cotton shirt and pants issued to the inmates. The dead man's clothes, torn in places, were stained with soil and blood. As Ben put them on, he felt the man's sweat and body heat on his own skin.

"Get them things offa his feet, and put 'em on. They're yours now."

Ben unlaced the prison-issued brogans, a size too large, and put them on.

"Now, put the dead sumbitch in that wheelbarrow," Hoke ordered.

Ben lifted the dead man's naked body with relative ease. It had been reduced to ninety pounds by overwork and malnutrition. He placed the body in the wheelbarrow.

"All right, now grab them handles and start pushing."

Ben pushed the dead man's body up a slight incline past a long, low building that housed the inmates. Behind the building, he saw a weed covered field.

After Ben disappeared from sight, Clayborne turned away and walked to his car without saying a word. The other men followed. On the drive to the camp, they had been jubilant, honking horns and shouting insults at Ben. Now, they were silent.

Ben heard the cars and trucks leaving the prison grounds. He thought about the men returning to their homes, to their families, and to warm meals. The reality that he'd eaten his last home-cooked supper and might not see his family again, slammed home as he pushed the dead man's body. Tears streamed down his cheeks. His head throbbed from the shovel blows. He'd been in the prison camp for less than fifteen minutes and thoughts of escape had already begun.

"God wiff me," he said under his breath. "Bu-Allah in my blood."

He repeated the words over and again. In saying them, he found succor and a strength he knew he didn't possess himself.

Hoke ordered Ben to stop after five minutes of pushing. When he set the wheelbarrow down, Ben noticed that the field was covered with almost indiscernible mounds of dirt. Jeder tossed the shovel on the hard packed ground at Ben's feet.

"Start diggin," he said. "I did this for the people of Lamar," Clayborne repeated to himself on the drive back home. A long silence ensued in his car. He focused on his thoughts while Thorpe, sitting in the passenger's seat, reflected on the day's events. Those in the trailing cars came alive again, laughing, honking horns, and cracking jokes.

"What we did today is highly irregular," Thorpe said at length, breaking the silence. He wiped his brow and rubbed his eyes. He'd worked hard, rising to the rank of police chief, and saw his career in law enforcement possibly coming to an end. "I thought those yahoos behind us were gonna burn the courthouse down. Jesus. I gave orders to shoot. If word ever gets out . . ."

A media storm surrounded Baxley, and the trial was something he didn't relish.

Clayborne welcomed the interruption of his own thoughts. He'd just doomed a man's life to further his own ambitions. "You gotta step on a few necks to get ahead," his father used to tell him. "Ask any politician."

"Don't worry about the media," Clayborne replied. "I'll make a call to the governor's office."

"Talmadge doesn't control the newspapers. What's he gonna do?"

"I don't know," Clayborne said. "That's why he's governor, and we're not. My daddy always said ol' Gene's got more tricks up his sleeve than Houdini. He can think about one or two steps ahead of the average man, and that makes all the difference."

"I'm concerned about that lawyer, Pendarvis. When he gets back to Atlanta, he's gonna spill some beans."

"Leave it to Gene," Clayborne said. "He's up for re-election. He needs my county, and he needs Appling County, too. He'll think up something."

"Well, I hope you're right. The papers around here won't make a big deal out of what happened after the trial, but if those damn Atlanta reporters come down here, I'll be lucky to get a job as night watchman at the tobacco warehouse."

After burying the prisoner, Hoke and Jeder took Ben to a shed where Silas, doing a life sentence for murder, served as the prison camp blacksmith. Ben stood in the doorway of the tiny outbuilding with one foot on a stump while Silas riveted a heavy steel shackle, thick as a man's finger, around the pants above the ankles. The strad, a heavy chain of thirteen links, connected the shackles and made it all but impossible for a convict to take a full stride.

"Make it good, Silas," Hoke said, inspecting each step of the operation. "I don't want another sumbitch escapin'."

"No, Suh!" Silas answered. "We sho don't want that."

"'Cause you know what happens when one runs off," Hoke said, his voice rising in intensity and anger.

"I knows, Cap'n."

"The warden gives the attending guard stinking yard duty!"

"I knows all 'bout it, Cap'n. I makes them shackles good an' strong. You can check it yo'self. I cain't hep it if sum of these mens gets a file and break a-loose."

"Well, you make sure those anklets are on good. This sumbitch has already done talked back once. He's already got ideas of running off, ain'tcha, Boy?"

"Don't talk back to the guards," Silas advised Ben. "Don't never talk back."

"He'll learn," Jeder said. "One way or another."

Silas affixed a three-foot long upright chain to the first chain with an iron ring the size of a silver dollar.

"Hold onto this chain," Silas instructed Ben. "If you don't, it drag on the ground. Another man step on it, and you gonna fall down."

Hoke grabbed the chains in his hands and pulled at them to ensure they were secure.

"They good, Boss," Silas said. "Ain't no man getting outta them chains by hisself. Now, wiff some hep from another man, that something else."

Hoke and Jeder followed Ben, his chains clanking as he walked, to the long building that served as sleeping quarters. Hoke directed Ben to a wooden post near the building. Four U-shaped rings stuck out at one-foot intervals on the post. Jeder ordered Ben to slip the upright chain onto the third post ring, which forced Ben to a standing position.

The two guards sat in the shade of the building as the sun beat down on Ben. From where he stood, Ben could see his Sunday clothes and leather shoes on the ground. He looked down at the stripes he now wore, realizing that he was being transformed from man to animal—to be treated like a beast of burden and worked like one. A barbed wire fence encircled the camp, and a pine forest surrounded the fence on all sides. Inside, was hard packed Georgia soil, baked to a hard surface by the unrelenting sun—*a hog pen*, Ben thought. Hogs were for butchering.

Forty-five minutes after sundown, the first of five trucks rumbled through the prison camp gate. Ben watched as shackled black convicts jumped from the back of the truck and walked, two-by-two, toward the building.

The warden, a small, thin man named Samuel Knox, seemed to materialize out of thin air, and stood at the building's entrance. Knox had wrangled the job through his connections with the local courthouse gang. As County Warden, he ran his prison camp with absolute authority.

"Who the hell is this son-of-a-bitch?" he asked Hoke.

"They brought him from Baxley."

"I don't have any paperwork on him."

"The police chief there said we had to take him, or they were gonna burn the courthouse down."

"Who? Thorpe?"

"Yep."

"Hell, he shoulda called ahead. I can't be taking every damn nigguh they throw in jail."

"I told him that. I called your house but couldn't get a hold of you."

"I was fishing. Where'd you get those extra stripes?"

"Sumbitch Mongo died. We chunked his ass in a hole and give this one his clothes."

"We think Mongo died," Jeder added with a snicker. "Least, we buried his black ass."

Knox turned to Ben.

"What you in for, you black son-of-a-bitch?"

Ben glanced at him then looked at the ground. He didn't like what he saw. The warden's skin had turned red from years of sun exposure. His eyes were coal black, and he sported a crew cut.

"They say I kilt a man," Ben replied.

"Shot a preacher," Jeder added.

The warden eyed Ben more closely.

"So you're the one. I heard about that murder. Shot a white preacher. Well, hell, you gonna wish they sent you to the chair."

Ben felt the little man's stare for several more moments before the warden walked to the front of the building.

"Come by me!" he called out to the convicts. "Come by me!"

Two other guards checked the convicts' shackles as the warden examined each man for signs that he hadn't adequately exerted himself during the day's labors. Occasionally, he'd smell a prisoner to ascertain his degree of filth. Each man counted off as he entered the building.

"Any one of you sons-of-bitches who don't want to put in a full day's work is gonna regret it!" he called out.

Ben watched as four more truckloads carrying twenty men each arrived in the prison yard and disgorged their cargoes. Two trucks carried white prisoners, and two carried more black convicts. The scene repeated itself as the men approached the building in two rows, their chains clanging as they walked.

After the final group waited outside the building, Hoke escorted Ben to the end of the line. When the warden finished inspecting the last two men, they entered the doorway and counted off, "Eighteen. Nineteen."

"All right. Let's go," Hoke said.

The warden eyed Ben up and down as one of the guards inspected his chains.

"There are one hundred and forty odd prison camps in the state of Georgia," Knox told Ben. "You done picked the worst one in the bunch, 'cause I'm the meanest son-of-a-bitch there is. Welcome to Hell."

Hoke shoved Ben forward with the barrel of his shotgun. He stumbled into a dimly lit room that served as a washing area for one hundred prisoners. Three tin basins with two faucets each served as the only means for a cursory cleaning before dinner. No soap or towels were provided to the men, who washed their faces, necks, and hands, and used their stripes to dry off.

Ben gagged at the stench of human filth that permeated the room.

"Get your feed!" he heard a voice shout from the other end of the building.

Ben walked past the basins and followed as other men filed

through another door into a long room that served as the sleeping area. The floors, walls, and ceiling were made of rough-hewn pine boards. An occasional iron-barred window allowed air in. A row of metal cots covered with dirty mattresses and pillows lined both sides of the room. Between the rows sat six open toilets down the center of the room. Ben looked on with disgust as he followed a smaller man in front of him. He soon passed through another door into a mess hall of long tables with benches. The men walked by a counter where each grabbed a tin plate onto which was placed a six-inch square corn pone, three slices of fried pig fat, and a small ladle of sorghum. They then scurried for the end positions on the benches. The ones unfortunate enough to occupy the middle were forced to sit and swing their legs over the bench.

Not a word was spoken the entire time. Ben sat at a table near the back of the room and looked at his plate with revulsion as the men around him eagerly lapped up their food.

"Better eat up," the man next to him said softly so he wouldn't be overheard. He was in his mid-thirties with skin almost as dark as Ben's. His hair was straight and wavy with a red tint to it.

Ben dipped the corn pone in the syrup and quickly downed it, but he couldn't bring himself to swallow the undercooked pig fat.

"Let me have it," the man said. "They beat you down you if you don't eat up."

Ben looked up to see if he was being observed and slipped the man the remainder of his food.

The dinner was over in a few minutes, and the inmates shuffled back into the sleeping area. Ben estimated that less than an hour had transpired between the time they unloaded the trucks and reentered the sleeping quarters for lights out. One hundred convicts sat on their cots for the final event of their day, a ritual they all knew was coming and could do nothing to prevent.

The warden and a number of guards entered the room.

"Which sons-of-bitches didn't want to work today?" the warden asked.

The guards walked up and down the room to identify men they thought hadn't fully discharged their debt to society that day. Mostly, they chose men at random. Two whites and the man Ben gave his food to, were fingered.

"That sumbitch talked back," he heard a voice say.

Ben looked up and saw Hoke pointing at him. The "dog finger" they called it on Sapelo, when someone pointed and accused another of a misdeed. He stared at the finger with a sick feeling in his stomach, not fully aware of what lay ahead.

"Bring 'em," said the warden in a weary voice, as though he was being inconvenienced and delayed from attending to more pressing duties.

The four men were marched back into the mess hall where a bench had been pulled away from one of the tables. In his hand, the warden held a six-foot leather strap, three inches wide, and a quarter inch thick.

"Drop 'em," he said to the first convict, a white man. The prisoner pulled his pants down without protesting. Two guards laid him on the bench and pulled his shirt up. They tied ropes around his arms and legs and pulled them taut.

"The strap was outlawed in Georgia ten years ago," the warden announced. "But inside these gates, I'm the law. Understand? So, you don't want to work?"

He reared back and flailed the strap across the man's back. Ben looked on in horror, now fully cognizant of his own impending punishment. The strap fell across the man ten times. Ten times, he cried out in pain. The little black man next to Ben simply made a clicking noise with his mouth. When it was over, the convict was ordered to rise, his back and buttocks bleeding. He stood up unsteadily and readjusted his shirt and pants to stave the blood flow. "Next son-of-a-bitch!" the warden called out.

Ben watched the other white convict receive his licks and cry out with each stroke.

Black an' white mens wearin' black and white stripes, he thought. *Dey all bleed de same red.*

Again, the little man next to him made clicking sounds, as if he was a detached observer saying, "That's a damn shame, but what can I do about it?"

"Next!" the warden called out.

"Coming, Boss!" the little man said. He quickly bared his backside and stretched out on the bench.

"So, you son-of-a-bitch. You don't want to work, huh?"

Ben thought he was going to pass out at the man's cries. None of the men begged for lenience, knowing full well that doing so was futile and would only result in more lashes. When his turn came, Ben resolved he would not cry out in pain. He was from the line of Bu-Allah and Ebo warriors. He had survived one lynching and had single-handedly run the Altamaha.

"Next!" shouted the warden after ten licks.

Ben reluctantly took his place on the bench.

"Kill a white preacher? Hell, that'll get you extra licks, you black son-of-a-bitch!"

Excruciating pain shot throughout his body at the first blow. Only the guards holding him down with ropes prevented Ben from rising off the bench. After the fifth lick, he felt as though his insides were exposed to the lash.

"Son-of-a-bitch!" Knox said, pausing to adjust his grip. "Won't yell? How about I give you a few more!"

Ben lost count after the twelfth lash, but still he wouldn't make a sound. *I am the son of Jesse! The son of Ben! The son of Bu-Allah!* he repeated mantra-like.

"Ain't nobody ever seen nuthin' like it," he heard his father's voice say. "You gots de strength of de Ebo an' de mind of Bu-Allah."

Just when he thought he might lose consciousness, the beating ceased.

"All right, get this son-of-a-bitch outta my sight," he faintly heard the warden say.

When he got up, Ben's legs wobbled like jelly. He pulled his pants up and his shirt down as the others had done to staunch the blood flow. He felt ashamed for having been beaten, but when he glanced at the three convicts lining the wall, they looked at him with approval. He was the newest initiate of an elite fraternity, the brotherhood of lost souls condemned to a Georgia prison camp.

"All right," said the warden, wiping sweat from his brow, "you boys give me a decent day's work tomorrow and maybe we don't have to do this again."

Ben slowly followed the three convicts who filed back into the sleeping quarters. He fell in a heap onto Mongo's former cot, his backside aflame with excruciating pain.

The little man lay on the next cot.

"Be on your stomach," he said told Ben. "You won't get stuck to the mattress with all that blood."

A guard walked down the middle aisle and slid a thick chain through each convict's iron ring. Two other guards attached the long chain to the walls at either end of the room. They repeated the procedure for the prisoners lying on the other row of cots.

Ben lay awake, staring at nothing and pondering the day's events. Occasionally, a convict needing to use a toilet would call out to the guard on duty.

"Getting up, Boss."

"Get up," came the reply, followed by the clanking of chains.

Jesus hep me, Ben thought. *We gots to wear dese chains twenny-fo hour. Gots to ax a man if can I use de toilet. God cum tek me.*

For a fleeting moment, he thought of divulging Clayborne's name to the authorities. Damn his promise to a white man. Then he recalled the three men who had come to his porch. Naomi and Geneva's safety came first. He could suffer for them. *Jesus suffer fo me. I suffer fo dem.* He could die for them, not for Clayborne Cutler. Thoughts of a quick death began to fill his mind. Escape or death. Either way, he'd be free of the nightmare called a Georgia prison camp.

God wiff me. Bu-Allah in my blood, he repeated silently.

He looked up at the ceiling from his cot long after the overhead light bulbs went dark. He had imagined the dull gray ceiling to be an overcast sky, a dim veil behind which were spirits that would one day reveal the secret of flight to him. When he was a child, the old folks on Sapelo had spoken of slaves who brought that secret from Africa with them. Coastal plantation owners advertised in newspapers as far away as Virginia for the recapture of runaways, but his folks knew that the escaped slaves had already flown back to Africa—that they always had the power to do so.

"Seen dem rise up lak a buzzard in de air," the older ones recounted. "Dey say de magic words, 'Kum buba yali kuni buba tambe. Kum kunka yali kum kunka tambe.' Dey say it quick like. Den dey rise off de groun' an fly away. Dey fly back to dey tribe. Nebuh cum back. No suh. Nebuh cum back to dis day!"

Outside, two outdoor lights lit up both ends of the building. After a while of swatting bed bugs, he felt a wisp of a breeze flowing through one window and over his body.

Just before he drifted off to sleep, he saw a movement at the window across the room from him. He opened his eyes and saw Mongo's spirit standing outside, staring back. He seemed to be speaking, trying to tell Ben something, but Ben couldn't make out the words. He realized that Mongo's spirit was still intact, whole, undamaged. His soul had already gone on, Ben believed.

Whether it was to heaven or hell, he couldn't say, but he realized that while the warden and his guards could mangle his body, they could never touch his soul or his spirit.

"The body is a temple," he heard Reverend Williams say very distinctly. His voice rang out so clearly that Ben raised his head to see if the island preacher had somehow slipped into the room. "Tear it down, and the spirit will rise up again!"

Bone-weary from the past week's events and loss of blood, Ben lay his head back down and, a few moments later, fell into a deep slumber.

CHAPTER 23

"Come on!" Eli called out as they ran through the Sapelo woods. Ahead, through an opening between an oak and a pine, stood his wife Saundra, calling Ben to come to her. He looked down every so often to avoid tripping on tree roots, but every time he looked up, she was still the same distance away.

"Come on!" said his cousin. He looked just as he had when Ben knew him in his prime. "Ben, Saundra calling you!"

Ben stopped to catch his breath and listen for his wife's voice, but all he could hear was the sound of a chain moving rapidly across metal.

He awoke with a jolt and let out an involuntary howl. During the night he had turned over onto his back, and the blood had stuck to the mattress. When he rose up, the dried blood ripped open his wounds, causing them to seep. Searing pain shot through his body as a guard pulled hard on the building chain, which rattled through each convict's iron ring. Those who didn't rise fast enough to hold their ring taut were pulled from their beds and dragged by their feet to the cot next to them.

"Hold the chain ring!" the little man on the cot next to him said. "Hold it tight!"

Ben sprung forward the grabbed his ring just as the building chain ran through it.

"Let's go! Let's go!" the guards yelled, beating tin trays together.

He looked outside at the pitch black. It was well before sunrise. A few minutes later, he was seated once again on a mess hall bench next to his new friend.

"Whut time it is?" Ben asked. "Same time every day. Three-thirty."

His response was masked by the sounds of ninety-eight other men coughing and clearing their throats. Breakfast consisted of a cup of weak coffee, fried dough made of grease and white flour, three pieces of pork sides, and another dose of sorghum syrup.

"Best eat up," the little man said. "This the best meal of the day. You gonna need it."

Fifteen minutes later, the inmates filed outside into the prison yard. Guards had set out flares that cast an eerie glow on the men in stripes.

"Come by me! Come by me!" the warden called out.

The prisoners assembled into five groups of twenty. Two guards, bearing shotguns and pistols, were assigned to each group. The convicts stood in rows of two. Each man held his upright chain toward the man next to him as a guard threaded a squad chain through the iron rings. The squad chain ensured that no man could move more than five feet from the next prisoner.

The inmates in Ben's squad counted off as they stepped up into the tarp-enclosed truck that would transport them to their destination.

"Eleven," the little man in front of Ben shouted as he got onto the truck.

"Twelve," Ben called out as he stepped up.

Hoke and Jeder were assigned to the group Ben was with. They sat in the front of the truck with the driver. When they reached the prison yard gate, another guard counted the prisoners again before securing the back of the truck.

The little man sitting next to Ben lit a home-rolled cigarette. In the light of the flame, Ben could see a glint of mischief in his eye. He drew deeply on the cigarette and held out a hand to Ben.

"They call me Roos," he said. Ben shook his hand. "I'ze Ben."

"We can talk now," Roos said once the truck picked up speed. "They cain't hear nuthin' we saying back here no how."

The headlamps of the trailing truck occasionally flooded the interior, allowing Ben to more closely examine the other occupants. Most seemed to be between twenty and forty-years-old.

Roos introduced Ben to his fellow prisoners beginning with the men on the opposite bench.

"That there Pigmeat. Next to him, Black Jack and Poo Doo. There go Hump Man . . ."

Each man in turn acknowledged Ben in some fashion. When he got to the convict sitting next to Ben, the man threw up. The others laughed.

"He always throw up in this wagon," Roos said. "Hey, Leroy. Man, you gonna need that food later!"

More rounds of laughter.

"Cain't hep it," Leroy responded. He reached into a fold of his pants, withdrew a piece of saved cornbread, and began to eat.

Before long, the truck following them pulled onto a side road, plunging the men into darkness once again.

"Where dey tekkin' us?" Ben asked.

Roos laughed aloud and took another long drag on his cigarette as the truck engine strained on an incline and the rolling prison lurched forward.

"We working on a new road. A new highway for the gov'na and the people of Georgia. Yes, sir. Going to work for the peoples."

"Man, they beat you last night. Why you laugh?" Ben asked.

"'Cause, they beat every man sooner or later. Everybody get the strap. Now, I'm free from it for a while. Might be six months befo they call me out again."

Ben tried to figure out the direction the truck was headed. They had turned right out of the prison camp gates, but had turned several more times since then.

"Which way we goin'?"

"To the river," Roos replied. "The gov'na building bunch of highways and bridges and fixin' up the rails. He must be plannin' to move everyone up north down to Georgia. He gots mo' highways than I gots sweethearts, and that's a lot."

"Hey, man, what they put you in here for?" asked Pigmeat, a man about Ben's age.

Ben didn't reply. The law said he killed a preacher. He believed he killed off a whole family. Even in the darkness, Roos could see his reluctance to talk about it. He recalled what Warden Knox said about Ben having murdered a white minister.

"He in for a traffic vi'lation," Roos responded, attempting to deflect attention from Ben.

"Traffic vi'lation?" Pigmeat replied. "Whatchoo talkin' 'bout, traffic vi'lation?"

"Yeah. He slipped on a banana peel, and the judge give him time for speeding!"

Howls of laughter shattered the darkness, startling Hoke and the others in the cab.

"You hear that?" Hoke said to Jeder, shaking his head. "Dumb ass nigguhs. You can beat 'em all you want, and the next day they're laughin' it up."

"They ain't human," Jeder agreed. "Bunch of animals."

In the back, the other men picked up on the thread of Roos's extemporaneous attempt at levity.

"Hey . . . uh . . . why Pigmeat in here?" Blackjack asked Roos.

"Pigmeat?" Roos said, drawing on the cigarette. He stood up and assumed his place as impromptu host of the proceedings.

"He and two white mens was brought up in front of the judge. One whitey was accused of taking a horse and the other for taking a cow. 'Guilty or not guilty?' the judge asked the first man. 'Not guilty, Your Honor,' the white man said. 'I been owning that horse ever since he was a li'l colt.' 'Case dismissed,' say the judge. Judge turned to the next fella. 'Guilty or not guilty?' 'Not guilty,' the man say. 'I been owning that cow ever since she was a little, bitty calf.' 'Case dismissed!' Then the judge turned to Pigmeat. 'Guilty or not guilty?' Pigmeat look at them other two fellas and say, 'Not guilty, Your Honor, Suh. I been owning that wagon ever since it was a wheelbarrow!'"

Howls of laughter rocked the back of the truck, but Ben didn't find the situation he was in a laughing matter. He squirmed on the hard bench, trying to find a position that didn't exacerbate the pain on his backside.

"What Poo Doo in for?" another prisoner asked Roos.

"Ol' Poo Doo? He got arrested for sassing his white boss."

"Sassing the boss?"

"Yeah. One day, the boss man say 'How do I look?' Poo Doo say, 'Boss, you looks mighty.' 'What you mean mighty?' boss man says back. 'Why, you looks noble. Just like a lion,' Poo Doo tell him. 'Poo Doo,' boss man say, 'when you ever seen a lion before?' 'I seen one down yonder in the field the other day,' Poo Doo say. 'Fool! That wasn't no lion. That was a jackass.' 'Well, Boss, whatever is was, you look just like him!'"

Ben sputtered, but resisted laughing along with the others who exploded with howls. Another voice in the dark asked Roos why Leroy got sent to the prison camp. Roos didn't hesitate, and launched into another tall tale.

"Leroy in here for exposing hisself to a white lady."

"What you mean?"

"Leroy bone-lazy. He got tired working that ol' cotton patch when someone told him Miss Liza was looking for someone to tend her petunia garden. Next day, he go to Miss Liza house and knock on the back door. Miss Liza open the door and ask Leroy, 'What you want?' He say, 'I'm the man come to work in your petunia garden.' Miss Liza say, 'Can I see your testimonials?' Leroy say, 'I reckon, Miss.' That's when he made his mistake and pulled down his drawers."

Ben tried to resist, but the laughter shot out of him like a cannon ball and reverberated around the back of the truck along with that of the other men. Hoke reached out of the cab window and banged hard on truck's side with a club. The back of the truck went silent.

"I knew I'd get you to smilin'," Roos said after a few moments passed. "Cryin' ain't gonna get you no where 'round here. You might as well belly laugh when you get the chance."

"How long you got?" Ben asked after another mile had passed.

"I gots ten mo' year," Roos replied. "Ten outta twenny. How long they gave you?"

Ben paused. Other nearby men who had been conversing stopped talking when Roos asked the question.

"Fo'ty year," Ben replied.

Roos whistled long and low.

"Ain't but four ways you leave here. You work out—make your time. You pay out, if you got two thousand dollar to buy parole. You die out, or you run out. Oh yeah, they is a fifth way. If you happen to be best friends with the gov'na, he can let you out. Me, I ain't the gov'na's best buddy. I ain't got no two thousand dollar to buy out. I plans to work my way outta here. Mongo, he tried to hang it out on the limb. He run out, but they caught him. Hound dogs treed him the next day. Then, they put him in the hotbox, and he die out. Either way, run out or die out, he gone. He free from this place."

The truck ambled on for another thirty minutes down a winding, bumpy logging road before coming to a halt. Hoke peered through the gate with a flashlight and counted the men while Jeder stood a few feet back with his shotgun at the ready. Hoke and the driver then raised the tarp to allow air inside, but they didn't unlock the gate.

"Whut dey doin'?" Ben whispered.

"It still slam dark. They waitin' fo big red," Roos replied. "They ain't lettin' us offa this truck until the sun come up."

In the dim first light of day, Ben had a vague feeling he was not far from the confluence of the Ocmulgee and Oconee Rivers, where the Altamaha began. In his mind, he saw himself floating downstream, holding onto a log, all the way to Sapelo. He'd navigated the river before. He knew the route and the dangers. Before long, the first rays of the sun crested the pine treetops.

"Let's go! Let's go!" Hoke called out as the driver let down the back gate. The crew of twenty convicts shuffled one at a time through the narrow metal door and jumped to the ground below. In the growing light, Ben saw a crudely-made roadbed nearby. In the distance, he saw a corridor of open space, roughly hewn through the dense pine forest. A barrel filled with picks and shovels sat twenty yards from the truck. Prisoners lined up and marched toward it. Two piles of dirt, thirty feet high, sat on one side of the roadbed.

"Whut we doin'?" Ben asked Roos.

"We gradin' road. A cement highway going right through here. Like a string pulled tight. Skrate, like a arrow," he said, imitating an archer pulling a bowstring taught. "Gonna be the fanciest highway in the South."

Ben shuffled in his manacled feet toward the barrel and grabbed a shovel. A mile ahead, he could hear the sounds of heavy machinery starting up.

"The highway men up ahead knockin' down trees and layin' down dirt. We come up behind and smooth it down. See them stakes?"

Roos pointed to small wooden stakes hammered into the soil by a survey crew a few days earlier. The stakes were scattered in ten-foot intervals the width of the roadbed, and as far as the eye could see. Some stuck out an inch or two above the ground, others were exposed six inches or more.

"We here to cover them stakes with the dirt, flush at the top. The road gots to be high in the middle and drain left and right. The stakes tell how high the road need to be in the middle and on the sides. We spread the dirt; the crew behind us put down gravel rock. Then, the next crew put down concrete on top of that. You lucky you on the lead crew today. Layin' down dirt ain't nuthin.'"

"Whut de men do wiff de trees?" Ben wanted to know.

"They gots tractors and ox teams come in here and haul them away. Take them to a lumberyard and cut 'em up."

Ben knew that once they crossed the river, the company that would collect the trees on the other side would likely be Cutler Land & Lumber.

Soon, another truck pulled up to the site, and twenty more prisoners piled out. The newly-arrived inmates were given flat, wide metal pans that required two men to maneuver. Several men were assigned to the dirt piles where they shoveled soil into the pans. The pans were hauled onto the roadbed where Ben and his crew spread the dirt until each stake was covered. On a good day, sunup to sundown, the chain gang could grade a mile of roadway.

Hoke and Jeder, like most prison camp guards, found fault with each convict's work and showered them with curses and threats as a means of maintaining order. They kept a close watch on the men. If one of them escaped, the warden would assign them to prison yard duty again with a cut in pay.

"That there is Bulldog," Roos said in a low voice amidst the clinking of chains, clanging of shovels, and picks loosening rock. "His real name Hoke, but we call him Bulldog."

Ben quickly glanced at the guard and noticed the resemblance. "Do de Bulldog bite?"

"Oh, yeah," Roos acknowledged. "Buckra bite. I seen him shoot a man had heat stroke. Man couldn't even move. Said he was disobeying orders."

Roos looked cautiously around to make sure he couldn't be overheard.

"You fall down sick out here, they shoot you dead and say you tried to run off. They ain't got no sick beds back to the camp. You get cut with a pick ax, they chain you to the whippin' post all day. But you lame fo life. Not me. No suh. I gots to have my legs when I get outta here."

"Do I hear talkin'?" Bulldog shouted.

"No, Boss!" nineteen convicts yelled back.

"I thought I heard talkin'!"

"Wipin' it off," Roos called out.

"Wipe it off," Bulldog replied.

Roos wiped his forehead and went back to work spreading dirt.

"If I catch one of you sumbitches talkin'," Bulldog said, "the warden's gonna know about it!"

Every other hour, a prisoner carried a pail of water to the crew and dispensed a ladleful to each convict. Ben followed Roos's lead in rolling up his shirt to allow the sun's penetrating rays to dry the blood and air-heal the wounds on his back.

"Lay 'em down!" Bulldog called out at exactly eleven-thirty.

The convicts dropped their shovels and picks, and shuffled to a shaded area where tin plates were stacked in a wooden crate. Another box held six-inch square corn pones. A prisoner dished boiled red beans from a galvanized iron bucket onto Ben's plate as he passed by. When he sat down to eat, he noticed worms in the mix. One spoonful also informed him that much of the dish's consistency was comprised of sand.

Roos saw the look on Ben's face and laughed.

"I told you breakfast was the best meal of the day." Ben looked over at Bulldog and the other guards, who were sitting twenty yards away eating fried chicken and drinking lemonade.

"Don't worry 'bout them," Roos said. "We can talk during lunch."

He lit up another cigarette.

"Why dey call you, Roos?" Ben wanted to know. Roos laughed, revealing two missing teeth.

"I used to have a way with the women. Oh, yes.

Yes, Sir. I could make the women folk smile. Plenty women. All kinds. You name it. They called me Rooster. That what they called me. Rooster. Roos. Now, with one woman, they is enough trouble. But two or three, like I sometimes had going at one time . . ." He shook his head and laughed. "That's trouble guaranteed, Man, I'm telling you. Double-trouble! Serious. That's serious trouble—guaranteed."

Ben recalled his trip to St. Catherine's Island with Eli to see the young girl, the father with the shotgun, and their narrow escape, and he recalled the man in Waycross telling him of Eli's numerous romances.

"Dat why you in here?" he asked. The smile left Roos's face.

"That exactly why I'm in here. Exactly the reason. Most every girl I knew had a boyfriend somewhere. Sure enough, one fella, who she said weren't even around no more, he come at me with a blade. I carried a blade, too, so I cut him. Self defense. A man come at you with a knife, and you ain't gonna do nothin'? Naw, man. Uh-uh. The man trying to kill me! I just defending myself, and they send me away for twenny years. Twenny long, hard years. And I'm halfway there. My mama trying to get me release, but they won't listen to her. They just keep tossing us niggas and po whites in here to lay down the roads. You gots to be strong, Ben, to survive in here. Don't look a guard in the eye. A guard tell you to do something, you do it. Don't say something first. Let them talk first. Don't ask no questions. Say, 'Yes, Sir. Yes, Boss. I'll take care of that right away, Boss.' Just like that. That all you gots to say, and you be all right. If you don't, man, they put you in them stocks and pull your arms from you sockets while the warden whip you. You pass out. Or they put you in that metal box in the sun. When you wake up, you tied up like a hog for butcherin'. You seen Mongo? Man, it worse here than in slave days. Least you could have a woman if you a slave, and children. Up in here, you got nothin'. It worse than slavery. It worse than Hell. I don't care what no preacher man say. If . . . look here . . . look here, now . . . if Hell is worse than this, then the Devil is worser than the warden. Anyone worser than the warden is one bad dude in my book. That's all I'm saying. The warden is the baddest man they is. Them judges, when they send you here, they sending you to the baddest place they know to send you. It the worst place they is on God's green earth. It the worst place, and the warden the worst man they is, 'cause he run the place. See what I'm sayin'? He *run* the place. Don't matter what the law says. He is the law. If Hell worse than this, the Devil worse than the warden. If Hell ain't worse, then Warden Knox worser than the Devil hisself."

Roos took a long drag on his cigarette before snuffing it and putting it back in his shirt pocket. Ben looked around and noticed that most of the other prisoners had stretched out on the ground and had fallen fast asleep.

"Get some rest," Roos told Ben. "Big Red gettin' high in the sky. Big Red gonna whup some ass this afternoon, for sure. So get ready."

"Let's go back!" Bulldog hollered at 1:00 on the dot.

At the sound of Hoke's voice, twenty men rose to their feet and quickly shuffled back to their previous positions. Up ahead, Ben saw surveyors peering through instruments atop tripods and other men pounding wooden stakes into the ground at varying heights.

"Pick 'em up!" Bulldog called out.

Twenty convicts picked up their shovels and picks and went back to work. The rest of the afternoon was a repeat of the morning. Bulldog kept a watchful eye on Ben. Despite his wounds, he easily kept pace with the other men.

"Lay 'em down!" Bulldog shouted when the sun finally dipped below the tree line.

The prisoners shuffled single file past the tool barrel, placed their picks and shovels in it, then climbed back into the truck where the slow, bumpy ride back to prison camp was repeated in reverse.

"Congratulations," Roos told Ben on the way back. "You done survived yo first day."

The evening procedure, like everything else, was a repeat of the day before.

"Come by me!" Warden Knox called out when they returned to the prison yard.

This time, after their meals had been served, only two men were picked at random for beatings. Ben, listening from his cot, covered his ears as the men screamed after each blow. One of them was Leroy, who was accused of talking without permission that morning. Bulldog fingered him. He received extra lashes and had to be carried to his cot.

In the early hours of the morning, something caused Ben to wake up. It was Mongo again, staring at him through the window. Soon, the spirits of other men, black and white, began to appear.

"Go home," Ben wearily whispered to them. "Go home."

CHAPTER 24

"Miss Evelyn, would you come in here?"

It was a question spoken as a command. The door between Clayborne Cutler's office and Evelyn Barrow's desk usually remained opened. In Obediah's day, a steady fog of cigarette and cigar smoke had poured through the doorway past her desk and out an opened window. O. C.'s office had been ground zero for the local power brokers who controlled commerce in and around the county. Now, Clayborne held court from that same office, with a mixture of the old guard and up-and-comers about his age. Among them was Tremont Rogers, whom Clayborne had known since grade school.

Three weeks had passed since Ben Jordan was spirited away from Lamar's collective conscience to the prison camp. Salty Hoffer had gone into debt defending himself. As far as the townspeople of Lamar were concerned, Salty's days as a purveyor of goods and services were over—a fact he realized before the trial even began. He had been the lone white man implicated in the pastor's death. Threats on his life were made both in person and in hand-scribbled notes left at his door. When he found the words "Preacher Killer" scrawled in black paint across his store window, he knew it was time to leave Lamar. He needed the money to cover his legal bills and to start a new life elsewhere. He was willing to sell his coveted property to anyone but the Cutlers.

Tremont sat in a leather chair across from Clayborne's desk.

"Miss Evelyn," Clayborne said, "Ol' Tree here is buying the Hoffer property downtown."

"Well, congratulations," Evelyn said matter-of-factly.

At five-one, she looked the part of a prim and proper lady. Her hair, once auburn, had grown gray in the service of the Cutler family. She'd been Obediah's right hand for twenty-five years. Now, in her early fifties, she was Clayborne's confidante, a woman who knew when to hear things and when not to, when to see and when to be seen. Obediah had more than a few skeletons in the Cutler Land & Lumber Company closet. Clayborne had just begun to add his own. Evelyn knew all of them, and she vaguely suspected a connection with the Dodge murder. She couldn't put her finger on it, but Clayborne's behavior changed after news of the murder came out; not in a way the average person would notice. Only someone intimately familiar with his ways might see the signs— someone who had known him since he was a boy. Obediah once confided to her that his son cleared his throat and looked away whenever he had something to cover up. He had told her this when a ten-year-old Clayborne and some friends were found with stolen watermelons after having denied they knew anything about it. His father thought it humorous, and let Evelyn in on the family secret. Since the murder, Clayborne had been doing a lot of throat clearing and looking in the other direction. He thought of Evelyn as one of the company's most valuable assets and potentially one of its greatest threats. But her loyalty was unwavering, and Clayborne knew it. Her status in the community was held aloft in direct proportion to her status in the company, and she wasn't about to undermine that by revealing state secrets.

"Miss Evelyn," Clayborne continued, "Old Salty is selling out at a bargain basement price, but Tremont needs a little cash to buy the property. I believe we have a couple thousand in the vault."

"We do."

"Good. Would you please go and get it?"

"I'll be right back, Mr. Cutler," Evelyn replied. Tremont looked around the room.

"You don't keep the safe in here?"

Clayborne frowned and shook his head.

"Oh, no. Daddy learned years ago not to keep money in here. No matter how much security we put in, someone always found a way to get at the safe. Only Evelyn and I know the hiding place. Well, us and Daddy. But he's not talking."

"Let me get this straight. You want me to buy Hoffer's place and set up a shop?"

Clayborne snuffed a Lucky Strike and leaned forward in his chair.

"No. Just buy the property. In a year, you sell it to me."

"Hell, Clay. Why don't you just buy it yourself?"

"I don't want to be tainted with the Hoffer name. Let things cool down. But here's the real reason why I called you."

He leaned closer.

"You know my daddy was skint with the money, right?"

"Tighter than Dick's hatband."

"We must have Scottish blood or something. Anyway, his daddy never trusted a bank, and Daddy never trusted them either. Every dime he ever made is in a safe here and squirreled away in deep holes on Cutler property. I came home to take over the business and find Cutler Land & Lumber is flush with cash. I mean, Tree, lots of the stuff. There's a lot of big shots in Atlanta in mansions, and they got nothing now. Not a penny. Everything they had was in the banks. But I'm sitting on a damn mountain of cash, and . . . I got an idea. This new highway is coming right through Lamar.

Hoffer's store is right on the corner. Hell, Tree, there are other little towns down the line that the new road is going through. Why not buy up downtown lots there? Put in tourist home or a filling station on the corner. All up and down the highway all the way down into Florida."

Tree's face lit up.

"Damn, Clay. I'm beginning to see what you're driving at. All these tourists coming through here . . ."

"They got to stop to buy gas somewhere. If not in Lamar, then the next place. Most of these small town yahoos still haven't figured out what this highway means. Commerce. Industries moving in. Jobs. New schools."

Clayborne pulled an envelope out of his top desk drawer.

"I'm starting a new company: Cutler Industries. And I want you to be a part of it. We're going to expand into other areas besides lumber. With the new highway, comes other business opportunities, like housing construction. Builders need timber to put up houses, and we got the timber. I got a contract right here. It's all legal and ready to go."

"What do you want me to do?"

"Go home and look it over. If you want in, bring it back, and sign it here. Miss Evelyn will witness. Then, go scout these towns. Let's buy some properties. But don't do anything until after you get Hoffer's store."

Evelyn entered the room with an envelope filled with bills.

"There's twenty-five hundred dollars in there," said Clayborne. "Whatever is left in there after you deal with Hoffer is yours."

He slid the contract toward Tremont.

"All right," Tremont said, picking up the money and the contract. "I'll be in touch."

"Don't think too long on it," said Clayborne. "Things are gonna move pretty fast once we get this new company going."

Soon after Tremont left, Evelyn entered the room.

"Mr. Cutler, there's a colored woman waiting outside to see you."

"Colored woman? What does she want?"

"She's that man's sister. The one who shot Reverend Dodge. You told her to come by sometime this week."

Clayborne lit a cigarette.

"Oh yeah. Mama's been complaining about Millie getting too old to keep up the house."

"You looking for a new house maid?"

"Yep. You know how Mama is. Once she gets it in her head someone ain't pulling their weight, you can't talk her out of it."

"Should I have her come in?"

"No. I got some work to finish up. Tell her to wait." He leaned back in his chair and recalled the day Ben went to the prison camp. Clayborne had stayed long enough to see the guard hit Ben with the shovel, and it made his stomach turn, but he continued to tell himself that it was all for the good of Lamar and the surrounding county. Ben was making a supreme sacrifice and didn't know it.

Clayborne heard the phone at Evelyn's desk ring. A few moments later, she poked her head inside the door.

"Governor Talmadge is on the phone," she said, just the least bit out of breath.

Clayborne motioned with his hand, waving it back and forth.

"Send it in here," he replied.

As she closed the door, he took a deep breath. Obediah Cutler's business connections with the sitting governor predated Talmadge's election to State Agriculture Commissioner in 1926. Talmadge spread his influence among the dirt-poor farmers through a department newspaper that carried his advice on agriculture and views on politics at no cost to him. The farmers responded by electing him governor in 1932, a two-year term that was about to expire. With the next election looming, Clayborne could readily guess the purpose of the call. Gene Talmadge didn't rely so much on the courthouse gangs that ran local affairs, as the farmers who ultimately cast their votes, but he did depend on a few prominent locals to keep him abreast of the political winds that blew through their counties.

"Governor, it's good to hear from you," Clayborne said when he picked up the ringing phone. "How're you doing?"

"Fine, fine," Gene Talmadge replied. "How's your pretty little wife doing? I haven't seen Claudette 'round here in a coon's age."

"She's doing fine . . . expecting a new addition to the family before too long."

Clayborne knew the perfunctory conversation would be short. Talmadge had a dozen irons in the fire and dozen more on deck. He had heard his father talk to enough men in power to know that the crux of the call would come next.

"That's great. Congratulations," Talmadge replied. "Between you two, that baby's got to be one fine looking child."

"Thank you, Governor. And thanks again for helping us out on that little incident in Baxley. We never heard a peep from the Atlanta press."

"Not at all. I just gave them another scandal to write about. They forgot about Baxley pretty quick. Say Clay," Talmadge continued after clearing his throat, "I hear you put on quite a show getting that rowdy crowd at the courthouse to settle down."

Clayborne rose to his feet. Something in the governor's tone of voice disturbed him. Talmadge could be calling to offer a position of importance or to take Clayborne to the woodshed for stepping on the wrong toes.

"Oh, hell, it was the Cutler name that did it, Governor," Clayborne replied as casually and self-effacing as possible. Sweat broke out on his brow.

"Your daddy was a fine man, Clay. We had us some good times hunting and fishing down on the Altamaha. But I got to tell you,

I'm a little concerned about some rumors going around up here that you got your eye on statewide office. People are talking about Clayborne Cutler and the next governor in the same breath. Is there any truth to that?"

Clayborne leaned hard against his desk. The conversation had taken a serious turn for the worse. Talmadge was just coming into his own as a political force, and he had designs for his son, Herman, to succeed in his footsteps. An upstart politician from middle Georgia, the Talmadge base, would have to be squashed one way or another. Governor Talmadge had a reputation for being dictatorial and vindictive. A road or bridge project could materialize or evaporate at the governor's whim. In an instant, Clayborne saw his hopes for the new highway coming through Lamar slipping from his grasp. He felt as though a heavyweight had just sucker-punched him. He fell back into his leather chair.

"No, Governor, that is absolutely not true!" Clayborne shot back. "That is just some crazy talk, I can assure you. All I was doing was trying to keep one of my workers from getting his butt lynched by that mob. That's all that was going on there."

There was a long pause on the other end—an eternity in Clayborne's mind—as Talmadge thought things through, possibly consulting one of several men who were always present in the Governor's Atlanta office.

"I don't know," Talmadge replied at length. "What I'm hearing is that those boys wanted to tear the place up one minute, and were eating out of your hand the next. A man who can turn a crowd like that can go a long way in Georgia politics. Now, the only reason I'm calling you is because your papa and me go back a ways."

"I appreciate that, Governor." Clayborne wiped the sweat from his forehead. "My daddy was a loyal Talmadge man, and so am I. Fact is, I'm trying to expand Daddy's business. Hell, I ain't got time or the inclination for holding office."

Clayborne held down a button, which triggered a buzzer on Evelyn's desk.

"Well, I hope not. I'd hate to see that highway heading for Lamar turn off toward Hazlehurst. You know, those farmers over there need a highway, too."

"I'd hate to see that happen, too, Governor. In fact," he said motioning for Evelyn to sit down at her typewriter and begin typing, "I heard the same crazy rumor about me running for office, and I got my secretary working on a statement right now refuting it on Cutler Land & Lumber letterhead. Here, listen."

He held the phone out as Evelyn typed gibberish on the Royal typewriter.

"You hear that?" Clayborne said, returning the phone to his ear, "I dictated it just a while ago. It says that I categorically deny any intention of running for office of any kind. I'm sending it to all the papers around here. I'll send you a copy first if you want."

"No, no. That won't be necessary," the governor replied. "I just wanted to hear it from you. You know how rumors get started. I just wanted to hear it from your lips. Now, tell me this, how you enjoying that county fertilizer inspector job? Your daddy did a good job on that for me for a long time. How you liking it?"

"I like it just fine, Governor."

"Gene. Call me Gene, Clay."

A smile spread across Clayborne's face. He had turned the crowd surrounding the Baxley courthouse to his advantage, and he had just averted another potential disaster. He motioned for Evelyn to stop typing.

"I like it fine, Gene. But I'd like it more with a five percent raise."

The governor burst into laughter. Clayborne heard Talmadge repeat his statement to other men in the background. They, too, found it amusing.

"Damn, Son, I'm glad you're on my team. You are just the man I need down in middle Georgia. We got an election coming up soon, Clay. We're gonna need all the support we can get. These big city fellas are looking every which a way to knock me off this throne. Do you reckon you could put together a rally outside Lamar? I'll be heading through there in a month or so."

"You can count on me, Gene. My daddy didn't let you down. I won't either. Hell, we got more votes here than people. You just let me know how many you need."

More laughter.

"It would sure be nice," Clayborne continued, "if you could be here for the dedication of the highway when it reaches Lamar. I can guarantee one hell of a turnout."

"Well, that sounds like a good idea to me. I'll have someone in my office contact you."

"I think we can get an ordinance to have that stretch of road through town renamed Talmadge Boulevard without any problem."

"Sounds good to me," the governor replied. "Well, it's been good talking with you, Clay. You tell that sweet wife of yours I said hello. And congratulations on that baby."

"If it's a boy, we'll name him after you."

"All right. Now, you tell Claudette ol' Gene says hello, you hear?"

"Will do. Thank you for calling."

Clayborne hung up the phone and slumped heavily into his chair, his armpits soaked with sweat. He looked at his hands. The palms were clammy, and his fingers trembled. Something told him that he wasn't out of the woods yet with Gene Talmadge. Lamar and Atlanta were separated by four hours of highway, enough to keep rural Georgians guessing what transpired in the halls of the state capitol and men in the governor's office trying to outguess the power brokers of rural Georgia. The distance was enough to drive men to distraction. Both depended on the other for votes and building projects. Clayborne knew that a steady stream of men with interests at odds with his own, constantly filed into the governor's office. Some of them might have designs on what Clayborne rightfully considered to be his highway.

All for naught, he thought to himself as he leaned back in his chair and collected his thoughts.

He replayed his talk with Gene Talmadge in his mind. Though it had ended up well, something gnawed at Clayborne. Had he really convinced the governor? Was a press release enough to squelch the rumor? He'd killed one man, ruined another, and incarcerated a third on the bet that a highway would pass through Lamar. He would be damned if a delegation from another town would convince Talmadge to nudge the road in their direction.

Clayborne looked at his hands again and slowly curled them into fists. Evelyn noticed the coloring of his face and an extreme change in his countenance. It was as though a person other than the young, handsome man now sat before her. What she saw was a man, an older man, filled with rage. For a moment, when he turned his gaze on her, she feared for her safety.

"I need train tickets for me, Mayor Reynolds, and Dyson Porter. Then call that hotel across from the capitol building in Atlanta and reserve a couple rooms."

"Yes, Sir."

"I swear to God, Miss Evelyn," Clayborne said as she stood to leave, "I swear to God if that bastard Talmadge diverts that highway away from here, I'm going to put a bullet through his heart. You hear me?"

"I hear you, Mister Cutler."

"I'm not kidding. You can put me down for the biggest liar in Lamar if I don't shoot him myself if he shifts that road. I swear to God I will."

"Yes, Mister Cutler."

Evelyn started out the door, then looked back.

"Oh. Mister Cutler. What about that colored lady?" Clayborne sat staring at his desk brooding.

"What colored lady?" he asked.

"The one outside. The domestic."

He ran his fingers through his wavy hair, still mulling over what he would do if the highway actually got diverted, envisioning himself gunning down the governor.

"Tell her to be at the back step of my house Monday morning at eight sharp."

CHAPTER 25

"A long steel rail!"

Whump!

"And a short cross tie!"

Whump!

"Gonna hammer that nail!"

Whump!

"'Til the day you die!"

Whump!

Each time Blackjack, the leader of the chain gang, sang out the words, a chorus of pick axes descended into the rock-strewn soil laid out before them.

"Keep up the lick, boys," Bulldog called out to two crews of ten men chained together. They stretched across the eighteen-foot wide roadbed, leveling the dirt to the height designated by wood stakes the surveyors set out. Soil crews comprised of convict laborers, dug dirt from surrounding farms. More men in stripes loaded the dirt onto trucks one shovelful at a time with a synchronized rhythm. Other crews broke rocks for the gravel bed that would be laid on top of the dirt base. Lucky farmers got a new pond and a new highway to move their produce to market. The state of Georgia received free labor from a system held over from a post-Civil War prisoner lease program, which grew in corruption and inhumanity with each passing decade.

"It ring like silver!"

Whump!

"And it shine like gold!"

Whump!

"When you hear that whistle!"

Whump!

"It time to go!"

Whump!

A chain gang at the highway site unloaded the dirt trucks. Another crew kept the dirt spread before the line of men in stripes to which Ben belonged. Clay soil had to be broken down with pickaxes and the soles of prisoners' brogans. Behind Ben, a row of convicts from another prison camp further leveled the ground with shovels. Those who couldn't keep up the lick, would feel the warden's strap later that night.

By the second week of Ben's incarceration, he had lost twenty pounds and would soon be indistinguishable weight-wise among his fellow inmates. He had already determined that he would escape no matter what had been prophesied about him on Sapelo. He might have to wander for forty years, but nothing in the prophecy said he had to be under the thumb of a petty tyrant.

After a few weeks, the days had already blurred into a seamless routine of hard labor, food, sleep, and more hard labor, punctuated by a continuous stream of threats, taunts, beatings, and demeaning remarks by guards. Georgia law required that convicts be issued a clean set of clothes each week, usually on Saturdays, but the warden pocketed extra money where he could, and laundry expenses were reduced by half. Knox's inmates received clean stripes twice a month. The few literate ones were allowed to write relatives and receive two dollars a week from family members, provided the warden or his guards didn't first pocket the money. Money could be used to buy cigarettes or bribe a guard to look the other way. Ben soon learned that he was the only black in the camp who could read and write. Half of the guards watching over the prisoners were illiterate. The remainder struggled with reading, and wrote on a third grade level.

"Lay 'em down, boys!" Bulldog called out at precisely eleven-thirty.

"Damn, Blackjack," Roos said, after the gang he and Ben were chained to had gobbled down their lunch of beans and cornbread. He stretched out on a patch of shaded ground with the rest of the men. "You gonna sing us all the way down to Florida before the day's done."

"Boss man tol' me to pick it up," Blackjack replied. Intermittent clouds had been rolling across the sky all morning, threatening rain, but never releasing it on the parched land. If it did rain, work would slow to a crawl, and the guards wanted the tempo to increase. "Bulldog say we falling too far behind the men up ahead."

"Man," Roos replied, "they got machines to knock out them trees, and dynamite to move out them stumps. All we got is a pick and shovel, and we chained together! How we supposed to keep up?"

"I'm just doing what the man tell me to do," Blackjack answered before turning over to catch a short nap.

Roos had likewise almost drifted off along with the others when he felt a nudge on his elbow.

"Hey, Roos. How you get out?" a voice whispered.

Roos opened his eyes and looked around to be sure he couldn't be overheard.

"What?" he whispered in reply.

"How you get out," Ben repeated.

"Man, you just got here. What you talking 'bout?" Roos checked his surroundings again and lowered his voice even more.

"Well, first, you sho as hell don't cut out on Monday. They looking for nigguhs who are fed and rested after Sunday to run off on a Monday. Second thing, you don't wait 'til Friday or Saturday when you dog tired from pulling hard all week."

"How Mongo get out?" Ben wanted to know.

Roos smiled. Some felons smuggled files into camps, wore down the rivets holding the shackles together, and replaced them with bolts they filed down to look like rivets. When the opportune time came, they stole into the woods. If the guards didn't shoot them down with their shotguns, they had a thirty-minute window before the hound dogs were brought in. By then, a general alarm would go out to the surrounding communities. All the roads would be shut down. Usually, the escapee was captured within a few hours.

"Mongo," Roos replied, "paid a guard to look the other way. It was a guard named Cletus. Clete give him a fifteen-minute head start. But them dogs treed ol' Mongo. The warden let Clete go, but he put Mongo in the sweatbox. That why we get water every other hour. We s'posed to get water on the hour, but the warden punishing us so's the next man thinking 'bout running off will think twice 'cause he know the warden gonna take it out on the men he left back to the camp. See those white boys behind us? They get water every hour, just like we 'sposed to."

"Mongo shoulda took to de river," Ben said.

"Nigga didn't know how to swim. Besides, that river still ten mile from here."

"He shoulda tek a creek. Dogs don't smell a man on de water."

"Creeks done dried up. You want to escape from this, you wait 'til we get some rain."

Ben thought about it for a few moments. "Dey can see de tracks in de mud."

"But the creeks swell up."

Ben looked at Roos and smiled.

"You come wiff me."

"No, Suh. I up for parole. I ain't going nowhere. Now, get you some sleep. Big Red gonna come out when these clouds move on. He gonna kick someone's ass before he slip over that horizon."

Ben looked south, down the long tunnel that had been carved out of the woods. On sunny days, he didn't need Bulldog to announce when eleven-thirty rolled around. He had learned to use himself and his fellow crewmen as human sundials, to tell the time of day by the shadows they cast on the ground. The angle of the sun and its orientation overhead told him. Looking down the long alley of stumps that lay between them and the heavy equipment up ahead, something caught his eye.

"Hey, Roos," he said.

Roos had almost drifted off to sleep.

"Now what?" he said without opening his eyes.

"De road turnin' west," Ben said.

"Road ain't turning west. We going south. Dead south, like a arrow."

Ben tapped Roos's leg.

"Naw. Look."

Roos slowly sat up and squinted in the direction Ben was looking. The bulldozers had cut a swath through the forest that turned sharply to the right and disappeared from view.

"Damn," Roos quietly said. "The road is turned. They must be going to Alabamy."

As he spoke, Ben felt something light land on his shoulder. A moment later, another raindrop hit his hand. He raised his face skyward and closed his eyes in bliss as the water droplets fell with more frequency.

Roos laughed so hard the guards looked over at him.

"God-water!" he said, cackling with delight. "Warden can't keep God-water from coming down."

He stood, raised his face toward the clouds, and opened his mouth wide. Most of the other convicts followed his lead while the guards scrambled for the relative shelter of nearby trees and parked trucks.

"Best take it in," Roos said. "This the only bath you gonna get 'til it rain again."

That Sunday afternoon, a wiry fifty-year-old Evangelical named Augustus Youmans showed up at the prison camp. He was one of several local preachers who rotated in and out of the area prison camps delivering sermons designed to instruct and inform the convicts, and to justify the actions of the warden and men who guarded them. Youmans usually performed his sermons in a perfunctory manner and departed quickly afterward. In the seven years he had been coming to the camp, he had yet to engage in meaningful conversation with any of the men incarcerated there. He had baptized a number of them during that time, but none had spoken freely to him. Though he'd grown up on a hog farm, the preacher refused to sermonize from inside the mess hall where the stench of human sweat, vomit, and excrement was unbearable. His sermons were strictly outdoor affairs.

At three o'clock the prisoners assembled in a semi-circle beneath the lone oak that provided shade in the prison camp. They were to listen attentively throughout the service. If anyone uttered a sound, it was only to be in affirmation of the sermon. Violators of this rule were severely punished once the minister left the grounds.

Youmans's brand of preaching was not what Ben had expected. The message he and his fellow men needed to hear was one of hope. What the warden of Ben's private hell wanted was to stamp out any glimmer of hope his prisoners might have once possessed. He needed broken men swinging pickaxes and shoveling Georgia dirt, not men with the prospect of a future. Such men, especially new arrivals, might think of ways to escape.

Ben thought of nothing but escape since wheeling Mongo's body in the wheelbarrow. As he took his place near the edge of the semi-circle, he considered the advice Roos had given him. Youmans soon took his place at their head, Bible in hand, and opened with the Lord's Prayer. When he finished the prayer, his eyes seemed to burn with the same intensity Ben recalled seeing in Clayborne's just before the Methodist pastor was killed.

"As I look out among you, I see murderers, thieves, evil-doers of all kinds," he told them. "In the eyes of the law, you are one step up from an animal."

Ben looked at Roos, who just smiled and nodded.

"Animals have no rights," the preacher went on. "We slaughter them for their meat and their hides. Fortunately for you, we are a Christian people, and we don't slaughter our convicts. Man's law may see you as no better than one of God's lowliest creatures, but God still sees you as His children. With that comes certain covenants, and one of those is that if you fall out of His will—that is to say that if you do evil—God, in His unerring wisdom, will bring judgment against you! He has put on His earth chosen men, like Warden Knox, who are given authority by God to carry out his instruction."

The guards stood behind Ben and the others, watching for anyone who got distracted or fell asleep. Knox sat in a chair near the preacher, his piercing eyes searching each man for signs of inattentiveness. Occasionally, a convict would lower his gaze or follow the flight of a bird overheard. The warden pointed the man out, and within a few moments, he would feel the butt of shotgun come down hard between his shoulder blades.

"Foolishness is bound in the heart of a child," Youmans continued, "but the rod of correction shall drive it far from him! You may be God's children, but you have fallen out of His favor. Every one of you. These guards are God's instruments. When one of them smites you, it is nothing more than God's rod of correction. The harder they come down on you, the more you can be assured that God loves you. He wants to make you perfect in His sight."

"You boys listen to what the preacher is telling you," Knox interjected.

"We listening, Boss," someone replied.

"Let every soul be subject unto the higher powers," said Youmans, reading from scripture, "for there is no power but of God: the powers that be—the judge who sent you here, the warden and his guards-are ordained by God."

"Amen," came the reply from another convict.

"Whosoever therefore resisteth the power, resisteth the ordinance of God, and they that resist shall receive to themselves damnation. For rulers are not a terror to good works, but to the evil . . . For he is the minister of God, a revenger to execute wrath upon him that doeth evil!"

"Amen," Roos said, joining the chorus. "Better 'amen' once in a while," he whispered to Ben, who sat next to him.

"You have been judged by man," Youmans continued, "but one day, you will be judged by God. You may not fear your fellow man, but scripture tells us to 'fear him which hath power to cast into Hell, where they will be tormented day and night for ever and ever!'"

"Amen," Roos said.

"You may think this prison camp is the worst place on Earth to be, but believe me, it is just a glimpse of what awaits you if you don't change your evil ways. When you rebel against man's laws, you rebel against God! When you disobey those who were put here to instruct you, you disobey God!"

"Y'all hear that?" said the warden. "Johnson? Roos? Y'all listening?"

"Yes, Suh!" Roos replied.

"Let no man deceive you with vain words, for because of these things cometh the wrath of God upon the children of disobedience."

"Amen!"

"The Bible tells us that God Almighty will repay each one of you according to your deeds. The Bible tells us that 'six things doth the Lord hate: yea, seven are an abomination unto Him: a proud look, a lying tongue, and hands that shed innocent blood, a heart that deviseth wicked imaginations, feet that be swift in running to mischief, a false witness that speaketh lies, and he that soweth discord among brethren.'"

"That's right, that's right. Amen," came the chorus of responses accompanied by nodding heads and knowing looks.

"We glory in tribulations, knowing that tribulations worketh patience."

For the first time in his life, Ben questioned the authority of a man chosen by God to preach the Word. Rupert Bright had taught him that preachers were anointed by God, but this wasn't the message of hope he had been brought up hearing in the First African Baptist Church on Sapelo and in Lamar. There, the preacher might remind members of a congregation about their transgressions, but there was always a seed of hope for redemption. Youmans's message was one of damnation without hope of salvation. By then, Ben's mind was far away. He saw himself sitting in the pew in Lamar with Saundra next to him and Naomi in her lap. He envisioned the men and women sitting on separate sides of the church on Sapelo.

"Amen," he occasionally responded in unison with the other convicts, even though he hadn't heard what the white preacher said. In his mind, Ben was replaying previous sermons in his head, soaking up scripture of hope.

As his mind drifted further in distance and time, he barely noticed Warden Knox pointing to a prisoner he felt wasn't paying enough attention to the sermon. Jeder stepped over prisoners and came at the unsuspecting man from behind just as he'd done a hundred times in the past.

"If any of you seek vengeance," Youmans said, "Consider this warning. 'To me belongeth vengeance and recompense,' saith the Lord.'" Ben was dimly aware that Youmans was speaking, but for some reason he tuned into these words, as if they portended an event close at hand.

Jeder shuffled between two rows of chained convicts.

"'Their foot shall slide in due time,'" the preacher read as Jeder leaned over the unsuspecting convict and raised the shotgun over his head.

"'For the day of their calamity is at hand, and the things that shall come upon them make haste.'"

Jeder brought the butt down abruptly below the base of the man's neck.

An instant later, Ben heard an explosion and instinctively fell forward along with everyone else wearing stripes. He turned and saw Jeder staring straight at him, a stain of crimson spreading across his upper body. Blood streamed from his neck. Part of the guard's face had been shot off by the shotgun he still held in his hand. He stared at Ben in disbelief.

"Goddammit, Jeder!" Warden Knox bellowed, overturning the chair as he jumped up. "I told you a thousand times to watch out . . ."

Jeder turned his gaze toward the warden. His mouth opened, but no words came out. A rivulet of red coursed from his lower lip and down his throat. Ben looked on as the guard's eyes rolled up into the back of his head and the gun fell from his hand to the ground. Prisoners scattered left and right, making way for his lifeless body, which fell face down onto the ground, stirring up a small cloud of dust. In that moment, Ben saw the man's spirit leave the body.

Knox's face turned red while he shouted orders at the prisoners and guards. Youmans stared open-mouthed at the scene unfolding before him. A cacophony of threats filled the afternoon air as guards forced the convicts to lie face down on the ground. Hoke and another guard pulled Jeder's body out of their midst.

"Put that son-of-a-bitch in the jack!" Knox ordered.

The guards dragged the prisoner Jeder struck to a device through which his arms and legs were stretched while he sat on a bench. A lever enclosed his wrists and ankles in the stocks, and the bench was pulled away, leaving him suspended in mid-air, his hands and feet protruding on the other side. He would hang there in excruciating pain for an hour before being released, where he would remain paralyzed on the ground for another half hour, until he slowly regained the use of his limbs.

"Sermon's over," the warden informed Youmans, who remained transfixed, unable to speak or move while the guards took their anger out on the convicts. He watched men in stripes stomped on, beaten, and kicked for no reason other than the fact that they were defenseless.

"Sam," Youmans said at last, turning to Warden Knox, "I know these men deserve to be here, but this right here, what your boys are doing, ain't right."

"Augustus," Knox replied, putting his hand on the preacher's shoulder and staring him down, "You leave the administration of Georgia's laws to me, and I'll leave the workings of God's law to you. Deal?"

Youmans looked at a man being kicked in front of him. He caught Ben's eye just as a black jack came down on him. Ben didn't flinch. In the short time he'd been incarcerated there, he had felt enough blows of a gunstock or a club to take them in stride. It was all that the preacher needed to know. What he witnessed was not an aberration. He looked at the Bible in his hand, then back at Ben.

"All right," he told the warden. "You're in charge here."

When they got to the gate, he turned and stared back at Knox, eye-to-eye and held up the Bible.

"But I swear by God that some people are gonna know what goes on out here."

Knox looked at the ground and kicked it with his foot. "They're gonna know what? That a prisoner grabbed Jeder's gun during a worship service and turned it on him? Hell, I got a dozen witnesses," he said, pointing at the guards. "They saw the whole thing. Besides, I know all about that woman up in McRae."

Youmans's face fell.

"How do you know about that?"

Knox smiled. "I got my sources. So you better watch what you tell folks. You just come out here once a month for an hour or so. Trust me, couple weeks in here, and you'd be doing the very same thing."

The warden held out his hand.

"Come on now, Augustus. No hard feelings. These boys are just doing their jobs. You don't know nothing about what it takes to keep these prisoners in line."

"I ain't seen that woman in over a year."

"And you ain't seen nothing out of the ordinary here today either," Knox replied. "I'll see you back here in a month. Okay?"

Youmans reluctantly took the warden's hand. "Yeah. See you next month."

CHAPTER 26

Geneva wore a faded calico dress and black pumps on her two-mile walk to the Cutler estate outside of Lamar. On her right arm, she carried a black purse. Inside the purse was the root Dr. Crow had given her, wrapped in a cotton napkin. The root hadn't left her side since she returned from Sapelo. To her, it held immense power, a power called upon by generations of African voodoo practitioners who passed along their knowledge by word of mouth to a chosen few. That power could only be released if the root was planted in the proper location.

The driveway from the main road wound through a forest before opening up to a ten acre pecan orchard. A brick bridge crossed a creek that led to a small lake on her right. Up ahead, the ambling two-story house sat in the shade of an oak with a wrap-around porch encircling three sides of the first story. Across from the house stood a barn that held Obediah's rusting Ford Model A pickup truck and a horse-drawn buggy. Between house and barn stood two towering pines joined at the trunk. The drive bent sharply beyond the tree and curved around to a newly-built garage behind the house.

The Cutler home rested on a series of brick pillars four feet high. Drawing closer, Geneva heard voices through an open window.

She eyed the diagonal crisscross pattern of wood strips extending from the porch to the ground. If, as Dr. Crow had instructed her, she was to bury the root under the front steps, she would have to find a way to get through the latticework.

"Damn it, Mama, the son-of-a-bitch is turning that highway to Hazlehurst. I know he is!" Geneva heard Clayborne say loudly.

The coming highway had become a topic of interest to the citizens of Lamar, and it was no secret that Clayborne was spearheading a group of prominent citizens bent on bringing a bigger commerce pipeline through the area.

"I don't like that language!" an elderly woman replied.

"Sorry, Mama. But you know what ol' Gene—the people's man, the poor dirt farmer's friend—did? He sat right there in front of the mayor, me, and the others, and swore all up and down that the highway was coming through Lamar."

Geneva tread softly, rounding the side of the house to the back where she couldn't hear the conversation anymore. On the far side of the home, she noticed a two foot wide opening in the latticework. To her right was a gravel parking area, on which sat a new Packard Sport Phaeton, a late model Ford pickup, and a Hudson motor car Clayborne had purchased a few years earlier. His idea of a vacation was to catch a train up north with Claudette, purchase a new car, and drive to Niagara Falls or some similar destination before making the long trip home. In contrast to his father, who bought only one automobile in his life, the Ford truck, Clayborne had purchased two cars since Obediah's death. He enjoyed stirring up the town by driving his shiny new vehicles into Lamar. Bets were placed about the make and model long before he arrived. Driving down through many states and hundreds of towns, he was keenly aware of the potential of automobile travel and the industries that might evolve around it. On his trip home with the Packard, thoughts of building motels and service stations to accommodate the influx of cars moving through central Georgia, took shape in his head. The further south he drove, the scarcer the motels and gas pumps became, but he knew that would change. The migration of autos would soon seep down to Georgia as well-to-do northerners sought warmer climes. Many would follow the new highway straight through Cutler Industries territory.

The only kink in Clayborne's plans was the man sitting in the governor's office who directed the paths of road projects with a flick of his pen.

Geneva turned the corner and followed a brick footpath leading to the back door. A garden plot filled with vegetables, herbs, and flowers took up a quarter of an acre behind the house. As she approached the rear entrance, she smelled fried bacon and freshly-brewed coffee through a screen door at the top of three wooden steps. She was relieved to see the backside had no covering beneath the house. Only a low row of holly bushes blocked the crawl space, but there was plenty of room for a slim woman like herself to slip in behind.

"Then I say," she heard Clayborne continue through the door, "'Governor, when Claudette has that baby, we're going to name him after you.'"

Clayborne's voice boomed down a hallway from an interior room.

"'It's all decided. If it's a boy, he'll be Eugene Cutler. If it's a girl, she'll be Genette.' He looked me in the eye, shook my hand, and said he would be proud to be the godfather. So Dyson Porter and I are all smiles as we're leaving. We think it's in the bag. But the mayor knows politicians like a dog knows ticks, and he's shaking his head like he's not so sure about it. He tells me he knows what it's like to look someone in the eye, tell them one thing, then turn around and do something else. Said he does it all the time."

Geneva looked down and saw a small trowel lying in a wicker

flower basket. Her heart began to pound as her gaze darted from the trowel to the crawl space. *Cain't plant dat root unner de fron' poach step*, she thought, *but dem back steps . . . dat sumtin' else.*

"So I go down the hall to the highway commissioner's office to speak to an old buddy of mine," Clayborne went on.

It was obvious to Geneva that no one had noticed her arrival.

"You remember Josh Mobley—I brought him home one semester—Josh shows me a map. That damn road is ten miles on the other side of the river. Then it goes blank until way south of here. So between here and the Florida border, it can go east or west or straight through Lamar. He told me even they don't know where it's going, which is probably the truth, but it sure as hell didn't show the highway coming through here! And there I was, just a few minutes before, nodding and bowing and saying, 'Yes, Governor. No, Governor'—just like Evelyn Barrow talks up to me. I may be a big man down here in Lamar, Mama, but up there, I'm just a damn secretary!"

"Keep your voice down," his mother said. "Don't you have a colored woman coming here to replace Millie?"

"Yes, Mama. Ben Jordan's sister. She's supposed to be here in a few minutes."

"Not that nigruh man who shot Pastor Dodge!"

"Yes, Mama. I'm helping them out."

"I don't want her in this house! You understand me?"

"Christ, Mama, you told me to replace Millie!"

"I don't care. You shouldn't have asked *her*! If she's got a brother that can shoot down a preacher in cold blood, there ain't no telling what she might do. She could burn the house down! And with your wife expecting . . . No. Turn her away."

"All right, Mama. Settle down. I'll take care of it."

Geneva thought her pounding heart would burst. God, Dr. Crow, or both had brought the elements together, placing her in the perfect spot at the perfect time to plant the root. She had hoped to plant it at her leisure as an employee of the household. Now, she saw her opportunity slipping away. Without hesitating, she grabbed the trowel and bent low under the crawl space, pausing a moment to let her eyes adjust to the dark. She knew that if a dog had been under the house, it would have already come out barking.

She reached between her legs, grabbed the back skirt hem, then pulled it to her belly and tucked it under her belt. Soon, she kneeled beneath the back door. The dirt under the house was bone dry and compact, but the recent rain had softened the ground beneath the steps. She dug quickly, keeping an ear out for the sound of Clayborne's voice. After digging a few inches, the trowel hit a piece of brick discarded during the home's construction. It made a distinct clinking sound. Geneva froze as she listened to the voices above.

The ranting continued, but she also heard footsteps approaching. They were lighter than a man's and swifter than an old woman's. She heard the screen door open. The footsteps paused right above her. Geneva peered through cracks and saw the outline of a woman descending the steps. The door slapped shut against the doorframe as the woman bent down and picked up the basket.

"God help me!" she said with a sigh. "Living with that woman . . ."

The woman was in her early twenties, with a model's face and long, dark hair tied into a ponytail with a white ribbon. She wore a red and white-checkered dress that revealed a shapely body and a stomach that protruded with child. She entered the garden while Geneva carefully placed the root into the hole in front of her and quietly covered it up. As she patted the dirt, Geneva looked up and saw the woman abruptly come to a halt and turn back toward the house, stopping at the foot of the steps.

"Clay!" she called through the screen door.

"Mama and I are talking!" came the reply.

"You're not talking. You're shouting, and it's giving me a headache!"

"What is it, Honey?"

"The trowel's missing."

"Well, I don't have it!"

"It was in the basket just a few minutes ago."

"Maybe you dropped it somewhere. Keep looking!"

"Thanks for nothing," Claudette said to herself as she turned away from the door and retraced her steps to the garden.

Geneva pressed down firmly on the ground one more time and backed further under the house. She recalled the opening in the latticework on the far side of the house and crawled toward it. It took her less than a minute to reach the opening, squeeze through the hole, and walk out onto the back part of the driveway. She rubbed her hands together to get the dirt off as best she could. Her dress, safely hiding soiled knees, was free of dirt. If anyone mentioned the smudges on her shoes, she would attribute it to the walk from town.

She pulled a handkerchief from her purse and daubed beads of perspiration from her face before rounding the back side of the house. Claudette searched for the missing tool along a row of squash while Geneva approached the back steps as if for the first time. She casually dropped the trowel onto a row of monkey grass bordering the path.

The voices inside the house grew louder. Geneva climbed the steps and knocked on the screen door. The voices didn't abate. She knocked again, this time a little harder.

"Are you here about the housework?" Claudette called out from the garden.

Geneva turned quickly, pretending to be startled by Claudette's sudden appearance.

"Yes, Ma'am," she replied, eyeing Claudette's belly.

"They can't hear you in there. Let me go and get Mister Cutler for you."

Geneva stepped down as Claudette set her basket on the path. She disappeared inside the house. A minute later, Clayborne returned alone. He stood on the top step, holding the screen door open.

"Hello . . ." he began, trying to recall her name.

Geneva," she replied.

"Geneva. Thanks for coming all the way out here. I didn't see you coming up the drive."

"Is dis a goot time, Missa Cutluh? I can cum back."

"No, no. Me and Mama are just having a little discussion. Only, the thing is, we can't use you right now. Something's come up."

"Oh," Geneva said, feigning ignorance of the conversation she'd overheard.

Clayborne reached for his wallet and pulled out two bills.

"Look," he said, "I want to help out with Ben's wife."

"No, Suh. She dead. She pass on 'fo he went off to de prison farm."

"Oh," he said. "Didn't know that."

"Ben don't know yet. I ain't tol' him. It too much all at one time fo him."

"He's got a little girl, doesn't he?"

"She up in Manhattan, New Yoke wiff my sisters. Dey tekkin' care of her."

"Then, here," he said, holding the bills out for Geneva. "Maybe you can use this."

Geneva looked at the money, but kept her hands latched onto her purse.

"Naw, Suh. I don't need nuthin' fo me. But I wuz wonderin' if you know de gov'ner."

Clayborne paused. "I do."

"I hear de gov'ner can let Ben outta dat camp, Missa Cutluh. He can write a note and get Ben release."

Clayborne looked away and coughed.

"Governor Talmadge? Pardon a negro prisoner with this election coming up?"

"Cain't you talk to him, Missa Cutluh, after de 'lection?"

Geneva's eyes momentarily strayed to the steps. In her mind, she saw the root buried beneath them. Clayborne stood over the spot where it lay dormant. Soon, it would come alive. Each day, as he crossed the steps, its power would grow.

Claudette had come to the door and saw Geneva look down. She interpreted it as a sign of dejection.

"Sure he can," she said, putting her hands on her husband's shoulders.

"Don't go making promises for me," Cutler snapped. "I can't even get Gene Talmadge to bring a highway through here."

Geneva raised her eyes and began to back away. "Okay, Missa Cutluh. I reckon I be goin' now."

"Hold on. Jacob, my yardman, will be around in a little while. He can give you a ride back to town."

"No, tank you, Missa Cutluh. I can walk."

"Clay. Give her the money!" Claudette said as Geneva turned to go.

"She won't take it."

Geneva bent down, and picked the trowel out of the monkey grass.

"You missin' dis?" she asked.

"That's it!" Claudette exclaimed.

"I told you you dropped it," Clayborne said. Claudette slapped him playfully on the arm.

"You always think you know everything."

"Maybe I do. I know I married the prettiest woman in the state of Georgia."

The two focused their attention on one another while Geneva retraced her steps and disappeared around the corner of the house. In their minds, she thought, she was already forgotten, the ghost of a memory at best.

But she wouldn't forget. Nor would the root she planted beneath the back steps.

CHAPTER 27

The day it poured rain down on Ben's chain gang was the last day they worked on the highway for months. Their work was redirected to the maintenance of lesser roads and railroad feeder lines in need of repair.

One stiflingly hot and humid morning, the crew's truck headed in the pre-dawn dark to a new worksite. In the back, Roos began to alternately imitate the warden and the preacher, Youmans, his antics once again partially illuminated by a truck following closely behind.

"You nigguhs listen up to what the preacher man telling you!" he said, using his warden voice.

"Yessuh, Boss. We a listenin! Amen, Boss!" came the replies from the other convicts.

"Now," Roos continued, adopting Youmans's persona, "the Lawd done put you pickaninnies down here to make us a road to heaven!"

In the cab of the truck, Bulldog used a flashlight to check his watch. Governor Talmadge was due to be in the area, barnstorming from one political stump speech to the next. Word was that he was resting at his home in McRae overnight, and would be in Lamar that day for a big rally. The whine of the engine and creaks and groans of the axles, drowned out the inmates' voices.

"You boys hear what the preacher say? You best listen up!" Roos said, imitating the warden to the delight of the others.

"We a listenin', Boss! Amen, Boss! Go ahead, preacher. Go ahead!"

"Thank you, Warden," Roos continued, shifting to his Youmans voice. "Now, like I was a-sayin', the good Lawd done put you here to build us roads just like your gran'pappy and your pappy was put here to pick us cotton!"

Howls of laughter filled the back of truck.

"Now, that there cotton gots to go to market! It can't be sittin' up in these here warehouses. So, the good Lawd done give you something more to do. You can pick that cotton and build a road to get it to market! You boys listening?"

"Yessuh, Boss! We a-listenin'! Amen, Boss!"

Ben unsuccessfully tried to stifle a laugh. Leroy puked his breakfast on the floor of the truck.

"Now, looky here, Leroy," Roos said, imitating the warden again. "That there food you done puked up is paid for by the good people of the state of Georgia!"

Leroy wiped his mouth and spat. He rubbed his right calf, swollen and bleeding from the constant irritation of metal on skin; "shackle poisoning" the convicts called it. Asking for medical attention or complaining about it would only get an inmate's skull busted.

"Sorry, Boss!" he said.

"Well, don't let that be happenin' no more. We don't cotton to no disrespectin' of the people's tax money. Seems to me you should be more grateful they givin' you a bed an' three meals a day! Now, enough 'bout that. Time fo you niggahs to sing me a hymn. Who got a song?"

After a moment's pause, a solemn voice rang out in the dark. A dozen other voices, including Ben's, soon joined in. It was a hymn he knew well.

Down in your soul you better get you humble,
Humble, humble, oh humble in my soul,
Stop and let me tell you 'bout Chapter One
The Lawd God's work has just begun
Stop and let me tell you 'bout Chapter Two
The Lawd, He let them mourners through
Stop and let me tell you 'bout Chapter Three
The Lawd, He set them pris'ners free!

The men shouted the last line with gusto. Spirituals were their only open expression of hope and defiance in the suffocating oppression of prison camp life.

Thirty minutes later, the truck crossed a bridge and came to a stop on the south side of the Ocmulgee River. When the trucks unloaded, Ben saw a chain gang comprised of white convicts file off the truck behind them. He looked around to get his bearings, and realized he stood next to the state road that went southeast to Lamar. Their job that day was to follow the white convicts who cut the tall grass with sling blades, and pick up bottles, tin cans, and other trash that had accumulated on the roadside. One of the white men in stripes did a double take at Ben as he passed by, but said nothing. To speak without permission would invite a reprisal from the guards overseeing them.

By mid-morning the crews had covered two miles of highway. Burlap litterbags the convicts carried required emptying every half a mile. Jeder's replacement, an acne-scarred man named Carson walked ahead of the crew. Bulldog followed closely behind with the butt of his shotgun resting on his hip.

Just before 10:30, sunlight reflecting from the bumper of a convertible with the top down, caught Ben's eye. He glanced up as the newly-polished Packard Sport Phaeton went by with Clayborne Cutler at the wheel. He drove at a good clip toward the bridge crossing over the river. Three other men were in the car with him.

"Ooh, Jesus," Roos whispered. "That there one mighty fine automobile."

Ben said nothing. He picked up a rusted can and dropped it in his sack.

"Lay 'em down!" Bulldog called out an hour later.

His words were echoed by one of the guards overseeing the white crew. Twenty burlap sacks and twenty sling blades hit the ground simultaneously. Ben's crew sat down to eat lunch in the shade of the tree line that paralleled the road. The white convicts settled in ten feet behind them. Bulldog stood on the road facing them, his gun at the ready. Carson stood behind the two chain gangs while the remaining guards ate.

Roos smiled as he finished his beans and cornbread.

"Damn. They must think someone fixin' to escape," he said, settling back in the tall grass for a nap. He pulled his cotton cap down over his face.

Ben was still eating when a pebble fell in front of him. A few moments later, another one hit him lightly on the back.

"Hey," said a voice from behind.

Ben glanced at a white convict with cropped red hair.

"Remember me?" the man said.

Ben turned for a better look.

"Naw, Suh. I 'fraid I don't."

The man patted himself on the chest with both hands. "It's me. Billy. Remember? From the river? You helped me across in your canoe!"

The man Ben looked at seemed a mere shadow of the confident shyster he had helped escape from the posse hot on his trail. His face was sunburned and gaunt, but the same mischievous grin and spark of roguish adventure remained in his eyes.

"Yessuh, I 'member you," Ben said. "You wuz headin' fo de swamp."

"And you were taking your cousin's body downriver. Did you make it home?"

"Yessuh, I did. Got him buried decent."

Billy smiled broadly. "Well, I made it to the Okefenokee. But then, like a damn fool, I had to come out. They caught me not too far from here. I should have never left the swamp."

The men sitting near Billy chuckled. Ben thought to himself for the umpteenth time that he should have never left Sapelo.

"Did you see de Devil?" Ben asked.

"No," Billy replied. "Never once saw him in the swamp. But I know for a fact that he is disguised as the warden of the prison camp I now call home."

Both whites and blacks snickered at hearing this and glanced nervously at the guards to make sure they hadn't been overheard.

"Son of a bitch beats us like rented mules, which, in fact, is what we are."

"Cain't be no worser than what we got," Roos said from beneath his cap.

"They sent you away fo gamblin'?" Ben asked.

"Not for gambling," Billy replied. "Remember that posse that was after me?"

"I 'member."

"One of them was a little peckerhead named Sonny."

"I 'members him. He tried to drown me affer you got away. I seen him cross de river wiff he dog."

"Well, I never saw him after that, but he must have found out where I was going. They found him dead on the edge of the swamp, half eaten. That's why I'm wearing stripes. They said I killed him and tossed him to the gators. I got into a poker game at a house near Homerville. Someone must have recognized me from a poster. Next thing I know, I'm in the hoosegow with my head split open."

Billy leaned forward and revealed a four-inch scar on his scalp.

"I told you you should have gone out to Texas," said the white man chained to him. "You would have cleaned up there."

"Anyway," Billy said, returning his attention to Ben, "here I am, and here you are. What did they accuse you of?"

"Dey say I shot a man."

"Did you?"

"Naw, Suh. I ain't never kilt no one."

"Do you know who did it?"

There was a long pause as those within listening distance went quiet, waiting for Ben's response. Before he could answer, their attention was drawn to the sound of tires on the highway approaching from the bridge. All eyes turned toward the road.

Bulldog looked in the direction of the car and squinted.

"It's him, boys!" he called out to the guards who were eating. They sprang to their feet and circled the convicts with shotguns at the ready.

The shiny Packard soon came into view, followed by a black Buick. The whine of the tires diminished as the cars slowed to a halt. Clayborne was still at the wheel. This time, there were four men in the car with him. The one sitting directly behind Cutler wore a white seersucker suit. When Clayborne brought his auto to a stop, the man stood up. A pair of red suspenders flashed for an instant beneath his coat. His dark yellow-brown face was thin and boyish, but his eyes projected an intensity that attracted those looking at him. His head, more rectangular than oval, seemed too large for such a wiry body. Combined with long, thin lips that created a slit for a mouth when closed, the casual observer might mistake him for a life-sized puppet, but there was no mistaking that this was a man used to giving orders and having others defer to him.

"How you doing?" he said, extending his hand to Hoke.

"Just fine, Governor," Bulldog replied. "How about you?"

"Can't complain. I've been on this road all morning. You and your men are doing a fine job keeping our highways maintained. Without you, this state would shut down in about six months. Ain't that right, boys?" Talmadge said to the men in the car.

"That's right, Gene," the men replied in unison, nodding their heads.

Ben noticed that Clayborne didn't speak up. He had been scanning the men in stripes for a familiar face. When he saw Ben, their eyes locked.

"Who's running your camp?" the governor asked. "Warden Knox, Sir," Bulldog answered.

"Sam Knox. I know Sam. He's a damn good man, ain't he, fellas?"

"Damn good!"

"You tell him ol' Gene says hello."

"I'll do that, Governor."

"Can I count on you and these other guards voting for me come election day?"

"You sure can, Governor!"

"Well, all right," Talmadge said. He sat down and waved. Clayborne released the clutch and sped away.

All eyes watched the cars until they were out of site. Several guards huddled around Bulldog, who feigned nonchalance at having spoken one-on-one with Governor Talmadge.

"Well, well, well," Billy said at length. "So that's what the governor of the state of Georgia looks like. Do you know that, with one stroke of his pen, he can pardon a man for any crime? You could be wearing stripes in the morning and eating a big, juicy steak in the nicest restaurant in Atlanta by evening."

The white convicts speculated on the first meal they would eat once they got out of the prison camp. Ben thought about his favorite foods, too.

I miss rice, he thought. *Could live on beans and rice. Saundra couldn't never cook rice right, bless her.* He smiled. *She liff de lid to check on it. Rice don't like dat. It like to simmer 'bout a hour, den it ready to cum out de pot.*

The whites continued to talk among themselves while the blacks remained quiet.

Roos hadn't raised up once during the entire exchange between Bulldog and the governor, but he had been observing from beneath the brim of his cap.

"Hey," he said softly to Ben, "that white man at the wheel was looking at you."

Ben said nothing.

"Who he is?"

Ben shrugged. "He just a man."

"He could spring you outta this place. He know the gov'na."

Clayborne had looked tired to Ben. He couldn't put his finger on exactly what it was, but the glow he once recalled seeing in Cutler's face was gone.

"He just a man," he repeated.

CHAPTER 28

Clayborne remained quiet and moody on the drive to Lamar. Fiery daggers of guilt and shame penetrated his heart the moment his eyes met Ben's. He'd driven by many a chain gang since Ben's incarceration and never once looked at them on the chance one would be the man he sent away. This day, he'd broken that rule.

Under his seat was a pistol. He had sworn to Evelyn that he would shoot the governor if he reneged on the highway deal. The more Talmadge, Mayor Reynolds, Dyson Porter, and Tremont Rogers bantered in the car, the more sullen he became, replaying the last several hours in his head.

Clayborne and the entourage from Lamar had waited for more than an hour at the bridge for Talmadge to arrive. The governor, known for stopping to talk with farmers on his travels, infuriated members of local courthouse gangs by arriving late for their well-planned political rallies. His timing was calculated to build anticipation in the crowds that waited breathlessly for the spectacle to begin. Most of the people who flooded into Lamar that day traveled from other counties by car and horseback. To Talmadge, it was theater—the voters were his adoring audience, the speaker's stand, his stage. He was the leading man who had long ago perfected the art of the grand entrance.

Cutler had overseen the committee that planned the fish fry preceding the rally. Letters and phone calls went out to solicit volunteers three weeks in advance. A committee headed by Claudette was established to procure food consisting of 5,000 pounds of fried fish, 100 gallons of sweet pickles, and 50 barrels of tea. Another committee was set up to construct a speaker's platform and long, high tables at which people could stand and eat. The wood was donated by Cutler Land & Lumber. The police chief secured additional officers from surrounding communities to assist with traffic control. Lamar's high school marching band drilled for two weeks in the summer heat, rehearsing the governor's grand entrance. Mayor Tom Reynolds, envisioning a possible position in the governor's next administration, practiced his introductory speech in front of a mirror at night.

The event was originally scheduled to take place inside the high school gymnasium, but crowd estimates swelled a few days prior to Talmadge's arrival. People had begun to arrive in Lamar by Thursday, finding a place to sleep with relatives, at the Lamar Inn, or camping on the outskirts of town. A speaker's platform was built beneath a stand of oak trees adjacent to the high school football field. The grand entrance would have to change, forcing Doug Ballard, the band instructor, to reconfigure the route the marching band would take.

When the governor's Buick sedan finally arrived at the Altamaha River, Clayborne was urinating from the bridge. He had purposely waited until Talmadge's car came into view before unzipping his pants. It was his way of saying what he thought about the governor making him, Mayor Reynolds, Porter, and Tremont wait in the broiling sun.

A pickup truck rolled to a stop behind the Buick. Inside were three men in overalls with deep-tanned faces from the forehead down. They looked like hard scrabble farmers—just the kind of voter the governor wanted to attract. Their steadfast gazes followed the governor's every move.

"Damn, Cutler," Talmadge said, grinning when he stepped from the sedan, "I didn't build this bridge so you could have a personal lavatory."

The men in the truck thought it was the funniest thing they had ever heard. Clayborne smiled.

"Sorry, Governor. I'm just a little excited about the rally this afternoon. You're going to sweep every county around here after today is done."

"That's what I want to hear," the governor replied as he shook hands with Mayor Reynolds, Porter, and Tremont. "Okay, boys," the governor said to the men in the truck, "you know what to do."

The truck sped away and disappeared down the road as Talmadge climbed into the back of Clayborne's car. They followed in the truck's wake with the Buick following close behind them. A few miles later, the governor tapped Clayborne on the shoulder and told him to pull over so he could talk with the guard overseeing the chain gangs. This only further infuriated Clayborne, who saw his plans for a well-organized rally being thwarted by the governor's delays. But to Talmadge, the guards represented voters who would tell their friends and relatives that the governor of Georgia took time from his busy schedule to talk to constituents. His popularity resided with the common man, the dirt farmer, the laborers with grease and soil under their fingernails. His power came not from a state legislature that thwarted his efforts, but from the government agencies he ruled with a despot's hand, agencies whose control he had wrested by any means possible.

Clayborne listened while Talmadge related anecdotes about past political contests and spoke about issues of the day, including his growing animosity toward President Roosevelt's New Deal policies that included educational opportunities for blacks. In his mind, he replayed the moments he and Ben Jordan had looked at one another. He could only hold Ben's gaze for a few seconds before turning away. He made a mental note to send some money to Ben's sister, whose name he had already forgotten. Evelyn could look it up for him. She wouldn't take it from his hand, but she might not be so picky receiving cash through the US mail.

"Governor," Porter said as they sped down the highway to Lamar, "them folks in Atlanta are raising a big fuss about those hogs you sold. Even people in Lamar are starting to talk about it. What are you going to tell them?"

Talmadge grinned broadly and leaned back against the seat. He had purchased eighty-two boxcar loads of hogs for the state and sold them to Chicago meat packing plants without proper authorization. The deal lost money, and his political rivals were using it, along with accusations of nepotism, funneling state monies to secret bank accounts, and various other charges, to build their case for his impeachment.

"I'm not sure what I'm going to say," he replied.

"You could say you made a mistake," Mayor Reynolds offered. "These folks around here will understand."

The governor frowned at the suggestion.

"Tom," he said, "that's why you won't ever be governor. You will admit your mistakes. I never do. I *know* the dirt farmer. Hell, I was one. He understands what it is to get beaten down but keep on getting back up. You got to take a negative and make it a positive. They hung Jesus on a cross. Now, the cross is the symbol of salvation. Can you imagine using the electric chair as a religious symbol? Take that Liberty Bell. The damn thing is a useless hunk of metal, but it is our symbol of freedom. So, I just got to sit here and figure out a way to turn that sow's ear into a silk purse. And I still got about a half hour to do it. So, y'all let me think it over for a bit."

Ten minutes later, when it appeared that the governor had dozed off, he reached out and tapped the mayor on the leg.

"You know what? I think I'll take your advice. I will admit I did wrong, at least partially."

Clayborne sat stewing in the front seat. The governor hadn't broached the one subject that was the sole reason for all the time and expense he and his colleagues had invested in the day's event.

"Governor Talmadge," he said at length, "how's that new highway coming?"

The car went silent. Mayor Reynolds, Porter, and Tremont bristled as the words were spoken. They knew, and the governor knew, what the political rally was really all about. If the Lamar event went well, and if Talmadge won the election, the town might be rewarded by being part of the newest north-south artery connecting Florida to points north. With one sentence, they feared, Clayborne may have squelched the deal beyond repair.

"Highway's coming along just fine," Talmadge replied without batting an eyelash. "Almost got everything from the Tennessee line to the Altamaha done and most of the links from Florida up to Waycross."

What he didn't say was if the final link would bend the highway around Lamar or through it.

"Say, Clayborne," said the governor, tapping Cutler on the shoulder, "pull this car over to the shoulder. I need to talk to you."

The mayor, Porter, and Tremont watched nervously as the governor and Clayborne got out and walked on ahead. The Buick with the governor's driver pulled to as stop behind them.

"Son of a bitch," Dyson Porter said when they got out of hearing distance. "There goes the highway."

The mayor rubbed his face with both hands. "Clay just said what we're all thinking, but personally, I wish he'd kept his big mouth shut."

As president of the local business owner's association trying to attract industry to the area, it would be Porter's unpleasant task to inform the other members that their hopes and dreams for becoming a hub of commerce had been dashed on the outskirts of town on the very cusp of victory.

The men watched as Talmadge and Cutler came to a halt a few hundred feet away. Ahead of them, the undulating black top presented the illusion of standing water in the road. The two turned and began walking back toward the cars. This time, it appeared that Clayborne was doing most of the talking.

"I can't watch," Porter said, popping a seltzer tablet in his mouth.

"I don't know," Mayor Reynolds replied. "Gene's got his hand on Clay's shoulder. That's a good sign."

"Well, I'll be damned," Tremont said, watching as the governor and Clayborne appeared to be treading on top of the mirage. "Some of these folks around here think ol' Gene Talmadge can walk on water. Well, I got proof."

When Clayborne and the governor got back in the car, neither man's countenance seemed to have changed.

"Well, Governor, we still having this rally?" the mayor asked cheerily. Inside, he expected the worst. Talmadge eased into the back seat of Cutler's Packard. His smile and chipper demeanor was that of a seasoned politician who had learned not to let his face betray the doubt that overwhelmed his thoughts.

"Hell, yes!" Talmadge replied, poking Clayborne on the shoulder. "Let's get going!"

Cutler hit the gas. They soon left the state highway and made the final southwest leg of the trip on a county road that connected Lamar to the outside world. It was a road traveled mostly by locals, logging trucks, and the occasional salesman.

A mile outside of town, Police Chief Hawkins was waiting in his squad car as prearranged. When he saw Cutler's Packard, he turned on the siren and sped out in front of the oncoming cars. A few minutes later, people eating at the food tables heard the siren's wail in the distance. The silence, which pervaded the otherwise festive atmosphere, was broken by the announcement coming from the speaker's platform sound system that the governor was en route.

All eyes strained toward the parking area as the siren grew in intensity. Soon, another siren could be heard. A minute later, Police Chief Hawkins's vehicle came into view, followed by the red Packard, the governor's Buick, then another squad car. The high school band struck up a rousing version of Dixie as the first car came to a screeching halt with the others close behind. A cloud of dust filled the air, momentarily obliterating the cars from view. A few moments later, it blew past the automobiles and revealed a man in a white suit standing on the back seat of the Packard, waving enthusiastically.

A cheer erupted from the crowd as Talmadge hopped down from the car and stepped up onto a cart pulled by two mules and driven by a white haired farmer. The marching band entered the shade of the rally grounds two-by-two and followed a wide alley set between the tables that led to the speaker's stand. The cart followed closely behind with the governor waving and shaking hands along the way. Dirt-poor farmers, barely able to afford the annual three-dollar car tag fee, stuffed dollar bills into the governor's coat pockets.

Clayborne and the Lamar entourage followed on foot behind the cart, watching Talmadge work the crowd like an emperor returning from a foreign conquest.

"Christ!" Porter shouted above the din, "you'd think it was the second coming."

Ahead of the cart, Chief Hawkins and two policemen tried to clear a path as people filled the void behind the last members of the marching band.

"Keep a clear o' them wheels!" the farmer barked when women and children stepped too close to the cart.

Clayborne and his companions held onto the back of the wagon. The crowd pressed in on them, each person eager to touch the governor or shove a dollar bill into his pocket.

"What did he tell you?" the mayor asked Clayborne. "Do we have the road or not?"

Clayborne's expression didn't change.

"You'll see," he answered.

After several more minutes of mayhem, the cart came to a rest next to the stand where Talmadge stepped down and was greeted by a very pregnant Claudette Clayborne. Much to the governor's delight, she reassured him that their child would be named in his honor.

When Talmadge bounded up the short flight of steps, a deafening cheer erupted. Mayor Reynolds, red-faced from the sheer exhilaration of the moment and grinning broadly, followed closely on his heels, eager to bask in the reflective glow of the governor's popularity.

The cheering continued full throttle for five minutes. At length, Talmadge sat down in an attempt to quiet the crowd. Twice, the mayor approached the microphone to begin his introduction, and twice, his voice was drowned out by masses of farmers who had come to see one of their own who had "done good."

Clayborne, Porter, and Tremont sat in their designated places on the speaker's stand along with the other local dignitaries. The onlookers politely endured the mayor's well-rehearsed introduction, but a discernable electric buzz emanated from the crowd. They wanted to hear only one voice that day. The "voice of the people" sat behind the mayor, smiling, nodding appreciatively, and occasionally waving to his constituents.

When the mayor's introductions ended, the governor stood to another ovation that lasted three minutes.

"It's kind of hot out here," Talmadge said after the cheering subsided. "Y'all mind if I take my coat off?"

Three dignitaries reached up to help as he removed the seersucker coat. His red suspenders had become a symbol of the workingman—the rural farmers who saw themselves as unjustly ruled for decades by an urban elite. When the people saw his suspenders, they burst into another round of deafening applause.

"Chief Hawkins," he said, talking into the microphone and turning to face the police chief, "can you give us an estimate of the size of this crowd today?"

Clayborne noticed that the governor's dialect had changed considerably between the bridge and the rally site. He had been Phi Beta Kappa in college and could hold his own in the salons of Atlanta and Washington, but in rural Georgia, his vowels were stretched much longer than usual. His tone became more nasal the further from Atlanta he traveled.

"I estimate the size of this crowd to be around five thousand people," Hawkins replied.

Talmadge smiled and looked out at the horde before him.

"Well, that's got to be some kind of record 'round these here parts, ain't it?" he asked the police chief.

"I would definitely say we have set a record today, Governor."

More applause.

"Seems I recall from the Bible something about Jesus and his disciples feeding fish to five thousand," Talmadge replied with a coy smile.

Members of the crowd nodded in approval and congratulated one another for having been part of a history-making event, another trick Talmadge had learned. They had been well fed, stirred by his entrance and the marching band, and were part of a record-setting rally. All of that was just a prelude to the performance the seasoned entertainer was about to unleash.

"Well, I ain't exactly Jesus Christ, our Savior, but I sometimes feel like Him taking on them big-wig money-changers up there in Atlanta and Washington!"

Another burst of applause erupted. Clayborne glanced at the mayor who shook his head in collegial appreciation of the governor's moxie.

Talmadge thanked the other dignitaries on the stage and then asked the mayor, Porter, Tremont, and Clayborne to rise.

"Folks," the governor said, extending his hand in their direction, "these fellas have been working mighty hard to get a road to come through this town and this county."

The mayor, Porter, and Tremont held their breaths. The moment of truth was at hand.

"Well, I'm proud to announce that the newest north-south highway connecting Florida to the Midwest and the Northeast is coming right through downtown Lamar!"

Mayor Reynolds was the first to pump the governor's hand in appreciation. The crowd erupted into yet another round of cheers and whistles. Dyson Porter knew that his position as a community leader had just been solidified. Tremont Rogers realized that his land purchases for establishing motels with restaurants and filling stations up and down the highway would make himself, Clayborne, and Cutler Industries very wealthy. The only thought going through Clayborne's mind was that he wouldn't have to use the loaded gun under his car seat on the governor that day.

Talmadge could have left the podium there and then with every vote in the county secured, but election-day was a long way off, and he knew that the stump speech he would give in Tifton, Valdosta, and Moultrie later that week would have to be well-honed for other crowds. When the jubilant cheers subsided, he turned his attention to a tried-and-true speech formula perfected in the pulpits of evangelists across the Deep South. Instead of sin and the devil, Talmadge aimed his sights on big government, taxes, and elitists in the state and national capitols who knew nothing of the workingman's struggles. The governor railed for twenty minutes against the injustices perpetrated on rural Georgians. Before he had finished, the crowd was ready to tar anyone from the big cities, including his opponent. The second part of his speech, like those of Billy Sunday and other evangelists, would be one of hope. There was a way out. There was one way to salvation. For the dirt farmer, the route to deliverance from his earthly condition was through Eugene Talmadge.

"Friends," he said, pulling on his suspenders, "I admit that I'm no saint, but I do feel it is my sacred duty to fight for justice for every man and woman in the state of Georgia, and that includes every one of you. I can't clean up the capitol unless you send me back up there. You think the Pharisees messed things up back in the days of Jesus Christ, our Lord? You should see some of the shenanigans going on up in Atlanta. They make them folks in Jesus's day look like Boy Scouts!"

"We're on your side, Gene!" someone shouted.

It was one of the men who had followed Talmadge to the bridge in the pickup truck.

"Thank you, friend," the governor replied. "It sure gets lonely up there at the capitol. Sometimes, I feel like it's just me against them entrenched bankers, lawyers, and politicians. I feel like David when he was being hunted down by Saul and his men. Now, Saul ain't alive these days, but . . . you folks ever heard of Franklin Delano Roosevelt?"

The people responded with boos and taunts for the sitting president.

"What about the negroes?" someone yelled. Clayborne recognized him as another of the men from the truck. He and the other two were strategically placed in the crowd where they could prompt the governor on topics he wanted to discuss.

"I'm a-comin' to that, Brother," the governor said. "I just wish I could take each and every one of you up there to see what I have to put up with each day—just to see to it that you get a fair shake. Ain't nobody else doing it. There ain't one single banker up there looking out for you. There ain't one single lawyer up there looking out for your interests. There's just me, friends."

He pulled a red bandana from his back pocket, which drew more cheers, and wiped his neck and brow as if he momentarily stopped working in a field for a moment of respite.

"I know what it's like to pour plow dirt out of my boots, friends. I know what it's like to come inside the house at the end of the day beat down by the sun, clothes saturated with sweat, neck blistered, hands callused. I know what it's like to sit on the back porch and watch the sky for signs of rain. I know what it's like to kneel down by my bed at night and pray that the crop will come in so's I can pay off the bank loan. Friends, the poor dirt farmer ain't got but three friends on this earth: God Almighty, Sears Roebuck, and Gene Talmadge!"

This comment was met with thunderous applause.

"They say you stole them hogs!" one of his prompters called out after the cheers died down.

Everyone in the crowd knew about the hog debacle. The mayor glanced at Clayborne and Porter. This was the governor's big moment. His answer would be recorded by reporters sitting near the stage, and printed in papers across Georgia the next morning.

"What?" the governor asked, making sure everyone heard the question.

"They say you stole!" his man shouted even louder.

The smile on Talmadge's face disappeared. He turned away from the crowd for just a moment. In that moment, Clayborne saw his face transform from dark brown to a beet red. His nostrils flared and his eyes bulged. The governor hunched his shoulders and clenched both his fists. His limbs stiffened as he turned back toward the crowd. A few women gasped at the change in the governor's appearance.

"They say I stole!" Talmadge bellowed, spitting the words like machine gun bullets. He stared at the man who spoke and extended his right arm, pointing at him. The Atlanta reporter's hand quivered as he poised the pen over his writing pad. Talmadge's career dangled in the balance of the silence that hung over the five thousand.

"Sure I stole!" he said at last with a hint of sarcasm, pausing only a second to let the words sink in. "But I stole for you!"

Clayborne felt the vibration of the crowd's spontaneous roar through the pine boards at his feet.

"And you! And you! And you!" the governor howled, pointing at people in the crowd.

The ensuing cheers drowned the governor's words even though he shouted into the microphone. He turned to Mayor Reynolds.

"Genius son-of-a-bitch!" the mayor yelled, in disbelief and admiration, though no one could hear him.

Talmadge winked at him.

"That's why I'm governor and you're not!" he mouthed.

Clayborne looked at Tremont and shook his head. How the dirt farmer benefited by the governor's bungling of financial deals and hidden bank accounts wasn't something they dwelled upon. One of their own was in high office, sticking it to the fat cats and big wigs, and that's all that mattered to them. The governor was indeed correct when he said he understood the workingman's mind.

A few in the crowd acted out their rage at unseen enemies the governor had conjured up in their minds by attacking his prompter. Two policemen intervened and escorted him behind the stage. The governor saw this and made a mental note to pay the man extra for the jostling he took.

He spoke for another fifteen minutes, this time, comparing himself to Daniel in the lion's den, surrounded by ravenous politicians and a federal government increasingly bent on intruding into the lives of its citizens. One issue, the integration of blacks into white society, had become a poisonous topic south of the Mason-Dixon Line. As he spoke, one of his prompter's called out again.

"Hey Gene, what about the negroes?"

Each time, the governor had replied, "Friend, I'm a comin' to that." And each time, he proceeded to rail against taxes and a growing government bureaucracy. When he was done, he summarized his argument for another term, and made his final plea for the crowd's votes. The final applause was enthusiastic as he waved and pretended to make an exit.

One of the men planted in the audience shouted out and waved his arms. Talmadge, feigning puzzlement, sidled back up to the microphone and asked the crowd to be silent.

"I believe this fella has a question," he said.

"Gene! What about the negroes?" the prompter asked one last time.

Clayborne watched as Talmadge morphed once again from the Dr. Jekyll of platitudes into the raging, self-righteousness Mr. Hyde.

"Before God, Friend," he replied with well-rehearsed outrage, "the nigguhs will never go to a white school while I am governor!"

Clayborne thought the stage would collapse from the roar of approval surging from the crowd. The entire speech had led up to that moment. It was a pivot point designed to please the crowd, and it never failed. The governor raised his arms in victory, shook hands with the dignitaries, then assumed his place on the cart again. The marching band could hardly be heard above the din as people fervently pressed in, each person trying to touch the governor and put more money in his pockets.

Ten minutes later, the Buick pulled out of the parking lot behind the siren of the police chief's car. The three audience baiters climbed into their truck and headed to the next rally. Mayor Reynolds and Dyson Porter were nowhere to be seen. Clayborne and Tremont sat on the stage, watching the spectacle wind down from a vantage point above the fray.

"Well, Clay," Tremont said as the crowd slowly dispersed, "what did ol' Gene tell you on that little walk y'all took?"

Clayborne smiled. "You'll never believe it, Tree. First, he tells me not to worry. The highway is a done deal, though it's going to be asphalt, not concrete due to costs. Then, he starts telling me about his son."

"Herman?"

"Yeah. 'Hummon,' as he calls him. He said, 'Clay, you know my son, Hummon, is attending the university. Seems like I got to send someone over to Athens pretty regular to take care of some sort of mischief he's got himself into. He's a good boy, just a little rambunctious. Now, I know it wasn't too long ago that you were in college. You know what's going on in an undergrad's mind. I can't talk any sense into him, but I was hoping you could have a word.'"

"The governor asked you to talk to his son?" Tremont said. "He's running this state, and he's asking you to talk to his boy?"

Clayborne nodded. "Yep. He knows Daddy had to bail me out a few times when I was going to school up there. He's got big plans for Herman, and he doesn't want the kid sabotaging any political opportunities he might have once he graduates."

"What did you tell him?"

"I told him I'd be happy to talk to his son."

"And what are you going to tell 'Hummon'?"

"I'm going to tell him to get his head out of his ass and straighten up, that's what I'm going to tell him! This highway isn't finished yet. If Talmadge doesn't get reelected, Charmichael or Rivers could kill the whole project. I'm going to tell 'Hummon' to clean up his act until his dad's back in office. After that, he can do whatever the hell he likes."

He didn't tell his business partner the other conversation he had with the governor, which kept replaying in his mind.

"Governor," he had said, "there's a man on that chain gang back there named Ben Jordan who was convicted for something he didn't do. What do I have to do to get him paroled?"

"You're not talking about that preacher killer?" the governor had responded. A near photographic memory gave him the ability to recall names and past events.

"Yep. He didn't do it. The real murderer is still out here somewhere."

"I can't touch that one, Clay. I got nothing against black folks. Hell, I broke bread with my negro field hands at the lunch table each day when I was farming. But I can't be letting one out of a prison camp, especially someone accused of shooting a white preacher. You know that. Never give your political opponents bullets to use against you. If I paroled him, it'd be handing my enemies a stick of dynamite."

Cutler's dismay over the answer was apparent. Talmadge put his hand on his shoulder.

"Tell you what, Clay. We're replacing that old prison in Reidsville with a brand new state pen. You call my office in Atlanta. Ask for my secretary. Give her Jordan's name, and I'll see that he gets out of the prison camp. We can put him in the old prison 'til the new one is up and running."

CHAPTER 29

That night as Clayborne sat down to dinner, Ben lay stretched on a bench having his back laid open by the warden's strap. Hoke had fingered him again, this time, for conversing with a white prisoner from another chain gang. The beating was severe enough to warrant Ben's remaining chained to his cot the following day while his wounds healed. Geneva had finally written to tell Ben that Saundra died. The letter was opened as usual, and the money his sister enclosed was missing. He spent the better part of an afternoon contemplating a way out.

That evening, Roos recounted the day's events to him. Their chain gang had been assigned to dig the muck from a water main break in a nearby town.

"You know why a manhole cover is round?" he asked. "It 'cause a round plate can't fall through a round hole. A square plate can fall through a square hole. See what I'm sayin?"

Ben saw. He saw for the first time, a glimmer of hope for his escape. A five-minute head start and being free of chains would be the key to freedom. As it stood, he was hobbled by twenty pounds of chain weight. He couldn't take full strides while bound by them, and he would be easily spotted even if he managed to change clothes.

It was a problem Ben had been turning over in his mind since arriving at the camp. The Jordan family prided themselves on being educated and having the ability to think, a trait handed down by Bu-Allah to his children and their descendants. The warden and his guards could beat his body, but they could never touch his soul or his thoughts, which now turned ever more to freedom.

The problem he had struggled with was how to slip his feet through the round ankle rings. Roos had unknowingly presented him with the answer. If the ankle rings were somehow warped into a rectangular shape, Ben intuitively knew he could pull his feet through them. With a forty-year sentence, he saw no light at the end of the tunnel. The daily misery he endured was indeed a sentence worse than death. He knew how he would be freed of his immediate bondage. Now, it was just a matter of time for the opportunity to present itself.

Two days later, the truck carrying his crew drove in a vaguely familiar direction. When daylight finally broke, he realized that they were back at work on the new highway.

"Let's go! Let's go!" Bulldog barked, pounding on the side of the truck with his cudgel.

After two days of grading, the crew had worked its way to the forty-five degree turn the road took toward the west.

Two days and two miles later, the road bent sharply back east.

"It going to Baxley," Roos whispered to Ben. "This road headin' straight to Baxley. You mark my words."

Lamar and Baxley, Ben thought. *But it got to go through Lamar first.*

Ben kept his head down and said nothing. He could only guess what had transpired between Clayborne and Governor Talmadge, but he was confident that seeing the two together had something to do with work resuming on the project and the road's turn back toward Lamar.

Ahead of him, a new convict named Titus expertly wielded a pickax. He was tall, in his mid-twenties with arms thick as small pines. His tool hit the ground with the force of a small explosive, spreading debris further and wider than anyone else's. "Wait on the Lord," Reverend Douglas had preached at his church in Lamar. "The Lord will deliver you in His time, not yours!"

Ben kept his eye on Titus, knowing full well that it might be many months before the right moment presented itself. As it turned out, his opportunity for escape came later that evening.

"Any of you sons of bitches know how to swing a sledge-hammer?" Warden Knox asked as the men ate their evening supper in silence.

Titus and another man raised their hands. The warden questioned them about their work experience. Both claimed to have worked on railroads, which seemed to please him.

"Write their names down," he instructed Hoke.

"Any of you ever done any tree logging?" Knox asked the men.

Twelve convicts, including Ben, raised their hands.

"Don't raise your hand if you ain't never done no logging," he admonished. "If you get out there, and it turns out you don't know what you're doing, I'm gonna make you wish you ain't never been born."

Five arms went down. Knox questioned each of the remaining seven. Ben was the last.

"Where you done logging?" he asked. "Lamar," Ben answered.

"Who you work for around Lamar?"

"Missa Cutler."

The warden's eyes widened.

"Obediah Cutler?"

"His son was the one driving the governor last week," Bulldog said.

"You worked on one of Cutler's logging crews?"

Knox asked Ben. "Yessuh."

Knox stared him down for several moments. Ben no longer feared the warden's strap. What he feared more was missing out on what he sensed to be an opportunity that might not come around again for a long time. He waited as Knox looked at the list and counted the names Bulldog had written down.

"All right," he said, "put his name down, too."

That night as the other men slept soundly, Ben stared at the ceiling. He no longer looked at the windows where Mongo, Jeder, and the spirits of other dead men stood, their forlorn faces close to the glass.

A few hours after lights out, Ben felt Roos's finger poking his shoulder.

"I know where you can go," Roos whispered, "if you get out."

Ben turned his head and looked at his friend.

"Get out?"

"You thinking 'bout escaping. I seen your face after the warden put your name down. Mongo had that same look."

"Ever'body tink 'bout 'scaping," Ben replied. "Where you planning to go?"

"Home, I reckon."

"That island? The law will be waiting for you there.

All up and down the river, too."

"I gots nowhere else to go. Cain't go back to Lamar."

"Ain't you got family up north?"

Ben, in fact, had been toying with the idea of going to the Okefenokee like Billy Waters had done, even if it was the mother of all swamps and even if the Devil himself lived there.

"I gots sisters up north," he said. "How I'm gonna get way up dere?"

Roos surveyed the bunks around him to make sure the other men were sleeping.

"You know that train bridge over to Lumber City?"

Ben was familiar with the trestle that spanned the Ocmulgee River there. Traffic in the town's center, located close to the river-bank, often caused passing trains to slow down.

"Them freight trains have to ease through Lumber City," Roos told him. "I seen 'em crawling through there sometimes. See what I'm sayin'? You camp out by the bridge and jump on one of them northbound trains. But watch out for train bulls."

"What dat?"

"They men hired to keep hobos off the trains. They'll beat you worse than the warden. Just keep going north."

The 3:30 wake up came just as Ben had finally dozed off. The building chain almost pulled him out of his cot. Once outside, he and the other men whose names had been written down the night before were ordered to huddle to one side while the other convicts shuffled away toward the trucks. Ben positioned himself near Titus.

A minute later, Bulldog showed up with a bloodhound named Whitey, distinguished by a large patch of white fur on its back. Normally, the hounds stayed in pens and were brought out only when a convict escaped. The fact that one blue tick coonhound would accompany the men, meant fewer guards were available than the warden would have liked.

"Let's go!" Bulldog shouted.

The convicts lined up as usual to be chained together and loaded onto a truck. A few minutes out of the camp, Ben leaned over and spoke to Titus in a low voice.

"Say, you mighty good wiff dat pick?"

Titus smiled in the dark. "I the best they is swingin' a pick or a hammer. I can sink a spike faster than any other man."

"Can you bend up dis here ankle ring?"

Ben's question was met with silence, and he wondered for a fleeting moment if Titus would tell the guards what he asked.

"I can bend it up real good," came the reply. The truck headed in the same general direction of the new highway, but it drove for another twenty minutes before coming to a halt. This time, when the landscape came into view with the first light of day, Ben saw that he and the others were beneath a canopy of trees.

"Let's go! Let's go!" Bulldog shouted.

The men piled out of the truck and followed an elevated trail with low-lying water on each side. After a twenty-minute trudge through the woods, they stood awaiting their instructions while the chain that joined them together was removed.

"Listen up!" Bulldog said. "You're gonna clear out this scrub oak and dismantle these tracks. By the time they lay down enough dirt to get out here, I want this section clear of trees and the tracks pulled up. Now, there ain't nothing but swamp between here and the river. A man ain't gonna last two days in this place. If you run and one of us wings you, you ain't gonna live through the night. So, don't even think about escaping."

Ben realized that Bulldog, Carson, and Whitey were the only things standing between him and freedom. What Bulldog didn't realize was that Ben had grown up around marsh, woods, and swamps. The only thing he feared in a swamp was the Devil, and Billy Waters had taught him that even Satan can't be in every swamp at the same time.

The section of a railroad bed he had been assigned to clear was part of an abandoned rail spur destroyed by Sherman's march through Georgia, now overgrown with trees. Ben knew he was close to the Altamaha River. He could taste it in the air. The raised railroad bed was surrounded by swampy land fed by an oxbow lake once part of the main river. Soon, the sound of Titus's sledge-hammer dismantling steel rails from crossties, echoed through the woods. By the end of the first day, it was apparent that Ben knew the most about logging trees, and the other men deferred to his judgment regarding where to chop a tree so that it fell in the desired spot.

At night, Roos acted no differently toward Ben than before lest he arouse the suspicion of the guards or other convicts who might inadvertently give away Ben's plan. After the men had fallen asleep, Roos handed Ben his share of cornbread he had saved from the evening meal. Both men knew Ben would need all the sustenance he could get for the upcoming trek.

By Friday, Hoke and Carson had become somewhat relaxed in their oversight of the convicts. The heat and humidity had already taken its toll on three convicts who didn't leave the camp that morning due to heat exhaustion. Had he been observing more closely, Bulldog might have noticed that one of the convicts seemed to be in his element.

That afternoon, Ben positioned himself near Titus and the other sledge swinger who followed in the loggers' wakes, tearing up rails as the trees were cleared. Two other men accompanied them, using long iron bars to pry up the rails and crossties deeply embedded in the soil. The moment neither guard was looking, Ben lifted his left ankle onto a crosstie still firmly planted in the ground.

"You tink you can hit dat ankle ring?" he asked Titus.

Titus smiled and shrugged. "It ain't nuthin."

Ben braced himself. If Titus missed, Ben would be hobbled for life.

Titus reared the sledgehammer back. A moment later, the sound of metal on metal was muted as the ankle ring buried itself into the wood. Ben twisted his leg and loosened it. The ankle ring was bent into a distinct rectangular shape. There was no turning back. If Bulldog or Carson didn't spot the change at the end of the day, one of the guards back at the camp surely would.

"Now, de udder one," Ben said. Titus took dead aim at the right ankle ring. This time, Ben felt the tang of metal on metal reverberate up his leg. Again, the ring became embedded in the wood. It took several efforts to free himself, but the result, a severely warped ankle ring, was the same.

"Tank you," he said.

Titus said nothing. He reared back and delivered a mighty blow to the rail.

Ben casually walked to a tall water oak thick with leaves. It would be getting dark in an hour or so. He had been saving the tree as an accomplice to aid in his escape, timing its demise for the appropriate moment. Bulldog stood thirty yards away, admonishing two axmen to work harder. Carson was nowhere to be seen.

He instructed Julius, the convict he was working with, to sink his axe into the tree's base on its south side. Ben positioned himself on the opposite side of the tree, and alternated his blows with the other convict's. Before long, the tree began to creak. A few minutes after that, it teetered ominously.

"Keep a swingin'," he told Julius. "Give me two minutes."

Bulldog, standing twenty yards away, suspected nothing when the sound of only one axe man came from that tree's direction. Seconds later, the oak began its decent. Bulldog looked in that direction and saw the tree hit the ground. The tree stump, and the axe man standing next to it were hidden from view. He turned his attention back to the two men chopping on another nearby tree.

"Man gone!" Julius shouted a minute later.

Bulldog whirled and cocked his shotgun.

"Man gone!" he called out to the other guard. He ran to the tree stump where Julius stood. "Where'd he go?"

Julius pointed toward the river. "He gone off thatta way, Boss!"

Bulldog fired blindly into the woods. Lead shot spat from the gun barrels, spraying trees. He paused and listened, but there was no movement.

Hoke turned and jabbed Julius hard in the chest with the butt of his gun.

"Why didn't you call out sooner?" he shouted.

"I thought he was trimming the other side of the tree, Boss!" Julius pleaded, rubbing his sternum with one hand. "Soon as I didn't hear no mo' sounds over there, I called out."

"What the hell?" Carson gasped, running up on them with Whitey at his side.

"Goddamn nigguh run off," Hoke said bitterly. "What the hell do you think happened?"

"Sshh!" Carson replied. "I hear something."

Bulldog turned his attention to the woods. The ground there was soggy but not completely underwater. In the distance, they heard the sound of a man sloshing through standing water.

Bulldog picked up Ben's axe and let Whitey sniff the handle.

"Put these boys back to the truck and go get some help," Bulldog instructed Carson.

"You going after him?"

The standard procedure was to lockdown the other convicts, inform the warden or yard boss using the nearest telephone, and bring the dogs. Within forty-five minutes, every policeman in the area would be on the lookout for the fugitive. Local radio broadcasts would be interrupted with the bulletin.

"Hell, yes, I am," Bulldog said, checking his pump-action shotgun and ammunition. It crossed his mind to get a rifle from the truck, but in a dense wood, the shotgun was the best weapon for bringing a man down. "I'm going coon hunting."

CHAPTER 30

Ben timed his escape to coincide with the falling tree, counting on its final decent to mask the sound of the rattling chains as he ran through the woods. The strad chain made it impossible to take a full stride, but he managed to put a hundred yards between himself and the guards before tumbling to the soggy ground in a small clearing. He sat and kicked off both brogans, then reached with trembling hands for the ankle rings. Everything depended on being able to slip them off his feet. He grabbed the left ankle ring and strained as he pushed down on it, but it wouldn't clear his heel.

"Jesus, cum tek dis ring!" he said, gasping for air. Adrenaline pumped hard through his body, but pushing harder on the ring only wedged it onto his foot.

He grabbed a handful of mud from the soft ground and worked it onto the metal ring on his left heel, wiggling the ring until he felt it start to give. He applied more mud until the ring slipped off his foot. He worked the right ankle ring in the same fashion. Titus had done a better job with that one, and it slipped off his foot with relative ease.

"Tank you, Lawd!" Ben said. He grabbed the chain in his right hand and started running, laughing out of sheer joy as he took long strides, leapt over fallen logs, and splashed through soggy patches. He spied a slough and tossed the chain into it. For the first time since his incarceration, he was twenty pounds lighter and felt as though he was floating through the forest like he and Eli had done so many times on Sapelo.

Ben knew the river was not far, and it wasn't long before he reached an oxbow lake, which he crossed with ease. He hung close to the opposite bank and moved west, hoping that he had chosen the quickest route to the Altamaha.

Hoke wasn't the least bit concerned that his quarry had a five-minute head start. He had hunted that section of the river for years, and had an intimate knowledge of the terrain. Whitey picked up Ben's scent here and there and pulled at the leash, but Hoke already knew where Ben was headed and made a beeline for the Altamaha. There was about an hour of sunlight left. It would take that much time to reach the river.

When he reached the oxbow lake, he held his shotgun, pistol, and ammo over his head and walked while Whitey swam by his side. On the other side, Ben's scent pulled Whitey toward the setting sun while Bulldog pulled his leash in a southerly direction.

"C'mon!" he growled. Whitey whimpered and reluctantly followed his master. Hoke knew the oxbow lake surrounded a finger of land that extended from the Altamaha half a mile to the north. While Ben ran for his life around the edge of the small peninsula, Hoke moved at a measured pace in a straight line to the river.

Fifteen minutes later, Ben got his first glimpse of the Altamaha as the descending sun turned the water's surface into a slowly moving golden highway. When he reached the northern bank, he fell to his knees next to a log and caught his breath. He removed the top of his uniform in anticipation of swimming to the far side some three hundred feet away. He remained kneeling, surveying the river current with his eyes, when he heard a twig snap.

"Well, looky here," a voice said.

Ben turned and saw Hoke grinning, his shotgun pointed in the air. Whitey was by his side straining at the leash to take in Ben's scent.

"Dumb-ass, sumbitch. Where you think you're going?"

Bulldog looked down and saw that Ben's chains were missing. "How'd you get rid of them chains?"

Ben made no answer.

"Huh? What's a matter? Tired of working for the state of Georgia?"

Again, Ben made no reply until Hoke leveled the gun at his chest.

"Go ahead an' shoot," Ben said. "I ain't goin' back."

Bulldog's finger tightened on the trigger. He had killed would-be escapees before, one in cold blood. A fresh breeze blew up the river from the east just as he was about to unload the round into Ben's chest. Ben welcomed the breeze, and, for the first time since arriving in the prison camp, he felt Bu-Allah's spirit. Another thought crossed Hoke's mind as he looked at the half-naked convict standing before him. He decided he would have some fun with Ben before killing him. He would let the drowning man thrash around in agony while filling him with gunshot.

"Looks to me like you was studying on how to get to the other side? Well, go right ahead. Be my guest. But leave that log where it is. Go on . . . go and jump in the river."

Ben hesitated, suspecting a trick. He turned his head and looked at the river. The breeze pushed against the current, forming small ripples on the water's surface. It was a sign.

"What's a matter now?" Bulldog said, mocking him. "Can't swim? Damn. You shoulda thought about that before you ran your stinkin' butt off the chain gang."

Ben looked back at Bulldog with sad eyes.

"You wants me to jump in de water, Boss?" Bulldog cocked the gun and aimed it at Ben's head. "Hell yeah, I want you to jump your black ass in the water. Let's go!"

Ben took a deep breath and plunged headfirst into the river, just as he and Eli had done a hundred times on the Sapelo dock. Hoke released Whitey's leash and stood ready to pump Ben with lead the moment his head broke the surface. Most of the drowning victims he knew of were black children who ventured too far out into the river and got caught in its current. The few blacks he personally knew couldn't swim. Area swimming holes were for whites only. He expected Ben to immediately pop up and flail helplessly.

After thirty seconds passed, the only sound Hoke heard was the dripping of sweat from his brow falling into the water. At sixty seconds, he lowered his gun and looked over at Whitey, who sniffed the shore where Ben had stood.

"Black sumbitch sunk like a damn stone," he said, disappointed over having been denied his game of cat and mouse. "Mule-headed bastard would rather drown than come up for air. Fine with me."

As he turned to leave, Whitey jerked his head up and stared across the water. Hoke heard a loud splash and wheeled in the direction of the sound. In the remaining reflection of light on the water, he glimpsed the back of Ben's head sixty feet away and a little downstream. He sprayed the river with pellets as the head disappeared again beneath the water.

"The hell!" Hoke yelled. "Son-of-a-bitch can swim! Keep an eye on him, Boy," he told Whitey. "Sumbitch has got to come up again."

Bulldog stepped up to higher ground, knowing full well that Ben would soon be out of the shotgun's effective range.

"Come up," he said, aiming the gun at the next logical spot for Ben to reappear. "Bring your black ass on up again."

Ben's head broke surface a minute later, this time a third of the way across the river and even further downstream. Bulldog fired two ineffectual rounds as Ben disappeared underwater again.

"God-o-mighty!" he shouted. "Son-of-a-bitch!" He pulled the pistol from his holster and aimed, realizing it would be a miracle if he put a bullet into a man from that distance. On a calm surface, he might have an outside chance of bouncing a round off the water, but with the choppy surface stirred by the breeze, that option was gone.

Ben rose up three more times for air before reaching the far shore. Hoke emptied his handgun without hitting his target.

"Go on and run!" Bulldog called out as Ben, exhausted, stumbled onto the far bank and crawled into the woods. "I'll be on your trail in two hours and have your sorry butt by midnight! By dawn, you'll be back in the bullpen! Go on and run, damn your black ass!" He took Whitey's leash and turned to go.

Ben lay on the ground breathing hard. He watched through the veil of trees as Bulldog and the hound disappeared into the woods. They would be back to pick up his trail in a few hours. He estimated it to be about twelve miles west to the point where the Oconee and Ocmulgee merged to formed the Altamaha, and another eight miles by river to the railroad trestle near Lumber City. He could cover the twenty miles on foot in ten hours, but that would leave a trail for the hounds to follow. He decided to cover the entire distance wading knee deep in the river.

As darkness fell, the steady breeze that had served as a shield for his escape died down.

"Tank you, God. Tank you, Bu-Allah," he said, rising to his feet.

He felt his strength return and walked back into the water. He thought about the Ebo tribesmen who walked chained together into the water chanting, "The water brought us here. The water will take us home." The river would take him to freedom. For how long, he had no idea, but each minute out of the shackles felt like an hour free from bondage to him.

He stepped into the river until the water reached his knees and began walking east toward Sapelo. With his hands or bare feet, a good tracker might be able to trace Ben's underwater footprints. Ben paralleled the shore for a couple of yards, then moved further out into the water where there was still very little current. He began to swim in the opposite direction, leaving the impression that he had gone east. Instead, he traveled west toward Lumber City. When he reached the bend in the river, he began walking chest high in the water.

Whitey picked up the baying of other hounds long before Hoke, and began to bark as well. Hoke listened until he, too, could hear them. He pointed his shotgun into the air and let off two rounds. Before long, he saw the lanterns and flashlights of men moving in his direction.

"Don't nobody shoot!" he called out. "It's me. Hoke."

"He's over here," a voice shouted.

A minute later, he met up with Warden Knox, Carson, and five other armed men.

"You get that son-of-a-bitch?" was the first thing out of the warden's mouth.

The words rolled off his tongue with a staccato, assembly line-like quality. Ben Jordan wasn't a man. He wasn't even human. In the warden's mind, he was on par with the dog at the end of his leash, only less valuable.

"Hell, no," Bulldog replied. "Sumbitch swam across the damn river up around Devil's Bend."

"You shoulda shot him!" Knox replied. "Should filled up the son-of-a-bitch with holes!"

"I fired a bunch of rounds. He swum underwater!" Knox glared at Bulldog in disbelief.

"Nigguhs can't swim underwater," Carson said.

"I ain't lyin'!" Hoke said, defensively. "Sumbitch swum most the way underwater. Damndest thing you ever saw. I heard a splash and thought it was a fish, but it was the dumb sumbitch coming up for air. Then he goes back under and pops up a minute later somewhere else. Hell, I emptied both guns, but he was out of range."

"I knew you should-a took the rifle," Carson said.

"Like hell you did!" Hoke said, turning on him. "You sat there and didn't say a word about it."

Knox shook his head. "All right, you two just shut up and listen. It's gone dark, and we've got an escapee on the other side. He's probably heading back to Lamar or thinking of going downstream back to that island he's from. So, Carson, I want you and Everett to stay on this side of the river . . ."

"Aw, come on, Warden," Carson protested, "He ain't smart enough to double-back."

"You do like I said!" Knox snapped. "If he can swim over there, he can swim back. The rest of you boys come with me."

CHAPTER 31

A little before midnight, Ben reached the confluence of the Ocmulgee and Oconee rivers. He'd stayed in the water for more than five miles before coming ashore. The lost spirits appeared to him every so often, but he ignored their presence. One slip up, and he, too, would be another wandering spirit on the river's shores.

Once or twice he had come within hearing distance of groups of men camping in the woods, probably Atlantans on hunting or fishing expeditions he thought. Each encounter slowed his progress as he waded around the group. Locals might be out coon hunting or running a still, but these men were loud, obviously not hunting for a fugitive. The relative lack of activity along the river gave him hope that anyone tracking him would think he was heading downstream.

The warden and his trackers had, in fact, reached that very conclusion, having found the point where he was last seen a few hours after sundown. Bryan Holtzclaw, one of the better trackers in the group, traced Ben's steps into the water up to his waist before confirming that his steps indicated that he was going downriver.

Knox called out to Carson on the north bank, telling him to move downstream. Both groups of men began trekking east, their coon dogs sniffing the ground. Both sides of the river were lit up with lanterns and flashlights south of Devil's Bend. The warden, riding in a boat powered by an outboard motor, cruised the river looking for signs of Ben perhaps drifting with a log. Several other boats with volunteers headed downriver with him.

An hour before dawn, the adrenaline sustained Ben's dash for freedom, began to wane. The paltry diet and hard work of the labor camp had taken its toll on his body. For the last hour, he became increasingly aware of the fact that without food, his hopes of escape would come to nothing.

"A tired, hungry man don't tink right," his father once told him.

Ben felt himself stumble. He had been surefooted with all of his senses on full alert. Now, his systems were shutting down. He didn't even notice the person sitting by the bank smoking a corncob pipe or the cane fishing pole extended out over the water in front of him.

"Mind the fishing line," the voice said.

It was an old woman.

"Sorry, Ma'am," Ben replied, attempting to act as if he had as much right to be there as anyone else. "I didn't see yuh."

"That's all right. Where you going in such a rush?"

Ben hesitated. It was still dark. He couldn't see her in the shadows. Perhaps, she couldn't see him either.

"I'ze goin' fishin', like you."

"Where's your fish pole. I don't see no pole."

Ben paused. He could run. He could dive into the water and swim to the opposite bank.

"I see your stripes, mister. I might be old, but I ain't blind. You done run off from a prison farm."

Her voice was firm, but unthreatening. With the river as a backdrop, reflecting what little moonlight was left in the night, the woman could easily see his features.

Ben considered his options for a moment. He had been spotted.

If she was alone, it might be an hour or more before she could bring the law to that spot. By then, he would be miles away, but something in her voice prompted him to reply.

"You is right, Ma'am. I is escape."

"Where's your shirt?"

"Back downriver, Ma'am."

He saw the tobacco in her pipe fire up as she puffed on the other end.

"You know where you're a-heading?"

"Yes, Ma'am. If it's all the same wiff you, Ma'am, I be on my way now."

He started to leave.

"Wait. Hold on there. Don't you want something to eat?"

Ben sensed a trap.

"No, Ma'am. I ain't hungry."

"Now, that's the first lie you told. Shame on you." He uneasily shuffled his feet in the shallow water. "You right, Ma'am. I is mighty hungry. But I don't wants to bother you none."

"You ain't bothering me none, Son."

"Is you white?" Ben asked. No white person had ever called him "son."

"I am."

"I'ze Negro," he said.

"I can see that. But you're one of God's children, just like me."

Ben knelt on one knee and rested his weary bones. "You ain't 'fraid of no convict?"

The woman chuckled. "I'm long past fearing any man," she replied.

"I wouldn't never hurt no one," Ben answered.

"I know, Son. I know. If you was a killer, you would have already tried something."

Ben sat down in the water. He felt as though he could fall asleep right there.

"If you can spare a little food, I be grateful," he said at length.

He saw the cane pole rise up and heard the fishing line cross the water near him, then he saw the woman rise to her feet.

"You think you can walk a half mile to the cabin?" she asked.

Ben slowly got up. He figured he just about had the strength to do that.

"Yessum. But you ain't gonna turn me over to the law is you?"

There was a short silence.

"No, Son. I ain't gonna turn you in. Now, if you want to end up back on a prison farm, go on ahead up the river. If you want to live, you best foller me."

Ben paused a moment. Everything she said seemed to be on the level. On the island, she was what the old timers called a *truth-mouth*. Her words so far had rung true in his ear, like the voices of the choir in his church. One off-key note would stand out from the rest. In her voice, in her words, he heard nothing off-key.

"I'ze comin', Ma'am," he said.

"Good. You can carry this."

He vaguely noticed a string of four catfish she had caught. The woods quickly enveloped him and his guide. The night grew more still the longer they walked, as if they had left the outdoors and entered a hushed cathedral. Ben stayed close behind the woman, following the sound of her footsteps. The first signs of dawn appeared in the sky high over the trees when they reached a log cabin. A shed was attached to it. Next to the shed was an old horse stall that housed a rusting Ford truck. Behind the stall sat a chicken coop.

"There's a hook on the outside wall," she said, tapping a spot under the lean-to with her cane pole. "Hang them fish there."

Ben felt with his hand and lifted the string of fish up onto the hook.

"Now, come on in this house. I want to see you better."

Ben started to enter when something caught his eye. He turned and saw an apparition, the spirit of a dead man standing a few feet from the cabin door. He turned his head and shuffled behind the woman into the cabin. He heard the thud of a heavy object being set high on one of the cabin's interior walls. A few moments later, the light from a lantern filled the twelve-by-twenty-foot room. The floor and ceiling were made of rough-hewn pine. A wood stove, a sink, and open shelves took up most of the space on the right side. A small pine table with benches on each end sat in the middle. Hugging the left wall was a cot large enough to hold a man. A door on the far end led to another, smaller room.

The woman's back was to him when she lit the lantern. Above her on the wall was a shotgun, the barrel still wet with morning dew. Ben had not seen it earlier and realized she likely had it trained on him the whole time they conversed by the river.

As she turned, the two looked at each other. She saw a mosquito bitten, half naked, dark-skinned man oozing blood from various nicks and cuts he'd picked up on his trek upriver. He saw a thin, white haired woman about five feet tall wearing a cotton dress that had been repaired many times. Her face was careworn, but her piercing blue eyes still burned with a fire that years of misfortune had failed to extinguish.

"What happened to your shoes?" she asked.

Ben looked down at his feet. They were covered in scratches from debris scattered on the river's bottom.

"I kick 'em off when I wuz swimmin' de river."

"Sit down at that table, and let me look you over," she said, circling him with her lantern.

Ben did as she directed.

"Uh-huh. Just like I thought," she said, shaking her head when she saw the wide scars on his back. "They been beating you poor souls."

"Yes, Ma'am. They beat us like we was a dog." She inspected him more closely.

"Son, you got buckshot all up in your neck and the back of your head. You just stay there while I get my kit."

Ben felt the back of his neck with his hand. His fingers lightly traced the small bumps of lead pellets, most of which were superficially imbedded in his skin. He recalled feeling a sting on the back of his head when he came up for air while swimming across the river, and he'd been vaguely aware of a continued discomfort on his neck since then. Now, in the cabin, weary, his adrenaline depleted, he began to feel his various wounds more intensely.

He watched the woman cross the room and rummage through a cabinet near the wood stove.

"My name Ben," he said.

She bent over and pulled a small sack from a shelf. "Faye," the woman replied, still searching for something. "Faye Worrell. There it is . . ." she said, grabbing a bottle near the back of the cabinet.

She returned to his side and set the sack and bottle on the pine table.

"Hold still now," she instructed as she liberally doused his neck with the bottle's clear fluid. He immediately rose up from the intense burning sensation.

"Stay put!" she said.

"Dat burn, Lady!"

"I know! It's supposed to sting. It's cleaning out every little wound. You don't want it getting infected, do you?"

Ben sniffed the air and sat back down. He well knew the odor from his dealings with Hoffer.

"Dat hard liquor, Ma'am," he said. "I know dat smell anywhere."

"Hush, and let me finish," Faye replied. She pulled a small, thick magnet from the sack and slowly waved it over his neck. Small metal pellets, attracted by the magnet's pull, dislodged from his neck and stuck to it. Faye put the magnet down and picked up a pair of tweezers.

"All right, now hold good and still!" she ordered, delicately picking the remaining pieces from Ben's skin.

When she was done, she doused the affected area again with the liquid.

"Ahh!" he yelped, rising to his feet and hopping around the room.

"You big baby," Faye said. "Now, you take this here rag, pour some of that distilled alcohol on it, and daub all them other cuts with it. I'm gonna go outside and clean them fish. We gonna have some fried catfish for breakfast. You think you can stand that?"

"Yessum," Ben replied.

"And keep your hand away from your neck. Let that alcohol work in. Daub them cuts real good, or I'll do it for you," she said, opening the cabin door and stepping outside.

"Yessum."

When Faye entered the room again, Ben was slumped over the table sound asleep, his head nestled in the crook of his right arm. He awoke a little while later to Faye's gentle prodding. When he opened his eyes, a plate filled with filleted catfish and scrambled eggs lay before him. He stared wide-eyed at the food.

"I'ze dreamin'," he said after taking in his surroundings and adjusting his eyes.

"You ain't dreaming. I got them eggs from the chicken coop out back. What you waiting for? Go ahead and dig in."

Ben looked up at Faye. "We ain't prayed yet."

"Well, go ahead," she told him.

He bent his head and breathed in the aroma of the meal.

"Our Fadda in Heavin, tank you fo lettin' me 'scape frum de camp. It worse dan anyting anyone ever knowed of. Watch over dem mens still in dere. I tank you fo directin' my steps an' bringin' me to dis here cabin. I tank you fo Faye. She a goot woman. She de best . . ."

"Amen. Now come on, and eat up," Faye said.

"I ain't done prayin', Miss Faye."

"Well, hurry up. Them eggs is gonna get cold!" He bent his head again.

"De world an' ever'ting in it belong to you, Lawd. We tank you fo dis food. Amen."

By midnight of the escape, Knox and his posse had covered ten miles of shoreline on both sides of the river without discovering a trace of Ben's movements. The woods increasingly lit up with locals as the night wore on. To them, hunting for escaped prisoners was a form of entertainment. The warden covered another ten miles of downstream river by boat before doubling back and meeting up with Hoke and his group again.

"Son-of-a-bitch ain't downriver," Knox said. The man steering the boat cut the motor and let it gently glide onto the sandbar where Bulldog and the others stood.

"He coulda drowned," Holtzclaw offered.

"Sumbitch can swim like a fish," Bulldog replied.

"He couldn't have swam this far," Holtz-claw replied. "I say his body will pop up somewhere in a few days."

"Unless he caught hold of a log."

Knox scratched his head. Ben Jordan was proving to be more of a challenge than he had anticipated.

"You know what I think?" he said. "I think the son-of-a-bitch went upstream."

"His tracks were heading down river," said Holtzclaw. "I'll swear on it. I'll swear on a Bible."

"Yep. But . . ." Knox replied after pausing to think, "the current is slack. He could have just as easily swum aways upriver. Hell, he could have crossed back over to the other side."

"He ain't that smart," Bulldog said.

The warden bit his lower lip. "Yeah. I keep hearing about how he ain't that smart." He wiped his brow and briefly looked out over the water. "But here we are," he continued, his voice rising in anger with each word, "after chasing his ass all night, and there ain't no gottdamn sign of him!"

Bulldog let out a disgusted sigh and set the butt of his gun on the ground. "So we've been out here all night going in the wrong direction?"

"Sure as hell looks that way. Your man is making a damn fool out of us."

"My man!"

"I put him under your charge! We got the whole countryside on the alert because you can't keep a handful of convicts on task. You've lost two men this summer. Now, I'm getting just the least little bit tired of this nonsense." Knox motioned for the man at the back of the boat to start the motor. "You boys go up to the road and catch a ride upriver. Then start tracking him west from Devil's Bend."

"You giving up?" Holtzclaw asked.

Knox turned and stared him down. "Hell, no. I'm just getting smart myself. I betcha anything that son-of-a-bitch Roos knows where he's heading."

CHAPTER 32

Eugene Clayborne Cutler, Junior entered the world at eight-and-a-half pounds one week before Ben's escape. His arrival in the Cutler household overshadowed news of the massive manhunt sweeping up and down both sides of the Altamaha from Lumber City to Sapelo Island. His son's birth was just one more in a series of fortunate events that assured Clayborne's ascendancy as a king-maker in the Empire State. He was flush with cash in a time when cash was scarce. The new highway through Lamar and middle-Georgia would become his personal path to more riches. With wealth came influence, and his ties to the Talmadge machine, also at its height of power, further solidified his emergence as a dominant player in state events.

In the course of Tremont's mission to acquire real estate along the highway's route, he had an epiphany. Cutler Industries could buy properties for far less between the towns rather than within their city limits. Instead of multi-story hotels, they would build motel courts comprised of free-standing bungalows arranged in a semi-circle around a restaurant and gas station. It was a concept Clayborne immediately endorsed. Cutler Industries could set up these establishments for a third of the cost of building them in-town. What's more, every cent of a traveler's dollar would be spent on Cutler property, not other hotels, restaurants, and filling stations.

At the same time the Cutler family enjoyed unbridled prosperity, the Jordan family struggled along with other families in the final days of what people were calling the Great Depression. Soon after Naomi had been snatched from her father's arms during his initial arrest, Geneva noticed a change come over her. She'd become more emotionally disconnected and cried very little. As Ben requested, Geneva had taken Naomi to live with Rona and Delphine in Harlem.

"Dis chile need islan' medicine," Delphine advised.

"Docta Crow after her for he own self," Geneva replied.

"Dey is Matilda. She know conjurin'. She make de white root."

"I ain't goin' back to Sapelo," Geneva declared.

She returned to Lamar just in time to learn of Ben's daring escape. Her neighbor, Lucille, caught her up on the latest news. Many of the local whites were involved in the search. The blacks stayed away from their favorite fishing holes on the river for fear of being mistaken for the fugitive. A large reward had been posted, and the law didn't care if he was taken dead or alive.

Geneva barely listened as Lucille informed her that Cutler put up money to bring her brother in alive, but when she mentioned the birth of Eugene Clayborne Cutler, Jr., Geneva's head jerked.

"Whut he name de chile?" she asked.

"Clayborne, Junior. Named for his daddy."

Geneva slumped back into her chair and covered her face with her hands.

"God forgive me," she muttered, recalling the name she had written for the root Dr. Crow made. She recalled the conjurer's words. His root would destroy anyone whose name was on the slip of paper.

Lucille assumed the shock of Ben's escape had overwhelmed Geneva and went to the kitchen to get her a glass of water.

"Dat root gonna turn on him, too," Lucille heard Geneva say when she returned.

"Who gonna turn on who?" she asked.

But Geneva was in another world and spoke as if Lucille wasn't present.

"Just like it did dem ol' Cales. Burn dey whole house down an' all dem peoples in it. But dis one even mo' pow'ful. I gots to tek it back."

"What you going on about, Geneva?"

"That Cutler boy. You don't unnerstan'. He in danger!"

"That little boy? He's a sick child. Something already wrong with him from what people say."

Geneva threw one hand up to her mouth and ran for the bathroom. She got two steps before vomiting on the floor.

She knew the root had already gone to work on the child.

While Ben slept on the cot in Faye's cabin, she went down to the river and sprinkled fish guts along the path to throw off his scent. She'd witnessed enough manhunts to know the law would eventually be combing the woods around her home.

An hour after daylight, she drove her late husband's truck the three miles to Lumber City, ostensibly for supplies. Her real purpose was to discover how far the dragnet for Ben's recapture had reached. She got her answer as soon as she reached the city limits where a roadblock had been set up.

"We're checking all cars in and out of town. No exceptions," the highway patrolman informed her.

"What are you looking for?" Faye asked.

"An escaped felon, Ma'am," he said, peering into the cab. "A nigruh fella from one of the prison camps. Ran off last night. They think he might've headed this way."

Faye watched in her mirror as another patrolman knelt behind the truck and searched under the carriage. To her left, she saw a freight train sitting motionless on the Ocmulgee River trestle south of the town. Two groups of men searched each boxcar, inside and underneath, moving down the line with the precision of a drill team.

"Okay, Ma'am. Thank you. You see anyone suspicious, contact the police department right away. You can go now."

She paused outside the grocer's store to inspect crates of vegetables while listening to a conversation between two men who were discussing the hunt. Faye learned the authorities were waiting for Ben in Lamar and on Sapelo should he try to seek shelter with family or friends in either of those places.

"Ol' Warden Knox and his posse searched that river all night from Devil's Bend south and halfway back up here," the first man said. "He thinks that preacher killer had an accomplice. It was all prearranged."

"If he did," his friend replied, "he's probably a hundred miles away from here by now."

"Either that or drowned. I say, if you can't pick up an escaped convict's scent with those hounds they got out there, he's a goner."

Faye returned to her cabin to find Ben sound asleep. He didn't awaken until noon when the aroma of freshly-cooked skillet cornbread stirred his senses. A kettle of water simmered next to it on the stovetop.

"Go on outside," she said. "There is an iron laundry pot next to the well. Fill it up with water. I'll be out directly."

She handed him a bar of homemade soap and a scrub brush.

"I want you to get in that basin outside and take a bath. I bet you ain't had a decent one in a while."

"No, Ma'am. We don't get no baths other than when it rain. But I'ze mighty clean affer being in dat river all night."

"You take this kettle with you. It's boiling hot, so be careful with it. Go on out and fill up that basin. There's a hand pump right next to it. Fill it half way, and pour this hot water in it. Then take off them awful pants, and get in it."

Ben hesitated.

"Strip down? Outside?"

"I'm not gonna be a lookin'. Now, stop messing around and hop to. This cornbread is just about ready, and I want to serve it hot."

The iron pot was five feet in diameter, like ones he'd seen people use on Sapelo to wash clothes. Ben pumped enough well water in it to bathe, then dumped the hot water in and enjoyed the first real cleaning he'd had in months. He was halfway through scrubbing when Faye opened the door and approached him carrying the same bottle she used to clean his wounds.

"Miss Faye, I'ze still cleanin'!"

"Don't stop on my account," she said. She hung a white shirt and cotton trousers on a nearby clothesline stretched between two trees. "These were my husband's clothes. I don't reckon I'll be a needin' them anymore."

She hung a towel on the line next to the clothes.

"Dry off, and put on them garments when you're done. And don't dawdle. When you come inside, I got a pair of his old shoes and a coat for you."

Faye picked up a stick and raised Ben's striped pants off the pump handle where he had placed them.

"Whut you doin' wiff dem britches?" he asked.

She held the pants over a steel drum used to burn yard trash and doused them with the bottle's contents.

"I'm gonna turn these filthy rags into ashes so's no hound can pick up the scent," she replied, striking a match against the metal with a free hand. The pants immediately burst into flames. She continued to hold them aloft, making sure they were fully engulfed before letting them fall into the drum.

"Dat real alcohol, Miss Faye," Ben said, reacting to the home-made liquor's flammability. "Dat some fine mash."

"Medicinal spirits," she corrected. "Now hush up and finish cleaning."

After a lunch of cornbread and fried okra with rice and gravy, Ben leaned on the table.

"Miss Faye, I tank you fo dese clothes an' dis fine cookin'. I gots no way to repay you."

"No need," she said.

He shook his head. "You de best woman I ever met 'sides my momma and wife. How cum you so nice? You white, an' I done 'scaped frum de law. I don't wants you gettin' in trouble fo me. I'ze outside de law. If you hep me, you outside de law, too!"

Faye smiled and looked him in the eye.

"Well, let me tell you something. There is man's law, and then there is God's law. 'For I was hungered, and ye gave me meat. I was thirsty, and ye gave me drink. I was a stranger, and ye took me in. Naked, and ye clothed me. I was sick, and ye visited me. I was in prison, and ye came unto me. . . . And the Lord shall say unto them, verily I say unto you, inasmuch as ye have done it unto one of the least of my brethren, ye have done it unto me.'"

"Dat right, Miss Faye. I heard dat in church all my life. Saint . . . uh . . ."

"It's from Saint Matthew. Now, whose law do you think I'm going obey? Man's or God's? Besides, I know a thing or two about what goes on inside of them prison farms. They came and took my Dallas away a few years back for making spirits. He weren't hurting nobody. But the revenuers got him and sent him to a camp and put him to work road building. They beat him down to where he wasn't nothin'. He was there two years. When he come home, he just withered away. This morning, when I was down to the river fishing, I heard you walking in that water from way off. I knew before I even saw you that God brung you from upriver for a purpose. No one was around to help my poor Dallas. But God has given me a chance to make it right. It's my Christian duty to help you."

Ben stared at a pine knot on the surface of the table. "I tink I seen yo husband, Miss Faye."

The smile disappeared from her face.

"Say what?"

"Is yo husband missin' he right hand?"

Faye jerked involuntarily.

"You knew my Dallas?"

"No, Ma'am. I seen his spirit outside yo door dis mornin'."

"His spirit?"

"Yessum. He a man 'bout my size?"

"Yes."

"Wiff he hand off? He right hand?" Faye looked at Ben in amazement. "You can talk to spirits?"

"No, Ma'am. I just sees dem. I ain't gots de power o'communicatin'."

"What was he doing?"

"He lookin' over de house, Miss Faye. He keepin' bad spirits frum comin' near."

She paused and took in the words. She had her husband buried in an unmarked grave a few hundred feet from the cabin.

"You can see bad spirits?"

"All dem spirits, Ma'am. Good an' bad."

Faye wiped her brow and collected her thoughts. "Dallas lost his hand when he was a young man working in a sawmill. Just after we got married."

"Yessum. Sawmillin' is dangerous work. Mighty dangerous."

"But he built this place with one good hand. Me and him together. We built that little barn out back where I keep the truck. Back then, we had a horse and carriage. Had a good life 'til they came and got him."

"Troubles is ever'where all de time, Miss Faye. Dat what my granmamma used to say. No gettin' 'round it. But, like I said, I don't wants to bring no mo' trouble down on you. Dis night, when the sun go down, I gonna be leavin'."

"Uh-huh," she said skeptically. "Where you going?"

"I gonna hop dat north train over to Lumber City. Dat de plan I had."

"That might have been a good plan last night, but not today. I drove into town while you were sleeping. The whole place is crawling with the law. They got the roads blocked and are inspecting every boxcar on every train coming through town."

Ben leaned back and rubbed his eyes. He let out a dejected sigh.

"I shoulda kep' goin' last night," he said.

"You wouldn't have made it to town. You were about to drop when you got this far."

"Den I hide out in de woods 'til everting die down."

"You'll do no such thing. Now, just let me think on this. You can't go to your home in Lamar."

"How you know 'bout Lamar?"

"I heard two men talking. One said you were the preacher killer from that trial over to Baxley everyone was talking about a while back."

"I ain't never kilt no preacher, Miss Faye."

"I know," she said. "I believe you. You don't strike me as the sort of man who could do that. You can't go to Lamar or Sapelo."

Faye paused and closed her eyes, imagining waves crashing on the shore.

"I ain't never seen the ocean," she said at length, opening her eyes.

"It big water, Miss Faye. Water all around. You go out on a shrimp boat 'bout ten mile, it just water an' sky. Dat all it is. Water an' sky."

"Well, where are you planning to go if you can't go to Lamar or back home?"

"I gots fambly up north."

"Where up north?"

Ben hesitated. He didn't want her to become further involved in breaking the law. "Tell me."

"Okay, Miss Faye. You been straight wiff me. I be straight wiff you. I gots fambly in New Yoke. De city."

"Uh-huh," she said, her mind working on the problem of getting him out of Georgia. "You know they'll wire the police up there to be on the lookout."

"I reckon dey might. But I gots to see my li'l girl one mo' time. New Yoke de place where I ask my sister to tek her. I don't tink I'll live dem fo'ty year de judge give me. Not in de camp run by Warden Knox."

Faye rose from her seat and spit out of an open window.

"Don't say that name in my house."

"Sorry, Ma'am. You knows him?"

"I reckon I do," she replied. Ben heard bitterness creep into her voice for the first time. "He used to be from around here. Back when we was fighting the Kaiser, all the boys signed up and went to fight, including my son, Brooks. But not little Sammy Knox. He come up with some excuse why he didn't have to go. Lots of good boys, including my Brooks, never came home."

"I'ze sorry, Miss Faye. De warden a hard man, but don't no one never say nuthin' bad 'bout him. Not even de preacher whut cum an' preach to us. Not even de guards. Dey all is 'fraid o' dat man. He de king over dat camp."

"He's a little tyrant is what he really is. And a coward! All tyrants is cowards inside. That's why they keep folks down—to hide it from the others. But I know Knox. I knew his daddy and all them Knox boys. Most of them other boys were okay. But Sammy is just about worthless, a sorry excuse for a human being. And I know something else for a fact. He's a big man when he's holding all the cards. But put him on the wrong side of a gun, and he'll wet his pants . . . every time." She laughed.

"Miss Faye!" Ben said, grinning.

"I seen it. Seen it with my own two eyes. Seen his knees shaking and his lip quivering, right there in town. He was mouthing off to one of them Peavey boys when he was out and about and full of hisself. Brady Peavey pulls out a little pistol, a little bitty ol' gun, and Sammy Knox—the warden now—he soiled his pants. Right there in the street. That's how come he moved out of the county. He was a coward then, and he's a coward now. Believe me. He married lucky, and her pa had connections, so now Knox is a camp warden and county road commissioner. I reckon he's a mighty big man over there. And you watch. He's gonna try to use you to redeem himself in this town. If he catches you, he'll parade you all through downtown Lumber City before hauling you back to the camp. Well," she said, banging her fist on the table, "we will just see about that!"

The two sat silently, Faye rocking back and forth in her seat, ideas forming in her head. At length, she cupped her hand around her mouth and suppressed a laugh.

"Whatchoo happy 'bout, Miss Faye? We bofe in a heap o'trouble."

She stood, walked to the stove, and grabbed a small iron hook hanging from a nearby shelf.

"Looky here," she told Ben as she crossed the room to the cot. She pulled the bed aside and looped the hook through a metal rod painted black, wedged into a floorboard pine knot. When she lifted her arm and raised a trap door up from the floor. Ben's eyes widened.

"This is where Dallas kept most of his produce. Some of it's been aging for years."

Ben peered over her shoulder. Six steps led to a small cellar lined with dusty shelves. Rows of bottles and wooden casks covered in dust lined each shelf.

"Miss Faye, why you keep callin' dat moonshine med'cin? It hard liquor. You can drive de truck on dat stuff."

"Don't you know that everything under the sun has its good and bad?" she said, smiling. "The spirits that make men act like fools are the same spirits that cleaned up your wounds. I use it for medicine, so I call it medicine. Anyone who pours it down their gullet to act like a fool is a fool."

"Why you showin' me dat cellar?"

"Because I guarantee someone's bound to come snooping around here to make sure the Widow Worrell is safe from the escaped convict. Mark my words, these woods will be a-crawlin' with folks."

"Whut you gonna say if someone ax, 'You seen dat ol' convict?'"

"I'll tell the truth. I ain't seen no one around here wearing stripes lately."

"But you is seen me! Dat a lie. I don't want you getting in trouble wiff de law."

"It's not a lie. I ain't seen anyone around here *wearing stripes* lately. See? I'm telling them the truth."

Ben thought about it a moment. A grin spread across his face.

"Miss Faye, you a sma't woman. I wish you wuz my counselor at de trial."

"Now," she said, "if you hear anyone approaching, you jump down in the cellar. You hear? Don't even think about it. Just open it and get down them stairs quick-like."

"How you get de bed back in place?"

"You don't. Just push it down a ways next to the wall. Ain't no one gonna see that piece of metal down there. If three people come in here, make sure you hear three sets of footsteps leave. Some of these fellers are pretty crafty. One of them might hang behind the others to make someone think everyone has left."

"I'll listen real good. But whut you gonna say if I gets caught?"

"Don't you worry about that. I'll think of something when the time comes. Now, tomorrow morning, I've got to run down to Waycross. I got an idea about how to get you out of here."

CHAPTER 33

Geneva had two good reasons for visiting Sapelo Island. At her sisters' urging, she agreed to purchase a conjure for Naomi from the island's other witch doctor, Matilda, a "white" root doctor. Her powers lay in reversing hexes and ensuring good health and good fortune in love and money. Between prayer and the root, Rona and Delphine believed Naomi's emotional state would improve. The other reason for returning to the island was to ask Matilda for a spell that would reverse the root she had planted under Cutler's back steps.

The morning of Ben's second day of freedom, she arrived by train at the Thalmann depot where a cousin met Geneva and drove her to the Meridian Dock for the ferry ride to Sapelo. Matilda's clapboard home sat near a pond half a mile outside of the Hog Hammock settlement. When Geneva told her about Dr. Crow's hex on Clayborne Cutler, Matilda shook her head.

"De Stinger a pow'ful root," she said. "Cain't no one undo dat 'cept the one who made up de conjure. Docta Buzzard might coulda undid Docta Crow, but he dead. An' Docta Crow dyin'. Only he can tek it back."

Geneva looked up at Matilda with alarm.

"Docta Crow dyin'?"

"He real sick. Dat de risk of dem black roots. It like handlin' a snake. One day, it gonna rise up an' strike back. All dem black magic forces he been callin' on all dese years, dey comin' back to demand payment, an' he gots to pay wiff he life."

Geneva understood the urgency with which Dr. Crow wanted to pass his knowledge on to an apprentice, and was all the more relieved for getting Naomi off the island permanently.

"I can mek up a root fo de girl," Matilda said, "but you hafta see Docta Crow to reverse out dat udder one. You go now. Go on an' see him dis very day. Cum back affer dat, an' I'll have your conjure ready. Go on, now."

The sky grew dark as Geneva walked through the island forest to Dr. Crow's shack. Her steps became more timid and her resolve diminished more the closer she got to it. When she reached the narrow trail that led to his doorstep, the storm that had been brewing unleashed fresh gusts of air. Dead leaves and loose forest debris scattered and danced around her. Tiny sand granules blew in her eyes, forcing her to keep her head down as she inched forward. Ghostly hands seemed to reach out and swipe at her.

"Jus' a swingin' vine," she told herself. Her eyes remained fixed on the footpath a yard or two in front of her. After ten minutes of surviving the gauntlet of spirits, real or imagined, she reached the gate, an arched trellis covered in vines. She looked up and saw the tiny structure, its roof covered with fern. On the roof sat an owl, keeping watch. She had never seen one in midday before, and understood it to be a sign of significant import. The root doctor's donkey looked out from its stall. Overhead, the two towering oaks kept the premises in a permanent state of semi-dark even on the brightest days. Now, with clouds quickly closing in, her surroundings seemed to be suddenly engulfed in an otherworldly twilight.

"Docta Crow!" she called out. "It me, G'neva Jordan."

No one responded. She never knew him to go anywhere without his faithful donkey. It was possible he had turned himself into an animal and was visiting another part of the island. He might have transformed himself into a crow and flown to the mainland or to one of the other barrier islands. As the wind picked up, the intimidating shack began to look more like an inviting shelter.

"Docta Crow!" she said a little louder.

She reached out to knock on the door, but it opened unassisted.

"Just de wind blowin'," she told herself.

She gingerly opened it wider and stepped inside, allowing her eyes to adjust to the gloomy interior. After a few moments, she noticed a white root sitting on the workbench by the window on her left. She started for it, but came to a stop when she heard a gurgling noise. On the bed in the opposite corner of the room, she saw what she thought at first to be a corpse partially covered by a blanket. She tentatively moved closer and saw that it was Dr. Crow lying on his back, his eyes closed, his mouth open. The gurgling sound grew louder as she neared.

"Docta Crow," she whispered. "It me. G'neva Jordan. I cum to see you. We gots to tek off de curse you giff me."

His eyelids flickered.

"Docta Crow?" she said, reaching out and touching his arm.

She leapt back at the sight of his glazed eyes opening wide. He stared at her—through her—to a realm she couldn't see. His lips moved as he tried to form words, but she heard nothing other than the steady gurgle of fluid on his lungs rising from his throat.

"We needs to undo dat curse you giff me," she repeated, the urgency rising with each word. "Dey is a chile with de same name I wrote on de paper."

He moved his head like a blind man, trying to hone in on her voice.

"De chile dyin', Docta Crow! He innocent . . . You said de blood on you, but . . ."

Her shoulders slumped forward. She hung her head, convinced he couldn't hear or comprehend.

"Is you here?" she asked. In her heart, she knew he was already moving to the next world.

She fell to her knees by his bedside. Tears formed in her eyes as she began to pray.

"God forgiff dis man fo all he sin. Fo callin' on dark powers. Fo givin' me dat root! God forgiff me fo plantin' dat root against Missa Cutluh an' he chile!"

Her voice rose to a grief stricken moan as she rocked back and forth, sputtering prayers of forgiveness and healing, tears streaming down her cheeks and onto the floor. Outside, the wind picked up. The thunderclaps she'd heard in the distance increased in intensity and seemed to be moving in her direction, like giants on the march. The room turned dark. She strained to see through a small window above the bed when she felt an ice-cold hand reach out and touch her shoulder.

She looked down and saw the root doctor, his body convulsing in the throes of agony, pointing toward the workbench with the other hand. Geneva turned her head and saw the root glowing white hot in the darkness. He pushed her toward the root. The gurgling noise rose and fell as his body continued to contort in pain. She hurried to the workbench and grabbed it, thinking the root might be a conjure created to relieve his suffering. When she returned to his bedside a few moments later, his body had become relaxed, and the noises emanating from his throat had ceased.

"Docta Crow," she said, holding the still glowing conjure out to him, "here de root."

His glassy eyes formed slits as he opened them one last time. He reached out and pushed the root back toward her. Geneva put it in her pocket. His eyes closed for the last time, and his breathing became shallower. A minute later, his breathing stopped altogether.

Geneva stood over him for a while before she remembered why she had come. The medicine man was dead. She could do nothing about that, but Ben, Naomi, and the Cutler child were still alive and she had work to do.

She pulled the blanket over Doctor Crow's head. When she turned to leave, the front door flew open. Outside, hail the size of baseballs hammered the ground. For a moment, she thought they would come through the roof. She took another step and stopped in her tracks at the sound of a fast approaching freight train. In the next instant, an explosion shook the entire hut. Geneva fell to the ground, screaming while the forces of nature pulled her body back toward Dr. Crow's lifeless body. She flattened herself and clawed at the dirt floor as a vortex of debris whirled around her. Something icy latched onto her leg. She screamed, but couldn't hear herself. Geneva dug her fingers deeper into the dirt. Her body lifted off the ground, and she struggled to breathe. Just as she felt herself being pulled into another world, two unearthly howls rose above the din, and the icy grip on her leg was no more. As quickly as the raging tempest began, it ended. She heard the freight train heading out to sea, followed by more thunderclaps.

When the cacophony died down, she realized that she still screamed, continuing to yell out of fear, shock, and as a confirmation of being alive. Geneva slowly recovered her faculties and tried to make sense of her surroundings. Before her, a narrow tunnel led to a shaft of light. She crawled toward the light, fully believing that she had been propelled into the afterworld along with Dr. Crow's soul. With great effort, she pulled herself through a slim opening and crawled another ten feet through the wreckage of the root doctor's home before attempting to rise and stand on trembling legs. Her clothes, torn to shreds, hung from her like rags. Her body was covered with dozens of nicks and cuts. Her fingers bled. Overhead, a bright shaft of light poured down on her through twisted oak limbs now stripped of their leaves. One of the oaks that had towered over Dr. Crow's shack partially lay on top of it, flattening the entire structure.

She started to walk off when a snort nearby caught her attention. Dr. Crow's donkey had survived the storm without a scratch.

"Come on," she said, removing two fence rails. "Come on wiff me. We gonna fine you a new home."

Halfway back to her parents' house, she remembered the white root and felt inside her pocket. It was still intact.

The next day, Matilda's eyes grew wide as she stared at the object Geneva held in her handkerchief. She had been expecting Geneva's return to her house twenty four hours earlier, the day the tornado rolled across the island's mid-section.

"Where you get dat?" the medicine woman asked.

"Docta Crow."

Matilda jerked her head up. "Docta Crow wuz took out by de whirlwind."

She, like many of the other islanders, had already been to the scene of the destruction. Dr. Crow's body was nowhere to be found.

"Dat weren't no whirlwind, Miss Tilly," Geneva responded. "God and de Devil hisself wuz wrestlin' over he soul."

"An' you wuz in it?"

"Yes, Ma'am. I seed an' heared de whole fight. I crawl outta dat mess and tek he donkey to Momma an' Poppa house."

"Dat ol' donkey survive?"

"Not a scratch! Not a scratch on de donkey. But looky here . . ."

Geneva raised the hem of her skirt to reveal three long gashes on her left leg.

"Dem is claw marks," Matilda observed. "Big ol' bird done dat."

Geneva shook her head. "It wuz Docta Crow! He grab a holt of my leg. I didn't notice it 'til I got home. My clothes were tore up, Miss Tilly. Tore up good. But I cum out whole like a baby frum de womb. God done had he eye on me while he whuppin' up on de Devil. I heard dem fightin', Miss Tilly. De Devil wuz a-howlin' and a-carryin' on like you ain't never heard befo."

Matilda studied the wounds on Geneva's leg for a moment. Both knew the scars would remain there for life. Geneva had already decided to buy white stockings to cover them up once she returned to the mainland.

"Wuz he still alive when you got dere?"

"Yes, Ma'am. He wuz makin' awful noises all up in his throat. He pointed at dis here root like he wanted me to tek it. Den he body rattle like a bag o' bones, an' he up and died."

"Sho nuff?"

"Dead as a nail, Miss Tilly. Ain't a drop o'life leff in he body. Den dem two start to fight over he soul. Lawd haff mercy, but dey fought right dere all over an' 'round dat place. When I cum to, de whole house wuz on top o' me. I crawl outta dere fast as I can. I seen de donkey an' tek him home. He tied up out back o' our house right now. Daddy say if you wants him, cum on an' tek him."

"Uh-uh," Tilly replied. "I don't want nuthin' frum dat man. Don't want nuthin' of his."

She eyed the root again.

"But I will tek a look-see at dat root. Set it on de table."

Geneva did as she was told and stepped back as if the thing might explode. She watched Matilda bend down and gently loosen the threads holding the felt cloth together.

"Whew, doggie!" the white root doctor said, meticulously inspecting the conjurer's contents with a pointed stick. "He sho put de works in dis here one. Didn't leave nuthin' out." She smiled and looked up at Geneva. "You know whut dis is?"

Geneva slowly shook her head.

"Dis here a root to reverse out dat other one he give you. Tek dat curse off real good."

"How he know I wuz cumin' back fo it? How he know dat?"

Matilda shrugged her shoulders. "He dip real deep into dat dark magic, Chile. Dat how he know dem kinda tings. But he payin' de price now. If you wuz to ax me, I say de devil won de fight fo he soul. I don't know, but dat my personal opinion."

"I don't know nuthin' 'bout dat," Geneva replied. "Where he soul is now up to de Lawd. Onliest ting I know is Docta Crow mek me write de name of de man on a piece of paper."

Matilda opened a desk drawer and pulled out a newspaper clipping and a pair of scissors.

"Tek dem scissors an' cut out de name of de man you wanna reverse de root on."

Geneva reached down and picked up the clipping, an article about a new highway going through central Georgia. Featured prominently in the story was the name "Clayborne Cutler."

"How you know who de man is?" she asked Matilda.

The white root doctor smiled but said nothing.

Geneva carefully clipped Clayborne's name from the article and slid it into the root.

Matilda then picked up a small, wooden box and held it out for her to see. In it was another, smaller root made of yellow felt stuffed with tiny medicinal plant cuttings, soil from a healer's grave, and handwritten Bible verses.

"Dis root fo to cure Naomi of worries," she said. "You bring a lock of de chile's hair?"

Geneva held out a piece of folded waxed paper containing a small clipping of Naomi's hair. Matilda removed the hair and placed it inside the root before sewing it tightly together.

"Put dis under de chile's bed. She won't have no mo' bad dreams, an' she be pert fo you know it."

Geneva put money on the table. She hesitated before turning to leave.

"What else you tinkin'?" Tilly asked. "Sumtin' else on yo mind."

"You right," Geneva said. "I wuz wonderin' if dey is anyting fo my brudder, Ben. He run off frum de law."

Matilda sighed loudly and looked Geneva in the eyes.

"Ol' Ruth done prophesied on him when he wuz born. Dat prophecy cum true, Chile. Ain't nuthin' no one can do, 'cept tek it to de Lawd."

CHAPTER 34

The same day the tornado passed over Sapelo, Faye walked down to her favorite fishing hole before sunup, and caught three catfish. The first light of dawn filled the sky when she returned to the cabin and saw a car parked in the yard. She hung the string of fish on the outside hook. As she approached her front door, three men got out.

"Miss Worrell," a voice said. She recognized it as belonging to a deputy on the county police force.

"It's me, Rembert," he said, "and Hiram."

"I know who you two are," she replied. "Whatchoo you want?"

"We're looking for that escaped convict, Ma'am. They think he mighta come up river somewhere around here."

"Oh? How come they think that?"

"'Cause ain't nobody popped up in the river downstream, and every man east of here has been combing the woods. So, it looks like he may have headed this way."

"Well, there ain't no man wearing stripes around here."

"If it's all the same to you, we'd like to look around the place and walk down to the river once the light gets up."

"Okay by me," she said.

"Why don't you boys come on inside, and I'll make a pot of coffee."

"That sure sounds good," Rembert replied.

Faye lit the lantern and turned up the wick, which illuminated the room to reveal Rembert, Hiram, and a man whose cheeks and neck showed acne scarring. Each one toted a shotgun.

"Y'all sit down," she said. Her gaze cut to the far wall as they sat on the table benches. She noticed the cot had been pushed back from its usual position. If Ben was safe in the cellar, he could hear every word they spoke.

"Hiram here has been deputized to help us hunt down the convict," Rembert said.

"Who is this fella?" Faye asked, motioning toward the third man.

"I'm Scott Carson, Ma'am," he answered.

"He's a guard over at Sam Knox's prison camp," Rembert informed her. "He was there when the prisoner got away."

"Sure 'nuff?" Faye said, pouring water into a pot and placing it on the stove. "I thought you kept them boys chained up real good."

"We do, Ma'am," Carson replied. "But some of them are real crafty. We think one of the men swinging a sledgehammer freed him up, but that one ain't talking, and we never found no chains. But the warden talked to another prisoner who knew the escapee real well."

"Talked to?" Faye asked as she stoked the stove fire.

An awkward silence followed before Rembert spoke.

"Miss Worrell's husband served time in a camp," he told Carson. "Government men caught him making shine."

"I know what goes on in them camps," she said.

"Miss Worrell," Rembert added, "you know we didn't have nothing to do with them taking your husband."

"I know," she said. She turned her attention back to Carson. "Did the other convict have anything to say?"

Carson shifted nervously in his seat.

"No, Ma'am," he replied. "The nigguh didn't say nothing."

"I suppose the warden took a strap to him," she said.

"Yes, Ma'am. He beat him down real good." He paused a moment. "Too good."

"He killed the negro," she said.

Carson hesitated. "No, Ma'am. Nigguh just up and died. Warden don't never kill no one."

"Uh-huh," she said. "Wardens never do. Seems to me you boys could do a better job of keeping an eye on them convicts so's they don't run around the countryside preying on good folks."

"We try, Ma'am. Sometimes, they just run off. But we catch 'em. We ain't never let one get away."

"We best get going," Rembert said. "There's a reward out, and these woods are gonna be crawling with folks pretty soon. All them fools gonna come around here and start messing up any tracks he mighta left. Carson, you stay at the cabin with Miss Worrell 'til we get back in case he shows up here. And if any of them bounty hunters come around, tell them we got things covered here. Send them on downriver a ways."

Carson yawned deeply and nodded.

Faye kept her eyes on Rembert and Hiram through the cabin windows as they looked around outside.

"How long you been living out here?" Carson asked.

Faye watched the movements of the men outdoors and didn't like what she saw. They began to study the ground in the yard in the growing light.

"Since I been married," she replied, her attention fixed on the others. "Going on fifty years, I reckon."

She saw Rembert and Hiram consulting for a few moments before walking back toward the cabin. There was a knock on the door. A moment later, Rembert opened it and poked his head inside.

"Carson. Get out here," he said.

"What is it?" Faye said.

"Now, don't be alarmed Miz Worrell," Rembert said, "but you got tracks in your yard. Looks like a man's footprints. And they come to your front door. These are fairly recent tracks, Ma'am."

"Coulda been one of them men tracking the convict. You said they're all around here trying to get the reward money."

"Could be," he said, lowering his voice. "Best not take that chance, though. You had anyone visiting in the last day or so?"

She shook her head. "But you know we get all sorts of strangers around here with the river nearby and the highway and them train tracks. Dallas and me used to feed a man or two every month a few years back when things was real hard and folks were shifting place to place looking for work."

"Has anyone stopped by since yesterday?"

"No," she said.

"I think we better check out your cabin real good and the barn out back."

"Please do!"

"You stay right here," he said, walking into the bedroom, gun at the ready. He emerged a few moments later, and shook his head.

"Nobody back there. Let's go check out the barn."

While Rembert and the other men inspected the back area, Faye moved the cot back to its usual position. They returned to the cabin a few minutes later.

"Did you look under the truck?" she asked.

"Yes, Ma'am. We searched both the barn and the truck real good. Now, here's what we decided. Me and Hiram are gonna go on back into town and fetch one of the hounds they brung up from the camp. They got the escapee's bed mattress, so the dogs got his scent real good. We're gonna bring one of them back here and search the area all the way down to the Altamaha. Carson is gonna stay here with you."

"I'll shoot the son-of-a . . ." Carson began. "Sorry, Ma'am. I'll shoot him down if he comes near."

"That's all very well for you men to talk about dogs and shooting people," Faye said. Her voice trembled with a touch of agitation and fear. "I can't take much more of this."

"Ma'am, you can come into town with us."

"No, Sir! I'm going to my sister's place over to Pineview. I want to get as far away from this nonsense as I can."

"Suit yourself, Miz Worrell. But if he's around these parts, we'll have him by noon."

"You go and get those hounds. Just don't let them in my house," she replied, fearing they would find the trap door. "Otherwise, do whatever you like. But I'm leaving!"

Faye started packing in the bedroom after Rembert and Hiram left. Carson stood by the kitchen window peering out into the woods for signs of movement. She noticed his yawns grow in frequency and duration and decided it was time to go implement an impromptu plan of action. She entered the large room with a frayed canvas suitcase she stuffed with overnight clothes.

"What would you do if you were in my shoes?" she asked. "Do you think I should stay? What if there's a gunfight or he tries to burn down the cabin?"

Carson turned from the window. His eyes were bloodshot from several sleepless days of a manhunt.

"Ma'am?" he said.

"Do you think I should leave or stay? What would you do?"

She pulled a small glazed jug from one of the shelves and placed it on the sink. In it was a quart of her late husband's brew from an especially potent batch of distilled liquor.

"Ma'am," Scott said again, his gaze fixing on the object with the cork in its spout, "Is that what I think it is?"

She looked innocently at him and held up the jug. "This? It's medicine."

"It looks like something that holds shine. That wouldn't be left over from your husband's still would it?" She smiled. "Dallas left a few samples around that the government didn't get a holt of. But I use it strictly for medicinal purposes, like this little cut I got on my finger this morning baiting a hook in the dark."

Carson eyed the jug, and licked his lips as she first removed a wax seal, then the cork stopper, and poured a trickle over the tip of her finger.

"You mind if I take a look at that?" he said, sitting wearily on the bench.

"No. I don't mind," Faye replied. She placed the jug on the table and pushed it toward him.

Carson held his nose over the spout and inhaled. A moment later, his eyes bulged and he gasped for air.

"Whew! That's some honest-to-God white lightning!"

Faye giggled. "I call it medicine. It'll cure all kinds of ills."

Carson yawned again.

"Including drowsiness," she added.

His ears perked.

"Ma'am, Warden Knox has had me, Hoke, and the others up for two days and two nights straight. We ain't slept a lick."

"How about some more coffee?"

He paused and eyed the jug.

"You said this stuff can cure the drowsies?"

"If you take the right amount. Too much, and you know what will happen."

"I know," he said. "It'll knock you out like a light."

"Well," she said, reeling in her catch, "you want some more coffee or some medicine?"

He looked at the jug and back at her.

"I'm about sick of drinking coffee. I think I could use some of your . . . uh . . . medicine."

"Okay," she said, "hep yourself."

She watched Carson pour a quarter of a mug full. "This enough you reckon?" he asked.

"That's about right," she said.

He lifted the mug to his mouth and hesitated before throwing his head back and downing the contents. He put the mug down and waited for the anticipated eruption which struck three seconds later, when the vapors traveled up his windpipe and into his sinus cavities.

"Jesus—Glory—Halleleujah!" he yelped as he shot off the bench and hopped across the room, breathing fast and hard, beating his chest with one fist. His face turned red. Tears formed in his eyes. A minute later, he was still reeling from the effects.

"Good god, Ma'am!" he said with a laugh. "That there is some mighty fine medicine. I ain't never been this wide awake!"

Faye grinned. "Well, I'm glad you think so. I forgot something in the back room. I'll be back in a little bit."

"Take your time, Ma'am," he said, moving back to the window.

She stayed in the bedroom and shuffled things around, pretending to search for a lost item, all the while keeping an ear out for movement in the other room. Twice in the course of five minutes, she heard the sound of liquid being poured and Carson gasping for air.

"I clean forgot all about them fish," she said, walking back into the big room. "I'll clean 'em and fry 'em up. By the time them boys get back from the river, you can have some breakfast. After that, I'm leaving."

"I'll come outside with you," he said.

"No, no. You stay at the window. If anyone comes out of the woods, I'm sure you'll see them and come to my rescue. Might even tempt the prisoner to show himself."

Her advice seemed sound to Carson. With her out of sight again, he could take one last hit of her late husband's exceptional product. Faye cleaned fish at the outside sink and peered in the window where she saw Carson once again throw his head back. This time, he stumbled clumsily about the room.

She came back in the cabin a few minutes later to find him passed out on the cot, half his body on it, his legs hanging off on one side.

"Glory be!" she mouthed between clenched teeth, seeing that he blocked her next move.

Faye poked his shoulder several times to make sure he wouldn't wake up. Then, she knelt by the cot.

"Ben!" she whispered loudly.

"Yessum," he replied.

"Don't make any noise. There is a man on the cot here. I'm gonna get the truck, then I'm gonna get you out of here. You hear?"

"Yessum."

Faye took her suitcase outside and pulled the Ford alongside the cabin. She got out, opened the passenger door, and lifted up the seat to reveal a hidden compartment big enough to hold a man. Years before, her husband had modified the interior to hide jugs of moonshine. He had cut the seat in half and hinged it so that either side could be lifted.

She entered the cabin again, gingerly walked past Carson, and grabbed an apron hanging on the wall. Faye wrapped it around the leg of the cot resting on the trap door. She then leaned back and pulled on both ends of the apron, straining with every inch of her ninety-pound frame. Fortunately for her, Carson was not a large man, and the end of the cot where his head lay slowly inched away from the wall. When both legs of the cot completely cleared the doorway, she knelt down next to it and tapped on the floor with her knuckle.

"Come on out!" she whispered loudly, her tone urgent but calm. "Hurry! Open up!"

A moment later, the trap door cracked.

"Carson still here?" Ben whispered.

"Shhh!" she replied, holding a finger to her lips.

"Hush up, and come out of there."

The hinges creaked as Ben lifted the doorway higher. Faye looked up at the guard, but he didn't stir. "Come on," she said impatiently, "we don't have time to sit here jawin'."

He stepped out of the cellar and turned to see Carson three feet away.

"Miss Faye, dey got me surrounded. Dey gonna have dem dogs here soon. Ain't no use in me runnin' an' gettin' you in trouble wiff de law."

"Hush. Slide him back to the wall."

Ben carefully lifted the front of the cot and moved it to its original position. As he did so, Carson turned onto his back. Faye and Ben remained motionless, waiting for his eyes to open. Instead, he began to loudly snore.

"Out cold," she said. "Just like I hoped for. But I didn't reckon he'd get on the cot."

She picked up her suitcase and pushed Ben toward the door. Once outside, Faye motioned for him to use the stepping stones that ran from the front door to the drive.

"Step up into the cab and get down into that," she instructed, pointing at the open seat and the space beneath it.

Ben's eyes lit up at seeing her plan unfold.

"Miss Faye, you gots mo' hidin' places dan ol' Bruh Fox."

"Stop jawin', and climb inside! They'll be back here afore too long."

Ben climbed into the hidden compartment where he contorted his body to fit in the cramped space. Faye closed the seat on top of him and cranked the motor. A few minutes later, they were on the highway heading away from Lumber City toward Jesup.

"Get comfortable," she said. "I don't want you crampin' up and making noise in case we come up on a road block."

"I comf'table," he answered.

"I'm sorry 'bout your friend."

Half a minute passed before he responded. Ben knew his escape would cause some hardship for the other convicts, especially those on his gang, but he didn't foresee the warden going after Roos the way he did.

"Tank you, Miss Faye," he said. "God in heavin mete out he justice in good time. But I still worried 'bout de men whut cum to yo cabin. Dey know you headin' to yo sister house."

"Well, that's what they think. I'm not going to my sister's house in Pineview. I'm going to my cousin's in Gardi, on the other side of Jesup."

"Dat gettin' close to Sapelo," Ben replied. "De law lookin' fo me down dere."

"I've been studying on that all night, Ben. And I got a plan."

"What de plan is?"

"You'll see soon enough.

On the outskirts of Hazlehurst, Faye rounded a bend in the road and came upon a roadblock set up by the town's police.

"Hush up, now," she said. "We're coming up on a barricade."

The officer in charge looked inside the truck cab as she came to a stop.

"How do, Ma'am," he said, tipping his hat. "Mind if we look under your truck? There's an escaped convict."

"I know all about it. You go right ahead, Officer," she answered.

His inspection, like the one near Lumber City, was quick, but when he returned to the driver's window, he noticed something curious.

"Ma'am, my daddy's got the same model truck as this one, and I know the seat of his truck ain't nearly as high as this 'un."

Ben held his breath and waited for the officer to ask Faye to step out of the cab. She burst out with a short, convincing, and disarming chuckle.

"This seat is high!" she said, patting it. "My late husband—God rest his soul—added a few inches to it 'cause he was just a short fella, and I'm a little old lady. I think sometimes them folks in Detroit is making cars for giants. You'd think they'd make some for us little people, too, wouldn't you?"

The policeman grinned and nodded.

"I hear you, Ma'am," he said, looking over his shoulder. No other cars were approaching, and he had time to kill. "Personally, I do a little re-engineering of my own on that squad car sitting over there. Me and my brother did some modifying, and now that thing will get up to a hundred on a good stretch of highway. Someone tries to run any shine through this town, I'll catch him. Guaranteed."

"Well, good luck to you, young man," she said, putting the truck into first gear.

"Thank you, Ma'am," he replied, stepping back. "You drive safe, now."

Another roadblock at the Appling County line was of a shorter duration, but yielded the same results.

"Miss Faye, de poleece ever'where," Ben said after they cleared the second search.

"Don't you worry about the police. Didn't I say I had a plan? Isn't God watching out for you?"

He cracked his side of the seat open a few inches for air.

"Yessum. You sho did say you had a plan. An' God sho is watchin' out fo me. Sometimes I tink he tek he eye offa me 'cause he gots other tings to do, but most de time, he watchin' out purty good."

Seven miles outside the town limits of Jesup, Faye felt the first sickening lurches of a truck running low on fuel.

"Gracious!" she blurted. "If it isn't one thing . . ."

She thought the truck had enough fuel to reach Jesup and was reluctant to stop at a filling station on the off chance a nosey gas station attendant might overhear Ben moving or ask questions about her seat like the policeman.

"You runnin' out of gas, Miss Faye," Ben said.

"I know," she replied distractedly, her voice rising in anger at herself. "This is the *very* thing I didn't want to happen. Goodness!"

She pulled the truck to the side of the road, cut the engine, and set the brake.

"Miss Faye . . ."

"Let me think," she replied, rubbing her temples. Her best option, she thought, would be to flag down a ride and claim Ben worked for her, but with a manhunt in full swing, it was an option fraught with dire consequences. He wouldn't be allowed inside a car driven by whites. If they were fortunate enough to hail a truck, he would have to ride exposed in the back of the truck. Then there would be questions from the driver. Where are you from? Where are you going? Did you hear about that prison camp escapee? What's your man's name? Where is he from?

"Miss Faye," Ben said again.

"I'm thinking," she replied.

"But Miss Faye, dey is fuel under dis here seat."

"What are you talking about?" she said, exasperated at the turn of events. "What fuel?"

She heard some shifting beneath her. A moment later, he opened the hinged seat and held out a gallon jug. "Yo husband leff sum med'cine. Dey is two of dem jugs down here."

"Ben! Do you think it will run on this?"

"Miss Faye, if dis here med'cine is strong as dat stuff in de house, you gonna haff trubble keepin' de truck frum flyin' to Jesup."

"Well, stop jawin' and pass me them jugs!"

Faye stepped out of the cab and poured the contents into the gas tank. When she got back in the truck and closed the door, she said a little prayer.

"Lord, please let this motor start up," she said aloud.

"Miss Faye, you best get a good grip on dat wheel."

The Ford flung gravel and left tire rubber on the road once the motor engaged and she let the clutch out.

"Mercy!" she cried, struggling to keep the truck in the right lane.

"Miss Faye, keep her on de road!"

"I'm trying, Ben. I'm trying!"

"Dat some ser'ous med'cine in dem jugs. It cure man and machine."

"Stop talking. I need to concentrate," she said, laughing.

A little while later, they entered Jesup city limits and pulled into a lot next to the train depot.

"Stay put," she told Ben, before walking inside the depot and inquiring about the train schedule. She returned a little while later with two large biscuits stuffed with ham from a nearby restaurant.

"Here," she said, flipping the passenger seat up and passing the food to him. "Eat this."

Ben gulped down his breakfast as she explained her plan to him.

"My Dallas used to bring some of his best produce here," she said. "He'd sell it to porters working on the passenger trains, and they'd sell it up north or down in Miami, depending on which way the train was a'going. There was one train, the *Sundowner*, would come through here twice a week like clockwork, and he'd drive here to meet it. I checked the schedule, and sure enough, it should be stopping here pretty soon like always."

"Which way it headed?"

"Going north. Just like you want."

"How you gonna get me on dat train, Miss Faye?"

"Don't know. But you will be on it."

She sat behind the wheel and observed people coming and going.

"Ben," she said after finished the first biscuit, "you can see spirits, right?"

"Yessum. I sees spirits."

"How 'bout dreams. Can you interpret them?"

"I gots sum o' dat power, Miss Faye. One o' my aunts had de power to tell people whut dey dreams mean, real good. I reckon I may be able to."

"I had a dream last night," she said after a long pause. "I've had this dream for going on three nights in a row. Even before you come up the river."

"Whut you dream, Miss Faye? Don't leave nuthin' out."

He took a large bite of the second biscuit.

"I was fishin' down to the river when I caught a big catfish. The biggest ol' thing you ever saw. It was wriggling and shaking, trying to get loose. All a sudden, all these little bitty catfish jumped up out of the water at me like they was trying to get at the big one. They just kept a-comin'. One after the other."

Ben stopped eating.

"Dat it, Miss Faye?"

"That's the dream. I wouldn't think nothing of it, but it's come to me three nights now."

Ben took a small bite and chewed it absentmindedly before speaking. "I knows whut de dream mean, Miss Faye," he said, his tone slightly downcast but matter-of-fact.

"Oh?"

"Yessum. Dat big catfish be me. Dem li'l cats is de law. All dem mens is lookin' fo me. Dey won't never stop 'til I get caught. De law got a arm dat stretch a long way, Miss Faye. I know dey gonna catch up wiff me one day. But I just wants to see my girl one mo' time. If I do dat, I don't care no mo' whut dey do. I been free fo a few days, and you treated me real nice. Dat mem'ry can carry a man fo many a year."

"Okay," she said, "the law might catch up with you. But not today. You hear?"

"I hear you, Miss Faye. Not today. No sir. Not dis day."

Forty-five minutes later, a passenger train arriving from Florida slowly pulled into the station.

"Come on," she said. "We got to do this fast while there is commotion on the platform."

Ben wiped perspiration from his face as he climbed out of the seat.

"Here," Faye said, handing him ten one dollars bills.

He stared at the money and shook his head.

"No, Miss Faye. I cain't tek yo money. You done too much already."

"You take it!" she said, stuffing the bills into his shirt pocket. "Now, we don't have much time. So do as I say."

"Yessum, Miss Faye."

Ben put on the coat she'd given him as they approached the last passenger car. The platform came alive with travelers and porters. One of them, a little man with buck teeth and a perpetual smile, stepped down from the train. Faye approached him with Ben close behind.

"Is there a porter named Robert working this train?" she asked.

The man looked up at her as he bent to pick up two pieces of luggage.

"Yes, Ma'am. I'll go and get him for you."

A minute later a tall, rotund man in his late forties stepped onto the platform.

"Yes, Ma'am," he said, tipping his hat, "Someone said you asked for me?"

"You're Robert?"

"I am," he said, smiling broadly.

"I'm Dallas Worrell's widow," she said, lowering her voice. "You do remember him? He used to sell . . . you know . . ."

"Sure, I remember Mister Dallas," Robert replied. "I ain't seen him in a while. You say you're his widow?"

"Yes."

His smile disappeared. "I'm sorry he passed on, Ma'am. He was a good man. A fine man."

"The law got a hold of him."

"I'm sorry, Ma'am."

"Yes, yes," she replied impatiently, "Look here Robert, I have another package for you."

"Oh?" he said, looking around to see if the conductor was nearby.

She stepped closer and lowered her voice further. "Can you take this man?"

Robert looked over her shoulder at Ben and made a quick assessment.

"The law after him too?"

She nodded.

"You buy a ticket, Ma'am?"

She shook her head. "Too risky. They'll be looking for negro passengers."

"You did right," he said.

Robert scanned the platform again. People were moving quickly. Some passengers disembarked, others got on, still others popped inside the station to make phone calls or head across the street to the drugstore. He paused a moment before speaking again.

"The baggage compartment gonna be a tight squeeze," he told Ben.

Ben's expression didn't change. Compared to sunup-to-sundown backbreaking road labor, an all night ride in tight quarters would be a luxury.

"Dat mighty fine wiff me," he replied.

"If the law finds you, I'll tell them you're a stowaway who snuck on the train when I wasn't looking. Okay? I don't know how you got aboard. I ain't never laid eyes on you. Understand?"

"I unnerstan," Ben said. "Ain't no one seen me get on."

Robert's eyes lowered and fixed on a large square box bound by leather straps that sat on the platform, cargo to be shipped from Jesup to someone up north.

"Ma'am, I'd be happy to deliver that package for you," he said loudly enough for passersby to hear. He pointed at the box. "If your man would go ahead and grab that freight, and put it on the train . . ."

Faye motioned for Ben to do as the porter said.

"Yessuh," Ben replied. He stepped over to the heavy bundle and lifted it onto his shoulder with some difficulty.

"You two best say your good-byes," Robert whispered to Faye. "Once he gets up those steps, he ain't coming back off."

"God bless you, Miss Faye," Ben said as he passed her.

Faye reached up and patted his shoulder as he went by. She started to speak, but the words wouldn't come out.

She watched him labor with his burden up the steps of the passenger car.

"Can you get him to New York City?" she asked Robert.

"Yes, Ma'am. We'll get that package to New York. Don't you worry about that."

Faye reached into her purse.

"No, Ma'am. Your cargo is paid in full."

"But I want to give you . . ."

"Step lively!" Robert called out to the other porters and platform workers. "This train departs in five minutes!"

"He'll need food," she protested. "Let me at least pay . . ."

"Awful sorry 'bout Mister Dallas, Ma'am," he said.

He tipped his hat and climbed onto the first step.

"I'll take real good care of your package," he said.

"Bye, Ma'am."

Faye stepped back, making room for other passengers to board. A few minutes later, the train slowly pulled away from the depot. She looked in each window as they passed by, hoping to catch a last glimpse of Ben, but by then he was well tucked away where no passenger or train conductor would find him.

She watched the *Sundowner* pick up speed, taking precious cargo with it. Soon, the train was out of sight.

CHAPTER 35

A little after seven o'clock that evening, Robert opened the door to the luggage compartment and set a tray atop a stack of suitcases that hid Ben from view. The head porter flipped on a switch, turning on a single overhead light bulb.

"Supper," he said.

A few minutes after he closed the door and left, the smell of cooked food overpowered Ben's reserve. He peeked out from his hiding place and saw the tray. On it was a dish covered with a metal warmer, a small plate of rolls, another plate with a large slice of coconut cream pie, a glass of water, and silverware rolled up in a white napkin. Ben carefully removed the warmer and breathed in the aroma of several pieces of sliced steak which the chef had carved off other customers' meals, a vegetable medley, and a baked potato stuffed with butter, sour cream, and bacon bits.

"Lawd a'mercy," he said, his mouth watering at the sight. Roos and the other convicts often talked about the meal he saw in front of him, but the likelihood of his ever enjoying one again had seemed remote to Ben just a few days before. He prayed long and hard before devouring the food.

When he was through, he turned off the overhead light and returned to his hiding place. There, he resumed his vigil, absorbing the rhythm of the train as it moved along the tracks, occasionally swaying gently around curves. He listened for voices and footsteps, but soon fell asleep.

An hour later, he heard the compartment door open and close again, followed by voices just outside.

"Come on. Let me have a look!" one of the men said in a raspy, high-pitched voice.

"I told you, Scat, ain't nobody in there."

The second voice he recognized as Robert's.

"Then what you pick up that tray for? I know you got a woman in there. Come on, let me have a look."

"No! Now, go on. And don't come snooping around here no more."

"I ain't snooping. Just coming to pull down the berths. Come on, man. I know she's in there. Just gimme one look."

"You want a look?"

"Yeah, I want a look."

"You sure?"

"Sure, I'm sure! Stop playing around now."

"Okay."

Ben heard the door open and saw the light come on. "See. I told you ain't nobody in here," Robert said. "Uh-huh," the second man said, "then what is them crumbs doing on that suitcase? She's back behind that pile, I bet."

"You want to see?"

"I told you I did."

Robert instructed Ben to come out of his hiding place. He reluctantly appeared and saw the porter Faye first spoke to on the Jesup depot platform.

"You satisfied, Scat?" Robert asked the little man. "Now, you in it. This here man is running from the law."

Scat's jaw fell as anticipation of viewing a female stowaway turned from disappointment to alarm.

"The law after you?"

Ben nodded.

"And now, mister-had-to-see-in-the-luggage-room, you have stepped your foot right in it, too!" Robert informed Scat.

"I ain't never seen him," Scat replied.

"You may not have seen him, but now you gonna help me get him to New York City. And you better help me watch out for the conductor to see that he don't come snooping around here either."

"What you did?" Scat asked Ben.

"Never mind what he did," Robert snapped. "Take that tray back to the kitchen. Then get on back to your bed making."

Robert watched Scat disappear down the corridor before turning his attention back to Ben.

"You get enough to eat?"

"Yessuh. Dat wuz sum mighty fine food."

"Folks will be getting along to bed before too long.

There's a restroom back here on the left if you need to go. Best take care of any business you need to tend to now while folks are dining."

"I'm okay," Ben assured him.

"All right. I'll be back to check on you later."

Ben remained alert for several hours before succumbing to the *clack-clack* of steel wheels on rails as the *Sundowner* plied its way across the mid-Atlantic states. He fell into a deep sleep and dreamed he was on the river again, taking Eli's body back to Sapelo.

"The river like a snake," the old man had warned him before he took his cousin's body downriver. "It shaped like a snake, always twisting and turning, and you riding on his back. You gots to watch out the whole time, or he'll rise up and bite you. When the river bites, ain't nothing you can do."

Ben dreamed he was in the belly of a serpent, winding its way north, but he was at peace. This snake couldn't rise up and bite him. It had already consumed his flesh. It was justice for escaping the full punishment of planting the fatal root against the Cale family. As the dream progressed, the snake turned into a giant fish, and he realized he was Jonah, being transported from danger to a large city. The dream continued to take unexpected twists and turns, culminating with the vision of the carcass of a rotting catfish that lay on a riverbank in the pitch-black night. He was relieved when the night instantly turned into day, and he awoke to realize that the light bulb was on in the cramped room he'd been sleeping in.

"Psst. It's me."

It was Robert's voice.

"You in there?"

Ben found that he had somehow made enough room to sink down into a curled sleeping position on the floor and struggled to rise. When he finally came out of his hiding spot, Robert closed the door behind him and sat atop a large, leather trunk. He opened the top of a thermos and poured black coffee into the lid.

"Want some?"

Ben shook his head. "No, tanks. Where is we?"

"Somewhere in Virginia," Robert replied. "We'll stop over in D.C. in a few hours and be in New York City by morning."

"You ain't going to bed?" Ben asked, eyeing the thermos of steaming coffee.

Robert laughed. "Lord, no. I got a room full of poker-playing men down the hall and a berth full of passengers. Some of them are old. Some got sick kids. These white folks is up all night. I don't get no sleep on the *Sundowner* run. Maybe a few little naps here and there during the day."

Ben grinned. "I always heard you porters got it good."

"Yeah," Robert said. He took a sip of coffee and put his feet up on piece of luggage. "We don't work in the fields or swing a hammer, but taking care of white folks ain't as easy as it looks. All the high-yellows get to work in the dining car, 'cause the company doesn't want us dark-skinned negroes upsetting people while they eat. We don't upset no one shining their shoes, or making their beds, or fetching things. God help the porter who gets off the train in the South and doesn't tip his hat to a white woman or step aside for a white man. Don't get no sleep on a train, and if you're lucky, you sleep in a bug-rid bed some other man just slept in at overnight stops. Now, Scat, that little man who was in here earlier, he got a wife and kids in Miami and another wife and kids up in New York. He got home-cooking and a warm bed on both ends. Me, I just ride the rails and make a few dollars picking up things at one depot and selling them down the line. I'm not complaining, but it ain't easy."

"Nuthin' easy dese days."

Robert agreed and leaned heavily against the wall behind him.

"Where you going in New York?" he asked. "To see my sisters," Ben answered.

"Where are they?"

"Dey in New York."

Robert rolled his eyes and grinned. "Where in New York? It's a big town."

"Manhat . . . Man-something."

"Manhattan?"

Dat sound 'bout right."

"Where in Manhattan?"

"In de black settlement, I suppose."

Robert chortled. "Man, you got to narrow it down more than that. They probably in Harlem."

"Yeah! Dat it!"

"Okay. Where in Harlem?"

"Uh . . ." Ben thought hard. It was their custom for Geneva to open the letters his sisters had written to them and to address envelopes with their replies. He had never given much thought to memorizing their address. "I cain't 'member."

"A hundred and tenth street? A hundred and twenty-fifth?"

Ben tried to recall the address on the letters they had exchanged. A number popped into his head.

"I tink dey say one hundred and thirty or forty-sumtin."

"Okay. That's Harlem. Where on a hundred and thirtieth?"

Ben shrugged. "Dey ain't never said."

Robert tilted his cap up and wiped his eyes with a handkerchief.

"Must be west hundred and thirtieth. You know where they work?"

"One of dem work in de factory. De other work fo some rich white folks."

"Do they talk like you?"

"Yessuh. Least, dey use-ta talk like me."

"Well," Robert said, thinking it over, "I reckon Scat can find them."

Robert yawned and stretched his arms.

"What time it is?" Ben asked.

Robert stared at his watch, letting his eyes adjust in the dim light. "About twelve midnight. Almost time for the 11:59."

Ben looked at him quizzically. "The 11:59? What dat?"

"You ain't never heard of the Death Train?"

Ben shook his head. "No, Suh."

"Well," Robert said, straightening up, "every man who rides the rails knows about the Death Train." He leaned forward. "If you ever hear a train whistle at 11:59 at night, you have exactly twenty-four hours to clear up your earthly concerns, 'cause at 11:59 the next night, the Death Train is going to carry you away."

Robert stared at his watch again and looked up after a minute had passed.

"Ten seconds past midnight," he said. "No train whistle."

"I reckon we okay fo another day," Ben answered.

Dawn broke over New York City as the *Sundowner* pulled into Penn Station. Ben left the train amidst a group of men carting trunks into the train terminal. He stared wide-eyed at the building's immense interior, thinking it the largest structure in the world. Scat led him to a small room and told him to wait until he or Robert returned from the payroll office. Half an hour later, both he and Robert showed up.

"This is where we part ways," Robert told Ben. "I got another train to catch."

Ben took his hand and shook it.

"I tank you."

Robert held out a crisp five-dollar bill. "Miss Faye from Georgia told me to give this to you," he lied.

"I can't tek no mo' money frum Miss Faye," Ben replied.

"You go on and take this," Robert said, placing it in Ben's hand. "Otherwise, some less deserving man gonna get it."

Ben reluctantly put the bill in his coat pocket.

"Scat is going to take you to his apartment," Robert continued. "He lives up in Harlem, too."

"That's right," Scat chimed in. "I'll help you find your sisters. Any of them good looking?"

"Hush up that kind of talk. For a little man, you got enough women to worry about."

"I'm just asking . . ."

"Now, be careful who you talk to," Robert warned. "Both of you. If there is a reward out, and folks find out, someone gonna turn you in. The law probably watching your sister's place right now, so be real careful."

"That right," Scat agreed. "Can't trust nobody these days."

Robert and Scat's ears perked to an announcement made over a loudspeaker, which Ben couldn't quite hear or understand.

"That's your train," Scat told Robert.

Robert started to leave and stopped at the door. "Remember what I said. Be careful who you talk to, black or white."

"Come on," Scat said. "We gonna catch another train in Grand Central."

"We in New Yoke?" Ben asked.

"Yep."

"I don't wanna catch no train. I wanna stay in New Yoke!"

Scat laughed aloud. "We ain't leaving the city."

"You mean we catchin' a train to get around in de same town?"

"Yep."

Ben shook his head. "Dis here sum big place."

Scat laughed even harder.

Once outside the station, Ben stared wide-eyed at the towering structures, some still under construction, which loomed overhead.

"Lawd a'mighty," he repeated under his breath. He felt as though he'd been reborn into a new world a million miles and a million years away from the simple life on Sapelo and the shackled confines of the prison farm. He'd seen pictures and heard stories of the big cities, but nothing had prepared him for the onslaught of sounds and images that bombarded his senses.

He followed Scat east on 34th past the Empire State Building and north on Park Avenue to Grand Central. Each step brought renewed wonderment to Ben, who could not have imagined or dreamed of such a place on his own.

"If heaven anyting like dis," he told Scat, "it sho gonna be a big time."

"Just wait 'til we get to Harlem. You'll see a big time then."

Ben closed his eyes and prayed when the train to Harlem pulled away from the crowded underground platform. He looked out the window a few minutes later and saw they were enshrouded in darkness. Soon, he felt the train car rise, then fly like a bat out of a cave and burst onto the hard belly of a concrete and steel world spread out to infinity in all directions. The buildings weren't as tall now, but they stretched out as far as he could see.

"Lawd, lawd, lawd," he mumbled.

As the train proceeded on the elevated track to Harlem, Scat chatted incessantly, excited to be back in New York with spending money in his pocket.

"I got apartments in New York and down in Miami with a woman in each place. It's what they call burning the candle at both ends," he said, laughing at his own humor. He lowered his voice and tapped Ben on the knee with his forefinger. "The secret is don't never tell the wife how much money they pay you."

He patted the wallet in his coat pocket.

"I got money here for Barbara. She's my woman up here. She pays the New York rent."

Scat took off his hat and removed a small wad of cash stuffed in the lining.

"This here money is for Wanda. She's down in Miami."

He pulled an envelope containing tip money from the recent trip on the *Sundowner*.

"And this here *my* money for the clubs." He laughed. "You see? You got to keep separate accounts. One for your women, one for you. See what I'm saying?"

Ben shook his head.

"De law allow you two wifes?"

Scat smiled. "If you have two wives, it's bigamy. If you have three wives, it's called polygamy. If you have just one wife, it's monotony!"

This statement brought about a burst of laughter from Scat and several men who overheard him. Ben thought about Roos entertaining his fellow convicts in the back of the prison farm truck each morning, giving them a few moments of laughter in an otherwise bleak existence. He smiled at Roos's memory, which Scat mistook for approval of his joke.

"Don't you worry about me finding those sisters of yours," he assured Ben. "I know women. I know how they think, see? Finding them is gonna be a snap."

Ben sat silently, gawking with growing anxiety at the breadth of the city, which seemed to grow in immensity the further they traveled. Until that moment, the largest towns he'd seen were Waycross and Baxley. Manhattan, with its hundreds of paved streets filled with traffic and hemmed in by manmade canyons, disoriented and distressed him. It would be harder for the law to catch up to him there, but he couldn't imagine finding his sisters or Naomi among the multitudes.

"All de people's in de whole world must be in dis place," he blurted, interrupting Scat's tales of the Savoy Ballroom, the newly opened Apollo Club and other Harlem hangouts.

"Man, you ain't seen nothing yet," Scat replied, laughing aloud, "This is just lower Manhattan. Wait 'til we get up into Harlem. They got more clubs, lounges, cafes, taverns, rib joints, dance halls—you name it—than you can shake a stick at. You can go to a different club from eleven at night 'til breakfast, every night for a month, and not go to the same place. See, I sit in with a band called the Jazz Cats when they in town. The bandleader, man named Gussy, he lets me get up there and sing sometimes. I don't always remember the words and make up stuff. Jazz players call that *scat*. That's how come I got my nickname. After we get you situated, and I get back from the next Miami run, I'll show you around. I know a club I might can get you a job pushing a broom or working in the kitchen. You know how to cook?"

Ben shook his head. "I work in de lumber bidness. An' I can build roads."

"That's all right. We'll get you some work somewhere. There's lots of work 'round Harlem. Plenty of work for a black man across the river, too."

Ben shook his head as the city continued to unfold before him. "You mean dey is mo' New Yoke City dan dis?"

Scat laughed even harder. "Oh yeah. This is just Manhattan. There's Brooklyn, Queens, the Bronx, Long Island . . . Shoot, you ain't seen nothing," he repeated as he leaned closer to Ben and lowered his voice again. "This is the best place in the world to hide from the law. You're just a drop in the bucket here. We'll go to my place, get some breakfast, then we'll head up to a hundred and thirtieth, and start looking for your family. We'll find them before night comes, guaranteed."

Back in Lamar, Geneva stood at the entrance of the drive leading up to the Cutler home. Black crepe hung around the two brick pillars marking the property's entrance. Streams of black and white visitors, their faces solemn, their eyes downcast, passed through the gates in cars and on foot. She didn't need to be told why they were coming, even though she had just arrived in town after her brief stay on Sapelo. However, she held out hope that the death in the family was that of Clayborne's mother.

"Who dead?" she asked Willie, who led a delegation consisting of the black logging crew and their wives.

"Clay, Junior," he said, removing his hat. "How he die?" she asked.

"Don't nobody know. They say Miss Cutler went to the crib yesterday, and he was dead. The good Lord needed another young un' up in Heaven, I reckon."

"I know that's right," Willie's wife affirmed. "Little babies ain't hurt nobody."

Geneva walked in stunned silence as the words replayed in her head.

"I reckon it murder," she told herself when she got home. She made a little fire in the back yard and burned Dr. Crow's final conjure.

CHAPTER 36

The search for Delphine and Rona produced no results on Ben's first day in the city. That night, he slept on the floor of Scat's crowded apartment, but got little sleep. When he closed his eyes, the day's images came flooding in like a movie reel, relentlessly replaying city scenes. He stayed awake most of the night taking in the night sounds, listening to babies crying in adjoining apartments, and hearing Scat make love to Barbara.

Scat remained discreet in his search, focusing mainly on black employees of neighborhood grocers and retail shops.

"I wish we had a picture of your sisters," he told Ben mid-morning on the second day of their search.

"I ain't never seen no picture of dem," Ben replied. "You don't have cameras down there in Georgia?"

"We gots cameras. My folks don't believe in picture tekkin'. Dey say it steal a man's soul."

Scat bent double with laughter. In his occupation, he had traveled across most of the United States east of the Mississippi. He'd overheard the conversations of leading politicians, sports figures, writers, and entertainers of the day. Now, walking the streets of Harlem, in the midst of a renaissance, Ben's dialect and ways seemed like something out of the distant past.

"Man, this is the 1930s!" he said. "You got to get in step with the times. Forget all of that slave talk. A camera picture don't steal no one's soul no more than the man in the moon."

Ben thought about roots Dr. Crow had prepared against islanders in the past. The power of his conjures often required a piece of the person's identity—a lock of hair, a clipped fingernail, a patch of cloth, or a name written on a piece of paper. It was commonly known that a person's photograph represented the Holy Grail for root doctors. It comprised a person's entire identity.

"All I know, it whut de ol' folks say," Ben replied, believing an elder's word to be the final authority on a subject.

Between runs to Miami and back, Scat searched the surrounding neighborhoods by day and visited Harlem's clubs by night. A week after Ben had been in the city, Scat secured a job for him at a nightclub called The Basement. There, he met a young singer named Billie just getting her start as an entertainer. She was particularly interested in his descriptions of life in the Deep South. When he told her about Eli's lynching, she promised Ben his cousin's death would not be forgotten.

Ben's work consisted of helping in the kitchen and cleaning up during the morning hours after the club closed its doors. He received five dollars a week for his labors and a room on the third floor of the same building that housed the club.

After a few weeks of working from ten at night until eight in the morning and scouring the neighborhoods in his spare time, Ben became increasingly despondent over his chances of locating Naomi. Perhaps, his sisters had moved back to Sapelo, he speculated. He couldn't write home or have anyone inquire on his behalf. He knew mail and telegrams would be watched carefully. Anything coming from New York would alert authorities to his whereabouts.

One evening, he cleaned up a tray of spilled drinks in a back room of the club where several games of poker were underway. Ben felt the eyes of one gambler, a white man, follow him across the room. A few minutes later, he stepped into the alley behind the club to set out a trashcan. He felt something touching his body and looked up. In the streetlight he could see mist-like raindrops descending. He stretched his arms wide and lifted his face to the heavens, opening his mouth to let the droplets hit his tongue just as he and Roos had done.

"God water!" he said.

He had been standing in that position for several moments when he heard a familiar voice from behind.

"I thought it was you," the voice said.

Ben turned and saw the outline of someone standing in the doorway of the club's back stairwell. The man stepped out of the shadows and into the light. He wore a pinstriped suit and patent leather shoes. In his left hand, he held a deck of cards. His red hair seemed to sparkle as tiny droplets landed on his head.

"It's me, Ben," the man said. "Billy!" Ben craned his neck and squinted. "Missa Billy? Is that sho'nuff you?" The man laughed.

"Of course it's me. But I go by the name of Billy Street now."

"Is you done serving yo time?"

"You could say that. As far as I'm concerned, I'm done."

"You mean you cut out an' ran?"

"You better believe it! Just like you. Folks are still talking about your escape. You inspired me and some other fellas to get out of there."

"How you get out, Missa Billy?"

Billy grinned and rubbed his thumb and forefinger together.

"Times are hard, my friend. Some guards will look the other way for the right price. One of them gave me a half hour head start. After that, the hand of Providence took over. I was fortunate enough to come upon the home of an accommodating lady who took a shine to me. I told her my story and did a little sweet-talking. Next thing I know, I'm driving to Chattanooga to catch a train. And here I am."

"Missa Waters, I know dat ain't de whole story."

"No, Ben, it's not. Fact is, I sort of borrowed her car and some of her cabbage—that is, cash—for the train ticket. But I feel she got her money's worth. Besides, they can trace the car tag to her. So really, she's just out a few dollars for train money."

Ben eyed Billy's new suit.

"Missa Billy, where you get dat outfit?"

Billy laughed. "Ben, would you believe I sweet-talked another little gal up here soon as I got off the train?"

"Missa Billy, I surprised you ain't sweet-talk some gal on de train."

"Ben!" a voice called from the bottom of the stairwell. "Where you at? I got some tables need clearing!"

"Comin' Boss!" Ben replied.

"Look here, Ben," Billy said, "I told you the hand of Providence was at work, and I meant it. You and me are twin spirits journeying through this life. How else can you explain our meeting up on the river like that, then as prisoners on the highway, and now here in New York City? Do you believe in predestination and reincarnation?"

"I don't know nuthin' 'bout dat, Missa Billy. I believe in de resurrection."

"Close enough. It's my firm belief that we've met many times in the past, and we'll meet again in the future. But for now, in this time and place, we are both in the same predicament. You once saved my life, now I'd like to return the favor."

"Missa Billy, dat ain't necess'ry."

"It is if you wish the cosmic forces to remain in balance."

"I don't wanna put nuthin' outta balance, Missa Billy."

"Good. Now look, they're already closing in on me. I can feel it. Know what I'm saying? If you got any family around here, you can bet your bottom dollar the law has men watching them, waiting for you to slip up."

Ben recalled the letters he received from Geneva while at the prison farm, some of which discussed his daughter's situation in New York. All of the letters had been opened.

"I searchin' fo my li'l girl up here."

"Ben!" the voice from below called. "Never mind him," Billy said. "He de boss man!"

"He's a mere bump in the road on our journey through life. Now, here's the plan, Ben. I'm moving up north to Toronto. If you're interested, have a bag packed this time next Friday. I'll be by to pick you up."

"Where you gonna get a car, Missa Billy?"

Billy pulled out a wad of cash from his pants pocket. "Been working the joints around here. 'Bout got enough to go legit."

"I cain't go 'til I find my li'l girl," Ben said.

Billy stared intently at Ben for a few moments. "Suit yourself, Ben. But I'm checking back here for you in a week. Okay?"

"Yessuh, Missa Billy."

"Next Friday."

"Yessuh."

"Ben! You seen a white man come up there? With red hair?" the voice called again.

Billy winked at him. "That's my cue," he said. He stuffed the cards into a coat pocket and hurried down the alley. "Same time next week. I'll be at the end of the alley," he called out before disappearing around the corner.

Eight o'clock in the morning of the following day Ben, too, felt the hand of Providence at work when Robert showed up at the club.

"You find them sisters of yours yet?" he asked.

"Naw, Suh. Dis town too big. Plus dey mighta went back home far as I know."

Robert chewed a toothpick and thought for a few moments.

"But Scat say he know women. How dey tink. He gonna find dem . . ." Ben began.

"Scat's too busy chasing skirts to be thinking about your problem," Robert interjected. "Tell me where you've been searching."

Robert listened intently while Ben described the numerous places he and Scat had looked. He closed his eyes and visualized the area they covered as Ben spoke.

"Hmph," Robert said disapprovingly. "Scat *thinks* he knows women. He's been looking everywhere except the one place only women folk shop at."

"Where dat?"

"Your sisters stitch clothes?"

Ben's eyebrows shot up.

"Dey sho do. Dey mek dey own dress."

"I bet you two haven't been inside one single sewing shop."

"Naw, Suh. We ain't."

"All right then. Put down that mop, and follow me."

Robert led Ben to different clothing stores around Harlem for two hours before locating a shop that looked promising. Inside, a woman in her twenties stood rearranging bolts of cloth on a table.

"May I help you?" she said smiling but somewhat surprised to see two men enter the store.

Robert removed his fedora. "You sure can, Miss. Me and my friend are looking for two females."

The woman cross her arms defensively. Her smile disappeared from her face. "This ain't that kind of place, Mister."

She turned to call the proprietor.

"No, no!" Robert interjected. "We're looking for this man's sisters."

He pointed at Ben, who stood next to the door, his hands behind his back.

"Okay," she replied, still suspicious of their intent. "Their names are Rona and Delphine."

She shook her head. "I don't know any Rona and Delphine. Do you have a photograph?"

"No, but he thinks they may live somewhere in this neighborhood."

"Lots of folks live here," she replied. "Lots more are moving in every day."

"You right, Miss," Ben said. "Dey is mo' negro folk in dis here place dan I knew dey wuz in de whole worl'." The young woman's eyes widened as Ben spoke. "Say that again," she said.

Ben looked quizzically at Robert.

"Repeat what you just said," he told Ben.

Ben cleared his throat. "I say, de is mo' negro folk in dis here . . ."

"I know where your sisters are," she said, interrupting him. "Two ladies come in here once in a while who talk just like you."

"Does dey haff a li'l chile wiff dem?"

She looked at Robert for an interpretation.

"Do they come in here with a little girl?"

She smiled brightly. "Yes! Uh . . . uh . . . Naomi! They're always talking to her. They say her name all the time. A cute little girl."

Ben stepped forward. "Where dey live?"

She rubbed her chin and thought for a moment.

"I don't know exactly where they live. They pay in cash, so we don't have an account with them. But they always come in from the left and leave to the left, so I'd say they live up the street that way," she said, pointing in the direction Ben and Robert had just come.

Several more inquiries along the same street led them to a three-story tenement building. They waited until almost dark before

Ben recognized Rona walking toward him along the sidewalk. In one hand, she held a cloth bag containing groceries. Naomi was nestled in the crook of her other arm.

Ben started to run after them, but Robert held his arm.

"Hold on, Man. These streets have a thousand eyes. Just play it real cool. You can hug and kiss on your family all you want once you get inside."

His words were barely out of his mouth when Rona saw Ben. She dropped the grocery bag and ran to him. The heads of passersbys turned as the reunion between brother and sister, father and daughter unfolded on the sidewalk. Rona wailed loudly at the sight of her brother, causing Naomi to cry. When Ben took his daughter in his arms, she cried even louder.

"Come on, Man!" Robert said, hustling Ben and the others inside. "Get on inside this building!"

Rona stopped halfway up the steps. "My groceries!"

"Go on in," Robert said, somewhat irritated. "I'll get 'em."

Ben remained inside the apartment with his sisters for three days, catching up on events and eating home cooked meals. Most of the time, Naomi stayed in his arms or asleep in his lap.

Robert's greatest fear was realized the morning of the fourth day when Delphine was about to leave for work. A sharp rap on the door startled Rona, who stood next to the stove, cooking Ben's breakfast. He sat at the table feeding Naomi when he heard men's voices and the sounds of leather-soled shoes on the apartment's hardwood flooring.

"Ben Jordan?" a voice said.

He turned in his chair and saw four men in plain clothes, three of whom surrounded him.

"Yessuh," he responded. "You're under arrest," the one closest to him said.

Naomi's eyes took in the strangers and all that transpired

around her.

Ben held his finger to his lips as Rona let out a yelp. He bent down and gently kissed Naomi on her forehead, then handed her to Delphine, who stood trembling with fear next to him.

"Don't upset de baby," he said.

As his sister took her from Ben, Naomi started crying, clinging to her father.

"I didn't know about this man being here!" a fourth man, the black landlord, protested.

"You evil!" Delphine shouted at him. "You an evil man fo bringin' de law. Ben ain't kilt no one, an' every white man in Lamar know it!"

"You two better start looking for another place to live," the landlord replied. "I don't need the police raiding my properties. I want you out of here by sundown!"

Naomi watched Ben being escorted away in handcuffs as her aunts alternately cried and shouted at the men taking her father from her.

The evening of Ben's extradition back to Georgia, a late model Buick came to a stop at the end of the alley behind The Basement nightclub. The man inside the car waited a half hour before cranking the car and heading to Canada.

CHAPTER 37

The sweatbox measured six feet long by three feet wide by two feet high, barely big enough for an average size man to stretch out. The men of Warden Knox's prison camp called it the hot box or the coffin for good reason. It was reserved for the worst offenses—for anyone who attacked a guard, attempted to escape, or proved too bull-headed to be broken. A man could last several days with water in milder weather, but three days in July or August was a death sentence.

The man unfortunate enough to be placed in the hot box had to crawl inside. The sensation of the hinged door swinging shut and being bolted was that of being locked inside a tomb. The box lay flat on the ground to maximize exposure to the sun where temperatures inside could reach 120 degrees. Small slits carved into the four sides functioned less as a means of ventilation than tiny portals for the entombed to suck air through during late afternoon when the air inside and out became stifling.

Ben's body dripped with sweat inside the box the first morning of his reincarceration in the prison camp. Any weight he had gained during his brief time of freedom was gone in the first twenty-four hours.

Some men broke quickly, screaming for relief from muscle

cramps and claustrophobia, clawing the interior until their finger-nails were bloody. The guards and convicts alike waited for Ben's cries, but they never came.

He had mentally prepared himself for his time in the box the entire return trip from New York to the camp, traveling in heavy chains, accompanied in a mail car by three policemen, two of whom never left his side.

Along the way, his father's words echoed in his head. "Dey can tek ever'ting you got. Dey can break yo body. But de spirit, de soul—cain't no man touch!"

The warden didn't lay a hand on him between the train station and the camp. Knox put the inmates and guards on notice not to acknowledge Ben's existence under penalty of the lash or loss of jobs. No one was to speak to him or make eye contact.

"Come by me!" Knox yelled as the convicts filed out of the bullpen and lined up in the prison yard. Ben wore an iron collar around his neck, connected by a thick chain to shackles on his ankles and wrists.

Bulldog paraded Ben in front of the other convicts while Knox reminded them about the hopelessness of attempting to escape.

"See this son-of-a-bitch?" he said, pointing at Ben as Hoke pulled the chain, walking him back and forth along the lineup of men. "You're looking at a dead man. He already cost another son-of-a-bitch, Roos, his life, and he cost the state of Georgia a lot of money and manpower tracking him down."

But none of that mattered to Knox. The thing that really angered him was the cost to his reputation. He lost sleep at night replaying his confrontation with Faye upon her return to Lumber City. Rembert Hall had brought her into town for questioning by Wade Scott, the sheriff. Knox insisted on being present, along with Hoke. While her answers satisfied Rembert and Scott, they only served to infuriate the warden.

STEPHEN DOSTER

"If you didn't know he was hanging 'round the place," Knox said, his voice loud and insistent, "then how in the hell was his scent all down in your liquor cellar! My dogs tracked him into your house and down under that trap door. Explain that!"

"Well, that's about what I expect out of you," Faye had replied with equal disdain. "I can't help it if your man comes in my house and goes down there when I'm out catching breakfast. You're the one let him escape in the first place! Then you got the nerve to come up here and start looking for a scapegoat. That's just like you—a coward. Always were, always will be!"

"Miss Worrell was concerned about her safety," Rembert said, supporting her story. "She told us she was leaving town."

"To take that son-of-a-bitch to a train depot! I bet he's on his way up north somewhere," Knox shot back, his eyes red with anger.

"Watch your language," Sheriff Scott interjected.

"Around who?" Knox said. "Her? I oughtta slap the bitch for what she done!"

Faye let out a long, full-throated laugh. "You? Little Sammy Knox? Yeah, you're a big man when it comes to beating helpless men or little old women. But you weren't so tough around these parts growing up here. You weren't so tough facing down Brady Peavey as I recall."

"Just shut up," Knox warned. "We were kids."

"Ha! You was twenty years old and too coward to fight in the war."

"Miss Worrell . . ." the sheriff began.

She ignored him and turned to Hoke. "Messed in his drawers like a two year old. The whole town knows about it. Just ask anyone."

Knox delivered a roundhouse to the side of Faye's head that sent her tumbling across the floor, but she got up laughing.

"Like a two-year-old," she repeated. "Coward then, coward now!"

The sheriff and his deputies escorted the warden to the county line. Knox swore Hoke to secrecy about what Faye had said, promising unnamed perks in exchange for his silence.

Now, Knox had Ben Jordan back in chains. All was right with his world once more.

"What do we do with a man who runs off?" the warden asked one of the older convicts.

"Put him in the box," the man replied.

"Put him in the box," the warden repeated. "Take a good look at this piece of trash. Next time you see him, he's gonna be roasted like a leg of lamb. Now," he said, turning to Hoke, "get that son-of-a-bitch outta my sight."

"Come on," Bulldog said, pulling hard on the chain, causing Ben to tumble to the ground. He whispered to Ben through pursed lips as Ben regained his feet. He, too, had a secret he didn't want revealed. If word got out he'd foolishly played cat-and-mouse with Ben, it could cost him his job. "You tell anyone about what happened at the river, and I'll shoot you dead where you stand."

By mid-morning of the second day in the box, Ben heard footsteps approaching.

"Hey, you still alive?" a voice asked. He recognized it as belonging to Carson, who had been relegated to prison yard duty for allowing Ben to escape. "Speak up."

"Yessuh," Ben gasped, his throat parched and swelling from the rising heat.

"He's still in there, warden."

Ben heard Knox reply from the shade of a tree near the entrance gate.

"Well, give the son-of-a-bitch one cup of water and a chunk of corn pone. I don't want him dyin' on us just yet."

That evening, when the convicts returned from their labor, several offered words of encouragement as they walked from the trucks to the bullpen. Ben heard their screams later as they were punished for the infraction.

Bulldog and several of the other guards gathered around the hot box each evening and placed bets as to how long he would last.

"I say the sumbitch don't last 'til mornin'," he heard Hoke say. "Nobody lives three days in there this time of year."

"I'll take that bet," another guard replied. "I give him 'til noon."

Ben lay inside panting from fatigue, adjusting to the heat dissipation as the night air cooled the outer shell, but he felt no animosity. It was his punishment for aiding in the death of God's anointed, Pastor Dodge, and for planting the root against the Cales. He had separated himself from God. In his mind, it was only right that he should be separated from his only child.

"Dey can break yo body. But de spirit, de soul—cain't no man touch," he murmured.

His father's words and voice returned to Ben more frequently and louder each time until they seemed to echo off the sweatbox's interior before landing on his ears.

He passed into and out of consciousness during the night, never sure if he was asleep or dreaming.

"You part Bu-Allah, part Ebo. Nobody ever seen nuthin' like dat. Never."

He heard his father's voice clearly, as if he was kneeling beside the hot box, speaking through its outer shell.

Ben didn't stir at three-thirty in the morning of the third day when the trucks backed up into the yard to load prisoners for a day of labor. When he awoke, it was with a jolt. The sun beat down from high overhead. Carson served the daily ration of water, but Ben's throat was too swollen to drink it down or take any food. He could barely open his eyes or comprehend Carson's demands to eat.

"He's going fast, warden!" Carson called out.

When the sweatbox door swung shut for what he thought would be the last time, Ben tried to open his eyes again. To his surprise, the interior was brightly lit, as if he was staring directly into the sun. As his eyes widened and acclimated to the intense brightness, a figure dressed in white clothing slowly emerged from the light, filling Ben with renewed strength. He stared for what he thought was an eternity before the figure fully emerged into a man of regular build. The box's interior was no longer small enough to hold a single man but large enough to accommodate more people than had ever existed. Ben dared not take his eyes off of the apparition for fear of losing it in the light, but he got the sense that he was now in another place with no borders, surrounded by infinite space.

"Is you a angel?" he finally asked, still unable to fully see the man's face.

"Confess," the man said.

The voice was calm, almost hushed, but it washed over Ben, soothing his bodily afflictions like a balm on an open wound.

"You is a angel!"

The man didn't answer.

"I know I done sinned," Ben said at length, his voice returning to him. "I kilt dat fambly. I kilt de whole lot. I kilt de preacher man, too!"

"Confess to the anointed."

"I confess!" Ben said. "I coulda stayed Missa Cutluh hand, but I run off. I confess it!"

"Both of you must confess to one of God's anointed."

The man's voice grew fainter. He slowly moved back into the light until he became part of it. The light gradually dissipated as Ben's bodily pains returned in proportionate intensity. He heard a rattling sound that grew louder each moment, and he became vaguely aware that the sound was that of his body hitting the sweatbox as his muscles involuntarily jerked to and fro.

"Won't be long now," a voice said. Ben vaguely recognized it as belonging to Hoke, who was allowed to stay in the prison yard that day to witness Ben's final moments.

"Stick a fork in this one. He's about done," Hoke called out.

"Well, pull his black ass outta there," the voice from beneath the shade tree commanded.

Ben heard the hinged door swing open and felt two hands grab his clothes. He tried to tell them about the vision he'd had, but he could only mouth the words.

"Pull his ass all the way out!" Bulldog instructed a new convict who still wore street clothes.

"Yessuh," the convict replied. "I'ze pullin' real good, boss."

A few moments later Ben lay in a fetal position on the ground, his body twitching in the midday sun.

"Take them clothes off, and put his on," Bulldog instructed the man.

Ben's eyes jerked open occasionally, taking in the sight of a black man about his age, stripping. He soon became aware that the stripes he wore were being removed from him and that his body was being lifted into a wheelbarrow.

"You wanna see him?" Hoke yelled.

"Hell no. Just go bury his ass," Knox replied.

Hoke and Carson walked behind the new convict, who pushed the wheelbarrow holding Ben's body. Though Ben couldn't move or speak, he was acutely aware of the fact that they were taking him to the prison camp's burial ground. Halfway there, the sun's rays were blotted out by dark clouds rapidly moving across the sky.

"Take a good look," Carson told the newly arrived convict. "That's what happens when you try to escape."

"I don't think he dead, boss," the convict offered.

An instant later, the man felt a blow from Hoke's shotgun butt across the back of his head.

"Nobody asked you!" he told the man, who staggered before dropping to one knee. "Get your black ass up, and move that wheelbarrow!"

Hoke and Carson stood nearby while the man dug a hole wide and deep enough to hold Ben's contorted body.

Ben's lips would move from time to time, causing the convict to halt his work.

"You buryin' a live man," he said at last, no longer able to keep silent.

"Goddammit!" Hoke said, moving toward the man with intent to crack open his skull.

"Hold on," Carson said, pulling on Bulldog's sleeve. He approached the wheelbarrow and poked Ben's shoulder several times with the barrel of his gun. "I ain't buryin' no man alive, nigguh or no nigguh."

Ben simultaneously felt the sharp jabs of Carson's gun and looked down from above, watching the three men and the events taking place around his body. In that moment, he realized that his spirit was hovering over them, waiting for its final release. He watched Carson lean closer in an attempt to detect breathing. At the same time, he felt the cold, wet raindrops falling onto his face. Several drops landed on his lips, lubricating them enough to open and close.

"His lips are still moving," Carson said.

Bulldog looked up at the sky with irritation, then back at Ben and the hole in the ground.

"That's just muscle contraction," Hoke replied. "He's dead!" He looked at the convict. "Chuck his ass in the hole before it turns to mud, or I'll put a bullet in your damn head, and you'll go in it, too!"

The man sighed deeply. He pulled Ben's body out of the wheelbarrow and gently slid it into the hole.

"All right," Hoke said, "cover it up!"

The convict slowly slung a shovel full of dirt onto Ben's legs. Then another.

"Quick-like!" Bulldog shouted as the rain began to fall harder.

The man reluctantly shoveled another batch of dirt, tears welling in his eyes.

"Sorry, Man," he said to Ben.

Ben, still overseeing these events from above, felt his spirit slowly descend to his body as the rain revived it. His eyes flickered open and shut. The rain came down harder.

The convict stared at him, then looked up at Hoke.

"Man ain't dead!" he said, again, this time crying as the words came out.

Bulldog sent him sprawling with a blow to the back of his head. "If that son-of-a-bitch moves, shoot him," he instructed Carson. He picked up the shovel and piled dirt on top of Ben's body, cursing with each shovel load.

The convict lay on the ground groaning from the blow. Blood trickled from his skull onto the ground, where it mingled with rain and soil. A minute later, only a portion of Ben's face remained exposed. Hoke filled a shovel full of dirt and turned to dump it, when a shrill whistle came from the direction of the warden's office.

He and Carson strained to hear as someone shouted something they couldn't make out through the pouring rain.

"Sounds like Knox," Carson said.

"Can't be," Bulldog replied. "He don't like getting wet."

He turned to toss in the dirt. Carson grabbed his arm.

"No, look. It *is* him."

They watched as the warden walked at a quick pace toward the burial ground.

"What the hell does he want now?"

"He's yellin' about something," Carson answered. "Looks pretty damn mad."

"He's always pretty damn mad."

"Get that nigguh Jordan outta that grave!" Knox shouted.

"What?" Hoke asked.

"Get him out! Get him out now!"

"What the hell? He's dead!"

"He ain't dead," the new convict said weakly, turning over on the ground and clutching his head.

"Get that goddam body outta there, right now!" Knox yelled, his voice strained, his face beet red.

The new man scrambled into the hole and removed dirt from around Ben's face.

"Carson, go fetch Doc Langer," Knox commanded. "What for?"

"Go! Run, goddammit! If the doctor ain't here in a half hour, you can start lookin' for work somewheres else!"

"Jesus," Hoke said as Carson disappeared in the rain, "You told me to bury the sumbitch!"

Knox caught his breath and watched the convict struggle to pull Ben's body out of the grave.

"I just got off the phone with Governor Talmadge. He wants that black son-of-a-bitch moved to the prison over in Reidsville. Now, if you got a problem with that, I suggest you take it up with the governor."

CHAPTER 38

Geneva visited Ben at Reidsville once a month, keeping him abreast of events outside the prison walls, especially of Naomi's progress.

"She a sma't girl. Rona say she de sma'test girl in she school. Naomi gots powers she don't even know she have."

"She see spirit?"

"She see all sorts of tings. She see spirit. Dead peoples. Wanderin' spirit. She talk to spirit. Dat why Docta Crow want her so bad. He knew she gots de power. She got de power to see tings frum way back, Ben. She see tings dat happen on Sapelo befo we wuz born. She see tings frum Africa. Frum way back befo dem slaves cum over on de ship, frum 'cross de water. But she don't know whut dese tings is. She tink she dreamin'. Naomi got de power an' don't even know it. She a root docta on de New Yoke street an' don't nobody know it. Not even her."

"She happy, Neva?" Ben wanted to know.

Geneva paused and looked down.

"Naomi laugh all de time, Ben, but dat don't mean she happy. Delphine say she ain't cry since dem New Yoke poleece tek you frum her. When she get hurt, she laugh. She laugh when she oughta cry. Delphine say Naomi don't know how to cry no mo' since you leff."

Ben's sisters honored his wish to not to reveal his true identity. To Naomi, he was a cousin the family rarely spoke of. By the time she could talk, visits to Sapelo ceased altogether on the chance wagging tongues might slip and inform Naomi of her true connection to the man incarcerated in the Reidsville State Penitentiary. As she grew up, her powers grew dormant through disuse until she could no longer see visions of the past. By the time Naomi graduated from high school, she could no longer see spirits.

Conditions in the segregated state pen, while harsh, were a luxury to Ben compared to his time in the prison camp. The most striking difference was that he was no longer fettered by chains, and the inmates received three substantial meals each day compared to prison camp fare. He still performed hard manual labor, but the threat of the lash ceased, and he was allowed visitations by family members. Each night, he stared at the concrete ceiling, envisioning a starry sky above just as he did in the prison camp. It meant freedom from shackles, freedom from walls. He still dreamed of flying away to his home like the Africans once did to escape slavery.

One day, he heard a radio playing a new song. He recognized the voice as belonging to the young singer named Billie who had befriended him in Harlem. She had promised Ben that Eli's death would not be forgotten. Tears trickled down his cheeks as the words rolled off her tongue and echoed down the concrete corridors of his cellblock.

Southern trees bear strange fruit
Blood on the leaves and blood at the root
Black bodies swinging in the southern breeze
Strange fruit hanging from the poplar trees

As the years passed, Naomi occasionally sent Ben letters, which he savored and kept in the cell he shared with three other men. In

October of his twenty-fifth year behind bars, Ben was reading one of her letters when news spread through the facility that an important prisoner, a black man in his early thirties, had been delivered to the prison in the dead of night and placed in solitary confinement. Eight days later, Ben saw him in the exercise yard. He sat on the ground, his back to a wall, writing on a small tablet. Ben noticed an aura about the man. He wiped his eyes and blinked, recalling the apparition he'd seen in the prison camp sweatbox and the angel's message.

Ben hesitantly approached and came to a stop ten feet away. The inmate, aware of Ben's presence, stopped writing and looked up.

"Yes, Sir," he said in a resonant and assuring voice. His eyes were tired, his face, haggard from enduring over a week in a tiny, roach-infested cell.

Ben advanced a few steps closer.

"I Ben Jordan," he said.

The man took in Ben's features and nodded.

"Good to meet you, Brother Jordan. My name's Martin."

"I know," Ben replied. "I been readin' 'bout you in de papers."

"What can I do for you, Brother Jordan?"

Ben looked around and hedged closer. He sat down across from him.

"I'ze a sinner, Reverend," he said.

Martin smiled. "We're all sinners. You, me, these men, the guards watching over us."

"Yes, but," Ben began, leaning closer, "I kilt a fambly. Dey house burn up."

Martin's eyes narrowed. "You burned their house down?"

Ben looked around to make sure he couldn't be overheard.

"Yessuh. I planted a root on dem."

"A root?"

"A conjure. Docta Crow mek one up 'cause my cousin, Eli, got hung."

"Your cousin was lynched?"

"Yessuh."

"And you took vengeance into your own hands?"

Ben briefly bowed his head, then looked up.

"Yessuh."

Martin stroked his cheek and thought for a moment.

"Conjuring is some serious business. That's the devil's domain."

"I know."

"Have you repented, Brother?"

"Yessuh. Many times. I pray to God ever'day dat he forgive my trespass as I forgive dem who trespass on me."

"And they sent you to prison for planting a root?"

"Naw, Suh. Dat de real reason I had to talk wiff you. I in here fo killin' a preacher."

Martin studied Ben's face closer.

"You murdered a preacher?"

"Naw, Suh. I coulda stayed de hand of de man who done it—a white man. But I didn't. I run off."

"What happened to the other man?"

Ben shook his head.

"Nuthin'. He free as de wind. Dey give me fo'ty year. Don't nobody know who de other man is 'cept me an' him and God Almighty."

Martin leaned closer.

"What is it you want from me, Brother Jordan?"

"I seen a angel," Ben told him. "He come to me twenny-five year ago. De angel say I must confess to a man of God. I kilt a man of God, so I gots to confess to one. Dat were whut he told me."

"Twenty-five years is a long time," Martin said. "Why did you wait until now?"

"Not all preachers is men of God," Ben replied. "But you is. I seen it frum 'cross de yard. If you ain't a man of God, I don't know what is."

"Okay," Martin replied, "I'm listening, Brother."

He sat and listened as Ben recounted the evening that he and Clayborne Cutler met behind the rectory and fired shots into the house, how he was almost lynched outside the Appling County courthouse, and how the apparition appeared to him in the sweatbox of the prison camp. When he was done, Martin leaned back against the exercise yard wall and closed his eyes.

"Do you forgive me?" Ben wanted to know. "De angel say I have to confess, an' I done it."

"Your sins are forgiven," Martin assured him, "but not by me. Only the God of Abraham, the God of Isaac, and the God of Jacob can do that. You have done what is right in God's eyes, and you have more than paid your dues to society."

"But what about de other man? De angel say we bofe have to confess or we bofe face de same judgment?"

"God doesn't hold you accountable for another man's transgressions."

Ben looked away and shook his head.

"It was a angel sent by de Lawd . . ."

"Well," Martin replied, "when God speaks to a man, he better do what the Lord says. As far as I'm concerned, your sin debt has been paid."

"Tank you, Reveren'. But how cum you in here?"

Martin smiled. "They said I was driving without a license."

Ben's head jerked up, startled by the words.

"Sho 'nuff? Dey put you in here fo dat? In solitary? Dis a state prison. It fo hard mens."

This time, Martin laughed. "They didn't put me in here, Brother Jordan. God did. And now I know why."

"You do?"

"It's so I can meet men like you. I was thinking how rough I had it lately, like I might not make it to the Promised Land. But what I've been through has been nothing compared to your journey.

All that road building you and prisoners like you were doing was really smoothing the way for people like me. Now, I got to help smooth it out even more for the next generation. I'll be out of here pretty soon if everything goes right. But you . . . How many years did they give you?"

"Fo'ty year, Reveren'. Fo'ty long year."

Martin shook his head. "I can't promise anything, Brother Jordan, but I'll see what I can do about getting your sentence commuted."

"You can do dat?"

"I can try. A black man being charged with killing a white preacher in the Deep South is something a politician, North or South, won't want to touch with a ten-foot pole."

"I don't mind payin' my dues, Reveren'," Ben replied. "I gots fambly, and I gots de Bible. Dat all a man need. When I feelin' real low, I say, 'Out de depths haff I cried unto you, oh Lawd.'"

Martin smiled approvingly and joined Ben's recitation of Psalm 130. Their voices reverberated across the exercise yard. Other inmates stopped what they were doing and listened.

"Lord, hear my voice. Let thine ears be attentive to the voice of my supplications. If thou, O Lord, should mark iniquities, who shall stand? But there is forgiveness with thee, that thou mayest be revered. I wait for the Lord, my soul doth wait, and in his word do I hope. My soul waiteth for the Lord more than they that watch for the morning. I say, more than they that watch for the morning."

"Amen!" said some of the men who had been shooting hoops.

The moment was shattered by the sound of a metal door opening and slamming against a wall.

"King!" a voice called out.

Ben looked up and saw two guards approaching. They were accompanied by another man dressed in a three-piece suit and carrying a briefcase.

"Looks like I'm getting out of here," Martin said. He extended his hand and looked Ben in the eye. "Take care of yourself, Brother Jordan. You're in my prayers."

CHAPTER 39

"Hey, Pops. You okay? Pops?"

Luke, the Greyhound bus driver, shook Ben's shoulder.

"Pops! You all right, Man?"

Ben let go of the metal rail in front of him and looked up.

"Suh?"

"I said, are you okay? You been staring off into space. I thought you were having a seizure."

"He may be epileptic," another bus passenger offered.

"You okay?" Luke repeated.

Ben looked around him and realized he was no longer in the Reidsville penitentiary. He was in the front seat of a Greyhound bus stuck in traffic on a bridge spanning the Altamaha River. After serving a forty year sentence, he was finally heading home to Lamar.

"Yessuh. I fine."

"You sure?"

"Yessuh. I sure."

Luke announced to the rest of the passengers that the pulp truck had been up-righted and that they would soon be moving again. A few minutes later, a state patrolman motioned for him to proceed along the opposite lane around the accident.

Ben turned and glanced at the Altamaha one more time, afraid to look at it too long for fear it might induce more memories. He needed to stay focused on the present. He needed to complete the mission the angel had commanded of him.

"We'll be in Lamar in just a little bit," the driver told him.

Twenty minutes later, the sign welcoming travelers to "Lamar, Ga. Population 8,600", came into view. A small row of stores on either side of a large food market appeared on the outskirts of town.

"Lawd, God in heaven," Ben whispered as the bus passed new houses and the recently-constructed Cutler Elementary School.

His initial elation over leaving the prison grounds slowly gave way to feeling of trepidation. He sat paralyzed when the Greyhound came to the stop and a new passenger climbed the steps of the bus.

Luke checked the man's ticket, then turned to Ben. "Okay, Pops," he said. "You're home."

Ben swallowed hard and rose from his seat.

"You're gonna do fine," Luke encouraged. "Don't forget. You got a man to see."

"Dat right," Ben replied, his resolve returning by degrees with each step. "I gots to see a man about he soul." The bus pulled away, leaving a small whirlwind of dust in its wake. He soon saw a diminutive woman with gray hair and wearing her best Sunday dress and white stockings, emerge from a storefront. Ben stared long and hard at Geneva. She looked very different in broad daylight than she did inside the prison with its bright, fluorescent lights. She embraced him and quietly sobbed into his chest.

Ben put his arms around her and gently hugged.

Geneva pulled a small white handkerchief from her pocketbook and daubed her eyes. The decades-long struggle to secure her brother's release had taken its toll on her frail body, but her spirit remained unvanquished. Despite her efforts to secure lawyers, appeal to governors, and request church leaders to intercede on her brother's behalf, Ben had remained behind bars while men convicted of more heinous crimes served their sentences and left prison. Governors had served their terms in office and moved on. Church leaders rose through the ranks and retired or died off. Everyone but her brother, it seemed to Geneva, got on with his life while Ben remained in limbo year after year.

She had taken in washing and sewed clothes for generations of Lamar's best families. She'd watched their children grow up, leave town, and eventually move back. An occasional envelope postmarked Toronto, Canada always seemed to arrive filled with cash just when Geneva needed it most. Most of her spare funds went toward educating Naomi, who earned a degree in education and eventually took a position as an assistant professor of English at a northern university.

Now, Ben's wilderness journey was over. She intended to see that he got the most of the remaining time allotted to him.

"You hungry?" she asked.

"I okay," Ben replied.

"I know you okay, but is you hungry?"

He'd been too anxious to eat for two days.

"I'ze mebbe a li'l bit hungry."

"Well, cum on," she said. "I got sumtin' warmin' on de stove."

The ten-minute walk from downtown Lamar to the house in Scott Hill, was spent in silence. Ben mostly stared at the ground, only occasionally looking up to see the stores and homes that had been erected in his absence.

That evening, the two spoke for hours of things and people past using the deep saltwater Geechee dialect they had grown up speaking on the barrier island. It was the language they shared when they were alone or when they didn't want others to understand what they were saying. It was the one thing that tied them to a time and place that nothing and no one could take away—not progress, not the police or a judge, nor the state of Georgia, or the federal government. Their language, their memories were theirs to keep.

It was well past midnight when Ben finally put his head on a pillow. His room and bed hadn't changed since he left. When he closed his eyes, images from the day's journey raced through his mind in rapid succession. When they became too overwhelming, he opened his eyes to still them. At length, he drifted off to sleep and again dreamed of the two-headed pine tree. This time, it had been felled; brought down with ax blows, not a clean saw cut, as if the work had been many years in the making. He counted the rings to determine their ages. Both trees had the exact same number.

"Dayclean," Ben said aloud when he awoke at first dawn, still in sync with the prison routine of his later years—wake before dawn, breakfast, work, lunch, recreation, work, supper, Bible, sleep, then awake before dawn again. It had become his life rhythm, an unvaried habit. He hadn't thought about dayclean since leaving the Baxley courthouse in chains. He quietly rolled out of bed wearing a pair of denim bib-overalls and a red cotton long-sleeve shirt Rona and Delphine had sent as a coming home present. It had once been his year-round attire, even during the dog days of summer.

Ben eased the back screen door shut and crossed the railroad tracks. He walked to downtown Lamar just as he planned for the last ten years of his incarceration. The stores looked the same as the day before, only cloaked in shadows. He was pleased to see that tall crepe myrtle bushes, planted by a long-gone garden club, still lined both sides of the street. Wide sidewalks remained in front of two long rows of storefronts.

He walked to the corner and stood in front of what had once been Salty Hoffer's liquor store, now empty except for the Cutler Realty sign in the window advertising "Space Available." He looked in the large glass window at the vacant room inside and saw the reflection of a lean, balding man in his early-sixties with care worn eyes and graying hair.

"Been a long time," he murmured, recalling his nocturnal liquor runs with Hoffer. There, in the semi-dark, the town looked like he remembered it. "Been a mighty long time."

As he continued to peer inside, a tiny, brilliant fireball formed in the window. He followed the source of the light to a church at the end of the street, and realized the first rays of the sun were reflecting off the only Methodist steeple in a thirty-mile radius—a sign that God hadn't forgotten about the slain minister or Ben's mission.

Ben sighed and walked back toward the train tracks. "Lord haff mercy on de ghost-mens," he muttered. "Gots to see a man about he soul."

On the way back to his home, Ben passed an empty lot overgrown with trees and vines where Hoffer's home had once stood. Nothing remained of the one-story house, not even the chimney, whose bricks had been pilfered by poor families to help shore up the sagging foundations of their shotgun shacks.

He shook his head, trying to collect his thoughts. He was a black man with no formal education. Most of his sixty-two years on Earth had been spent behind bars. Who was going to hire him? Maybe he could get a job pushing a broom. He might become someone's yardman, weeding flowerbeds in the spring, mowing the lawn in the summer, raking pine straw in the fall. He thought about the old man he once overheard on Sapelo, a former field hand on the Spalding Plantation. "What me learn to read fo?" the man asked a visitor to the island, "Me ain't got no prospect." The same words echoed inside Ben as he approached his front yard.

When he entered the door, several neighbors and church members were seated in the front room. Ben recognized none of them save Deacon Thomas, now nearing his one-hundredth birthday. He was bent over. The vibrant voice that had once rumbled like thunder across church pews and echoed through forests had long been silenced by throat cancer. He took Ben's hands in his. Though he couldn't speak, his eyes told Ben what everyone else in the room said.

"We know you ain't killed no preacher. It's a doggone shame you went to prison and the real killer didn't. Welcome back, Brother Jordan. They should have let you out years ago. Years ago!"

A steady stream of visitors wearing their best clothes and bearing food trays, flowed in and out of the home until mid-afternoon. By two o'clock, Ben had to lie down.

"Too much," he told Geneva. "It too much fo me."

The next morning, Ben told her he needed a car ride.

"Where to?" she asked.

"I gots to see de Jesus Tree," he replied.

"What fo you wanna go dere?" she said. "It ain't de same no mo. Best keep de mem'ry like it wuz."

But he insisted. Geneva drove him in the used Chevy she'd acquired years before. She hadn't exaggerated in saying the place had changed. A few miles outside of town, they passed between two impressive brick columns, and were greeted with a large marker with the words "Tara Estates" chiseled on it. Clayborne and his wife had attended the *Gone With The Wind* premiere in Atlanta where they met the lead actors at a private reception after the movie. When he later opened up some of the Cutler timberland for development, Claudette had insisted the new neighborhood adhere to the movie's theme, complete with streets named O'Hara Avenue, Butler Drive, and Ashley Lane. The tract of forest had long since been replaced with homes built on riverfront property.

Ben directed her to where he thought Eli had been lynched. When she brought the car to a stop, they were parked in front of a two-story home. Ben stared at it and the well-manicured lawn, blinking his eyes in disbelief. In the middle of the yard, a lone pine tree towered high above.

"Still here," he said softly.

Geneva turned the engine off.

"Dis de spot," he said, rolling down the window and staring up at the pine. "Dis where dey strung up . . ."

She waited patiently as Ben's eyes took in the tree from top to bottom, expecting at any moment for him to say he'd seen enough and that she could drive them home. Instead, he got out of the car and walked toward the tree trunk as if drawn by an unforeseen force.

"You on white folk property," she called through the window.

A freckled, stocky man in his early forties stood near the garage, washing his car. Ben ignored him and circled the tree, staring up, searching for the limb from which his cousin had been lynched.

"Can I help you?" the man asked, approaching Ben.

"Yessuh," Ben said, turning toward him, "Does you needs a yardman?"

"Not really," the man replied, memorizing the license tag on the back of Geneva's car, "I keep the place up pretty good. You from around here?"

"Yessuh. I live in Lamar. Use to work fo Missa Cutluh."

"Clayborne Cutler?"

"Yessuh. Missa Clayborne an' he daddy, Obediah. I work fo bofe mens. Bofe of dem. My name Ben. Ben Jordan."

Geneva held her breath, concerned that her brother's name might register with the man, but most of the Tara Estates residents had been in Lamar for less than a generation. The man, an IBM typewriter salesman originally from Kentucky, had moved further south after college to cover the middle Georgia territory. He, like most of the newcomers, had never heard of the Dodge murder.

"Jack Carter," the man replied, eyeing him with newfound respect. "You say you worked for Mister Cutler?"

"Yessuh, I sho did. Use to log dese woods all 'round here." Ben slowly extended his arm in an arc from left to right. "Dis whole area. Use to log trees right here. Right on dis spot."

"Is that right? It's changed a little, huh?"

"It sho has, Missa Carter. It sho has."

Ben looked up and pointed to a spot on the trunk where the bark had been scarred like skin folded over an amputated arm.

"In fak, dey use to be a limb right dere. Big ol' limb stickin' out."

"Funny you should say that," the man replied. "Darnedest thing happened a few years ago. Some clouds rolled through here one afternoon, big black things. Didn't let out one drop of rain. Didn't make a sound except for one lightning bolt, and it struck this tree right where that limb was. Sheared it right off, like someone had climbed up there with a saw."

"De limb wuz dere," Ben said, "an' it poke out dis direction?" He motioned toward the driveway.

"You have a good memory. We'd be standing right under it."

"Uh huh, uh huh," Ben said absent-mindedly, thoughts running through his head. He mentally calculated how far out on the limb Eli's body had hung.

Jack looked at the license plate again, then back at Ben. He and the family were going away for a two-week vacation, and he needed someone to mow the yard in his absence. He had been considering one of the neighborhood kids, but the man looked like he could use the money.

Besides, he thought, *Ben's connected to the Cutlers, and I know the tag number of the car that brought him.*

"I tell you what," he said, "I do need someone to keep up the place while I'm gone. I was going to mow the lawn today, but if you can come back tomorrow . . ."

"Yessuh," Ben said, "I can be here tomorrow. Sunup."

"You got a mower?"

"Naw, Suh. But I can get one."

"Don't bother. There's one in the garage. It's gassed up. Come here, and I'll show you."

Geneva stayed in the car and watched as the two men crossed the lawn. Once inside the garage, Ben's gaze fell on the tool he was hoping would be there. On the opposite wall, a shovel hung on a four-inch nail.

"I reckon five dollars ought to cover your labor?" Carter asked.

"Yessuh. Five dollars is fine." "Why fo you wanna tek dat job?" Geneva fussed on the drive home. "You just outta prison."

He rocked contentedly back and forth in the front seat with a smile on his face. The morning's outing had turned out far better than he had expected.

"You gonna see, Neva," he replied. "Pretty soon you gonna see why."

CHAPTER 40

A few days later, Ben sat beneath the fig tree in back of his house, listening to neighborhood sounds. He recalled sitting there years before, listening to bird song for hours without interruption except for a distant church bell or the occasional train passing through town. Now, it seemed to him, loud music or the rumble of an overhead jet continually disturbed his quiet.

"Ben, we gots some guests!" Geneva called out through the screen door.

She knew from their days growing up on the island that it was best not to give her brother advance notice of visitors. He'd lose sleep worrying about what he would say or how he might act in front of company. Ben's years of prison routine only intensified his dislike of change.

"Wish they'd let me stay here," he once told one inmate, a lifer, who simply nodded, knowing fully well what Ben meant. Being outside for some convicts was the same as being on the *other side* to Sapelo islanders. Both were unknowns. Best stay where you are and stick to who you know and what you know.

Ben didn't bother to ask who the visitors were. He could guess. He'd been losing sleep anyway knowing that his daughter would eventually show up.

As he walked the dark hallway from the kitchen to the front of the house, the silhouette of a small figure with tootsie-roll hair darted past. When he reached the parlor, he saw a little girl sitting on the sofa next to a woman with exotic eyes and the Bu-Allah nose that appeared every so often among the descendants from Hog Hammock. The woman wore a yellow dress. A white, broad-brimmed hat rested on her lap. Outside, on the street, a new Ford Mustang glistened in the morning sun.

The woman rose to her feet and approached him.

"Unca Ben!" she cried out.

"Naomi," Ben said softly, embracing her for the first time in four decades.

The little girl remained on the couch, staring at him. He looked at his granddaughter with equal fascination. He could see his wife's features in her.

Naomi stood back, still holding his hands, and eyed his overalls.

"You look so good, Unca!" she said, with a giggle. He forced a smile. "Better dan stripes, I reckon." She had kept him apprised of her progress through undergraduate work as an English major and her pursuit of advanced degrees at northern universities.

"Whut you doin' wiff dat fancy diploma?" he asked.

"Unca, I'm moving to Georgia. I've accepted a position at Armstrong State in Savannah," she proudly announced. "I want Renee to be closer to her roots."

"Delphine and Rona also movin' back," Geneva added. "Movin' to de islan'. Dey say New Yoke goin' to de dogs."

"Harlem isn't like it once was," Naomi agreed. "It's used to be a great place to live, but now, it's really going downhill."

Ben's gaze moved back and forth between Naomi and the girl on the sofa, drinking in as much of them as he could.

"You teachin'?"

"She a principal," Geneva said.

"Assistant Professor, Aunt Geneva," Naomi replied with another giggle.

Her laugh was the one constant in her life, and it lifted Ben's spirits each time he heard it. It had helped her through her divorce from a man from the Dominican Republic who had used her to secure residency in the United States. After he left her for another woman, she went through several more romances before marrying a second time. Though short in duration, that marriage had produced Renee, the child on the sofa who couldn't keep her eyes off the man she instinctively knew to be of her own blood.

"Granpa!" the little girl blurted out.

Naomi laughed nervously. "No, no, Renee. This is Uncle Ben."

"He's Granpa!" the girl insisted.

Naomi laughed louder. "Honey . . ."

"Let her say Granpa if she want to," Geneva said.

"Won't hurt nobody."

Naomi stifled a giggle with her hand. "You're right, Aunty." She led Ben to the sofa. "Unca Ben, this is Renee."

"Hi," Renee said.

Ben slowly dropped to one knee and held out his hand. "Miss Renee," he said, his voice wavering, "Can I gets a hug?"

Geneva and Naomi looked on, expecting the girl to pull away out of shyness. Instead, she bounced off the sofa and leapt into her grandfather's arms with a force that almost knocked him over.

"Gently!" Naomi said, tossing her head back and laughing.

"She a good girl!" Geneva said encouragingly.

As Naomi looked on, memories from her own childhood began to stir.

Renee squeezed Ben hard around the neck and burrowed her head into his cheek. He hugged back gently as though embracing a carton of eggs while at the same time wishing to squeeze forty years of lost time into the moment.

"Oh, Granpa," Renee said as the tears rolled down his cheeks and onto her hair, "You don't have to cry. I'm here now."

After lunch, Renee nestled in Ben's lap in the shade of the fig tree while Geneva and Naomi sat around the kitchen.

"Granpa, you were locked up a long time, weren't you?" Renee asked him.

Ben looked at her, then at the ground at his feet.

"A long time, Miss. Dat whut happen when you do some bad ting."

"I know," she replied with a grin. "Mama puts me in the corner sometimes and makes me look at the wall. I try to think of things. Sometimes, I turn around and look outside, but I'm not supposed to."

Neither said anything for several minutes before Ben spoke.

"I know what you talkin' 'bout. I made up all kinds of tings in my mind. But mostly, I just looked out de window."

Renee swung her thin legs beneath the chair and made chirping sounds at the birds.

"Why you went to prison, Granpa?" she asked. "I done a bad ting," he said without hesitating. "Did you hurt somebody?"

He wiped perspiration from his forehead.

"I didn't hurt nobody, but I coulda stop de man who did, and that just as bad as doing de ting."

"You know," said Naomi, watching from the kitchen, "this is so weird . . . I seem to remember sitting out there with my father under that old fig tree just like they're doing."

"You do?" Geneva said, trying to hide any sign of emotion that might betray her. "You wuz just a li'l baby den."

"I know, but I'm having some serious déjà vu right now, Aunt Geneva."

"Day-zaw who?"

Naomi laughed. "I wish y'all could have saved some photographs of him."

"Well, Chile, we wuzn't never much on tekkin' pictures."

"I wish we had taken more photos of Harlem when I was growing up. It has sure changed since Aunt Delphine and Aunt Rona first moved there."

"Lamar haff changed, too." said Geneva, attempting to steer the conversation away from Ben. "I 'member when dis street wuz dirt. Shoot, I 'member when most de roads 'round here wuz dirt."

"I guess the Cutler family still owns most of the town," Naomi said.

"All of it! Cutler own all dat property. Ever'one of dem shops on de main block, includin' de movie house. An' he own de property where de fillin' station wuz. He got dat, too!"

Naomi turned in her chair and straightened the hem of her dress.

"I suppose I should give Mr. Cutler a call and let him know I'm in town."

Geneva crossed her arms and stared out the back door.

"Hmph," she grunted.

"Aunt Geneva, did I say something wrong?"

"Hmph," Geneva grunted again, rocking to and fro.

"It a free land. You can call dat man when you in town if you want to."

"He did pay for my education," Naomi said.

Geneva turned toward her. "Chile, it time you know sumtin'. When you wuz a li'l girl, Missa Cutluh give me some money to put in de bank account to build up fo your education. But dat ain't what put you through school."

"It's not?"

"No, Honey-Chile. De money I put in dat account wuz washin' an' sewin' money an' money frum a man in Canada who say Ben once save he life. It wuz washin' an' sewin' money dat put you into college, plus dem . . . dem . . ."

"Supplemental scholarships?"

"Dat right. But it wuzn't no Cutluh money!"

Naomi put her hand to her mouth to stifle a laugh. "Sorry, Aunty," she said, embarrassed over her habit of laughing or giggling at inappropriate moments.

"I knows you laugh when you nervous," Geneva told her. "Ain't no need to apologize to me, Chile."

"But what about. . . ?"

"Missa Cutluh's money?" Geneva smiled and pointed outside. "I spend all dat, ever' bit of Cutluh money on lawyers trying to get yo uncle outta prison. Ev'ry Cutler dime of it!"

That evening, Ben lay in bed staring at the ceiling just as he had done in the prison camp and at Reidsville. Some nights, he felt himself flying back to Sapelo, hovering over the island, but never landing. Though he had confessed his sin to a preacher, he believed he couldn't die in peace or return to the island until Cutler confessed as well. The spirits of his ancestors wouldn't allow it. Bu-Allah, dead for over a hundred years, wouldn't allow it. More importantly to Ben, the angel had told him both he and Cutler must confess. Their very souls were at stake. When he felt his resolve wane at confronting the richest, most powerful man in the region, Ben remembered his encounter with the angel. Replaying the memory gave him courage to fulfill his mission.

CHAPTER 41

Clayborne Cutler saw something moving out on the long driveway leading up to his house. At first, he thought it was a deer, but he soon realized the figure stood upright, moving slowly, but steadily. Soon, he could see it was a black man wearing a broad-brimmed straw hat and overalls. He assumed from the measured gait and the sloped shoulders that the visitor was about the same age as him. As the figure drew nearer, Cutler saw the small burlap bag in the man's left hand.

"Don't want none," Clayborne barked when Ben got within talking distance. "Whatever it is you're selling, I got one. If I ain't got one, I can go get it myself."

Ben kept moving, slowly approaching the wraparound porch of the Cutler home. To his right, he passed a two-headed tree that split into a V six feet above the ground. Two towering pines sprang from the shared trunk to a height of seventy feet.

"I been dreamin' 'bout you all my life," he murmured to the tree. It had been cut down in his last dream. He'd counted the rings. Now, he knew for certain who the other man was Tiny Ruth had prophesied about many years before.

"I see a tree sproutin' frum de earth," she had told his parents. "It a pine tree wiff two heads. Dis baby's soul tied to some'un else.

De tree will reach up to de sky. De two heads cum into dis world together an' will leave together."

He turned to his left and allowed his eyes to adjust to see the man on the porch, shaded from the morning sun's glare.

"I lookin' fo Missa Cutluh."

"That's me," Clayborne replied.

Ben stopped and looked more closely at the man on the porch. He wore faded pajamas and sat in a wheelchair with a bottle of oxygen set in a metal basket. The man lifted nicotine-stained fingers to his lips, alternating between drags on a cigarette and inhaling deeply from an oxygen mask.

"I lookin' fo Missa Clayborne Cutluh," Ben said, thinking he must be talking to an elderly relative.

"Damn it to hell, you're talking to him! Now, state your business!"

Ben's jaw went slack. The sparse white hair Clayborne still possessed, dangled precariously from the back of his head to his shoulders like loose wisps of spider's thread. His voice, though raspier and deeper, sounded somewhat like the man Ben had once known. The only real evidence that this was indeed, the same Clayborne Cutler, could be found in the fierce eyes that burned with enmity and bitterness. Ben had seen that look many years before behind the Methodist church rectory. He crossed a small plot of yard toward the steps.

"Ain't nobody invited you up here on this porch!"

"Missa Cutluh, it me. Ben Jordan. Don't you know me?"

"Hell, yeah, I remember you, Ben Jordan," Cutler said. "You got a lot of nerve coming out here like this, unannounced."

Ben climbed the five wooden steps to the porch and leaned against a supporting post near Cutler's wheelchair. He lifted his hat and wiped his brow with a white cotton handkerchief.

"Ain't nobody gots to know I here, Missa Cutluh," Ben replied. "Everyone in church."

"Well, state your business, then get the hell off my property. I posted no trespassing signs out there."

"I seen 'em, Boss. You posted dem real good. But whut I gots to say is real important. It bout life and deff."

Clayborne leaned forward in his wheelchair to study Ben more closely. A number of thoughts raced through his mind. Having the man accused of murder on his porch the first thing after his release might start people talking. But then again, why shouldn't Ben pay his respects to his former employer, the man who had saved his neck at the Baxley courthouse, and the man who had contributed money for his daughter's education? Besides, Cutler's wife was in Lamar attending church service. No one had to know Ben had even visited. Although Clayborne would never admit it, he craved the rare visitor who made the trip up his drive to see him.

"Hell," he said with a wave of his hand, "I reckon I can spare you a few minutes."

Ben leaned on the porch railing with his back against a post.

"I don't see many folks from the old days," Clayborne said after a few moments of silence. "Things have changed, Ben Jordan," he said. "Things have changed a lot since we last saw one another."

"Sho haff, Boss," Ben said, instinctively affirming Clayborne's superior social status, much to Cutler's pleasure.

Geneva had wanted him to accompany Naomi, Renee, and her to the First African Baptist church that morning. "It goot fo de soul," she said, but Ben told her he had an appointment to save a man's soul.

"Some folks don't know their place anymore," Cutler continued. "Young people don't have a lick of respect for their elders."

"No respec'!" Ben echoed, shaking his head. "No respec'."

Some of the younger blacks sent to Reidsville had referred to Ben and others his age as Uncle Toms for not standing up to the white man sooner. They didn't know how things had been in his day, and they didn't want to know. As far as they were concerned, he'd had his chance and blown it. They were going to change the world on their terms. Conditions at the state pen had deteriorated since its opening. Public outcry over prison camp abuses had shut them down, putting men like Warden Knox out of work. However, many of the prison camp guards had found employment at Reidsville. As the camps had died out, overcrowding at the pen increased. Still, Ben thought conditions were better than what he'd experienced under Knox. The younger inmates hadn't wanted to hear about that either.

"You know what I do these days, Ben?" Clayborne said. "I sit on this porch and watch the driveway. Used to be a steady stream of people coming up here—politicians needing middle Georgia votes, businessmen, reporters—big men in power and little people writing about men in power."

"Is dat right, Boss . . ."

"Herman Talmadge, Billy Stuckey . . . you name 'em. For years, if they were in this neck of the woods, they came to see me."

He paused, recalling days gone by, then shook his head in disgust.

"Then, a while back it got to be the ones coming up the drive were men either looking for my help to get into a state office or men on the way back down looking for a soft place to land. The last few years have been college kids working on their damn MBAs or some such garbage. They read all about me and Tremont Rogers. We wrote the book on setting up hotels up and down highways in the South. You ever heard of Holiday Inn? They copied my model. They won't admit it, but they did. And those Stuckey restaurants and gas stations, where do you think they got the idea for that?"

"Where dey get dat idea, Missa Cutluh?" Ben replied, clueless as to what Clayborne was talking about after spending four decades in another world.

Cutler thumped his bony chest with a crooked forefinger.

"Me! That's who. Hell, by the time these college kids get hired into a real business, everything they learned is going to be out of date. If one of them came up here now, you know what I'd tell him?"

"No, Boss. Whut you gonna tell him?"

"I'd tell him my daddy, Obediah Cutler, was right! He had it all over these big shots today. All we Cutlers know how to do is chop down trees, sell 'em, grow some more, and chop 'em down. That's it. All you got to do is one thing, and do it right. I should have never let Tremont talk me into diversifying. That was the big thing back then . . . getting into all those other lines of business. Nowadays, the only one who comes up here is someone who got lost taking a shortcut from Lamar to McRae, or people like you, the ghosts of Christmas past. Well, that's a fine how-do-you-do for someone who gave his life to this town. Used to be, I'd go into Lamar and people would gather around me. Gather 'round me, Ben. You hear what I'm saying?"

"I hear ya, Missa Cutluh."

"When that highway finally came through town . . . Hell, I owned downtown. I mean I owned it lock, stock, and barrel. Children would run up to me, Ben. Children! Where are they now? And their children?"

"I don't know, Boss."

"Now, they run the other way like I'm some ghoul. And they just named an elementary school after me. That's irony for you, Ben. You know what irony is?"

"No, Boss."

"It's that damn highway, Ben. That gottdamn highway! Full of empty promises. Brought money to this town, and made me rich. That same highway took money right on out of here, Ben. I fought hard to put Lamar on the map. Now, look at it."

"De town growed big, Missa Cutluh."

Clayborne shook his head in disgust. "It's drying up. Can't lease any space downtown. Not even . . ."

He stopped himself, avoiding the subject of Salty Hoffer and the corner building that had once consumed his waking thoughts. There was a time when Clayborne had considered it crucial to the launch of the empire he envisioned. Now, the space stood empty.

"It's that highway," he continued. "People in Lamar use it to leave town. They go to that indoor mall down in Brunswick or up to Macon on that highway. And they're going to those little strip malls. That's what they call them. Strip malls. I should have listened to my daddy. I should have stuck to timber. It's what we Cutlers know. Daddy was right, Ben. Daddy knew."

Ben rocked forward and nodded in affirmation as Josephine's words echoed in his head.

"I should have listened to my momma, Missa Cutluh. Shoulda never leff de islan.'"

Clayborne emitted a raspy gurgle of a laugh.

"Ben, you still talk like you just got off the damn boat from that island."

Ben scratched his head and smiled.

"De ol' peoples used to say, 'You can tek de man frum de islan,' but you cain't tek de islan' frum de man.'"

"Well, you can't tell a young man anything. I was full of piss and vinegar right out of school. Told ol' Gene Talmadge exactly what was on my mind. The governor of Georgia, Ben! There I was, this young little snot, talking man-to-man with the governor."

"Young folks is bold as lions, Boss."

"Yeah. They're bold. But they don't know anything. A man doesn't know squat until he turns fifty. Then, it's either too late, or he's been mighty damn lucky. I was lucky, Ben. Mighty lucky. I admit that. Most successful businessmen won't admit it. Just try finding someone else who will fess up."

Clayborne stared down the driveway, lost in thought. He turned around and faced Ben again after a long silence.

"I used to be in it, Ben. You know what I'm saying?"

"I hear ya, Boss."

"I used to run the show. Then, one day, you wake up and . . ."

"An' whut, Missa Cutluh?"

Clayborne shook his head and stared at his feet. "Show's over," he said almost inaudibly.

A long pause followed. Only the hum of a ceiling fan filled the silence. Ben cleared his throat.

"Missa Cutluh, whut you wuz sayin' 'bout fessin' up is de reason I here today."

Clayborne, whose mind often wandered to better days, pivoted his wheelchair and looked up at Ben.

"Oh?" he asked guardedly.

Cutler hadn't expected Ben to survive the prison camp, nor had he expected Eugene Talmadge to make good on his promise to transfer Ben to the Reidsville state penitentiary when the first cellblock had been built, but the governor never forgot a name or a face, and granting the seemingly insignificant requests of constituents became a useful tool in the arsenal he employed to retain power. Over the years, Clayborne had made discreet inquiries about Ben's incarceration, sometimes using his connections to surreptitiously block Geneva's efforts to gain her brother's release. It had been bad enough seeing Geneva at events in and around Lamar. She represented a painful reminder of an egregious injustice he perpetrated. If her brother's sentence had been commuted, he would also have returned to Lamar, and the guilt would have been magnified.

For her part, Geneva had made it a habit to be present at store openings, dedication ceremonies, and other civic gatherings so that Cutler could see her face. He was the only white man in town she allowed to see her eyes. All the others, she concluded, had either participated in Eli's lynching, Ben's false conviction, or had stood idly by, doing nothing to prevent either. She had witnessed Clayborne's slow, physical deterioration over the years, simultaneously pleased, guilt-stricken, and terrified at the power of Dr. Crow's conjure, a curse that did its daily work years after the medicine man's death.

"Missa Cutluh," Ben began, clearing his throat. He'd prepared for this moment for years, ever since his encounter with the angelic spirit in the sweatbox. But now, sitting face-to-face with the man whose eternal destiny was tied to his, the words came out unlike the way he had rehearsed.

"Missa Cutluh, dey is two confessions we gots to discuss."

"Oh?" Clayborne repeated, leaning closer.

"De first one is dat someone I know done planted a root against you. Dat why you a sick man."

Cutler hesitated, thinking he had misheard Ben. "A root?"

"Yessuh."

"The hell are you talking about, a root?"

"It a conjuh, Boss. A hex. De person plant it unnerneath yo back step. It whut make you all sick inside."

Clayborne sat up and let out a hoarse, winded laugh. The conviction with which Ben spoke such nonsense amused him. The more he thought about it, the more the notion caused him to laugh, triggering a coughing fit that produced a mouthful of dark liquid which he spat over the porch rail. When he sufficiently recovered, he turned to Ben.

"You want to know what's killing me? It's this . . ." He held aloft the cigarette in his hand.

"This is what's been doing me in."

"It de root, Boss. Ain't nuthin like it. Docta Crow give me one to plant against dem Cales, an' it burnt down dey house. De whole fambly!"

Cutler waved his hand dismissively.

"Jesus, Ben. Don't get me coughing again. Houses burn down all the time, and it ain't because of someone's hex. You think what you want, but leave that black magic mumbo-jumbo back on the island."

"It de trufe I'm talkin', Missa Cutluh!"

"Ben, I've been to the best medical specialists they got up at Emory. Every one of them says it's these cigarettes. Not one, to the best of my recollection, has said the first damn word about the cause being a root or whatever the hell you call it. I don't want to hear another word about it. Now, what was the other thing you wanted to 'fess up about?"

CHAPTER 42

Since Pastor Dodge's murder, denial became Clayborne Cutler's closest ally, a talent he had perfected through years of practice, regardless of who suffered. The greater good of the community and the state outweighed all other considerations, he told himself.

Pastor Dodge's death, too, had been for the greater good, he reasoned. An entire town's fate was at stake. So what if one or two men took a fall? They were martyrs in a good cause. "Great men are measured by the fruits of their labor," he told anyone who would listen. On the whole, many more good benefits than bad had befallen Lamar and its townspeople over the years. As he developed his denial skills, he eventually came to believe that Salty Hoffer had actually fired the fatal shot. Everybody in town knew it. The papers had covered the trial closely, leaving no stone unturned. It was there in black and white at the library and the courthouse for anyone to read. Salty had been acquitted, but another man went to jail for the crime.

Cutler spent a good portion of his later years contributing to worthy causes, establishing scholarships, and leading community drives. The town had reciprocated by naming a street, a school, and a new hospital wing in his honor, but in his heart of hearts,

Clayborne knew this day would come. Now, the man who had been sent to prison for his crime stood across from him, holding a cloth sack.

"De firs' confession," Ben began, shuffling the sack from one hand to the next, "wuz mine. De second confession haff to be frum you, Missa Cutluh."

Clayborne snuffed his cigarette and flicked the butt through the porch slats into the azalea bushes. He lit a new one, careful to keep the flame away from his oxygen mask.

"Uh-huh," he said, eyeing Ben's sack with suspicion. "And just what is it I'm supposed to confess?"

"Missa Cutluh, befo I wuz in de state pen, when I'ze still in de work camp, a angel of de Lawd cum to me."

Clayborne froze mid-motion, a cigarette dangling in one hand, the mask in the other.

"An angel?" he said at length.

"Yessuh. A angel from de Lawd cum to me. An' he say . . ."

"Whoa. Back up," Clayborne said in a condescending tone. "An angel came to you?"

"Yessuh!"

"Did anyone else see it?"

"Naw, Suh. I wuz in de sweatbox . . ."

"The sweatbox?"

"Yessuh. It a box wiff holes in it. Dey put me in dere when dey brung me back from New Yoke. Affer a couple days, I see a bright light. Outta de light cum a angel. De angel tell me I must confess to a man of God 'cause a man of God were kilt, an' I coulda stop de killin', but I didn't."

As he spoke, Cutler stared at him with growing impatience and incredulity.

"De angel say de man whut done de killin' must also confess or neither one of us gonna see our eternal reward! Dat whut he say."

Clayborne stared at Ben, his mouth agape, cigarette poised near his mouth.

"Hold on a second," Cutler said, "You're trying to tell me an angel came to you and told you to confess, and that this other fella, the one who did the killing, has to confess, too. Is that what you're telling me?"

"Yessuh, Boss. Dat it exactly."

Clayborne turned away and looked down the driveway. He shook his head a few moments before breaking out into another hoarse fit of laughter that caused him to convulse and cough up more dark phlegm, which he duly spat over the rail. This time, his recovery took a while longer. He breathed deeply into the mask for a few minutes before being able to speak.

"Jesus, Ben Jordan!" he said. "You're killing me. I haven't laughed this much in years."

"Ain't no laughin' matter, Boss," Ben replied, his serious expression unchanged. "Two souls in de balance. Me an' you!"

Cutler held up his hand imperiously, cutting Ben off.

"First of all, what you saw was all in your head, Ben. They put you in a box in the blazing sun for two days. Right?"

"Yessuh. Dat right."

"Well, there you go! You were dehydrated. Hallucinating. Seeing and hearing things that weren't real. That's all that was going on there."

Ben shook his head. He recalled hearing the same type of dismissal years before from logging crewmen on Sapelo who explained away his and Eli's island beliefs. It was so much superstition, they told Ben and his cousin—outdated folklore, easily disproved by science. He had learned the hard way that explaining away supernatural events didn't alter their existence.

"Naw, Boss. De angel wuz real! I seen him just like I lookin' at you right now!"

"So what do you want me to do?" Cutler shot back, irritated with the direction the conversation had taken. "You want me to help you track down Salty Hoffer so he can confess? Last I heard, about twenty years ago, he was sweeping floors in Mobile. He's probably dead by now."

"Missa Cutluh, I cum here so's I could tell you whut de angel say, 'cause you gots to confess!"

"Damn it, Ben," Clayborne responded angrily, "Don't start that again. I told you I didn't fire that shot! You weren't even there at the time!"

"De police say Missa Hoffer wuz in Waycross when de preacher kilt. How he gonna be in Waycross an' kill a man in Lamar? How he gonna do dat, Missa Cutluh?"

"Damn it to hell!" Clayborne said hotly, flinging the lit cigarette over the rail. "You come to my house on a Sunday morning and bring up this mess! Get the hell outta my sight, or I'll call the police on you!"

Cutler turned the wheelchair and started for the front door, but Ben blocked the path.

"Get the hell out of my way!" Cutler said, his face reddening.

"Hold on, Boss," Ben said, determined to maintain his ground. "We talkin' 'bout my soul an' your soul. Dis here a serious ting!"

"So is trespassing and holding a man against his will!" Clayborne barked with great agitation. "You just got out of prison. How'd you like to spend the rest of your born days there?"

"Missa Cutluh, I been waitin' fo'ty year to speak. Least you can do is hear me out."

Cutler reached for his mask, and breathed deeply as a plan formulated in his head. He kept a loaded gun in the foyer closet. He would tell the police he had to shoot Ben out of self-defense. Lamar's preacher-killer had gone on another crime spree, picking up right where he left off, terrorizing the town's leading citizens. Once a killer, always a killer.

"Okay," he told Ben between gulps of air. "Make it quick."

Ben placed the sack on the rocker and took a deep breath, collecting his thoughts.

"Like I tol' you, Boss, I done confessed to a preacher. De law sent Docta Martin Luther King to Reidsville . . ."

"You mean Martin Luther Coon!" Cutler interjected bitterly.

"Naw, Boss. Martin Luther King. He said he would try to get me out, but they kilt him, an' they kilt dat man, Kenn'dy, who coulda signed me out."

"Good riddance to him and Kennedy and his brother!"

"You gots to confess, Missa Cutluh. I don't want my soul to go to Hell. An' I know you don't want yo soul going dere, too!"

Clayborne rolled his eyes and took a final drag on the oxygen. "I'm not about to confess to something I didn't do! And even if I did do it, I'm not confessing to some preacher who's gonna run to the police."

As he spoke, Ben reached into the sack and withdrew a writing pad and a Bic pen. He held them out to Clayborne. "I wuz 'fraid you might say dat. So I gots an idea. You write out de confession on dis paper. Affer you pass on—which I hope God giff you a lotta mo' years—den I tek it to de preacher. Dat way, ever'ting be okay."

Clayborne let out a short, hollow laugh, this time being careful not to let it escalate into another coughing attack.

"Then you'll take it right to the police!"

"Naw, Boss!" Ben replied, genuinely wounded by Cutler's comment. "Dis a matter fo God, not de po-leece!"

"We had a pact, remember!"

"I 'member, Boss. I ain't tol' no one. I kep' my word."

Clayborne saw the determination in Ben's face and knew another tactic would be in order. If he couldn't order him out of the way, he could appeal to Ben's sympathy, a perceived weakness in others Cutler had learned to exploit. He slumped in his chair.

"Didn't I save you from that mob in Baxley?" he asked, his voice softening.

"Yessuh. You sho did."

"And didn't I get the governor to transfer you out of that prison farm before the pen was even finished?"

"I reckon so, Boss."

"And didn't I pay for your daughter's education?"

"Well, Missa Cutluh, I don't know nuthin' 'bout dat," Ben replied, having been informed of this matter by Geneva on her many visits to Reidsville.

"Take my word for it. I did! Listen to me; you're not thinking straight, Ben. You're a free man. Why do you want to go and dredge up all of this mess again? That's all in the past. You got to think about the future."

"I is tinkin' 'bout de future, Boss. I tinkin' 'bout eternity. De angel of de Lawd told me all 'bout it."

Cutler threw his hands up in disgust.

"Stop with this talk about an angel! They turned you into one of those gottdamn Bible thumpers! It was bad enough when Claudette got religion after little Clay died. I don't need to hear it from you!"

"Missa Cutluh, I wish you wouldn't use de Lawd's name in vain. It ain't right."

"I'm not using the Lord's name in vain!"

"You is! You . . ."

"Gottdamn it, Ben . . ."

"See! Right dere, Boss. You done it again. It a sin ever time you do it."

"Swearing a little is no sin."

"It in the good book, Boss. Any preacher can tell you."

Cutler threw his head back and laughed as loudly as his diseased lungs would permit.

"I don't need you to tell me about the good book, Ben Jordan. You want to know who killed Salty Hoffer? It was the good church-goers of this town."

He laughed again at the thought of how easily his plan had taken effect.

"I let the Bible-quoters do all the heavy lifting. I never once said Salty Hoffer killed Dodge. I just wondered aloud who would profit by his death. 'Seems to me whoever owns a liquor store in this town would want Dodge dead.' That's all I said. One little sentence, Ben Jordan. A death sentence."

Cutler snickered at his own clever turn of phrase.

"Then I sat back and watched those church folks try and convict Hoffer on the spot. You think I ran old man Hoffer out of town? Hell, no! It was those God-fearing bastards! And you want me to confess to one of their leaders? You must be insane."

"You didn't say nuthin while de whole town thought Salty done de killin'. Dat ain't right, Missa Cutluh. It ain't right."

"It was right for this town. Look around, Ben Jordan. This town prospered for the last forty years. It would be a whole different story if it was me they ran out of Lamar. Don't you lecture me about what is right."

"Is fo'ty year outta my life right?"

"We had a deal! I kept my end of it, and you kept yours. You got caught. Not me. No use crying over spilled milk."

"A man died, Missa Cutluh. A preacher man. Another man were ruin, an' I went to jail fo sumtin' I ain't even did. Ain't none of dat right."

"Damn it, Ben, I'm not gonna sit here and argue about who did what or what happened to who or why! That's all in the past."

"De past all I gots, Missa Cutluh," Ben replied, his voice getting loud with emotion. "I ain't gots no future. Whut I gonna do? Ain't nuthin' fo a old black man who done prison time. All I gots is de past from de moment you fired dat bullet on back. Ain't nuthin fo me affer dat."

"Don't you come around here raising your voice at me!"

"I'm just saying it ain't right, Boss. I gots me a troubled spirit, Missa Cutluh. I gots me a monstrous troubled spirit. I gots de most trouble spirit dey is."

He extended the writing pad and pen out for Clayborne to take.

"And you want me to confess to some preacher just because you 'gots a troubled spirit,'" Cutler mocked, "and because you had a gottdamn vision in a box?"

"It de only way, Boss! We kilt Passuh Dodge together. You gots to confess, or we doomed to perdition. The bofe of us!"

Cutler put his hands on the wheels of his chair, preparing to move forward. "Okay, you've had your say. Now, get off my property. We're done talking."

Ben widened his stance and held his arms out wide.

"I cain't let you go inside, Missa Cutluh. Not 'til we done."

Clayborne squinted up at Ben, his eyes blazing. "What did you say?"

"I say . . ."

"I heard what you said. Now, hear me. You got ten seconds to get off this porch, Ben Jordan, or suffer the consequences."

Ben shook his head and reached for the bag.

"Missa Cutluh," he said, slowly extracting a metal object from the bottom of the sack, "I didn't want to haff to go an' do this . . ."

Clayborne instinctively recoiled at the sight of the .45 caliber handgun, as if it was a water moccasin about to strike. He shoved the wheelchair backward until it slammed into the corner railing, causing the oxygen tank to rattle in its basket. For a few moments, he could say nothing. His eyes remained fixed on the murder weapon. Ben had retrieved it from Jack Carter's front yard after mowing the lawn. He had found the gun in the exact spot he'd buried it the night of Dodge's murder—inside a box, still covered in Cosmoline and wrapped in oily rags. Ben had spent much of Saturday evening cleaning and polishing the gun until it appeared to the casual observer to be in perfect working order. He brought the revolver to the Cutler home thinking that Clayborne would need more incentive than words to agree to a confession.

A full minute passed with neither man moving. Clayborne's eyes moved from the gun to Ben and back to the gun in stunned silence, unable to speak, not sure where to begin. His reaction confirmed that the object in Ben's hand was indeed the weapon that had put a bullet through Pastor Dodge's brain.

"Where'd you get that?" he said at length, unsure of what else to say.

"I bury it 'neath de Jesus Tree," Ben replied matter-of-factly. "Seven paces frum de trunk, right under where dey hang my cousin, Eli."

"All you had to do was throw the damn thing in the swamp!" Cutler angrily cried out as he slammed his fist on the wheelchair's arm support.

"De Devil live in de swamp, Boss!" Ben replied. "No tellin' de mischief he get up to wiff dat gun! But de Jesus Tree on holy ground. It where Eli soul went to heaven. It de safest place fo it. Cain't nuthin' touch it dere."

Clayborne slumped forward and slowly nodded his head as Willie Stokes's words came back to him. "Them Sapelo peoples is different, Boss. They ain't like most folk." For the first time, he understood why Ben was seen carrying a shovel the morning after the murder.

"Okay," he said warily, almost in a whisper. "Okay . . ."

Cutler extended his bony hand and took the pad and pen from Ben. "I see what's going on. You've done your time for something you didn't do, and you got nothing to lose. You come out here to an old man's house on a Sunday and threaten him with a gun . . ."

"No, Boss. Dat ain't it at all . . ."

". . . figuring you can force a confession out of him or shoot him down. Either way, you get your revenge. I understand. My checkbook is on the hall table. Just give me a minute."

"I don't wants no money, Missa Cutluh."

"Really? Not even a few grand? Is that enough to make you forget all this confession nonsense?"

"It ain't 'bout money, Boss."

"I see. Five grand."

"No, Boss."

"Ten thousand dollars, and that's final. Ten grand."

"No, Boss. I wants you to write out de confession. Like I say, I give it to de preacher when you gone." Clayborne stared hard at Ben.

"You don't want money?"

"No, Suh."

"Okay." He held out his hand. "Give me the writing tablet."

Ben watched closely while Cutler scribbled on the pad. Half a minute later, Clayborne tore off the top sheet and handed it to him.

"Okay, Ben Jordan," he said, "here's my confession. Now you can shoot a weak, defenseless old man. If that will help you think you've squared things up, go right ahead."

Clayborne watched with keen interest as Ben took the sheet, reached into an overall pocket, and extracted a pair of reading glasses. His interest turned into amazement when he saw Ben's eyes scan the page. In Cutler's youth, very few blacks or poor whites knew how to read. Even now, the literacy level among poor blacks and whites in and around Lamar had not greatly improved.

"Don't tell me you learned how to read in prison?"

Ben chuckled. The great-grandson of Bu-Allah not know how to read? That was amusing. But he found Cutler's comment not as amusing as what he had written.

I, Clayborne Cutler, am being held hostage on my front porch by that preacher killer, Ben Jordan, who is standing here holding a gun on me. It is the same gun he used to shoot Pastor Dodge.

"Missa Cutluh," Ben said, stuffing the page in his hip pocket, "I don't believe dat de confession de angel of de Lawd had in mind."

Clayborne looked up at Ben with scorn. "Well, you're just full of surprises, aren't you? I should have listened to Willie. He tried to warn me about you."

"Missa Cutluh, please put it down right dis time, an' don't fergit to ask de Lawd fo He mercy. Dat real impo'tant in dese type matters."

Ben unconsciously tapped the gun's barrel against his leg while he spoke. Clayborne took it to be a threat. As he poised the pen over the pad for a second time, a new thought occurred to him, one that eased his mind considerably. A confession obtained by force or threat of violence would be tossed out of court. He marveled that he hadn't thought of it sooner. Besides, he would immediately contact the police, tell them what had transpired, and that Ben had the murder weapon, further proving his guilt as the gunman.

"All right," he said, feigning resignation. "I'll write a confession."

Thirty seconds later, Ben had in his hand what he had come for.

I, Clayborne Cutler, did willfully and with premedita-tion, shoot and kill Pastor DeLong Stanton Dodge at his residence. God forgive me of my trespasses.

At the top of the page, Clayborne had scribbled in the date. His distinctive, swirling signature appeared immediately below the confession. Ben smiled and put the gun in the sack.

"Missa Cutluh," he said with great relief, his face aglow, "I can die a happy man now. My soul at rest." He carefully folded the page and gently slid it into his pocket.

"It is?" Clayborne said as Ben turned and walked to the steps. "Well, I'm happy to hear it." He rolled the wheelchair toward the steps, shadowing Ben's movements. "You go ahead and take that to the police, you hear. Go ahead. Be sure to give them that gun, too!"

Ben had no intention of leaving the premises with the weapon. He, too, knew what the consequences would be if it were found on him or his property. He also didn't want to put it immediately into Clayborne's hands as he was fairly certain Cutler would be tempted to shoot him with it. He'd heard of unearthed firearms going off unexpectedly, and Ben didn't want to take any chances.

"I don't need dis gun no mo', Boss. I gonna leave it wiff you."

"Don't you leave that thing here, Ben Jordan!"

"I don't wants de gun no mo', Boss," he said. "It ain't brung nuthin' but evil."

Ben placed the firearm in the sack and wrapped it tightly. He walked over to the double-headed pine tree and placed the bundle in the trunk's crotch.

Clayborne's eyes burned with anger. If he had his gun at that moment, he would have shot Ben in his tracks. He sucked hard on the oxygen mask.

"Go on. That's right," he called out as Ben slowly walked down the driveway. "Take it into town. Take that confession to the police. You hear? It ain't worth the paper it's written on. No judge in the world is gonna allow a forced confession in court. You hear me, Ben Jordan?"

Clayborne's denunciations increased in ferocity the further Ben got away from the house. Before long, the pauses between Cutler's curses increased as he stopped to take in oxygen.

The moment Ben was out of sight, Clayborne wheeled himself to the telephone in the foyer, his heart racing from exertion and rage. He dialed a number and breathed heavily into the mask while the phone on the other end rang.

"Get me Avery!" he barked hoarsely, gasping for breath between words. "I don't care if he's in church. Send somebody after him . . . Clayborne Cutler, that's who! Yes, of course it's an emergency! Well, have him call me at my house."

He hung up and reached into his basket, retrieved a prescription bottle, and put a pill under his tongue. After a few minutes, Clayborne's heart rate settled down enough to light another cigarette while he waited for the phone to ring.

Miles Avery, Jr., Lamar's chief of police, was no stranger to the Dodge case. He and his father, Miles, Sr., had found Dodge's body the day after the murder. His father spoke of the unresolved case until the day he died. Miles, Jr. possessed two files on the murder. One, the official records, he kept at Lamar's police station. The other file, his father's, he kept under lock and key at his house. Eventually, the most intimate details of the case were transferred to Avery's private files. His father often told him murders like this one were solved either by a deathbed confession or through a slip of the tongue. The particulars of the murder had never been released to the public, and the few men who knew the details, including Miles, Sr., had long since passed away.

Fifteen minutes after his call, Clayborne's phone rang.

"Cutler here," he said, some agitation remaining in his voice.

"Mister Cutler, this is Miles. How can I help you?"

"You can help me by arresting a man named Ben Jordan. He just got out of prison, and he was up here this morning threatening me with a gun!"

Miles stood in the pastor's office at the Methodist Church. He put a hand over one ear to block out the choir singing in the sanctuary on the other side of the office wall. He, too, was well aware of Ben's release from prison, but played ignorant.

"Ben Jordan, you say?"

"Yes! He's the one who killed your church's preacher when you were a little boy. Remember?"

"I vaguely recall, Mister Cutler."

"Well, you should. Your daddy found Pastor Dodge's body."

"And you say this Ben Jordan has been at your residence making threats?"

"Yes! He was over here, out on the porch. Forced me to sign a confession at gunpoint using the same gun he killed that preacher with. Now, that confession was signed under threat of death and isn't worth the paper it's written on. I'm not worried about myself, but I want you to put him behind bars where he can't do any harm to anyone else!"

"He forced you to sign a confession?"

"Yes!"

"A confession for what?"

"He's got it in his head that I killed that preacher, when everybody in town knows Ben Jordan shot Dodge while he was sitting at his desk working on a sermon."

For a moment, Clayborne thought the line had gone dead. On the other end of the phone, Miles felt his legs turn to jelly. He fell heavily into the office chair as if he'd been sucker-punched in the stomach. The fact that Dodge had been killed while sitting at his desk had never been released to the public. Of all the people still living in Lamar, only Avery and the real killer shared this knowledge.

Clayborne immediately had a vague awareness that he had blundered.

"Mister Cutler," Avery said after several moments passed, "I believe we need to talk. I'll send a squad car right over."

Cutler sat in stunned silence, replaying the conversation in his mind, dumbly listening to the dial tone before twice attempting to place the phone in its cradle. The hallway flickered before his eyes as the full realization of his error hit home. He suddenly felt faint. He started to light a cigarette but forgot what he was doing.

"I need a trial lawyer, a good one," he said weakly as he wheeled himself onto the porch. "Tremont Rogers can help me out there. No. Tremont died years ago. Daddy can help me."

The front yard and surrounding landscape seemed to swim in his vision. He descended the front steps as if in a dream, vaguely aware that he'd left the oxygen bottle behind.

"It's evidence," he said, eyeing the sack that held the gun.

He set his face resolutely toward the tree. He had to get the murder weapon first. Then he'd call Gene Talmadge. The governor would make things right. He always did. He had named his first child for the governor, hadn't he? That had to count for something.

Clayborne heard a scuffling noise and realized his feet dragged along the ground. He felt shadows closing in around him though no clouds were overhead.

"Mama," he called out feebly. "Daddy."

CHAPTER 43

Over four hundred people came to the funeral the following Wednesday. Grey haired dignitaries from around the state positioned themselves in the front pews of Lamar's First Baptist church. The balcony seats filled to capacity for the first time in years, and the overflow waited outside, listening to the sermon through speakers set up on the church steps. Those who eulogized the town's leading citizen spoke of his many charitable acts and recalled how it was he who had brought "the highway" to Lamar, how he'd gone toe-to-toe with Eugene Talmadge to ensure Lamar's citizens would prosper, how Middle Georgia's visionary built a small empire of roadside motels, restaurants and filling stations, whose model had been studied and emulated by several generations of businessmen.

After the church service, Claudette rode in a limousine to the graveyard. Ahead of her car, the black Weakley-Chambers Funeral Home hearse, driven by a man in maroon blazer, carried Clayborne's pine casket, elaborately decorated with wood inlays. At the cemetery, six pallbearers, consisting of one former Cutler Land & Lumber employee and five prominent men who owed their careers to Clayborne, carried the coffin to the Cutler section of the town cemetery. Claudette, dressed in black, sat beneath the Weakly-Chambers maroon-colored tent that had been set up over the graves of Obediah and his wife. Next to their graves was a smaller headstone with the name "Clayborne Cutler, Junior" chiseled on its face.

"I thought there would be more coloreds," she remarked to a cousin who clutched her hand. Cutler Land & Lumber had hired hundreds of blacks over the years, but only one black man, accompanied by a little girl, stood a respectful distance from the tent. He wore a new dark wool suit and held a black fedora in one hand. The girl wore a sparkling white cotton dress with pink trim.

"Who died, Granpa?" Renee asked, looking up at Ben.

"Missa Clayborne Cutluh," he answered. "I use to work fo he an' he daddy. Bofe mens."

The graveside service lasted twenty minutes. Ben couldn't hear much of what Pastor Gaines said. As he squinted in the hot sun, trying to detect an aura around the preacher, he overheard the comments of two men standing in front of him.

"I hear the police found him dead in the driveway," the first man said.

"The police?" asked the second. "What were they doing out there?"

"Don't know. Something funny was going on, though."

"They found him in his wheelchair?"

"No. The wheelchair ramp is in back of the house. Somehow, he got down the front steps by himself. They found him sitting under that tree—you know, the double pine—staring up at it, dead as a doornail. Stroke or heart attack or something."

"Sounds like he was out of his head."

"Must have been."

"What was he looking at? I mean, something had to be up in that tree to get him out of his chair. He's like a fish out of water without that oxygen tank."

"Whatever it was, Avery isn't telling anyone. It's all hush-hush from what I hear."

When the service ended, Claudette rose from her seat and hobbled through the throng back to the limousine that brought her.

Forty-five minutes later only the cemetery crew, Ben, and Renee remained. He stood nearby, holding his granddaughter's hand, watching workers disassemble the tent and prepare to cover the casket with dirt.

"Dat big marker," he told Renee, pointing to Obediah's simple Georgia marble headstone, "belong to Missa Obediah. He de one hire me. De one nex' to it belong to he wife. I never knew her real well." He paused and pointed at the small headstone. "Dat one de saddest of all. It belong to li'l Clayborne. He die when he were just a baby boy."

Ben studied Clayborne's headstone, an ornate monument much larger than his father's, with a foot-wide Doric column running from its base to a point eight feet above. A thick line representing a highway, traveled the length of the column with the names of Georgia towns on either side of it. The town of Lamar had been etched in large letters at its midsection. Ben followed the highway from top to bottom. He his eyes grew wide when he read the birthdate on the headstone: January 1, 1910.

"What are you looking at?" Renee asked, pulling on his sleeve.

His gaze remained fixed on the date. He stood still, as if in a trance. The recent dream of the two pines with the same number of rings laying side by side flashed through his mind. He didn't need Tiny Ruth to interpret the dream.

"Granpa!"

"Yes, Chile," he said, regaining his senses. "Whut you say?"

"What's wrong?"

"Ain't nuthin' wrong, Baby. I just noticin' de man, Missa Cutluh . . . he born de same day as yo Granpa."

As he turned to leave, a car approached and stopped nearby. Ben had been hoping to have a private word with Pastor Gaines, but he couldn't get close enough earlier. He had decided to go by the Methodist Church, but now it appeared he would have his chance.

The preacher smiled and nodded at Ben and Renee as he walked up to the open grave.

"Anybody seen my Bible?" he asked, a bit out of breath.

"Yes, Sir," one of the workers responded. "You left it on one of the seats. We set it over there." He pointed to a stack of folded chairs, ready to be carted back to the funeral home.

"Thanks," Gaines responded. "Sometimes, I think I'd leave my head behind if it wasn't screwed on." He picked up his Bible and turned to leave.

By then, Ben had positioned himself to intercept him. Though he detected no aura, he interpreted the fact that Gaines had returned to the cemetery as a sign from above.

"Missa Pastor," Ben said.

Gaines stopped and winked at Renee.

"Can I help you?" he asked Ben.

"Yessuh, you sho can," he replied, reaching into his inside coat pocket. "Dis here a very impo'tant ting."

Ben pulled out a crisp envelope. Inside was Clayborne Cutler's confession.

"It de mos' impo'tant paper dey is. I s'posed to giff it to a man of Gawd."

"Thank you," Gaines said, thinking it to be a modest charitable donation in honor of the recently deceased. "I'll take care of it."

He absent-mindedly shoved the envelope into his coat and hastily departed, late for the post-funeral reception at the Cutler home.

CHAPTER 44

Ben returned from the funeral tired, but he immediately changed into his comfort clothes—red long-sleeve shirt, bib overalls, and ankle high boots. After lunch, the four of them spent the afternoon sitting beneath the fig tree, talking about the old days. At one point, Naomi reached out her hand and took Ben's.

"You know, Unca," she said, "Renee keeps calling you Granpa. I never knew my father, but I imagine he was a lot like you. Would you mind if I called you Papa?"

Geneva's body jerked involuntarily in her chair. "Dat ol' wasp affer me again," she said, slapping the air around her in a clumsy attempt to cover her reaction.

Ben squeezed Naomi's hand. "No, Chile," he said, his throat tightening with emotion, "I don't mind. I know'd yo daddy real good. I know he wouldn't mind."

Naomi leaned closer and rested her head on his shoulder.

"Thanks, Papa," she said.

Renee climbed onto his lap and stroked her mother's head. After a few minutes, both had fallen sound asleep.

"She know!"

Geneva mouthed the words to Ben.

That evening, he stayed up late, mostly listening to Geneva and Naomi talk about her new job in Savannah and Renee's future. Ben went to bed close to midnight, emotionally and physically drained from the week's events. He lay on top of the bedspread with his boots on, and recalled the interview he'd had with Chief Avery at the police station a few days earlier.

"Missa Cutluh wuz my boss man," Ben had informed Avery. "We wuz catchin' up on de ol' days."

"How'd this gun get up in that tree?" Avery asked, placing the .45 caliber revolver on the table before Ben.

"I put it dere, Suh."

"Is this the murder weapon that killed Dodge?"

"I don't know 'bout dat, Suh. I ain't never seen who done it."

Avery nodded. Ben's reply matched exactly his testimony during the trial.

"But you think Cutler was the murderer?"

"I don't know, Suh. Dat 'tween Gawd and Missa Claybo'ne Cutluh. But dat wuz Missa Cutluh's gun. He wuz in de wood dat night of de killin'. I wuz just returnin' it to him."

Ben told Avery about the hanging tree and that he had buried the revolver beneath it for safekeeping. Miles paced the room, contemplating his next move. Everything Ben told him had been consistent with what he knew about the case. In Avery's mind, the real murderer was dead, and Ben had already served a long sentence for the crime. Avery had found Cutler's body by the pine, his eyes fixed on the sack wedged in the tree's trunk, his hand outstretched, attempting to grasp it. The police chief felt confident the coroner would conclude Cutler had died of natural causes. Bringing the case back to life would serve no purpose.

"Sometimes," his father once told him, "you got to open a case back up. And sometimes, you got to let sleeping dogs lie."

"Mister Jordan," he said, closing the Dodge murder case folder, "thank you for clearing some things up for me. I'll have one of my men take you back home."

Ben recalled the day's funeral and the afternoon under the fig tree with his daughter and granddaughter. Outside, he heard a train whistle in the distance. The clock by his bed glowed 11:59. "De death train," he murmured. He stared at the ceiling just as he had done many a night while incarcerated. To his amazement, the ceiling turned first into a vapor, then into a fine mist, and finally, into a clear black sky filled with more stars than there were grains of sand on Sapelo's beach. He felt his body rise from the bed and float up, above the house, effortlessly passing over the fig tree and high over the surrounding pines. He felt as though he floated on a current of air that pushed him ever higher toward a full moon.

"I'ze dreamin," he told himself. "De mos' beautiful dream dey is."

He looked down on the silvery landscape far below and noticed he was moving due east. Soon, the Altamaha River came into view, and he followed its sinewy course, mesmerized and thrilled by what was transpiring.

"Ize flyin," he said, "like de Africans."

He looked down and recounted his journey with Eli along the river's entire length. After what seemed like hours of uninterrupted ecstasy, he looked up and viewed the vast Atlantic shimmering on the horizon. Before long, the dense wooded landscape below gave way to soft, lush, open marsh. To his left, the lights of Darien went out one-by-one as its residents bedded down for the night. He slowly descended over the wide Doboy Sound and miles of marsh and saltwater tributaries. Two dolphins skipped effortlessly across the water, welcoming him home. He continued downward until he felt his feet would surely splash down into the sound, but instead, he glided over the remaining stretch of water like the pelicans he used to watch skimming inches above the sea on unseen air currents. Ahead, he felt shadows on the bluff, slowly coming into view. As he got closer, he could see their faces. His mother, Josephine, was the first he recognized. Next to her stood Jesse, his father. Behind them stood aunts and uncles. At last, his feet touched down on Sapelo soil, and he found himself embraced in their arms. More people, elders he knew as a child and others he innately knew to be his ancestors, arrived every moment. He stood in their midst overcome with euphoria, expecting to be awakened from the dream at any moment. But the dream didn't end. He couldn't get the words out fast enough as he met old friends he hadn't seen since leaving the island. Then, he looked up and saw Eli standing to one side, grinning from ear to ear, as youthful and as whole as he had ever been. They embraced for a long time, and still more people arrived. He felt a tap on his shoulder and looked up to see Rupert Bright. The deacon, smiling broadly, told him someone else was coming to greet him. He pointed in the direction of the deep woods. Hundreds of islanders made way for a tall figure with distinct Arabic features. Ben turned his head and slowly lifted his eyes to see Bu-Allah approach with outstretched arms.

CHAPTER 45

Geneva knew her brother had died in the night before she opened her eyes. She knew by the wailing coming down the hall from his room. Lights came on in houses up and down the street. Her neighbors, too, knew death had come in the night.

When she got to Ben's bedside, Geneva found the woman who could not cry was on her knees, bawling like a baby, her head pressed hard against her father's ribs, soaking his shirt and overalls with her tears.

"Dat right. You cry, Chile," Geneva told Naomi. "Dat fo'ty year of tears you gots inside. You cry all you want. Get it out."

"It's not fair!" Naomi bawled in anger, her hands clenched into fists. "It's not fair!"

"No, Chile, it ain't fair," Geneva said, soothingly. "Ain't none of it fair."

By then, Renee had come to her mother's side and began to sob with her, clinging to her grandfather's overalls.

"Dat right. You go on an' cry too, Hon. Bofe of you. Cry it out. Den, when you done, we gonna tek he body home to Sapelo. We gots to bury he bones wiff de bones of he ancestors. De spirit cum lookin' fo de body after three day. So, we gots to get him to Sapelo."

Naomi's shoulders shook uncontrollably as she sobbed.

"Don't stop cryin', Chile," her aunt encouraged. "Dat de bes' ting to do. But don't be sorry fo yo daddy. He soul in heaven wiff de Lawd our Gawd. He spirit already on Sapelo where de affer birth buried. He already wiff Momma and Papa, an' he cousin Eli, an' all de ol' folk. All of dem. Bu-Allah. Ever'one of dem. Cry fo de ones still here, Chile. Cry fo you an' your li'l girl. But don't cry fo yo daddy. He safe. He in de arms of Gawd an' fambly."

Naomi put her arm around Renee and squeezed her tightly.

Renee looked up at her mother. "We have to take Granpa home," she said.

Naomi nodded but could not speak.

"Dat right, Chile. Dat right," Geneva said. "De bones go in de ground. De soul go to heaven. And de spirit stay here on Earth."

ABOUT THE AUTHOR

Writer and oral historian Stephen Doster was born in Kingston-on-Thames, England, and raised on St. Simons Island, Georgia. He is the author of both fiction and nonfiction, including two oral histories. Doster's literary works are focused on Georgia and its coast. He holds degrees from the University of Georgia and Vanderbilt University and currently resides in Nashville, Tennessee, with his wife, Anne.

STEPHEN DOSTER

FROM OPEN ROAD MEDIA

OPEN ROAD

INTEGRATED MEDIA

INTEGRATED MEDIA

Find a full list of our authors and titles at www.openroadmedia.com

FOLLOW US
@OpenRoadMedia